THE WORLD'S CLASSICS

THE STEPPE
AND OTHER STORIES

ANTON CHEKHOV was born in 1860 in south Russia, the
son of a poor grocer. At the age of 19 he followed his family
to Moscow, where he studied medicine and helped to
support the household by writing comic sketches for popular magazines. By 1888 he was publishing in the prestigious
literary monthlies of Moscow and St Petersburg: a sign that
he had already attained maturity as a writer of serious
fiction. During the next 15 years he wrote the short
stories—50 or more of them—which form his chief claim to
world pre-eminence in the genre and are his main achieve-
ment as a writer. His plays are almost equally important,
especially during his last years. He was closely associated
with the Moscow Art Theatre and married its leading lady,
Olga Knipper. In 1898 he was forced to move to Yalta,
where he wrote his two greatest plays, *Three Sisters* and *The
Cherry Orchard*. The première of the latter took place on his
forty-fourth birthday. Chekhov died six months later, on
2 July 1904.

RONALD HINGLEY, Emeritus Fellow of St Antony's
College, Oxford, edited and translated The Oxford
Chekhov (9 volumes), and is the author of *A Life of Anton
Chekhov* (also published by Oxford University Press). He is
the translator of four other volumes of Chekhov stories in
the World's Classics: *The Russian Master and Other Stories*,
Ward Number Six and Other Stories, *A Woman's Kingdom and
Other Stories*, and *The Princess and Other Stories*. His transla-
tions of all Chekhov's drama will be found in two World's
Classics volumes, *Five Plays* and (forthcoming) *Twelve
Plays*.

THE WORLD'S CLASSICS

ANTON CHEKHOV

The Steppe
and Other Stories

*Translated with an Introduction
and Notes by*
RONALD HINGLEY

Oxford   New York
OXFORD UNIVERSITY PRESS

Oxford University Press, Walton Street, Oxford OX2 6DP

Oxford New York Toronto
Delhi Bombay Calcutta Madras Karachi
Petaling Jaya Singapore Hong Kong Tokyo
Nairobi Dar es Salaam Cape Town
Melbourne Auckland

and associated companies in
Berlin Ibadan

Oxford is a trade mark of Oxford University Press

Translations and editorial material © Ronald Hingley 1965, 1970, 1971,
1975, 1978, 1980
Introduction © Ronald Hingley 1991
Chronology © Oxford University Press 1984

This selection first issued as a World's Classics paperback 1991
Reprinted 1991

British Library Cataloguing in Publication Data

Chekhov, A. P. (Anton Pavlovich) 1860–1904
The steppe and other stories.—(The World's classics).
I. Title   II. Hingley, Ronald
891.733

ISBN 0-19-282663-8

Library of Congress Cataloging in Publication Data

Chekhov, Anton Pavlovich, 1860–1904.
The steppe, and other stories / Anton Chekhov:
translated with an introduction and notes by Ronald Hingley.
p.   cm.—(The World's classics)
Includes bibliographical references.
1. Chekhov, Anton Pavlovich, 1860–1904 — Translations, English
I. Title   II. Series.
PG3456.A15H56   1991   891.73'3—dc20

ISBN 0-19-282663-8

Printed in Great Britain by
BPCC Hazell Books
Aylesbury, Bucks.

CONTENTS

INTRODUCTION

THE present volume is the fifth selection of Chekhov's short stories to be brought out in The World's Classics, and it completes the paperback publication for this series of his entire œuvre as a mature fiction-writer. This means that the five volumes contain all those stories which received their first publication between March 1888 and the author's death in 1904. The text is that of the original hardback translation, The Oxford Chekhov, except that the stories are grouped differently and that textual variants have been omitted, as has much other scholarly apparatus.[1] The five volumes contain sixty titles altogether, and they maintain so high a level of excellence that many readers will rate them as the finest collection of short stories which any of the world's literatures has to offer. This high standard is maintained in the present volume, with a few minor reservations indicated below, and with the obvious exception of four trifles from the year 1892 which Chekhov himself excluded from his first Collected Works of 1899–1901; these are admitted here more for the sake of completeness than for their literary qualities.[2]

It is hoped that the completed paperback publication of these stories will help to correct the common view of Chekhov as a dramatist whose other work is comparatively unimportant. A playwright of genius he certainly was. But he surely deserves even greater admiration for what he achieved with the short story.

It is especially appropriate that this final selection should begin with, and take its title from, The Steppe, since it was the appearance of that renowned saga of the prairies which marked and brought about Chekhov's elevation from the minor to the major league among Russian writers. Its publication in the St

[1] The Oxford Chekhov (London and Oxford, 1965–80), vols. iv–ix.
[2] See pp. 239–46.

Petersburg monthly *Severny vestnik* ('The Northern Herald') in March 1888 remains the most important single landmark in the creative evolution of its author, then 28 years old.

Chekhov had begun his literary career in 1880 as the author of short comic items possessing little artistic merit. They were written for money (but then, all Chekhov's work was written for money) and published in various humorous magazines of the period. He felt obliged to maximize such earnings by churning out more and more 'balderdash', as he himself later called it. But a more serious sense of purpose was sometimes dimly discernible even at the outset, and this asserted itself increasingly. The result was that Chekhov, chiefly popular in his early twenties as a lightweight humorist, had nevertheless already begun—during the two or three years preceding the publication of *The Steppe*—to attract the attention of influential Russian critics and littérateurs. Older writers, of whom D. V. Grigorovich was the best known, began lecturing him on the need to take his talent more seriously, and to write less hastily.

The first fruit of this advice was *The Steppe*, and particular significance attaches to the status of the publication in which it appeared. *Severny vestnik* was one of the revered 'thick journals' in which almost all serious Russian literary works were first offered to readers. Now, nothing of Chekhov's had ever previously featured in any of these august literary monthlies, and so the importance of this promotion—from the pages of sundry despised or semi-despised weeklies and dailies—could be lost on no one. Everyone knew that if the young man was ever to rival his great predecessors—Dostoyevsky, Tolstoy, and the others—Thick Journal status was indispensable.

He now had 'lift-off'. This is at once evident from the quality of the story itself—written, curiously, enough, at high speed despite the insistence of Chekhov's seniors that he should pace himself. His reward was the immediate ecstatic reception accorded by ordinary readers, as well as by his self-appointed senior mentors and various influential reviewers, to a work which so clearly surpassed his most promising previous achievements. In the sixteen years of life remaining to him he was indeed to pace himself as he had been advised, becoming only a quarter as prolific—in terms of pages of fiction published per annum—as he had been during his eight-year-long immature phase. But the main point is that he first hit the highest level of the short-story writer's art with *The Steppe*, and that he afterwards rarely descended from it—even then for no more than the odd page or two.

Though *The Steppe* clearly pointed to Chekhov's future it is also important for its links with his past, since the background is that of his boyhood summer holidays—the Ukrainian and South Russian plains. The Chekhovs would camp there *en famille* on their way by horse- or ox-cart to visit the future author's paternal grandfather, Yegor, who had been a serf in youth, but who had since purchased his own and his family's freedom, and who had also become the manager of a vast Ukrainian estate. These details help to explain why Chekhov chose to make the central character of *The Steppe* a 9-year-old boy, and to present the world through the eyes of this youthful hero who is in many ways the author himself as a child. Here he was repeating on a larger scale the success of such early stories as *Boys*, *Grisha*, *Volodya*, *An Incident*, and *Sleepy*, which all centred, with varying degrees of humour and tragedy, on the lives of children. Perhaps Chekhov felt that *The Steppe* summed up all he had to say in fiction about children, for there were to be no comparable juvenile heroes in the fiction which followed. This is, incidentally, a substantial story by his standards, belonging in bulk as well as quality to a small group of later masterpieces of similar length: *The Duel*, *An Anonymous Story*, *Three Years*, and *My Life*. It is also remarkable for describing the most extensive journey in Chekhov's fiction. In 1887, some months before writing *The Steppe*, Chekhov had revived memories of his native prairies by revisiting his birthplace, Taganrog on the Sea of Azov, and by touring the surrounding area so familiar to him from childhood. Hence the echoes in the story of such characteristic features as the archaeologically significant *kurgany* (ancient burial mounds) and *kamennyye baby* (menhirs), the *buryan* (coarse grass and weeds), the oxen, the water-towers, the windmills, the kites, the Ukrainian peasants, the Cossacks, and above all the immense expanse of the seemingly endless plains. No other work of Chekhov's is so saturated with landscape.

Other noteworthy stories in this volume take us back again into southern landscapes familiar to the author. One of them, *The Beauties*, contains a recognizable portrait of his grandfather Yegor among other colourful locals. *Thieves* and *Peasant Women* too have their southern coloration, while *The Savage* evokes the Don Cossacks of the area in all the picturesque barbarity for which they were notorious—and which is often amusingly portrayed in Chekhov's correspondence.[3] Yet more exotic autobiographical resonances echo from *In Exile* and *Gusev*. These draw on the adventurous journey undertaken by Chekhov in 1890 across Siberia (the location of *In Exile*) to the Island of Sakhalin, an unsavoury penal colony; he returned by ship via the Indian Ocean, which becomes the last resting place of the Gusev who gives his name to the story. Otherwise the settings of the stories in this volume are somewhat vaguer, in Chekhov's more characteristic manner—rural, for the most part, and evoking the atmosphere of the central Russian countryside south of Moscow where he owned an estate in the 1890s.

By that time Chekhov himself had, in effect, become a member of Russia's social élite through his prowess in two of the liberal professions—the medical as well as the literary, for he was a qualified and sporadically practising doctor; he also became a landowner on a more than modest scale. Yet he never formally acquired the legal status of *dvoryanin* (member of the gentry) normal for a successful professional man or country squire. Moreover, as the stories in this volume so richly illustrate, he never forgot his origins as the son of a failed provincial grocer and grandson of a one-time peasant and serf.

In his work as a whole he chiefly focuses on the privileged class which he himself had joined as an outsider—that of the

---

[3] See *The Oxford Chekhov*, iv. 5; v. 4–5.

landed gentry, officials, and professional people; and also of the 'intelligentsia', a notoriously elusive group overlapping those previously mentioned. Eternal students, ailing university professors, bankrupt landowners, incompetent architects, fuddy-duddy grammar school masters, overworked doctors, conscience-stricken industrialists, self-deprecating, pompous, or ironical higher bureaucrats: for all their pathetic attributes (in much of Chekhov) these were yet members of the upper crust—as one look at the typical Russian peasant would at once make clear.

Typical of Chekhov such upper-crust characters indeed are, but just how far they are from exhausting his social range the present volume richly illustrates. It consists almost exclusively of stories in which the emphasis lies on characters from the less privileged levels of society.

The Russian underclass included principally, and at the lowest level, the peasantry, which accounted for four-fifths of the population, consisting mostly of illiterate, poor, and down-trodden individuals who retained the status of peasant in law without necessarily being employed on the land. As for the intermediate area between peasant and élite, one despairs of finding the right nomenclature, since 'middle class' suggests something foreign to Russian conditions. To the higher part of this intermediate stratum belonged the merchants and the clergy—as represented in *The Steppe* by Father Christopher and Kuzmichov. To the humbler class of intermediates belonged what might be called the junior NCOs of society— petty officials, artisans, parish clerks, hospital orderlies, and the like. Old-fashioned in their dress and customs, in which they often resembled the peasants rather than the gentry, and often speaking an 'earthy' form of substandard Russian, such persons also tend to adopt on Chekhov's pages a form of comic, pseudo-sophisticated speech which presents considerable problems to those translators who are aware of its special nuances. It is persons of this social category that the judge in *An Awkward Business* calls 'in-betweeners'—those who belong to neither of 'the two poles of society . . . professional people and peasants'.

Elsewhere in the same story they are described as 'neither peasant nor master, neither fish nor fowl'.

An Awkward Story presents what *The Steppe* lacks: a clash of social classes. The obstreperous hospital orderly Smirnovsky, an 'in-betweener' if there ever was one, is locked in conflict with his superior officer, the doctor, who falls over himself trying to be fair to this appalling lout, but who is comically doomed by Russian conditions to win the contest, however hard he tries, in effect, to lose it. It is one of Chekhov's most acute comments on the Russian class system. On rereading it I feel that I did it less than justice in my second biography of Chekhov, where its ineffectiveness is stressed—as I now think, wrongly. As for what rings like a dismissive sentence ('seldom did even Chekhov write so inconclusive a study of inconclusiveness'), that still seems to be true, but is surely a compliment to the story rather than the reverse.[4] For a very different confrontation, lacking the element of open conflict, between a gentleman and an 'in-betweener', readers may turn to the haunting *In the Cart* and to the relationship or non-relationship between Squire Khanov and the unfortunate schoolmistress Mariya.

If a Smirnovsky, if a Mariya can rate as Russian 'in-betweeners', what of the real social dregs? We shall meet them in plenty—not his horse rustlers (who formed a special élite of their own), but his Siberian exiles, his poor cobblers, his struggling coffin-makers, and their ilk. In *At Christmas* we sink to the pathetic world of the village woman Vasilisa so cruelly defrauded of her fifteen copecks by the scoundrelly Yegor. And in *Patch* our protagonist is a mere quadruped.

In three particularly eloquent stories Chekhov explores the gulf which separates the élite from this social stratum even lower than that of Hospital Orderly Smirnovsky. The eponymous hero of *Gusev* is an innocent, if somewhat brutal, peasant soldier, and is shown in contrast with the embittered intellectual Paul Ivanovich—by no means a privileged member of

---

[4] R. Hingley, *A New Life of Anton Chekhov* (London, 1975); repr. in paperback as *A Life of Anton Chekhov* (Oxford, 1989), p. 115.

society, but emphatically on the other side of the educational, linguistic, and class barrier to the dying soldier-hero. This plain tale of a ship's sick bay in the tropics ends with a burial of both men at sea, and consists of death-bed conversations that are characterized by the lack of effective communication between human beings which so fascinated Chekhov as a theme. Despite Paul Ivanovich's insistence on travelling third-class, and on airing his views in some splendid harangues, the rift between first- and third-class Russian remains unbridged at the time when both bodies are consigned to the ocean.

Two further stimulating variants on this theme are presented by *New Villa* and *On Official Business*. In the first, an engineer successfully bridges a river near a village. But his well-meaning wife can build no bridge at all between herself and the local villagers, for all her attempts to fraternize with Rodion, Stepanida, and their kind. A bemused and sorry crew—some kind-hearted men and women, some malicious hooligans— Chekhov's muzhiks, as always in his work, are presented in a manner militantly contrary to the stereotype of Russian populist and Slavophile literature about the noble peasant. He had many times flouted these canons before, and most notoriously in his story *Peasants* (which will be found in the World's Classics volume *The Russian Master and Other Stories*), but he evidently felt that the point was worth making again and again. Howls of anguish from Russia's embattled pseudo-progressive and trendy peasant-fanciers might annoy him, but he always stuck to telling the truth as he saw it.

A similar rift is that portrayed in *On Official Business*. A magistrate and a coroner have been summoned to conduct an inquest in a village. Here they make memorable contact with the local constable, or *sotsky*, a downtrodden elderly messenger whose life consists largely of trudging through snow drifts to deliver official forms. The *sotsky* of this story was modelled on the real-life *sotsky* of Melikhovo, where Chekhov had his estate.

The two least typical items represented here are, probably, *The Bet* and *The Head Gardener's Story*. With their disembodied settings and their powerful moralizing pretensions they might seem as far from Chekhov as it is possible to go. But they do have their parallels, reminding us of his experimental attempts of the late 1880s to purvey Tolstoyan messages in fiction, as also does *Rothschild's Fiddle*. These are not vintage Chekhov, perhaps, but they are more than mere curiosities. To this same small group may be assigned a better-known item—*The Student*, that tantalizing, brief, plotless study which Chekhov once puzzlingly described as his own favourite among all his works, and which he also claimed as a manifesto in favour of optimism. It is, like *Beauties*, one of the items which most appeal to those who like to discourse on Chekhov's 'lyricism'; 'for sheer lyricism this takes the biscuit', as I seem to remember one reviewer writing. But *The Student* also has its charm for those who, like myself, prize Chekhov more for his inimitable astringency.

As this brief survey indicates, the stories in this volume are not quite what many readers of Chekhov may have come to expect. As studies of the Russian underclass they are typical, perhaps, of an important minor enclave within his work rather than of his work as a whole. But they have nothing to lose from comparison with more familiar material. On the contrary, they enhance it, while also providing eloquent testimony to the power and flexibility of an art which everywhere transcends its sociological, its geographical, its psychological, and any other of its analysable or classifiable aspects.

SELECT BIBLIOGRAPHY

W. H. Bruford, *Chekhov and his Russia: A Sociological Study* (London, 1948).

The Oxford Chekhov. Tr. and ed. Ronald Hingley. Nine vols. (London, 1964–80).

Letters of Anton Chekhov. Tr. Michael Henry Heim in collaboration with Simon Karlinsky. Selection, Commentary and Introduction by Simon Karlinsky (New York, 1973).

Letters of Anton Chekhov. Selected and edited by Avrahm Yarmolinsky (New York, 1973).

T. Eekman, ed., *Anton Chekhov, 1860–1960* (Leiden, 1960).

Ronald Hingley, *Chekhov: A Biographical and Critical Study* (London, 1950).

—— *A New Life of Anton Chekhov* (London, 1976); also, the same in paperback, *A Life of Anton Chekhov* (Oxford, 1989).

Robert Louis Jackson, ed., *Chekhov: A Collection of Critical Essays* (Englewood Cliffs, NJ, 1967).

Karl D. Kramer, *The Chameleon and the Dream: The Image of Reality in Čexov's Stories* (The Hague, 1970).

Virginia Llewellyn Smith, *Anton Chekhov and the Lady with the Dog*. Foreword by Ronald Hingley (London, 1973).

A CHRONOLOGY OF
ANTON CHEKHOV

All dates are given old style.

1860   16 or 17 January. Born in Taganrog, a port on the Sea of Azov in south Russia.

1876   His father goes bankrupt. The family moves to Moscow, leaving Anton to finish his schooling.

1879   Joins family and enrols in the Medical Faculty of Moscow University.

1880   Begins to contribute to *Strekoza* ('Dragonfly'), a St Petersburg comic weekly.

1882   Starts to write short stories and a gossip column for *Oskolki* ('Splinters') and to depend on writing for an income.

1884   Graduates in medicine. Shows early symptoms of tuberculosis.

1885–6   Contributes to *Peterburgskaya gazeta* ('St Petersburg Gazette') and *Novoye vremya* ('New Time').

1886   March. Letter from D. V. Grigorovich encourages him to take writing seriously.
    First collection of stories: *Motley Stories*.

1887   Literary reputation grows fast. Second collection of stories: *In the Twilight*.
    19 November. First Moscow performance of *Ivanov*: mixed reception.

1888   First publication (*The Steppe*) in a serious literary journal, *Severny vestnik* ('The Northern Herald').

1889   31 January. First St Petersburg performance of *Ivanov*: widely and favourably reviewed.
    June. Death of brother Nicholas from tuberculosis.

1890   April–December. Crosses Siberia to visit the penal settlement on Sakhalin Island. Returns via Hong Kong, Singapore, and Ceylon.

1891   First trip to western Europe: Italy and France.

1892   March. Moves with family to small country estate at Melikhovo, 50 miles south of Moscow.

1895   First meeting with Tolstoy.

1896   17 October. First—disastrous—performance of *The Seagull* in St Petersburg.

1897   Suffers severe haemorrhage.

1897–8   Winters in France. Champions Zola's defence of Dreyfus.

1898   Beginning of collaboration with the newly founded Moscow Art Theatre. Meets Olga Knipper. Spends the winter in Yalta, where he meets Gorky.

          17 December. First Moscow Art Theatre performance of *The Seagull*: successful.

1899   Completes the building of a house in Yalta, where he settles with mother and sister.

          26 October. First performance by Moscow Art Theatre of *Uncle Vanya* (written ?1896).

1899–1901 First collected edition of his works (10 volumes).

1901   31 January. *Three Sisters* first performed.
          25 May. Marries Olga Knipper.

1904   17 January. First performance of *The Cherry Orchard*.
          2 July. Dies in Badenweiler, Germany.

THE STEPPE

THE STORY OF A JOURNEY

I

On an early July morning a dilapidated springless carriage—one of those antediluvian britzkas now used in Russia only by merchants' clerks, cattle-dealers and poor priests—drove out of N., a sizeable town in Z. County, and thundered along the post road. It rumbled and squeaked at the slightest movement, to the doleful accompaniment of a pail tied to the back-board. These sounds alone, and the wretched leather tatters flapping on the peeling chassis, showed just how decrepit, how fit for the scrap heap it was.

Two residents of N. occupied the britzka. One was Ivan Kuzmichov, a clean-shaven, bespectacled merchant in a straw hat, who looked more like a civil servant than a trader. The other was Father Christopher Siriysky, principal priest at St. Nicholas's Church—a short, long-haired old man wearing a grey canvas caftan, a broad-brimmed top hat and a brightly embroidered belt. The former was absorbed in his thoughts, and kept tossing his head to keep himself awake. On his face a habitual businesslike reserve was in conflict with the cheerfulness of one who has just said good-bye to his family and had a drop to drink. The other man gazed wonderingly at God's world with moist eyes and a smile so broad that it even seemed to take in his hat brim. His face was red, as if from cold. Both Kuzmichov and Father Christopher were on their way to sell wool. They had just been indulging in cream doughnuts while taking farewell of their households, and they had had a drink despite the early hour. Both were in excellent humour.

Besides the two already described, and the coachman Deniska tirelessly whipping his pair of frisky bay horses, the carriage had another occupant: a boy of nine with a sunburnt, tear-stained face. This was Kuzmichov's nephew Yegorushka. With his uncle's permission and Father Christopher's blessing he was on his way to a school of the type intended for gentlemen's sons. His mother Olga—Kuzmichov's sister and widow of a minor official—adored educated people and refined society, and she had begged her brother to take the boy on his wool-selling trip and deliver him to this institution. Understanding neither where he was going nor why, the boy sat on the box by Deniska's side, holding the man's elbow to stop himself falling, and bobbing about like a kettle on the hob. The swift pace made his red shirt balloon at the back, and his new coachman-style hat with the peacock feather kept slipping to the back of his neck. He considered himself extremely unfortunate, and was near to tears.

As they drove past the prison Yegorushka looked at the sentries slowly pacing near the high white wall, at the small barred windows, at the cross glittering on the roof, and remembered the day of Our Lady of Kazan, a week earlier, when he and his mother had attended the celebrations at the prison church. Before that he had visited the gaol at Easter with Deniska and Lyudmila the cook, taking Easter cakes, Easter eggs, pies and roast beef. The convicts had thanked them and crossed themselves, and one had given the boy some tin studs of his own manufacture.

While the boy gazed at the familiar sights the hateful carriage raced on and left them all behind. Beyond the prison black, smoke-stained forges flashed past, and then the tranquil green cemetery with the stone wall round it. From behind the wall cheerful white crosses and tombstones peeped out, nestling in the foliage of cherry trees and seen as white patches from a distance. At blossom time, Yegorushka remembered, the white patches mingled with the cherry blooms in a sea of white, and when the cherries had ripened the white tombs and crosses were crimson-spotted, as if with blood. Under the cherries behind the wall the boy's father and his grandmother Zinaida slept day and night. When Grandmother had died she had been put in a long, narrow coffin, and five-copeck pieces had been placed on her eyes, which would not stay shut. Before dying she had been alive, and she had brought him soft poppy-seed bun rings from the market, but now she just slept and slept.

Beyond the cemetery were the smoking brickyards. From long thatched roofs, huddling close to the ground, great puffs of thick black smoke rose and floated lazily upwards. The sky above the brickyards and cemetery was dark, and the great shadows of the smoke clouds crept over the fields and across the road. In the smoke near the roofs moved people and horses covered with red dust.

With the brickyards the town ended and open country began. Yegorushka took a last look back at the town, pressed his face against Deniska's elbow and wept bitterly.

'What, still howling, you old cry-baby?' asked Kuzmichov. 'Still snivelling, you mother's darling. If you don't want to come, stay behind—nobody's forcing you.'

'Never mind, Yegorushka, old son, it's all right,' Father Christopher rapidly muttered. 'Never mind, my boy. Call on God, for you seek not evil but good. Learning is light, they say, and ignorance is darkness. Verily it is so.'

'Do you want to go back?' Kuzmichov asked.

'Yes, I d-do,' sobbed the boy.

'Then you may as well. There's no point in your coming anyway—it's a complete fool's errand.'

'Never mind, son,' Father Christopher went on. 'Call on God. Lomonosov once travelled just like this with the fishermen, and he became famous throughout Europe. Learning conjoined with faith yields fruit pleasing to God. What does the prayer say? "For the glory of the Creator, for our parents' comfort, for the benefit of church and country." That's the way of it.'

'There's various kinds of benefit.' Kuzmichov lit a cheap cigar. 'There's some study for twenty years, and all to no purpose.'

'That does happen.'

'Some benefit from book-learning, others just get their brains addled. She has no sense, my sister—wants to be like gentlefolk, she does, and make a scholar of the boy. And she can't see that I could set him up for life, doing the business I do. The point is that if everyone becomes a scholar and gentleman there won't be anyone to trade and sow crops. We'll all starve.'

'But if everyone trades and sows crops there won't be anyone to master learning.'

Thinking they had each said something weighty and cogent, Kuzmichov and Father Christopher assumed a serious air and coughed simultaneously. Having heard their talk but making nothing of it, Deniska tossed his head, sat up and whipped both bays. Silence followed.

By now a plain—broad, boundless, girdled by a chain of hills—lay stretched before the travellers' eyes. Huddling together and glancing out from behind one another, the hills merged into rising ground extending to the very horizon on the right of the road, and disappearing into the lilac-hued far distance. On and on you travel, but where it all begins and where it ends you just cannot make out. Behind them the sun was already peeping out over the town and had quietly, unfussily set about its work. First, far ahead where the sky met the earth—near some ancient burial mounds and a windmill resembling from afar a tiny man waving his arms—a broad, bright yellow band

crept over the ground. Then, a minute later, another bright strip
appeared a little nearer, crawled to the right and clasped the hills.
Something warm touched Yegorushka's back as a stripe of light stole
up behind him and darted over britzka and horses, soaring to meet
other bands until the whole wide prairie suddenly flung off the penum-
bra of dawn, smiled and sparkled with dew.

Mown rye, coarse steppe grass, milkwort, wild hemp—all that the
heat had browned, everything reddish and half dead—was now
drenched in dew and caressed by the sun, and was reviving to bloom
again. Arctic petrels swooped over the road with happy cries, gophers
called to each other in the grass, and from somewhere far to the left
came the plaint of lapwings. Scared by the carriage, a covey of partridges sprang up and flew off to the hills, softly trilling. Grasshoppers,
cicadas, field crickets and mole crickets fiddled their squeaking, monotonous tunes in the grass.

But time passed, the dew evaporated, the air grew still and the dis-
illusioned steppe assumed its jaded July aspect. The grass drooped, the
life went out of everything. The sunburnt hills, brown-green and—in
the distance—mauvish, with their calm, pastel shades, the plain, the
misty horizon, the sky arching overhead and appearing so awesomely
deep and transparent here in the steppe, where there are no woods or
high hills—it all seemed boundless, now, and numb with misery.

How sultry and forlorn! As the carriage raced on Yegorushka saw
only the same old sky, plain, hills. The music in the grass was hushed,
the petrels had flown away, the partridges had vanished. Over the
faded grass rooks idly hovered—all alike, making the steppe more
monotonous still.

A kite skimmed the earth with even sweep of wings, suddenly
paused in mid-air, as if pondering the tedium of existence, then flut-
tered its wings and sped over the prairie like an arrow. Why did it
fly? What did it want? No one knew, and far away the mill flapped its
sails.

Now and then, to break the monotony, came the glimpse of a white
skull or boulder in the tall grass. A grey menhir loomed for a moment,
or a parched willow with a blue crow on its top branch. A gopher ran
across the road, and once again grass, hills and rooks flitted before the
eyes.

But now, thank God, a wagon approached—loaded with sheaves of
corn, with a peasant girl lying on top. Sleepy, exhausted by the heat,
she lifted her head to gaze at the travellers. Deniska gaped at her, the

bays craned at the sheaves, the carriage screeched as it kissed the wagon, and the prickly ears of corn brushed Father Christopher's hat.

'Look where you're going, dumpling!' shouted Deniska. 'Hey, balloon-face! Stung by a bumble bee, was you?'

The girl smiled sleepily, moved her lips and lay back again. Then a lone poplar appeared on a hill. Who planted it? Why was it there? God alone knows. It was hard to tear one's eyes away from the graceful form and green drapery. Was that beautiful object happy? There is summer's heat, there are winter's frosts and blizzards, and there are terrible autumnal nights when you see nothing but blackness, and hear only the wayward, furiously howling wind. Worst of all, you are alone, alone, alone, all your life. Beyond the poplar bands of wheat stretched their bright yellow carpet from the roadside to the top of the hill. The corn had already been cut and gathered into stooks on the hill, but at the bottom they were still reaping. Six reapers swung their scythes side by side, and the scythes cheerfully glittered, shrieking in shrill unison. The movements of the women binding the sheaves, the reapers' faces, the gleaming scythes—all showed how burning and stifling the heat was. A black dog, its tongue hanging out, ran from the reapers towards the carriage, probably meaning to bark, but stopped half way and cast a bored glance at Deniska, who shook his whip at it. It was too hot for barking. A woman straightened up, clutched her tormented back with both hands and followed Yegorushka's red shirt with her eyes. Pleased by the colour or remembering her own children, she stood motionless for a while, staring after him.

But then, after the glimpse of wheat, came another expanse of scorched plain, burnt hills, sultry sky. Again a kite hovered over the ground. Far away the mill still whirled its sails, still resembling a tiny man waving his arms. What a tedious sight! It seemed that they would never reach it, that it was running away from the carriage.

Father Christopher and Kuzmichov said nothing. Deniska whipped up his horses and shouted. Yegorushka had stopped crying and gazed listlessly about him. The heat, the tedium of the prairie had exhausted him. He seemed to have been travelling and bobbing up and down with the sun baking his back for a very long time. They had not done seven miles yet, but he already felt that it was time for a rest. The cheerful expression had gradually disappeared from his uncle's face, leaving only the businesslike reserve that lends an implacably inquisitorial air to a gaunt, clean-shaven face—especially if bespectacled, and with nose and temples covered with dust. But Father Christopher still gazed admiringly at God's world and smiled. Not speaking, he was thinking some serene, cheerful thought, and a kindly, good-humoured smile was stamped on his face. It also looked as if that serene, cheerful thought had been stamped on his brain by the heat.

'Well, Deniska, shall we overtake the wagons soon?' asked Kuzmichov.

Deniska looked at the sky, rose in his seat and whipped his horses. 'By nightfall, God willing.'

Barks were heard, and half a dozen huge prairie sheepdogs suddenly pounced at the carriage with ferocious howls as if from ambush. Extremely vicious, red-eyed with malice, their shaggy muzzles resembling enormous spiders, they surrounded the britzka and set up a hoarse bellow, jealously jostling each other, imbued with utter loathing, and seeming ready to rend horses, vehicle and people asunder. Deniska, who liked teasing and whipping, and who was glad of his opportunity, bent over with an expression of unholy glee, and lashed one dog with his whip. The dogs growled more loudly than ever and the horses rushed on. Hardly able to keep his seat, Yegorushka realized, as he looked at the dogs' eyes and teeth, that he would be torn to pieces at once if he fell off. Yet he felt no fear, and looked on with malicious glee like Deniska, sorry to have no whip in his hands.

The carriage drew level with a drove of sheep.

'Stop!' shouted Kuzmichov. 'Pull up! Whoa!'

Deniska flung his whole body back and pulled the horses up. The carriage stopped.

'Come here, man!' shouted Kuzmichov to the drover. 'And call your bloody dogs off!'

The old drover, ragged and barefoot, in a warm cap with a dirty sack on his hip and a long crook—a regular Old Testament figure— called off the dogs, doffed his cap and came up to the carriage. At the other end of the flock another no less patriarchial figure stood motionless, staring unconcernedly at the travellers.

'Whose sheep are these?' Kuzmichov asked.

'Varlamov's,' the old man answered loudly.

'Varlamov's,' repeated the shepherd at the other end of the flock.

'Now, did Varlamov pass this way yesterday or didn't he?'

'No, sir. 'Twas his bailiff as came past, and that's a fact.'

'Drive on!'

The carriage rolled on and the drovers were left behind with their vicious dogs. Yegorushka looked glumly ahead at the mauve horizon, and he now began to feel that the whirling windmill was coming nearer. It grew bigger and bigger until it was quite large and its two sails were clearly distinguishable. One was old and patched, but the other had been made with new wood only recently, and shone in the sun.

The carriage drove straight on while the windmill for some reason began moving to the left. On and on they travelled, and it kept moving to the left while remaining in view.

'A fine windmill Boltva has made for his son,' remarked Deniska. 'But why can't we see his farm?'

'It's over there, beyond the dip.'

Soon Boltva's farm did indeed appear, but the windmill still failed to retreat. Keeping pace with them, it watched Yegorushka, waving its shiny sail like some wizard of the steppes.

II

Towards midday the britzka turned off the road to the right, went on a little at walking pace, then stopped. Yegorushka heard a quiet, a most delectable gurgling, and felt a different air brush his face with its cool velvety touch. From the hill, that nature had glued together out of monstrous boulders, a thin stream of water jetted through a little pipe of hemlock wood put in by some unknown benefactor. It hit the ground, and—limpid, sparkling merrily in the sun, quietly murmuring as if fancying itself a mighty, turbulent torrent—swiftly ran away to the left. Not far from the hill the little brook broadened into a pool. The hot rays and parched soil thirstily drank it in, sapping its strength. But it must have merged with another similar stream a little further on, because dense, green, lush sedge was visible along its course about a hundred yards from the hill. As the carriage approached three snipe flew up from there with a cry.

The travellers settled down by the brook to rest and feed the horses. Kuzmichov, Father Christopher and Yegorushka sat on a felt rug in the sparse shadow cast by the britzka and the unharnessed horses, and began eating. After Father Christopher had drunk some water and eaten a hard-boiled egg the serene, cheerful thought—stamped on his brain by the heat—craved utterance. He looked at Yegorushka affectionately and chewed.

'I myself have studied, son,' he began. 'From my earliest years God imbued me with sense and understanding. And so, unlike other boys, I was rejoicing my parents and teachers by my comprehension when

I was only your age. Before I was fifteen I could speak Latin, and write Latin verse, as well as Russian. I remember being crozier-bearer to Bishop Christopher. After service one day, as I recall, on the saint's day of our most pious Sovereign Alexander the First of blessed memory, he unrobed in the chancel, looked at me kindly and asked: *"Puer bone, quam appellaris?"* And I answered: *"Christophorus sum."* And he said: *"Ergo connominati sumus"*—we were namesakes, that is. Then he asked me in Latin whose son I was. I answered, also in Latin, that my father was Deacon Siriysky of Lebedinskoye village. Noting the celerity and clarity of my answers, the Bishop blessed me, saying: "Write and tell your father that I shall not forget him and shall keep you in mind." Hearing this exchange in Latin, the priests and fathers in the chancel were also no little amazed, and each expressed his pleasure by praising me. Before I had grown whiskers, my boy, I could read Latin, Greek and French. I knew philosophy, mathematics, secular history and all branches of learning. God gave me a wonderful memory. Time was, if I'd read something once or twice I could remember it by heart. My preceptors and patrons were amazed, expecting me to become a great scholar and a church luminary. I did think of going to Kiev to continue my studies, but my parents disapproved. "You'll be studying all your life," said my father. "We'll never see the end of it." Hearing these words, I gave up learning and took an appointment. Aye, I never became a scholar, of course, but at least I didn't disobey my parents. I was a comfort to them in their old age, gave them a decent funeral. Obedience is more blessed than fasting and prayer.'

'I bet you've forgotten all you ever learnt,' Kuzmichov remarked.

'Of course I have. I'm past seventy now, praise be. I can still remember a scrap or two of philosophy and rhetoric, but languages and mathematics—I've quite forgotten them.'

Father Christopher frowned and pondered. 'What is a being?' he asked in a low voice. 'A being is an integral entity sufficient unto itself.' He flexed his neck and laughed delightedly. 'Food for the soul,' said he. 'Verily, matter nourisheth the flesh and spiritual sustenance the soul.'

'Learning's all very well,' sighed Kuzmichov. 'But if we don't overtake Varlamov we'll be taught a lesson we'll never forget.'

'He's not a needle in a haystack. We'll find him—he's knocking around in the area.'

The same three snipe flew over the sedge, their squeaks betraying alarm and vexation at being driven off the brook. The horses steadily munched and whinnied. Deniska attended them, trying to demonstrate his utter indifference to the cucumbers, pies and eggs that his masters were eating by plunging into the slaughter of the flies and horse-flies clinging to the animals' bellies and backs. Uttering a peculiar, venom-ously exultant guttural sound, he swatted his victims with gusto, grunting with annoyance when he missed and following each lucky fly that escaped death with his eyes.

'Deniska, what are you up to? Come and eat.' Kuzmichov sighed deeply—a sign that he was replete.

Deniska approached the mat diffidently and picked out five large yellow cucumbers—what they called 'yolkies'—not venturing to choose smaller, fresher specimens. He then took two black, cracked hard-boiled eggs, and—hesitantly, as if afraid of someone slapping his outstretched hand—touched a pie with his finger.

'Go on, help yourself,' urged Kuzmichov.

Deniska seized the pie decisively, went off far to one side and sat on the ground, his back to the carriage. There ensued a chewing noise so loud that even the horses turned round and looked at Deniska sus-piciously.

After his meal Kuzmichov got a bag containing something out of the carriage. 'I'm going to sleep,' he told Yegorushka. 'You mind no one takes this bag from under my head.'

Father Christopher removed his cassock, belt and caftan, seeing which Yegorushka was downright astounded. That priests wore trousers he had had no inkling, and Father Christopher was wearing real canvas trousers tucked into his high boots, and a short cotton jacket. With his long hair and beard, and in this costume so unsuited to his calling, he looked to the boy very like Robinson Crusoe. Having disrobed, Father Christopher and Kuzmichov lay in the shade under the britzka facing each other, and closed their eyes. Deniska, who had finished chewing, stretched out belly upwards in the sun's heat and also closed his eyes. 'Make sure no one steals the horses,' he told Yegorushka and fell asleep at once.

Quietness ensued. Nothing was heard but the horses' whinnying and chewing, and some snores from the sleepers. A little way off a single lapwing wailed, and there was an occasional squeak from the three snipe, which had flown up to see if the uninvited guests had left. The brook softly lisped and gurgled, but none of these sounds tres-passed on the silence or stirred the sluggish air. Far from it, they only made nature drowsier still.

Panting in the heat, which was particularly oppressive after the meal, Yegorushka ran to the sedge and surveyed the locality from there. He saw exactly what he had seen that morning: plain, hills, sky, purple horizons. But the hills were nearer and there was no windmill, for that had been left far behind. From behind the rocky hill where the stream flowed another—smoother and broader—hill loomed, with a small hamlet of five or six homesteads clinging to it. Near the huts neither people, trees nor shadows could be seen—the settlement might have choked in the hot air and withered away. To pass the time the boy caught a grasshopper in the herbage, held it to his ear in his closed hand, and listened to its pizzicato for some time. Bored with that music, he chased a flock of yellow butterflies flying up to the sedge to drink, and somehow found himself near the carriage again. His uncle and Father Christopher were fast asleep—a sleep that was sure to last two or three hours, to let the horses rest. How was the boy to get through all that time? Where could he escape the heat? No easy problem, that.

Without thinking, Yegorushka put his lips under the jet running out of the pipe. His mouth felt cold, and there was a smell of hemlock. He drank thirstily at first, and then forced himself to go on till the sharp cold had spread from his mouth throughout his body and water had spilt on his shirt. Then he went to the carriage and looked at the sleepers. His uncle's face still expressed businesslike reserve. Obsessed with his business, Kuzmichov was always brooding on it—even in his sleep, and in church during the anthem 'And the Cherubims'. Not for a minute could he forget it, and at this moment he was probably dreaming of bales of wool, wagons, prices and Varlamov. But Father Christopher—gentle, light-hearted, always ready to laugh—had never in his life known anything capable of taking a stranglehold on his entire being. In the many deals he had embarked on in his time he had been less attracted by the business side than by the bustle and contact with other people that are part of any undertaking. For instance, what interested him about their present journey was less the wool, Varlamov and the prices than the long road, conversation on the way, sleeping under the carriage and eating at the wrong times. From his expression he must be dreaming of Bishop Christopher, the Latin conversation, his wife, cream doughnuts and everything that Kuzmichov could not possibly be dreaming of.

Watching their sleepy faces, the boy unexpectedly heard someone quietly singing. It was a woman's voice—not near, but just where it came from and from what direction it was hard to tell. Despondent, dirgelike, scarcely audible, the quiet song droned on. Now it came from the right, now from the left, now from above, now from underground, as if an invisible spirit floated, chanting, above the steppe. Looking around him, Yegorushka could not tell where the strange song originated, but as his ears became attuned he fancied that the grass must be the singer. Half dead, already perished, it was trying—wordlessly, but plaintively and earnestly—to plead that it was guilty of no crime and that it was unfair for the sun to scorch it. It asserted the passionate love of life of a creature still young and, but for the heat and drought, potentially beautiful. Guiltless, it yet begged forgiveness, swearing that it was suffering agonies of grief and self-pity.

Yegorushka listened for a while, until the lugubrious chant began to make the air seem more suffocating, hot and stagnant than ever. To drown the sound he hummed to himself and ran to the sedge, trying to bring his feet down noisily. Then he looked all around and found the singer. Near the last hut in the hamlet stood a woman in a short petticoat, long-legged like a heron. She was sowing, and white dust floated languidly down the hillock from her sieve. That she was the singer was now patently obvious. Two paces from her a small bareheaded boy, wearing just a smock, stood stock-still. As if bewitched by the song, he remained immobile, looking downhill—probably at Yegorushka's red shirt.

The singing ceased. Yegorushka made his way back to the carriage and, having nothing else to do, started playing with the jet of water again.

Once again the song droned out. It was the same long-legged woman in the hamlet over the hill. Suddenly Yegorushka felt bored again, left the water-pipe and cast his eyes aloft. What he saw was so unexpected that he was a little frightened. On one of the large, awkward boulders above his head stood a chubby little boy wearing just a smock. It was the same boy—with large, protruding stomach and thin legs—who had been with the woman. Open-mouthed, unblinking, with a blank stare and in some fear—as if contemplating a ghost—he inspected Yegorushka's crimson shirt and the britzka. The red colour attracted and beguiled him, while the carriage and the men asleep under it stirred his curiosity. Perhaps he himself had not been aware that the agreeable red colour and his own inquisitiveness had lured him down from the hamlet, and by now he was probably amazed at his own boldness. Yegorushka and he surveyed each other for a while, neither speaking, and both feeling slight embarrassment.

'What's your name?' Yegorushka asked, after a long silence.

The stranger's cheeks puffed out still more. He braced his back against the rock, opened his eyes wide, moved his lips and answered in a husky bass. 'Titus.'

That was all the boys said to each other. After more silence the mysterious Titus lifted one foot, found a heelhold and climbed up the boulder backwards without taking his eyes off Yegorushka. Backing away, while staring at Yegorushka as if afraid of being hit from behind, he clambered on to the next rock and so made his way up till he vanished altogether behind a crest.

Watching him out of sight, Yegorushka clasped his knees and bowed forward. The hot rays burnt the back of his head, neck and spine. The melancholy song now died away, now floated again in the still, stifling air, the stream gurgled monotonously, the horses munched, and time seemed to drag on for ever, as if it too had stagnated and congealed. A hundred years might have passed since morning. Perhaps God wanted Yegorushka, the carriage and the horses to come to a standstill, turn to stone like the hills, and stay in the same place for ever?

The boy raised his head and looked ahead with glazed eyes. The distant, lilac-coloured background, hitherto motionless, lurched and soared off, together with the sky, into the even further beyond, dragging the brown grass and sedge behind it, while Yegorushka hurtled after the retreating perspective with phenomenal speed. An unknown force silently drew him along with the heat and the weari-some song careering in his wake. He bowed his head, closing his eyes.

Deniska was the first to awake. Something must have bitten him, for he jumped up and quickly scratched his shoulder with a 'damn you, blast you and perdition take you!'

Then he went over to the brook, drank and slowly washed. His snorting and splashing roused Yegorushka from oblivion. The boy looked at the man's wet face, covered with drops and large freckles that created a mottled effect. 'Shall we be leaving soon?' he asked.

Deniska checked the sun's height. 'Soon, that's for sure.' He dried himself on his shirt tail, assumed an air of the utmost gravity and began hopping on one foot. 'Come on, hop! Race you to the sedge!'

Yegorushka was drowsy and exhausted by the heat, but hopped after him all the same. Deniska was about twenty, a working coach-man, and was going to be married. But he was still a boy at heart. He was fond of flying kites, of racing pigeons, of playing knuckle-bones and tag, and he was always taking part in children's games and quarrels. His employers only had to go away or fall asleep for him to start hopping, throwing stones and similar antics. Noting his genuine enthusiasm when cavorting in juvenile company, adults found it hard not to remark what a 'great oaf' he was. But children saw nothing odd in their domain being invaded by a large coachman—let him play so long as he wasn't too rough. Similarly, small dogs see nothing strange in an unsophisticated big dog intruding on them and playing with them.

Deniska overtook Yegorushka, obviously delighted to do so. He winked, and—to show that he could hop any distance on one foot—proposed that the boy should hop along the road with him, and then back to the carriage without stopping. This proposal Yegorushka declined, being out of breath and exhausted.

Suddenly assuming an air even graver than that which he wore when Kuzmichov rebuked him or threatened him with his stick, Deniska cocked his ears and dropped quietly on one knee. A stern and fearful expression, as of someone hearing heretical talk, appeared on his face, and he fixed his eyes on one spot, slowly raised his hand—holding it like a scoop—and then suddenly flopped on his stomach and slapped the scoop on the grass.

'Got him!' he hoarsely gloated, rising to his feet and presenting a big grasshopper to the boy's gaze.

Thinking to please the grasshopper, Yegorushka and Deniska stroked its broad green back with their fingers and touched its whiskers. Then Deniska caught a fat, blood-gorged fly and offered it to the grasshopper. With sublime nonchalance—as if it were an old friend of Deniska's—the creature moved its large, visor-shaped jaws and bit off the fly's belly. They let the grasshopper go, and it flashed the pink lining of its wings, landed on the grass, and at once resumed trilling. They let the fly go too. It preened its wings and flew off to the horses minus a stomach.

From beneath the carriage a deep sigh proceeded—Kuzmichov had woken up. He quickly raised his head, cast a troubled look into the distance, a look that slid unconcernedly past Yegorushka and Deniska and showed that his waking thoughts had been of wool and Varlamov.

'Father Christopher, get up—time to start,' he said anxiously. 'We've slept enough, we'll have missed our deal as it is. Hitch up the horses, Deniska.'

Father Christopher woke up, smiling the smile with which he had dozed off. Sleep had so creased and wrinkled his face that it seemed half its usual size. He washed, dressed, unhurriedly took a small, greasy psalter out of his pocket, faced east and began a whispered recital, crossing himself.

'Time to be off, Father Christopher,' Kuzmichov reproached him. 'The horses are ready. Now, look here——'

'Just a minute,' muttered Father Christopher. 'Must read my doxology. Didn't do it earlier.'

'Your doxology can wait.'

'I have to do one section every day, Kuzmichov, I really do.'

'God would forgive you.'

For a full quarter of an hour Father Christopher stood stock-still, facing east and moving his lips, while Kuzmichov looked at him almost with hatred, his shoulders fidgeting impatiently. He was particularly enraged when—after each 'Glory!'—Father Christopher took a deep breath, quickly crossed himself and thrice intoned his 'Halleluja, halleluja, halleluja, glory be to Thee, O Lord!' in a deliberately loud voice so that the others had to cross themselves too.

At last he smiled, looked at the sky, put the psalter in his pocket, and said *'Finis'*.

A minute later the britzka was under way. It might have been going back instead of pressing on, for the travellers saw the same scene as before noon. The hills still swam in the lilac-hued distance and there still seemed to be no end to them. High weeds and boulders flitted past and strips of stubble sailed by, while the same rooks, and the same kite with its steadily flapping wings, flew over the steppe. More and more the air seemed to congeal in heat and silence, submissive nature became petrified and soundless. There was no wind, no cheering fresh sound, no cloud.

But then at last, as the sun began setting in the west, the prairie, the hills and the air could stand the strain and torment no longer, lost patience and tried to cast off the burden. Behind the hills, a fleecy ash-grey cloud unexpectedly appeared. It exchanged glances with the steppe, as if to say 'I'm ready', and frowned. In the stagnant air something suddenly snapped, and a violent squall of wind swirled, roaring and whistling, about the area. At once the grass and last year's vegetation raised a murmur, while a dust spiral eddied over the road and sped along the prairie, sweeping straw, dragonflies and feathers behind it in a gyrating black column, soared up into the sky, and obscured the sun. Hither and thither over the heath tufts of loose herbage raced off, stumbling and bobbing. One of them was caught by the whirlwind, pirouetted like a bird, flew aloft, turned into a black speck and vanished. After it swept another, and then a third. Yegorushka saw two such tufts clash and grapple like wrestlers in the azure heights.

Right by the roadside a bustard flew up. Bathed in sunshine, wings and tail gleaming, it looked like an angler's artificial fly or a pond moth whose wings, as it darts over the water, merge with the whiskers that seem to have sprouted in front, behind and on all sides. Vibrating in the air like an insect, the bird soared vertically aloft with a shimmer of bright colours, and then—probably scared by a dust cloud—swerved aside, the glint of it remaining visible for a long time.

Then, alarmed and baffled by a whirlwind, a corncrake sprang up from the grass. It flew with the wind, not against it like other birds, and so its feathers were ruffled, puffing it out to a hen's size, and giving it a furious, imposing look. Only the rooks—grown old in the steppe and accustomed to its upsets—calmly floated over the grass, or pecked nonchalantly and heedlessly at the hard earth with their thick beaks.

There was a dull growl of thunder from beyond the hills, and a puff of fresh air. Deniska whistled cheerfully, belabouring his horses, while Father Christopher and Kuzmichov held their hats and stared at the hills. A shower would not come amiss.

With a little more effort, with one more heave, the steppe would assert itself, it seemed. But an invisible, oppressive force gradually immobilized wind and air, laying the dust, until stillness reigned again as if it had never been broken. The cloud vanished, the scorched hills frowned, and the subdued air was still, with only the troubled lapwings somewhere weeping and bemoaning their fate.

Soon evening came on.

III

A large bungalow with a rusty iron roof and dark windows showed up in the gloaming. It was called a posting inn, though it had no stableyard, and it stood in the middle of the prairie with no fencing round it. A wretched little cherry orchard and some hurdles made a dark patch somewhat to one side, and under the windows stood sleepy sunflowers, their heavy heads drooping. In the orchard a miniature windmill rattled, having been put there to scare the hares. Near the house there was nothing to see or hear but the prairie.

Barely had the britzka halted at the porch, which had an awning, when delighted voices were heard from inside—a man's and a woman's. The door squeaked on its counterweight, and a tall, scraggy figure instantly loomed up by the carriage in a flurry of arms and coat-skirts. It was the innkeeper Moses. Elderly, very pale-faced, with a handsome jet-black beard, he wore a threadbare black frock-coat that dangled from his narrow shoulders as from a coat-hanger, flapping its wing-like skirts whenever he threw his hands up in joy or horror. Besides the coat he wore broad white trousers not tucked into his boots, and a velvet waistcoat with a pattern of reddish flowers like gigantic bugs.

Recognizing the new arrivals, Moses was first rooted to the spot by the onrush of emotion, then flung up his arms and uttered a groan. His frock-coat flapped its skirts, his back curved into a bow, and his pale face twisted into a smile, as if seeing the carriage was no mere pleasure but excruciating ecstasy.

'Oh, goodness me, what a happy days this is for me!' he reedily intoned, gasping, bustling and hindering the travellers from getting out of their carriage by his antics. 'Ah, what, oh what, to do next? Mr. Kuzmichov! Father Christopher! And what a pretty little gentlemans that is sitting on the box, or may God punish me! Goodness me, but why am I standing here? Why am I not asking the guests into the parlour? Come in, I beg you most humbly. Make yourselves at home. Give me all your things. Goodness gracious me!'

Ferreting in the carriage and helping the visitors out, Moses suddenly turned back. 'Solomon, Solomon!' he bellowed in a frantic, strangled voice like a drowning man calling for help.

In the house a woman's voice repeated the 'Solomon, Solomon!'

The door squeaked on its counterweight, and on the threshold appeared a young Jew—short, with a large, beaked nose and a bald patch surrounded by coarse, curly hair. All his clothes were too short —his exceedingly shabby cutaway jacket, his sleeves and the woollen trousers that made him seem as docked and skimpy as a plucked bird. This was Moses' brother Solomon. Silently, with no greeting but a rather weird smile, he approached the carriage.

'Mr. Kuzmichov and Father Christopher are here.' Moses' tone hinted at a fear of being disbelieved. 'Aye, aye, and such a wonder it is that these good peoples are paying us a visit. Well, Solomon, take their things. This way, my honoured guests.'

A little later Kuzmichov, Father Christopher and Yegorushka were sitting at an old oak table in a large, gloomy, empty room. The table was almost isolated, since there was no other furniture in the room except for a broad sofa covered with tattered oilcloth and three objects that not everyone would have ventured to call chairs. They were a pathetic simulacrum of furniture, with oilcloth that had seen better days, and with backs canted unnaturally far back so that they closely resembled children's toboggans. It was hard to see what amenity the unknown carpenter had envisaged when giving those chair backs that pitiless curve, and one might have thought that it was not his doing but the work of some itinerant Hercules who had bent the chairs to show his strength and had then offered to put them right, only to make them even worse. The room had a lugubrious air. The walls were grey, the ceiling and cornices were smoke-stained, and there were long cracks and yawning holes of mysterious provenance on the floor, as if that same strong man had kicked them in with his heel. The room looked as if it would still have been dark even with a dozen lamps hanging in it. Neither walls nor windows boasted anything resembling decoration. On one wall, though, a list of regulations under the Two-Headed Eagle hung in a grey wooden frame, and on another wall was some engraving in a similar frame. It was inscribed 'Man's Indifference'. But to what man was indifferent was not clear since the engraving had faded considerably in course of time and was profusely fly-blown. The room smelt musty and sour.

After bringing his guests in, Moses went on twisting, gesticulating, cringing and uttering ecstatic cries, believing all these antics essential to the display of supreme courtesy and affability.

'When did our wagons go by?' Kuzmichov asked.

'One lot passed this morning, Mr. Kuzmichov, and the others rested here at dinner time and left in late afternoon.'

'Aha! Has Varlamov been by or not?'

'No, he hasn't. But his bailiff Gregory drove past yesterday morning, and he reckoned Varlamov must be over at the Molokan's farm.'

'Good. So we'll first overtake the wagons, and then go on to the Molokan's.'

'Mercy on us, Mr. Kuzmichov!' Moses threw up his arms in horror. 'Where can you go so late in the days? You enjoy a bite of supper and spend the night, and tomorrow morning, God willing, you can go and catch anyone you like.'

'There's no time. I'm sorry, Moses—some other day, not now. We'll stay a quarter of an hour and then be off. We can spend the night at the Molokan's.'

'A quarter of an hour!' shrieked Moses. 'Why, have you no fear of God? You will be making me to hide your hats and lock the door. At least have a bite to eat and some tea.'

'We've no time for tea, sugar and the rest of it,' said Kuzmichov.

Moses leant his head to one side, bent his knees, and held his open hands before him as if warding off blows. 'Mr. Kuzmichov, Father Christopher, be so kind as to take tea with me,' he implored with an excruciatingly sweet smile. 'Am I really such a bad mans that Mr. Kuzmichov cannot take tea with me?'

'All right then, we'll have some tea.' Father Christopher gave a sympathetic sigh. 'It won't take long.'

'Very well then,' agreed Kuzmichov.

Moses, flustered, gave a joyful gasp, cringed as if he had just jumped out of cold water into the warm, and ran to the door. 'Rosa, Rosa! Bring the samovar,' he shouted in the frantic, strangled voice with which he had previously called Solomon.

A minute later the door opened and in came Solomon carrying a large tray. He put it on the table, gave a sarcastic sidelong look, grinned the same weird grin. Now, by the light of the lamp, it was possible to see that smile distinctly. It was highly complex, expressing a variety of feelings, but with one predominant—blatant contempt. He seemed to be brooding on something both funny and silly, to feel both repugnance and scorn, to be rejoicing at something or other, and to be waiting for a suitable moment to launch a wounding sneer and a peal of laughter. His long nose, thick lips and crafty, bulging eyes seemed tense with the urge to cachinnate. Looking at his face, Kuzmichov smiled sardonically.

'Why didn't you come over to the fair at N. and do us your Jewish impressions?' he asked.

Two years previously, as Yegorushka well remembered, Solomon had had great success performing scenes of Jewish life in a booth at the N. fair. But the allusion made no impression on him. He went out without answering and came back with the samovar a little later.

Having finished serving, Solomon stepped to one side, folded his arms on his chest, thrust one leg out in front of him and fixed Father Christopher with a derisive stare. There was something defiant, arrogant and contemptuous about his pose, yet it was also highly pathetic and comic because the more portentous it became the more vividly it threw into relief his short trousers, docked jacket, grotesque nose and his whole plucked, bird-like figure.

Moses brought a stool from another room and sat a little way from the table. 'Good appetite! Tea! Sugar!' He began to entertain his guests. 'Enjoy your meal. Such rare, oh, such rare guests, and I haven't seen Father Christopher these five years. And will no one tell me who this nice little gentlemans is?' He looked tenderly at Yegorushka.

'It's my sister Olga's son,' answered Kuzmichov.

'Where is he going then?'

'To school. We're taking him to the high school.'

Out of politeness Moses registered surprise, sagely twisting his head. 'Is very good.' He wagged his finger at the samovar. 'And such a fine gentlemans you'll be when you leave school, we'll all take our hats off to you. You'll be clever, rich, and oh so grand. Now, won't your Mummy be pleased? Is good, good.'

He was silent for a while and stroked his knee. 'Forgive me, Father Christopher.' He spoke with a deferential, jocular air. 'I'm going to report you to the Bishop for robbing the merchants of their living. I'll get an official application form, and write that Father Christopher can't have much moneys of his own if he has turned to trade and started selling wool.'

'Yes, it's a notion I've taken in my old age,' Father Christopher laughed. 'I've turned from priest to merchant, old son. I should be at home saying my prayers, but here I am galloping about in my chariot, even as a very Pharaoh. Ah, vanity!'

'Still, you will make much moneys.'

'A likely tale. I'll get more kicks than halfpence. The wool isn't mine, you know, it's my son-in-law Michael's.'

'Then why hasn't he gone himself?'

'Why, because—. He's only a young shaver. He bought the wool all right, but as for selling it—he has no idea, he's too young. He spent all his money, counted on making a packet and cutting a bit of a dash, but he's tried here and he's tried there, and no one will even give him what he paid for it. Well, the lad messes around with it for a twelve-month, and then he comes to me. "Dad," says he, "you sell the wool, be so kind. I'm no good at these things." Well, that's true enough. As soon as things go wrong he runs to his dad, but till then he could manage without his dad. Doesn't consult me when buying it, oh no, but now things have come unstuck it's daddy this and daddy that. But what can daddy do? If it wasn't for Ivan Kuzmichov daddy could have done nothing. What a nuisance they are.'

'Yes, childrens are a lot of trouble, believe me,' sighed Moses. 'I have six myself. It's teach the one, dose the other, carry the third round in your arms, and when they grow up they're even more nuisance. There ain't nothing new about it, it was the same in Holy Scripture.

When Jacob had small childrens he wept, but when they grew up he wept more than ever.'

Father Christopher agreed, looking pensively at his glass. 'H'm, yes. Now, me, I haven't really done anything to anger God. I've lived out my span as lucky as could be. I've found good husbands for my daughters, I've set my sons up in life, and now I'm free, I've done my job, I can go where I like. I live quietly with my wife, eat, drink, sleep, enjoy my grandchildren, say my prayers—and that's all I need! Live on the fat of the land I do, and I don't need any favours. There has been no grief in my life. Suppose the Tsar asked me what I needed and wanted now—there isn't anything! I have everything, thanks be to God. There's no happier man in all our town. True, I'm a great sinner, but then—only God's without sin, eh?'

'Aye, true enough.'

'I've lost my teeth of course, my poor old back aches and so on, I'm short of breath and all that. I fall ill, the flesh is weak, but I have lived, haven't I? You can see that for yourself. In my seventies, I am. You can't go on for ever—mustn't outstay your welcome.'

Struck by a sudden thought, Father Christopher snorted into his glass, and then laughed himself into a coughing fit. Moses, too, laughed and coughed out of politeness.

'It was so funny!' Father Christopher made a helpless gesture. 'My eldest son Gabriel comes to stay with me. He's in the medical line, a doctor with the rural council down Chernigov way. Well, now. "I'm short of breath and so on," I tell him. "Now, you're a doctor, so you cure your father." So he undresses me there and then, he does a bit of tapping and listening—the usual tricks—squeezes my stomach. "Compressed air treatment's what you need, Dad," says he.'

Father Christopher laughed convulsively until he cried, and stood up. ' "Confound your compressed air," says I. "Confound your air!" ' He laughed as he brought out the words and made a derisive gesture with both hands.

Moses also stood up, clutched his stomach and uttered a shrill peal of mirth like the yap of a pekinese.

'Confound your compressed air!' the chortling Father Christopher repeated.

Laughing two notes higher, Moses uttered a cackle so explosive that he almost lost his footing. 'Oh, my God,' groaned he in mid-guffaw. 'Let me get my breath back. Oh, such a scream you are—you'll be the death of me, you will.'

While laughing and speaking he cast apprehensive, suspicious glances at Solomon, who stood in his former posture, smiling. To judge from his eyes and grin his scorn and hatred were genuine, but so incompatible were they with his plucked-hen look that Yegorushka interpreted the challenging mien and air of blistering contempt as buffoonery deliberately designed to amuse the honoured guests.

After silently drinking half a dozen glasses of tea Kuzmichov cleared a space on the table in front of him, took his bag—the same one that he had kept under his head when sleeping beneath the carriage—untied the string and shook it. Bundles of banknotes tumbled out on the table.

'Let's count them while there's time, Father,' said Kuzmichov.

On seeing the money Moses showed embarrassment, stood up, and —as a sensitive man not wanting to know others' secrets—tiptoed from the room, balancing with his arms. Solomon stayed where he was.

'How much in the one-rouble packets?' began Father Christopher.

'They're in fifties, and the three-rouble notes are in ninety-rouble packets. The twenty-fives and the hundreds come in thousands. You count out seven thousand eight hundred for Varlamov and I'll count Gusevich's. And mind you get it right.'

Never in his life had Yegorushka seen such a pile of money as that on the table. It must have been a vast amount indeed, because the bundle of seven thousand eight hundred put aside for Varlamov seemed so small compared to the pile as a whole. All this money might have impressed Yegorushka at any other time, moving him to ponder how many bagels, dough rolls and poppy-seed cakes you could buy with it. But now he looked at it unconcernedly, aware only of the foul smell of rotten apples and paraffin that it gave off. Exhausted by the jolting ride in the britzka, he was worn out and sleepy. His head felt heavy, his eyes would scarcely stay open, and his thoughts were like tangled threads. Had it been possible he would have been glad to lay his head on the table and close his eyes to avoid seeing the lamp and the fingers moving above the heap of notes, and he would have allowed his listless, sleepy thoughts to become more jumbled still. As he struggled to stay awake he saw everything double—lamplight, cups, fingers. The samovar throbbed, and the smell of rotten apples seemed yet more acrid and foul.

'Money, money, money!' sighed Father Christopher, smiling. 'What a nuisance you are! Now, I bet young Michael's asleep, dreaming of me bringing him a pile like this.'

'Your Michael has no sense.' Kuzmichov spoke in an undertone.

'Right out of his depth, he is. But you *are* sensible and open to reason. You'd better let me have your wool, like I said, and go back home. Very well, then—I'd give you half a rouble a bale over and above your price, and that just out of respect——'

'No thanks,' Father Christopher sighed. 'I'm grateful for your concern, and I wouldn't think twice about it, of course, if I had the choice. But you see, it's not my wool, is it?'

In tiptoed Moses. Trying not to look at the heap of money out of delicacy, he stole up to Yegorushka and tugged the back of his shirt. 'Come on, little gentlemans,' said he in a low voice. 'I'll show you such a nice little bear. He's oh such a fierce, cross little bear, he is.'

Sleepy Yegorushka stood up and sluggishly plodded after Moses to look at the bear. He entered a small room where his breath was caught, before he saw anything, by the sour, musty smell that was much stronger than in the big room, and was probably spreading through the house from here. One half of the room was dominated by a double bed covered with a greasy quilt, and the other by a chest of drawers and piles of miscellaneous clothing, beginning with stiffly starched skirts and ending with children's trousers and braces. On the chest of drawers a tallow candle burnt, but instead of the promised bear Yegorushka saw a big fat Jewess with her hair hanging loose, wearing a red flannel dress with black dots.

She had difficulty in turning in the narrow space between bed and chest of drawers, and emitted protracted groaning sighs as if from toothache. Seeing Yegorushka, she assumed a woebegone air, heaved a lengthy sigh, and—before he had time to look round—put a slice of bread and honey to his lips. 'Eat, sonny, eat. Your Mummy's not here, and there's no one to feed you. Eat it up.'

Yegorushka did so, though after the fruit-drops and honey cakes that he had at home every day he thought little of the honey, half of which was wax and bees' wings. While he ate, Moses and the Jewess watched and sighed. 'Where are you going, sonny?' she asked.

'To school.'

'And how many childrens does your Mummy have?'

'Only me, there's no others.'

'Ah me!' sighed the Jewess, turning up her eyes. 'Your poor, poor Mummy. How she will miss you, how she will cry! In a year we shall be taking our Nahum to school too. Ah me!'

'Oh, Nahum, Nahum!' sighed Moses, the loose skin of his pale face twitching nervously. 'And he is so poorly.'

The greasy quilt moved, and from it emerged a child's curly head on a very thin neck. Two black eyes gleamed, staring quizzically at Yegorushka. Still sighing, Moses and the Jewess went up to the chest of drawers and began a discussion in Yiddish. Moses spoke in a deep undertone, and his Yiddish sounded like a non-stop boom, boom, booming, while his wife answered in a thin voice like a turkey hen's with a twitter, twitter, twitter. While they were conferring a second curly head on a thin neck peeped out from the greasy quilt, then a third, then a fourth. Had Yegorushka possessed a vivid imagination he might have thought that the hundred-headed hydra lay beneath that quilt.

'Boom, boom, boom,' went Moses.

'Twitter, twitter, twitter,' answered his wife.

The conference ended with her diving with a deep sigh into the chest of drawers, unwrapping some kind of green rag there, and taking out a big, heart-shaped honey-cake. 'Take it, sonny.' She gave Yegorushka the cake. 'You have no Mummy now, isn't it? Is no one to give you nice things.'

Yegorushka put the cake in his pocket and backed towards the door, unable to continue breathing the musty, sour air in which the inn-keeper and his wife lived. Going back to the big room, he comfortably installed himself on the sofa and let his thoughts wander.

Kuzmichov had just finished counting the banknotes and was putting them back in his bag. He treated them with no particular respect, stuffing them in the dirty bag without ceremony, as unconcernedly as if they had been so much waste paper.

Father Christopher was talking to Solomon. 'Well, now, Solomon the Wise.' He yawned and made the sign of the cross over his mouth. 'How's business?'

'To what business do you allude?' Solomon stared at him as viciously as if some crime had been implied.

'Things in general. What are you up to?'

'Up to?' Solomon repeated the question with a shrug. 'Same as everyone else. I am, you see, a servant. I am my brother's servant. My brother is his visitors' servant. His visitors are Varlamov's servants. And if I had ten million Varlamov would be my servant.'

'But why should that be?'

'Why? Because there's no gentleman or millionaire who wouldn't lick the hand of a dirty Yid to make an extra copeck. As it is I'm a dirty Yid and a beggar, and everyone look at me as if I was a dog. But if I had moneys, Varlamov would make as big a fool of himself for me as Moses does for you.'

Father Christopher and Kuzmichov looked at each other, neither of them understanding Solomon.

'How can you compare yourself to Varlamov, you idiot?' Kuzmichov gave Solomon a stern, dour look.

'I'm not such an idiot as to compare myself to Varlamov.' Solomon looked at the others scornfully. 'Varlamov may be a Russian, but he's a dirty Yid at heart. Moneys and gain are his whole life, but I burnt mine in the stove. I don't need moneys or land or sheep, and I don't need people to fear me and take off their hats when I pass. So I am wiser than your Varlamov and more of a man.'

A little later Yegorushka, half asleep, heard Solomon discussing Jews in a hollow, lisping, rapid voice hoarse from the hatred that choked him. Having begun by speaking correctly, he had later lapsed into the style of a raconteur telling Jewish funny stories, employing the same exaggerated Yiddish accent that he had used at the fair.

Father Christopher interrupted him. 'Just one moment. If your faith displeases you, change it. But to laugh at it is sinful. The man who mocks his faith is the lowest of the low.'

'You don't understand,' Solomon rudely cut him short. 'That has nothing to do with what I was saying.'

'Now, that just shows what a stupid fellow you are.' Father Christopher sighed. 'I instruct you as best I can and you become angry. I speak to you as an old man, quietly, and you go off like a turkey—cackle, cackle, cackle. You really are a funny chap.'

In came Moses. He looked anxiously at Solomon and his guests, and again the loose skin on his face twitched nervously. Yegorushka shook his head and looked around him, catching a glimpse of Solomon's face just when it was turned three-quarters towards him and when the shadow of his long nose bisected his whole left cheek. The scornful smile half in shadow, the glittering, sneering eyes, the arrogant expression and the whole plucked hen's figure—doubling and dancing before Yegorushka's eyes, they made Solomon look less like a clown than some nightmare fantasy or evil spirit.

'What a devil of a fellow he is, Moses, God help him.' Father Christopher smiled. 'You'd better get him a job, find him a wife or something. He's not human.'

Kuzmichov frowned angrily while Moses cast another apprehensive, quizzical look at his brother and the guests. 'Leave the room, Solomon,' he said sternly. 'Go away.' And he added something in Yiddish.

With a brusque laugh Solomon went out.

'What was it?' Moses fearfully asked Father Christopher.

'He forgets himself,' Kuzmichov answered. 'He is rude and thinks too highly of himself.'

'I knew it!' Moses threw up his arms in horror. 'Oh, goodness gracious me!' he muttered in an undertone. 'Be so kind as to forgive him, don't be angry. That's what he's like, he is. Oh, goodness me! He's my own brothers, and he's been nothing but trouble to me, he has. Why, do you know, he——'

Moses tapped his forehead. 'He's out of his mind—a hopeless case, he is. I really don't know what I'm to do with him. He cares for no one, respects no one, fears no one. He laugh at everybody, you know, he say silly things, he get on people's nerves. You'll never believe it, but when Varlamov was here once, Solomon made some remark to him and he gave us both a taste of his whip! What for he whip me, eh? Was it my fault? If God has robbed my brother of his wits, it must be God's will. How is it my fault, eh?'

About ten minutes passed, but Moses still kept up a low muttering and sighing. 'He doesn't sleep of a night, he keeps thinking, thinking, thinking, but what he thinks about, God knows. If you go near him at night he get angry and he laugh. He doesn't like me either. And there's nothing he wants. When our Dad died he left us six thousand roubles apiece. I bought an inn, I married, and now I have childrens, but he burnt his moneys in the stove. Such a pity. Why he burn it? If he not need it, why he not give it me? Why he burn it?'

Suddenly the door squeaked on its counterweight, and the floor vibrated with footsteps. Yegorushka felt a draught of air and had the impression of a big black bird swooping past and beating its wings right by his face. He opened his eyes. His uncle had his bag in his hand, and stood near the sofa ready to leave. Holding his broad-brimmed top hat, Father Christopher was bowing to someone and smiling—not softly and tenderly as was his wont, but in a respectful, strained fashion that ill suited him. Meanwhile Moses was doing a sort of balancing act as if his body had been broken in three parts and he was trying his best not to disintegrate. Only Solomon seemed unaffected, and stood in a corner, his arms folded, his grin as disdainful as ever.

'Your Ladyship must forgive the untidiness,' groaned Moses with an excruciatingly sweet smile, taking no more notice of Kuzmichov or Father Christopher, but just balancing his whole body so as not to disintegrate. 'We're plain folk, my lady.'

Yegorushka rubbed his eyes. In the middle of the room stood what indeed was a ladyship—a very beautiful, buxom young woman in a black dress and straw hat. Before Yegorushka could make out her features the solitary graceful poplar he had seen on the hill that day somehow came into his mind.

'Was Varlamov here today?' a woman's voice asked.

'No, my lady,' Moses answered.

'If you see him tomorrow ask him to call at my place for a minute.'

Suddenly, quite unexpectedly, about an inch from his eyes Yegorushka saw velvety black eyebrows, big brown eyes and well-cared-for feminine cheeks with dimples from which smiles seemed to irradiate the whole face like sunbeams. There was a whiff of some splendid scent.

'What a pretty little boy,' said the lady. 'Who is he? See, Kazimir, what a charming child. Good heavens, he's asleep, the darling wee poppet!'

The lady firmly kissed Yegorushka on both cheeks. He smiled and shut his eyes, thinking he was asleep. The door squeaked and hurried footsteps were heard as someone came in and went out.

Then came a deep whisper from two voices. 'Yegorushka, Yegorushka, get up. We're leaving.'

Someone, Deniska apparently, set the boy on his feet and took his arm. On the way he half opened his eyes and once again saw the beautiful woman in the black dress who had kissed him. She stood in the middle of the room, watching him leave with a friendly smile and a nod. As he came to the door he saw a handsome, heavily built, dark man in a bowler hat and leggings. He must be the lady's escort.

From outside came a cry. 'Whoa there!'

At the front door Yegorushka saw a splendid new carriage and a pair of black horses. On the box sat a liveried groom holding a long whip.

Only Solomon came out to see the departing guests off, his face tense with the urge to guffaw, as if he was waiting impatiently for them to leave so that he could laugh at them to his heart's content.

'Countess Dranitsky,' whispered Father Christopher as he mounted the britzka.

'Yes, Countess Dranitsky,' repeated Kuzmichov, also in a whisper.

The impression made by the Countess's arrival must have been considerable, for even Deniska spoke in a whisper, not venturing to whip his bays and shout until the britzka had gone several hundred yards and nothing could be seen of the inn but a faint light.

IV

Who on earth was the elusive, mysterious Varlamov of whom so much was said, whom Solomon despised, whom even the beautiful Countess had need of? Sitting on the box by Deniska, the dozing Yegorushka thought about that personage. He had never set eyes on Varlamov, but he had often heard of him and imagined him. He knew that Varlamov owned acres by their scores of thousands, about a hundred thousand head of sheep and a lot of money. Of his life and activities the boy only knew that he was always 'knocking around' in the area, and that he was always in demand.

At home the boy had heard much of Countess Dranitsky too. She also owned acres by their scores of thousands, many sheep, a stud farm and a lot of money. Yet *she* did not 'knock around', but lived on a prosperous estate about which people he knew—including Kuz- michov, who often called there on business—told many a fabulous tale. For instance, it was said that in the Countess's drawing-room, which had the portraits of all the Kings of Poland hanging on the wall, there was a big, rock-shaped table-clock surmounted by a rampant gold horse with jewelled eyes and a gold rider who swung his sabre from side to side whenever the clock struck. The Countess was also said to give a ball twice a year. The gentry and officials of the county were invited, and even Varlamov attended. The guests all drank tea made from water boiled in silver samovars, ate the oddest dishes—for instance, raspberries and strawberries were served at Christmas—and danced to a band that played day and night.

'And how beautiful she is,' thought Yegorushka, remembering her face and smile.

Kuzmichov must have been thinking about the Countess too, because he spoke as follows when the carriage had gone about a mile and a half. 'Yes, and doesn't that Kazimir rob her! Two years ago I bought some wool from her, remember? And he picked up three thousand on that deal alone.'

'Just what you'd expect from a wretched Pole,' Father Christopher said.

'But she doesn't let it bother her. Young and foolish she is, with something missing in the top storey, as folks say.'

Somehow Yegorushka wanted to think only of Varlamov and the Countess, especially the Countess. His drowsy brain utterly rejected mundane thoughts and became fuddled, retaining only such magical and fantastic images as have the advantage of somehow springing into the mind automatically without taxing the thinker, but vanish without trace of their own accord at a mere shake of the head. In any case the surroundings did not encourage ordinary thoughts. On the right were dark hills, seeming to screen off something mysterious and terrifying, while on the left the whole sky above the horizon was steeped in a crimson glow, and it was hard to tell whether there was a fire somewhere or whether it was the moon about to rise. The distant prospect was visible, as by day, but now the delicate lilac hue had disappeared, obscured by the gloaming in which the whole steppe hid like Moses' children under the quilt.

On July evenings and nights quails and corncrakes no longer call, nightingales do not sing in wooded gullies, and there is no scent of flowers. But the steppe is still picturesque and full of life. Hardly has the sun gone down, hardly has darkness enfolded the earth when the day's misery is forgotten, all is forgiven, and the prairies breathe a faint sigh from their broad bosom. In the grass—as if it can no longer tell how old it is in the dark—a merry, youthful trilling, unknown by day, arises. The chattering, the whistling, the scratching, the bass, tenor and treble voices of the steppe—all blend in a continuous monotonous boom, a fine background to memories and melancholy. The monotonous chirring soothes like a lullaby. You drive on, feeling as if you are dozing, but the brusque alarm call of a wakeful bird comes from somewhere, or a vague noise resounds, like a human voice uttering a surprised, protracted sigh, and slumber closes your eyelids. Or you may drive past a bushy gully and hear the bird that prairie folk call a 'sleeper', with its cry of 'sleep, sleep, sleep'. Or another bird guffaws, or weeps in hysterical peals—an owl. Whom do they cry for? Who hears them in the steppe? God alone knows, but their cries are most mournful and plaintive. There is a scent of hay, dry grass and late flowers—a scent dense, sickly-sweet, voluptuous.

Everything is visible through the haze, but colours and outlines are hard to make out. All seems other than it is. As you journey onward you suddenly see a silhouette like a monk's on the roadside ahead of you. It does not move, but waits, holding something. A highwayman perhaps? The figure approaches, swells, draws level with the britzka, and you see that it is a solitary bush or boulder, not a man. Such immobile, waiting figures stand on the hills, hide behind the ancient barrows, peep out from the grass, all resembling human beings, all arousing suspicion.

When the moon rises the night grows pale and languid. It is as if the haze had never been. The air is limpid, fresh and warm, everything is clearly seen, and one can even make out individual blades of grass by the road. Stones and skulls stand out a long way off. The suspicious monk-like figures look blacker and gloomier against the night's bright background. The surprised sighing resounds more and more often amid the monotonous chatter, troubling the still air, and you hear the cry of a wakeful or delirious bird. Broad shadows move over the plain like clouds across the sky, and in the mysterious distance, if you peer into it for a while, grotesque, misty images loom and tower behind each other. It is a little eerie. And if you gaze at the pale, green, star-spangled sky, free of the smallest cloud or speck, you will know why the warm air is still, and why nature is alert, fearing to stir. It is afraid and reluctant to lose one second's life. Of the sky's unfathomable depth, of its boundlessness, you can judge only at sea and on the moon-lit steppe by night. It is frightening and picturesque, yet kindly. Its gaze is languorous and magnetic, but its embraces make you dizzy.

You drive on for an hour or two. On your way you meet a silent barrow or menhir—God knows who put them up, or when. A night bird silently skims the earth. And the prairie legends, the travellers' yarns, the folk tales told by some old nurse from the steppes, together with whatever you yourself have contrived to see and to grasp in spirit—you gradually recall all these things. And then, in the insects' twittering, in the sinister figures and ancient barrows, in the depths of the sky, in the moonlight, in the flight of the night bird, in everything you see and hear, you seem to glimpse the triumph of beauty, youth in the prime of strength, a lust for life. Your spirit responds to its magnificent, stern homeland and you long to fly above the steppe with the night bird. In this triumph of beauty, in this exuberance of happiness, you feel a tenseness and agonized regret, as if the steppe knew how lonely she is, how her wealth and inspiration are lost to the world —vainly, unsung, unneeded, and through the joyous clamour you hear her anguished, hopeless cry for a bard, a poet of her own.

'Whoa! Hallo there, Panteley. All well?'

'Thanks to God, Mr. Kuzmichov.'

'Seen Varlamov, lads?'

'No, we ain't.'

Yegorushka awoke and opened his eyes. The britzka had stopped. A long way ahead on the right extended a train of wagons, and men were scurrying about near them. The huge bales of wool made all the wagons seem very tall and bulging, and the horses small and short-legged.

'So we're to visit the Molokan's farm next,' said Kuzmichov in a loud voice. 'The Jew reckoned that Varlamov was staying the night there. Good-bye then, lads. Best of luck.'

'Good-bye, Mr. Kuzmichov,' answered several voices.

'I tell you what, lads,' said Kuzmichov briskly. 'You might take my boy with you. Why should he traipse around with us? Put him on your bales, Panteley, and let him ride a bit, and we'll catch you up. Off you go, Yegorushka. Go on, it'll be all right.'

Yegorushka climbed down from his box seat, and several hands picked him up. They raised him aloft, and he found himself on something big, soft and slightly wet with dew. He felt close to the sky and far from the ground.

'Hey, take your coat, old chap,' shouted Deniska far below.

The boy's overcoat and bundle were thrown up from below and fell near him. Quickly, wishing to keep his mind a blank, he put the bundle under his head, covered himself with his coat, stretched his legs right out, shivering a little because of the dew, and laughed with pleasure.

'Sleep, sleep, sleep,' he thought.

'Don't you do him no harm, you devils.' It was Deniska's voice from below.

'Good-bye, lads, and good luck,' shouted Kuzmichov. 'I'm relying on you.'

'Never fear, mister.'

Deniska shouted to his horses as the britzka creaked and rolled off, no longer along the road but somewhere off to one side. For a minute or two the wagons all seemed to have fallen asleep, since no sound was heard except the gradually expiring distant clatter of the pail tied to the britzka's back-board.

Then came a muffled shout from the head of the convoy. 'On our way, Kiryukha!'

The foremost wagon creaked, then the second and the third. Yego-rushka felt his own vehicle jerk and creak as well—they were on the move. He took a firmer grip on the cord round his bale, gave another happy laugh, shifted the honey cake in his pocket, and fell asleep just as he did in his bed at home.

When he awoke the sun was already rising. Screened by an ancient burial mound, it was trying to sprinkle its light on the world, urgently thrusting its rays in all directions and flooding the horizon with gold. Yegorushka thought it was in the wrong place because it had risen behind his back on the previous day, and was further to the left now. But the whole landscape had changed. There were no more hills, and the bleak brown plain stretched endlessly in all directions. Here and there arose small barrows, and rooks flew about, as on the day before. Far ahead were the white belfries and huts of a village. As it was a Sunday the locals were at home cooking—witness the smoke issuing from all the chimneys and hanging over the village in a transparent blue-grey veil. In the gaps between the huts and beyond the church a blue river could be seen, and beyond that the hazy distance. But nothing was so unlike yesterday's scene as the road. Straddling the prairie was something less a highway than a lavish, immensely broad, positively heroic spread of tract—a grey band, much traversed, dusty like all roads and several score yards in width. Its sheer scale baffled the boy, conjuring up a fairy-tale world. Who drove here? Who needed all this space? It was strange and uncanny. One might suppose, indeed, that giants with seven-league boots were still among us, and that the heroic horses of folk myth were not extinct. Looking at the road, Yegorushka pictured half a dozen tall chariots racing side by side like some he had seen in drawings in books of Bible stories. Those chariots had each been drawn by a team of six wild and furious horses, their high wheels raising clouds of dust to the sky, while the horses were driven by men such as one might meet in dreams, or in reveries about the supernatural. How well they would have fitted the steppe and the road, these figures, had they existed!

Telegraph poles carrying two wires ran on the right-hand side of the road as far as eye could see. Ever dwindling, they vanished behind the huts and foliage near the village, only to reappear in the lilac-coloured background as thin little sticks resembling pencils stuck in the ground. On the wires sat hawks, merlins and crows, gazing unconcernedly at the moving wagons.

Lying on the last wagon of all, the boy had the whole convoy in view. There were about twenty wagons or carts, with one wagoner to three vehicles. Near Yegorushka's wagon, the last in line, walked an old, grey-bearded man, as short and gaunt as Father Christopher, but with a brown, sunburnt face, stern and contemplative. The old man may have been neither stern nor contemplative, but his red eye-lids and long, sharp nose gave his face the severe, reserved air of those accustomed to brood in solitude on serious matters. Like Father Christopher, he wore a broad-brimmed top hat—a brown, felt affair more like a truncated cone than a gentleman's topper. His feet were bare. He kept slapping his thighs and stamping his feet as he walked—probably a habit contracted in the cold winters, when he must often have come near to freezing beside his wagons. Noticing that Yego-rushka was awake, he looked at him.

'So you're awake, young man.' He was hunching his shoulders as if from cold. 'Mr. Kuzmichov's son, might you be?'

'No, his nephew.'

'His nephew, eh? Now, I've just taken off me boots, I'm bobbing along barefoot. There's something wrong with me legs, the frost got to them, and things is easier without boots. Easier, boy. Without boots, I mean. So you're his nephew, then? And he's a good sort, he is. May God grant him health. A good sort. Mr. Kuzmichov, I mean. He's gone to see the Molokan. O Lord, have mercy on us!'

The old man even spoke as if he was frozen, spacing out the words and not opening his mouth properly. He mispronounced his labial consonants, stuttering on them as if his lips were swollen. When addressing Yegorushka he did not smile once, and seemed severe.

Three wagons ahead of them walked a man in a long reddish-brown topcoat, carrying a whip. He wore a peaked cap and riding boots with sagging tops. He was not old—only about forty. When he turned round the boy saw a long red face with a thin goatee and a spongy swelling under the right eye. Besides this hideous swelling he had another specially striking peculiarity—while holding the whip in his left hand, he swung the right as if conducting an unseen choir. Occasionally he tucked the whip under his arm and conducted with both hands, humming to himself.

The next carter was a tall upstanding figure with noticeably sloping shoulders and a back as flat as a board. He held himself erect as if he was marching or had swallowed a ramrod, his arms not swinging but hanging straight down like sticks as he walked in a sort of clockwork fashion like a toy soldier, scarcely bending his knees and trying to take the longest stride possible. Where the old man or the owner of the spongy swelling took two steps he contrived to take only one, so that he seemed to be moving more slowly than anyone and to be falling behind. His face was bound with a piece of cloth, and on his head sprouted something resembling a monk's cap. He was dressed in a short Ukrainian coat all covered with patches and in dark blue oriental trousers over bast shoes.

Yegorushka could not make out the more distant carters. He lay on his stomach, picked a hole in his bale, and began twisting some wool into threads, having nothing better to do. The old man striding away below turned out less severe and serious than his face suggested. Having started a conversation he did not let it drop.

'Where are you going, then?' he asked, stamping his feet.

'To school,' answered Yegorushka.

'To school? Aha! Well, may Our Blessed Lady help you! Aye, one brain's good, but two is better. God gives one man one brain, and another man two brains, and another gets three, that's for sure. One's the brain you're born with, another comes from learning, and the third from living a good life. So it's a good thing for a man to have three brains, son. Living's easier for him, it is, and so is dying too. Dying—aye, we'll all of us come to it.'

After scratching his forehead the old man looked up, red-eyed, at Yegorushka, and went on. 'Maxim Nikolayevich, the squire from down Slavyanoserbsk way—he took his lad to school last year, he did. I don't know what he might be like in the book-learning line, but he's a good, decent lad, he is. And may God prosper them, the fine gentle-folk that they be. Aye, so he takes the lad to school, like you, since they don't have no establishment—not for learning proper, like—in them parts, that they don't. But it's a good, decent town. There's an ordinary school for the common folk, but for them as wants to be scholars there ain't nothing, there ain't. What's your name?'

'Yegorushka.'

'Yegorushka—"George", properly speaking. So your name-day's the twenty-third of April, seeing as how that's the day of the holy martyr St. Georgie-Porgie what killed the Dragon. Now, my name's Panteley—Panteley Kholodov. Aye, Kholodov's the name. I come from Tim in Kursk County myself, you may have heard tell of it. My brothers registered themselves as townsfolk—they're craftsmen in the town, they are. But I'm a countryman, and a countryman I've remained. Seven years ago I visited there, home that is. I've been in my village and in the town—in Tim, I've been, say I. They were all alive and well then, thank God, but I don't know about now. A few of them may have died. And time it is for them to die—they're all old, and some is older than me. Death's all right, nothing wrong with it. But you mustn't die without repenting, stands to reason. Ain't nothing worse than dying contumacious—oh, it's a joy to the devil is a contumacious death. But if you want to die penitent, so they won't forbid you to enter the mansions of the Lord like, you pray to the martyred St. Barbara. She'll intercede for you, she will, you take it from me. That's her place in heaven that God gave her so everyone should have the right to pray to her for repentance, see?'

Panteley muttered away, obviously not caring whether the boy heard him or not. He spoke listlessly, mumbling to himself, neither raising nor dropping his voice, but managing to say a great deal in a short time. His talk, all fragmentary and largely incoherent, lacked any interest for Yegorushka. Perhaps he spoke only to call the roll of his ideas—make sure that all were present and correct after the night spent in silence. Having finished talking about repentance, he went off again about this Maxim Nikolayevich from down Slavyanoserbsk way. 'Yes, he took the lad to school, he did, true enough.'

One of the carters walking far in front gave a sudden lurch, darted to one side, and began lashing the ground with his whip. He was a burly, broad-shouldered man of about thirty, with fair, curly hair and a healthy, vigorous look. From the motions of his shoulders and whip, from the eagerness of his posture, he was beating some live creature. A second carter ran up—a short, thick-set fellow with a full black beard, in a waistcoat with his shirt outside his trousers. He broke out in a deep, coughing laugh. 'Dymov has killed a snake, lads, as God's my witness.'

There are people whose intellect can be accurately gauged from their voice and laugh, and it was to this lucky category that the black-bearded man belonged, his voice and laugh betraying abysmal stupidity. The fair-haired Dymov had stopped lashing, picked his whip from the ground and laughed as he hurled something resembling a bit of rope towards the carts.

'It ain't a viper, 'tis a grass snake,' someone shouted.

The man with the clockwork stride and bandaged face quickly strode up to the dead snake, glanced at it and threw up his stick-like arms. 'You rotten scum!' he shouted in a hollow, tearful voice. 'Why kill the little grass snake? What had he done to you, damn you? Hey, he's killed a grass snake! How would you like to be treated like that?'

'Grass snakes oughtn't to be killed, that's true enough,' muttered

Panteley placidly. 'It ain't a viper. Look like a snake it may, but 'tis a quiet, innocent creature. A friend of man, it be, your grass snake——'

Dymov and the black-bearded man were probably ashamed, for they gave loud laughs and sauntered back to their wagons without answering these grumbles. When the hindmost wagon drew level with the place where the dead grass snake lay, the man with the bandaged face stood over the creature and addressed Panteley. 'Now, why did he kill the grass snake, old man?' he inquired plaintively.

Yegorushka could now see that the speaker's eyes were small and lack-lustre. His face looked grey and sickly, also seeming lustreless, while his chin was red, appearing extremely swollen.

'Now, why did he kill the grass snake?' he repeated, striding by Panteley's side.

'A fool has itchy hands, that's why,' the old man said. 'But you shouldn't kill a grass snake, true enough. He's a trouble-maker is that Dymov, see, he'll kill anything that comes his way. But Kiryukha didn't stop him when he should have, but just stood there a-chuckling and a-cackling. Don't take on, though, Vasya, don't let it anger you. They killed it, but never mind. Dymov's a mischief-maker and Kiryukha's just silly like. No matter. Folks are stupid, folks don't understand, so let them be. Now, Yemelyan won't never touch anything he shouldn't. Never, that's true enough, seeing as how he's educated and they're stupid. He won't touch anything, not Yemelyan won't.'

The carter with the reddish-brown topcoat and the spongy swelling —the one who liked conducting the unseen choir—stopped when he heard his name spoken, waited for Panteley and Vasya to catch up, and fell in beside them. 'What are you on about?' he asked in a hoarse, strangled voice.

'Well, Vasya here's angry,' said Panteley. 'So I said a few things to stop him taking on. Oh, my poor legs, they're so cold. It's because it's Sunday, the Lord's Day, that's why they're playing up.'

'It's the walking,' remarked Vasya.

'No, lad, no. It ain't the walking. When I walk it seems easier, it's when I lie down and warm meself—that's what does for me. Walking's easier like.'

Yemelyan, in his reddish-brown topcoat, took station between Panteley and Vasya, waving his hand as if that choir was about to sing. After a bit of a swing he lowered his arm and gave a grunt of despair. 'My voice has gone,' he said. 'Diabolical, it is. All night and all morning I've been haunted by the triple "Lord Have Mercy" that we sang at the Marinovsky wedding. I've got it on me brain and I've got it in me gizzard. I feel I could sing it, but I can't. I ain't got the voice.'

He brooded silently for a while and then went on. 'Fifteen years in the choir I was, and in all Lugansk no one had a better voice than me, belike. But then I have to go and bloody bathe in the Donets two year ago, and not one proper note have I sung since. A chill in the throat it was. Without me voice I'm like a workman with no hand.'

'True enough,' Panteley agreed.

'What I say is, I'm done for, and that's that.'

At that moment Vasya chanced to catch sight of Yegorushka. His eyes glittered and seemed even smaller. 'So there's a young gentleman a-driving with us,' he said, hiding his nose with his sleeve as if from shyness. 'Now, that's what I call a real 'igh-class cabbie! You stay with us riding the wagons and carting wool.'

The incongruity of one person combining the functions of young gentleman and cabbie must have struck him as most curious and witty, for he gave a loud snigger and continued to develop the idea. Yemelyan looked up at Yegorushka too, but cursorily and coldly. He was obsessed with thoughts of his own, and would not have noticed the boy, had it not been for Vasya. Not five minutes had passed before he was waving his arms again. Then, as he described to his companions the beauties of the wedding anthem 'Lord Have Mercy' that he had remembered in the night, he put his whip under his arm and started conducting with both his hands.

Nearly a mile from the village the convoy stopped by a well with a sweep. Lowering his pail into the well, black-bearded Kiryukha lay stomach down on the framework and thrust his mop of hair, his shoulders and part of his chest into the black hole so that Yegorushka could see only his short legs, which barely touched the ground. Seeing his head reflected from afar down at the well bottom, he was so pleased that he let off a cascade of stupid, deep-voiced laughter, and the well echoed it back. When he stood up his face and neck were red as a beetroot. The first to run up and drink was Dymov. He laughed as he drank, frequently lifting his head from the pail and saying something funny to Kiryukha. Then he cleared his throat and bellowed out half a dozen swear words for all the steppe to hear. What such words meant Yegorushka had no idea, but that they were bad he was well aware. He knew of the unspoken revulsion that they evoked in his friends and relations, he shared their feelings himself without knowing why, and he had come to assume that only the drunk and disorderly enjoyed the privilege of speaking these words aloud. He remembered the killing of the grass snake, listened to Dymov's laughter, and felt something like hatred for the man. At that moment, as ill luck would have it, Dymov spotted Yegorushka, who had climbed down from his cart and was on his way to the well.

'Lads, the old man gave birth in the night!' shouted Dymov with a loud laugh. ' 'Tis a baby boy.'

Kiryukha gave his deep-throated laugh till he coughed. Someone else laughed too, while Yegorushka blushed and conclusively decided that Dymov was a very bad man.

Bareheaded, with fair, curly hair and his shirt unbuttoned, Dymov seemed handsome and extremely strong, all his movements being those of the reckless bully who knows his own worth. He flexed his shoulders, put his hands on his hips, talked and laughed louder than the others, and looked ready to lift with one hand some weight so prodigious as to astound the entire world. His roving, ironical glance slid over the road, the string of wagons and the sky, never resting, and he seemed to be seeking something else to kill—as a pastime, just for a joke. He obviously feared no one, would stick at nothing, and probably cared not a rap for Yegorushka's opinion. But the boy now wholeheartedly detested his fair head, his clean-cut face, his strength, listening to his laughter with fear and loathing and trying to think of a suitable insult to pay him back with.

Panteley too went up to the pail. He took a green lamp-glass from his pocket, wiped it with a cloth, scooped water from the pail, drank it, then scooped again before wrapping the glass in the cloth and replacing it in his pocket.

Yegorushka was astonished. 'Why do you drink from a lamp?' he asked the old man.

The answer was evasive. 'Some drinks from a pail and some from a lamp. It's every man to his own taste. If you're one as drinks from a bucket, then drink away, and much good may it do you.'

Suddenly Vasya gave tongue in a tender, plaintive voice. 'Oh, the darling, oh, you beauty, oh, the lovely creature!' His eyes, glinting and smiling, stared into the distance, while his face took on the expression with which he had previously looked at Yegorushka.

'Who's that?' Kiryukha asked.

'A vixen, that be—a-lying on her back, playing like a dog.'

All peered into the distance, all looking for the vixen, but no one spotted her. Only Vasya—he of the lack-lustre, grey eyes—could see anything, and he was entranced. His sight, as Yegorushka later discovered, was remarkably acute—so much so that the brown wastes of the prairie were always full of life and content for him. He had only to look into the distance to see a fox, a hare, a great bustard, or some other creature that shuns humanity. To spot a hare running or a bustard in flight is not hard—anyone crossing the steppes saw those—but it is not given to everyone to detect wild creatures in their domestic habitat, when they are not running, hiding or looking about them in alarm. Now, Vasya could see the vixen at play, the hare washing himself with his paws, the great bustard preening his wings, and the little bustard doing his courtship-dance. Thanks to vision so keen, Vasya possessed, besides the world that everyone else sees, a whole world of his own—inaccessible to others and most delectable, presumably, for it was hard not to envy him when he went into raptures over what he beheld.

When the convoy resumed its journey church bells had started ringing for service.

V

The wagon line was drawn up on a river bank to one side of a village. As on the previous day the sun blazed away, and the air was stagnant and despondent. There were a few willows on the bank, their shadows not falling on the earth but on the water where they were wasted, while the shade under the wagons was stifling and oppressive. Azure from the reflected sky, the water urgently beckoned.

Styopka, a carter whom Yegorushka now noticed for the first time, was an eighteen-year-old Ukrainian lad in a long shirt without a belt and in broad trousers worn outside his boots and flapping like flags as he walked. He quickly undressed, ran down the steep bank and dived into the water. After plunging three times he floated on his back and shut his eyes in his delight. He smiled and wrinkled his face as if from a combination of being tickled, hurt and amused.

On a hot day, when there is nowhere to hide from the stifling heat, splashing water and a bather's heavy breathing are music in the ears. Looking at Styopka, Dymov and Kiryukha quickly undressed, laughed loudly with anticipated joy, and flopped into the water one after the other. The quiet, humble brook bombinated with their snorting, splashing and shouting. Kiryukha coughed, laughed and yelled as if someone was trying to drown him, while Dymov chased him and tried to grab his leg.

'Hey there!' shouted Dymov. 'Catch him, hold him!'

Kiryukha was laughing and enjoying himself, but his expression was the same as on dry land: a stupid, flabbergasted look, as if someone had sneaked up from behind and clouted him on the head with a blunt instrument. Yegorushka also undressed. He did not lower himself down the bank, but took a run and a flying leap from a ten-foot height. Describing an arc in the air, he hit the water and sank deep, yet without reaching the bottom. Some power, cold and agreeable to the touch, seized him and bore him back to the surface. Snorting and blowing bubbles, he came up and opened his eyes, only to find the sun reflected on the stream close by his face. First blinding sparks, then rainbow colours and dark patches twitched before his eyes. He hurriedly plunged again, opened his eyes under water and saw something dull green like the sky on a moonlit night. Once more the same power would not let him touch the bottom and stay in the cool, but bore him aloft. Up he popped, and heaved a sigh so deep that he had a feeling of vast space and freshness, not only in his chest but even in his stomach. Then, to make the most of the water, he indulged in every extravagance. He lay on his back and basked, he splashed, he turned somersaults, he swam on his face, on his side, on his back, standing up—just as he pleased till he grew tired. Glinting gold in the sun, the other bank was thickly grown with reeds, and the handsome tassels of their flowers drooped over the water. At one point the reeds quivered and nodded their flowers, which gave out a crackling noise—Styopka and Kiryukha were 'tickling' crayfish.

'Here's one! Look, lads, a crayfish!' shouted Kiryukha triumphantly, displaying what indeed was a crayfish.

Yegorushka swam up to the reeds, dived, and began grubbing among the roots. Burrowing in slimy liquid mud, he felt something sharp and unpleasant. Perhaps it really was a crayfish, but at that moment someone grabbed his leg and hauled him to the surface. Gulping, coughing, he opened his eyes and saw the wet, grinning face of the mischievous Dymov. The rascal was breathing heavily, seeming bent on further tomfoolery from the look in his eyes. He held the boy tightly by the leg, and was lifting the other hand to take hold of his neck when Yegorushka broke away with revulsion and panic, shrinking from his touch as if afraid of the bully drowning him.

'Idiot!' he pronounced. 'I'll bash your face in.' Then, feeling that
this was inadequate to express his detestation, he paused in thought and
spoke again. 'Swine! Son of a bitch!'

But this had no effect on Dymov, who ignored the boy and swam
towards Kiryukha. 'Hey there!' he shouted. 'Let's catch some fish.
Let's fish, lads!'

Kiryukha agreed. 'All right. There must be lots here.'

'Nip over to the village, Styopka, and ask the men for a net.'

'They won't lend us none.'

'They will, you ask them. Tell them it's their Christian duty, seeing
as we're pilgrims, or as near as don't matter.'

'Aye, 'tis true.'

Styopka climbed out of the water, quickly dressed and ran—bare-
headed, his wide trousers flapping—to the village. As for Yegorushka,
the water had lost all charm for him after the clash with Dymov. He
climbed out and dressed. Panteley and Vasya sat on the steep bank,
dangling their legs, and watched the bathers. Close to the bank stood
Yemelyan, naked and up to his knees in water, as he held the grass
with one hand to stop himself falling over and stroked his body with
the other. Bending down, obviously frightened of the water, he cut a
comic figure with his bony shoulder-blades and the swelling under his
eye. His face was grave and severe, and he looked angrily at the
water as if about to curse it for once having given him that chill in the
Donets and robbed him of his voice.

'Why don't you go in?' Yegorushka asked Vasya.

'Oh, er—I don't care to.'

'Why is your chin swollen?'

'It hurts. I used to work at a match factory, young sir. The doctor
did say as how that was what made me jaw swell. The air ain't healthy
there, and there were three other lads beside me had swollen jaws, and
one of them had it rot right away.'

Styopka soon came back with the net. After so long in the water
Dymov and Kiryukha had become mauve and hoarse, but set about
fishing with gusto. They first stalked the deep part near the reeds.
Here Dymov was up to his neck and the squat Kiryukha out of his
depth. The latter gasped and blew bubbles, while Dymov bumped
into prickly roots, kept falling, and got tangled in the net. Both
thrashed about noisily, and all that came of their fishing was horseplay.

'It ain't half deep,' croaked Kiryukha. 'We won't catch nothing
here.'

'Don't pull, blast you!' shouted Dymov, trying to work the net into position. 'Hold it where it is.'

'You won't catch nothing here,' shouted Panteley from the bank. 'You be only scaring the fish, you fools. Go to the left, 'tis shallower there.'

Once a huge fish gleamed above the net. Everyone gasped, and Dymov punched the spot where it had vanished, his face a picture of vexation.

Panteley grunted, stamping his feet. 'We've missed a perch—got away, he did.'

Moving off to the left, Dymov and Kiryukha gradually worked their way to the shallows, and fishing began in earnest. Having gone about three hundred yards from the wagons, they were seen hauling the net silently, scarcely moving their feet, while trying to get as deep and close to the reeds as they could. To frighten the fish and drive them into the net they flogged the water with their fists and raised a crackle in the reeds. Making for the other bank from the reeds, they trawled there, and then went back to the reeds, looking disappointed and lifting their knees high. They were discussing something, but what it was no one could hear. The sun scorched their backs, insects bit them, and their bodies had turned from mauve to crimson. Styopka followed, carrying a bucket—his shirt was tucked up under his armpits, and he held it in his teeth by the hem. After each successful catch he raised a fish aloft and let it glitter in the sun. 'How about that for a perch?' he shouted. 'And we've five like that!'

Every time Dymov, Kiryukha and Styopka pulled the net out they were seen grubbing in the mud, putting things in the bucket and throwing other things out. Sometimes they passed something that had got into the net from hand to hand, scrutinized it keenly, and then threw that out too.

'What have you got?' shouted voices from the bank.

Styopka gave some answer, but it was hard to tell what. Then he climbed out of the water, gripped the bucket with both hands and ran to the wagons, forgetting to let his shirt drop. 'This one's full,' he shouted, panting hard. 'Let's have another.'

Yegorushka looked at the full bucket. A young pike poked its ugly snout out of the water, with crayfish and small fry swarming around it. The boy put his hand down to the bottom and stirred the water. The pike disappeared beneath the crayfish, a perch and a tench floating up instead. Vasya also looked at the bucket. His eyes gleamed and his expression became as tender as it had when he had seen the vixen. He took something from the bucket, put it in his mouth and started to chew, making a crunching noise.

Styopka was amazed. 'Vasya's eating a live gudgeon, mates—ugh!'

'It ain't no gudgeon, 'tis a chub,' Vasya calmly answered, still munching.

He took the tail from his mouth, looked at it dotingly, and stuck it back again. While he chewed and crunched his teeth Yegorushka felt that what he saw was not a human being. Vasya's swollen chin, his lustreless eyes, his phenomenal eyesight, the fish tail in his mouth and the affectionate air with which he chewed the 'gudgeon'—it all made him look like an animal.

Yegorushka was beginning to find Vasya irksome, and in any case the fishing was over. The boy walked about by the carts, thought for a while and then plodded off to the village out of boredom.

A little later he was standing in the church, leaning his forehead on someone's back—it smelt of hemp—and listening to the choir. The service was nearly over. He knew nothing about church singing and did not care for it. After listening a while he yawned and began examining people's necks and backs. In one head, reddish-brown and wet from recent bathing, he recognized Yemelyan. The back of his hair had been cropped in a straight line, higher than was usual. The hair on his temples had also been cut back higher than it should have been, and Yemelyan's red ears stuck out like two burdock leaves, looking as if they felt out of place. Watching the back of his head and ears, the boy somehow felt that Yemelyan must be very unhappy. He remembered the man 'conducting' with his hands, his hoarse voice, his timid look during the bathing, and felt intensely sorry for him. He wanted to say something friendly. 'I'm here too.' He tugged Yemelyan's sleeve.

The tenors and basses of a choir, especially those who have ever chanced to conduct, are accustomed to looking at boys in a stern and forbidding way. Nor do they lose the habit even when they come to leave the choir. Turning to Yegorushka, Yemelyan looked at him rancorously and told him not to 'lark around' in church.

Yegorushka next made his way forward, closer to the icon-stand, where he saw some fascinating people. In front, on the right-hand side, a lady and gentleman stood on a carpet with a chair behind each of them. Wearing a freshly ironed tussore suit, the gentleman stood stock-still like a soldier on parade, and held his bluish, shaved chin

aloft. His stiff collar, blue chin, bald patch and cane—all conveyed
great dignity. From excess of dignity his neck was tensed, and his chin
was pulled upward with such force that his head seemed ready to
snap off and soar into the air at any moment. As for the lady, she was
stout and elderly, and wore a white silk shawl. She inclined her head
to one side, looking as if she had just done someone a favour and
wanted to say: 'Don't trouble to thank me, please—I dislike that sort
of thing.' All round the carpet stood a dense array of locals.

Yegorushka went up to the icon-stand and began kissing the local
icons, slowly bowing to the ground before each one, looking back
at the congregation without getting up, and then standing to apply his
lips. The contact of his forehead with the cold floor was most gratify-
ing. When the verger came out of the chancel with a pair of long
snuffers to put the candles out, the boy jumped quickly up from the
floor and ran to him. 'Has the communion bread been given out?' he
asked.

'There is none,' muttered the verger gruffly. 'And it's no use you——'

When the service was over the boy unhurriedly left the church and
strolled round the market place. He had seen a good many villages,
villagers and village greens in his time, and the present scene held no
interest for him. Having nothing to do, he called—just to pass the time
of day—at a shop with a broad strip of red calico over the door. It
consisted of two spacious, badly lit rooms. In one drapery and groceries were sold, while in the other were tubs of tar and horse-collars
hanging from the ceiling. From the second room issued the rich tang
of leather and tar. The shop floor had been watered—by some great
visionary and original thinker, evidently, for it was sprinkled with
embellishments and cabbalistic signs. Behind the counter, leaning his
stomach on a sort of desk, stood a well upholstered, broad-faced shopkeeper. He had a round beard, obviously came from the north, and
was drinking tea through a piece of sugar, sighing after each sip. His
face was a mask of indifference, but each sigh seemed to say: 'Just
you wait—. You're for it!'

Yegorushka addressed him. 'A copeckworth of sunflower seed.'

The shopkeeper raised his eyebrows, came out from the counter and
poured a copeckworth of sunflower seed into the boy's pocket, using
an empty pomade jar as measure. Not wanting to leave, the boy spent
a long time examining the trays of cakes, thought a little, and pointed
to some small Vyazma gingerbreads rusty with antiquity. 'How much
are those?'

'Two a copeck.'

Yegorushka took from his pocket the honey cake given to him by the Jewess on the previous day. 'How much are cakes like this?'

The shopkeeper took the cake in his hands, examined it from all sides and raised an eyebrow. 'Like this, eh?'

Then he raised the other eyebrow and thought for a while. 'Two for three copecks.'

Silence ensued.

'Where do you come from?' The shopkeeper poured himself some tea from a copper teapot.

'I'm Uncle Ivan's nephew.'

'There's all sorts of Uncle Ivans.' The shopkeeper sighed, glanced at the door over Yegorushka's head, paused a moment, and asked if the boy would 'care for a drop of tea'.

'I might.' Yegorushka made a show of reluctance, though he was dying for his usual morning tea.

The shopkeeper poured a glass and gave it to him with a nibbled-looking piece of sugar. Yegorushka sat on a folding chair and drank. He also wanted to ask what a pound of sugared almonds cost, and had just broached the matter when in came a customer, and the shopkeeper put his glass to one side to attend to business. He took the customer into the part of the shop smelling of tar and had a long discussion with him. The customer—evidently a most obstinate man with ideas of his own—kept shaking his head in disagreement and backing towards the door, but the shopkeeper gained his point and began pouring oats into a large sack for him.

'Call them oats?' asked the customer mournfully. 'Them ain't oats, they'm chaff. 'Tis enough to make a cat laugh. I'm going to Bondarenko's, I am.'

When the boy got back to the river a small camp-fire was smoking on the bank—the carters were cooking their meal. In the smoke stood Styopka stirring the pot with a large, jagged spoon. Kiryukha and Vasya, eyes red from smoke, sat a little to one side, cleaning fish. Before them lay the net, covered with slime and water weeds, and with gleaming fish and crawling crayfish on it.

Yemelyan had just returned from church and was sitting next to Panteley, waving his arm and humming 'We sing to Thee' just audibly in a hoarse voice. Dymov pottered near the horses.

After cleaning the fish Kiryukha and Vasya put them and the live crayfish in the pail, rinsed them, and slopped the lot into boiling water.

'Shall I put in some fat?' asked Styopka, skimming off the froth with his spoon.

'No need—the fish will provide their own juice,' replied Kiryukha.

Before taking the pot off the fire Styopka put in three handfuls of millet and a spoonful of salt. Finally he tried it, smacked his lips, licked the spoon and gave a complacent grunt to signify that the stew was cooked.

All except Panteley sat round the pot plying their spoons.

'You there! Give the lad a spoon!' Panteley sternly remarked. 'He's surely hungry too, I reckon.'

' 'Tis plain country fare,' sighed Kiryukha.

'Aye, and it don't come amiss if you've the relish for it.'

Yegorushka was given a spoon. He started to eat, not sitting down but standing near the pot and looking into it as if it was a deep pit. The brew smelt of fishy wetness, with a fish-scale popping up now and again in the millet. The crayfish slid off their spoons, and so the men simply picked them out of the pot with their hands. Vasya was particularly unconstrained, wetting his sleeves as well as his hands in the stew. Yet it tasted very good to Yegorushka, reminding him of the crayfish soup that his mother cooked at home on fast-days. Panteley sat to one side chewing bread.

'Why don't you eat, old 'un?' Yemelyan asked him.

The old man turned squeamishly aside. 'I can't eat crayfish, rot 'em!'

During the meal general conversation took place. From this Yegorushka gathered that, despite differences of age and temperament, his new acquaintances all had one thing in common—each had a glorious past and a most unenviable present. To a man, they all spoke of their past enthusiastically, but their view of the present was almost contemptuous. Your Russian prefers talking about his life to living it. But the boy had yet to learn this, and before the stew was finished he firmly believed that those sitting round the pot were injured victims of fate. Panteley told how, in the old days before the railway, he had served on wagon convoys to Moscow and Nizhny Novgorod, and had earned so much that he hadn't known what to do with his money. And what merchants there had been in those days! What fish! How cheap everything was! But now the roads had shrunk, the merchants were stingier, the common folk were poorer, bread was dearer, and everything had diminished and dwindled exceedingly. Yemelyan said that he had once been in the choir at Lugansk, had possessed a remarkable voice, and had read music excellently, but had now become a bumpkin living on the charity of his brother, who sent him out with his horses and took half his earnings. Vasya had worked in his match factory. Kiryukha had been a coachman to a good family, and had been rated the best troika driver in the district. Dymov, son of a well-to-do peasant, had enjoyed himself and had a good time without a care in the world. But when he was just twenty his stern, harsh father—wanting to teach him the job and afraid of his becoming spoilt at home—had begun sending him out on carrier's work like a poor peasant or hired labourer. Only Styopka said nothing, but you could tell from his clean-shaven face that for him too the past had been far better than the present.

Recalling his father, Dymov stopped eating, frowned, looked sullenly at his mates, and then let his glance rest on Yegorushka. 'Take yer cap off, you heathen,' he said rudely. 'Eating with yer cap on—I must say! And you a gentleman's son!'

Yegorushka did take his hat off, not saying a word, but the stew had lost all relish for him. Nor did he hear Panteley and Vasya standing up for him. Anger with the bully rankled inside him, and he decided to do him some injury at all costs.

After dinner they all made for the carts and collapsed in their shade.

'Are we starting soon, Grandad?' Yegorushka asked Panteley.

'We'll start in God's good time. We can't leave now, 'tis too hot. O Lord, Thy will be done, O Holy Mother. You lie down, lad.'

Soon snoring proceeded from under the wagons. The boy meant to go back to the village, but on reflection he yawned and lay down by the old man.

VI

The wagons stayed by the river all day and left at sunset.

Once more the boy lay on the bales while his wagon quietly squeaked and swayed, and down below walked Panteley—stamping his feet, slapping his thighs, muttering. In the air, as on the day before, the prairie music trilled away.

The boy lay on his back with his hands behind his head, watching the sky. He saw the sunset blaze up and fade. Guardian angels, covering the horizon with their golden wings, had lain down to sleep—the day had passed serenely, a calm, untroubled night had come on, and they could stay peacefully at home in the sky. Yegorushka saw the heavens gradually darken. Mist descended on the earth, and the stars came out one after the other.

When you spend a long time gazing unwaveringly at the deep sky your thoughts and spirit somehow merge in a sense of loneliness. You begin to feel hopelessly isolated, and all that you once thought near and dear becomes infinitely remote and worthless. The stars that have looked down from the sky for thousands of years, the mysterious sky itself and the haze, all so unconcerned with man's brief life—when you are confronted with them, and try to grasp their meaning, they oppress your spirits with their silence, you think of that solitariness awaiting us all in the grave, and life's essence seems to be despair and horror.

The boy thought of his grandmother, now sleeping under the cherry trees in the cemetery. He remembered her lying in her coffin with copper coins on her eyes, remembered the lid being shut and her being lowered into the grave. He remembered, too, the hollow thud of earth clods against the lid. He pictured Grannie in the dark, cramped coffin—abandoned by all, helpless. Then he imagined her suddenly waking up, not knowing where she was, knocking on the lid, calling for help and—in the end, faint with horror—dying a second death. He imagined his mother, Father Christopher, Countess Dranitsky and Solomon as dead. But however hard he tried to see himself in a dark grave—far from his home, abandoned, helpless and dead—he did not succeed. For himself personally he could not admit the possibility of death, feeling that it was not for him.

Panteley, whose time to die had already come, walked by the wagon taking a roll-call of his thoughts. 'They was all right, proper gentle-folk they was,' he muttered. 'They took the little lad to school, but how he's doing—that we don't hear. At Slavyanoserbsk, as I say, they don't have no establishment—not for book-learning proper like. Nay, that they don't. But the lad's all right he is. When he grows up he'll help his dad. You're just a little lad now, son, but you'll grow up and keep your father and mother. That's how 'tis ordained of God— "Honour thy father and thy mother". I had children meself, but they died in a fire, me wife and kids too. Aye, that they did. Our hut burnt down on Twelfth Night eve. I weren't at home, having gone to Oryol. Aye, to Oryol. Marya—she jumped out in the street, but she remembered the children asleep in the hut, she ran back and she was burnt to death along with the little ones. Aye, next day all they could find were the bones.'

About midnight Yegorushka and the wagoners once more sat by a small camp-fire. While the prairie brushwood blazed up, Kiryukha and

Vasya were fetching water from a gully. They vanished in the darkness, but could be heard clanking their pails and talking all the time, which meant that the gully must be near by. The firelight was a large, flickering patch on the ground, and though the moon was bright, everything beyond that red patch seemed black as the pit. The light was in the wagoners' eyes, and they could see only a small part of the road. In the darkness wagons, bales and horses were barely visible in outline as vague mountainous hulks. About twenty paces from the fire, where road and prairie met, a wooden grave cross slumped. Before the fire had been lit, while he could still see a long distance, the boy had spotted another such ramshackle old cross on the other side of the road.

Coming back with the water, Kiryukha and Vasya filled the pot and fixed it on the fire. Styopka took his place in the smoke near by, holding the jagged spoon, looking dreamily at the water and waiting for the scum to rise. Panteley and Yemelyan sat side by side silently brooding, while Dymov lay on his stomach, his head propped on his fists, and watched the fire with Styopka's shadow dancing over him so that his handsome face darkened and lit up by turns. Kiryukha and Vasya were wandering a little way off gathering weeds and brushwood for the fire. Yegorushka put his hands in his pockets, stood near Panteley and watched the flame devour the fuel.

Everyone was resting, reflecting and glancing cursorily at the cross with the red patches flickering on it. There is something poignant, wistful and highly romantic about a lonely grave. You feel its silence, sensing in it the soul of the unknown beneath the cross. Is his spirit at ease in the steppe? Or does it grieve in the moonlight? The prairie near the grave seems mournful, despondent and lost in thought, the grass is sadder, and the crickets appear to chatter with less abandon. Every passer-by spares a thought for the lonely spirit and turns to look at the grave until it is behind him and veiled in mist.

'Why is the cross there, Grandad?' Yegorushka asked Panteley.

Panteley looked at the cross and then at Dymov. 'Nicholas, might that be where the reapers murdered them merchants?'

Dymov reluctantly raised himself on an elbow and looked at the road. 'Aye, that it be.'

Silence followed. Kiryukha bundled some dry grass together with a crackling sound, and thrust it under the pot. The fire blazed up, enveloping Styopka in black smoke, and the shadow of the cross darted down the road near the wagons.

'Aye, they were killed,' said Dymov reluctantly. 'The merchants, father and son, were travelling icon-sellers. They put up near here in the inn that Ignatius Fomin now keeps. The old man had had a drop too much, and he started bragging about having a lot of cash on him —they're a boastful lot, of course, are merchants, God help us, and they needs must show off to the likes of us. Now, some reapers was staying at the inn at the time. Well, they heard the merchant's boasts and they took due note of 'em.'

'O Lord, mercy on us!' sighed Panteley.

Dymov continued. 'Next day, soon as it was light the merchants got ready to leave and the reapers tagged along. "Let's travel together, mister. It's more cheerful and less risky like, seeing as these be lonely parts." The merchants had to travel at walking pace to avoid breaking their icons, and that just suited them reapers.'

Dymov rose to a kneeling position, stretched and yawned. 'Well, everything went off all right, but no sooner had the merchants reached this spot than them reapers laid into 'em with the scythes. The son, good for him, grabbed a scythe from one of them and did a bit of reaping on 'is own account. But the reapers got the best of it of course, seeing there was about eight of 'em. They hacked at them merchants till there weren't a sound place on their bodies. They finished the job and dragged 'em both off the road, the father one side and the son the other. Opposite this cross there's another on the other side. Whether it still stands I don't know. You can't see from here.'

'It's there,' said Kiryukha.

'They do say as how they found little money on 'em.'

'Aye,' confirmed Panteley. 'About a hundred roubles it were.'

'Aye, and three of them died later on, seeing the merchant cut 'em so bad with the scythe. 'Twas by the blood they tracked 'em. The merchant cut the hand off one, and they do say he ran three miles without it, and was found on a little hummock right by Kurikovo. He was a-squatting with his head on his knees as if he was a-thinking, but when they looked at him the ghost had left him like, and he was dead.'

'They traced him by his bloody tracks,' said Panteley.

All looked at the cross and again there was a hush. From somewhere, probably the gully, floated a bird's mournful cry: 'Sleep, sleep, sleep!'

'There's lots of wicked folks in the world,' said Yemelyan.

'Aye, that there is,' agreed Panteley, moving closer to the fire and

looking overcome by dread. 'Lots of 'em,' he went on in an undertone.
'I've seen enough of them in my time—beyond numbering, they've
been, the bad 'uns. I've seen many a saintly, righteous man, too, but
the sinful ones are past counting. Save us, Holy Mother, have mercy!
I remember once—thirty years ago, maybe more—I was driving a
merchant from Morshansk. He was a grand fellow, a striking-looking
man he was, that merchant, and he weren't short of money. He was a
good man, no harm to him. Well, we're a-going along like, and we
puts up at an inn for the night. Now, inns in the north ain't like those
in these parts. Their yards are roofed in, same as the cattle sheds and
threshing barns on big southern estates—only them barns would be
higher.

'Well, we put up there, and it's all right. My merchant has a room,
and I'm with the horses, and everything's proper like. Well, I says my
prayers before going to sleep, lads, and I goes out for a walk in the
yard. But the night's pitch black—not a blind thing can you see. I
walks up and down a bit till I'm near the wagons like, and I sees a
light a-twinkling. Now that's a bit rum, that is. The landlord and his
lady have long been abed, it seems, and there ain't no other guests,
barring me and the merchant. So what's that light doing? I don't like
the look of things. So I goes up to it, and—Lord have mercy on us,
Holy Mother save us! Right down on ground level I sees a little window with bars on it—in the house, that is. I get down on the ground
for a look, and a cold chill runs right through me.'

Kiryukha thrust a bundle of brushwood into the fire, trying to do
so quietly, and the old man waited for it to stop crackling and hissing
before going on.

'I look in there and I see a big cellar—all dark and gloomy. There's
a lamp a-burning on a barrel, and there's a dozen men in there in red
shirts with rolled-up sleeves, a-sharpening of long knives. "Oho!"
thinks I. "We've fallen in with a gang of highwaymen." So what's to
be done? I run to the merchant, I wake him quiet like. "Don't be
afeared, Mister Merchant," says I, "but we're in a bad way, we are.
We're in a robbers' den." His face changes. "What shall we do, Panteley?" he asks. "I've a lot of money with me—'tis for the orphans. As
for my soul," says he, "that's in the Lord's hands. I ain't afeared to die.
But," says he, "I am afeared of losing the orphan fund." Well, I'm
proper flummoxed. The gates are locked, there's no getting out by
horse or by foot. If there'd been a fence you could have climbed over,
but the yard has a roof to it. "Well, Mister Merchant," says I. "Never

you fear, you say your prayers. Happen the Lord won't harm them orphans. Stay here," says I, "and don't let on, and happen I'll hit on something in the meantime."

'So far so good. I says a prayer, and the good Lord enlightens me mind. I climb on me carriage and, quiet as could be so no one will hear, I start stripping the thatch from the eaves, I make a hole and out I crawl. Then, when I'm outside, I jump off the roof and down the road I run as fast as me legs'll carry me—run, run, run till I'm worn to a frazzle. Happen I do three miles in one breath, or more. Then, praise the Lord, I see a village. I rush to a hut, bang on the window. "Good people," says I, and I tells them the tale. "Don't you let 'em destroy a Christian soul." I wake them all up, the villagers gather and off we go together. Some take rope, some cudgels, some pitchforks. We break the inn gate down and straight to the cellar we go.

'By now them robbers have finished sharpening their knives, and they're just going to cut the merchant's throat. The peasants grab the lot of them, tie them up and take them to the authorities. The merchant's so pleased he gives them three hundred roubles and me five gold coins—and he writes my name down so he can remember me in his prayers. They do say a mighty lot of human bones was found in that cellar later. Aye, bones. They'd been a-robbing of people and then burying them to cover the traces, see? Aye, and later on the Morshansk executioners has the flogging of 'em.'

His story finished, Panteley surveyed his audience while they said nothing and looked at him. The water was boiling now, and Styopka was skimming off the froth.

'Is the lard ready?' whispered Kiryukha.

'In a minute.'

Styopka—fixing his eyes on old Panteley, as if fearing to miss the beginning of another story before he got back—ran to the wagons, but soon returned with a small wooden bowl and began rubbing pork fat in it.

'I went on another journey with a merchant,' continued Panteley in the same low voice, not blinking his eyes. 'Name of Peter Grigor-yevich, as I now mind. A decent fellow he were, the merchant.

'We stay at an inn, same as before—him in a room, me with the horses. The landlord and his wife seem decent folks, kindly like, and their workers seem all right too. But I can't sleep, lads, there's something on me mind. A hunch it were, no more to be said. The gates are open and there's lots of folk about, but I'm kind of frightened, I don't feel right at all. Everyone has long been asleep, it's far into the night and it'll soon be time to get up, but I just lie alone there in me covered wagon, and I don't close me eyes no more than an owl do. And I can hear this tapping noise, lads: tap, tap, tap. Someone steals up to the wagon. I stick out me head for a look and there's a woman in nothing but a shift, barefoot.

'"What do you want, missus?" I ask and she's all of a dither, she looks like nothing on earth. "Get up, my good man!" says she. "It's trouble. The inn folks are up to no good, they want to do your merchant in. I heard it with me own ears—the landlord and his wife a-whispering together." Well, no wonder I'd had that feeling inside me. "And who might you be?" I asked. "Oh, I'm the cook," says she. So far so good. I get out of the carriage, go to the merchant, wake him up. "There's mischief afoot, Mister Merchant," says I, and so on and so forth. "There'll be time for sleep later, sir," says I. "But you get dressed now, before it's too late, and we'll make ourselves scarce while the going's good."

'Barely has he started dressing himself when—mercy on us!—the door opens, and blow me down if I don't see the landlord, his missus and three workmen come in. So they'd talked their workmen into joining in. "The merchant has a lot of money, and we'll go shares." Every one of the five holds a long knife—a knife apiece they had. The landlord locks the door. "Say your prayers, travellers," says he. "And if so be you start shouting," says he, "we shan't let you pray before you die." As if we could shout! We're a-choking with fear, we ain't up to shouting. The merchant bursts into tears. "Good Christian folk," says he, "you've decided to murder me because you've taken a fancy to my money. Well, so be it. I ain't the first, and I shan't be the last. Not a few of us merchants have had our throats cut in inns. But why kill my driver, friends? Why must he suffer for my money?" And he says it all pathetic like. "If we leave him alive, he'll be the first to bear witness against us," says the innkeeper. "We can just as well kill two as one—may as well hang for a sheep as a lamb," says he. "You say your prayers and that's that, it ain't no use talking."

'The merchant and I kneel down together, weeping like, and we start praying. He remembers his children, while I'm still young, I am, I want to live. We look at the icons and we pray—so pathetic like, it makes me cry even now. And the landlord's missus looks at us. "Don't bear a grudge against us in the other world, good people," says she. "And don't pray to God for us to be punished, for 'tis poverty as drove us to it." Well, we're a-praying and a-weeping away, and God hears us—takes pity on us, He do. Just when the innkeeper had the merchant by the beard—so he could cut his throat, see?—suddenly there's no end of a knock on the window from outside. We cower down and the innkeeper lets his hands fall. Someone bangs the window.

' "Mister Peter, are you there?" a voice shouts. "Get ready, it's time we left."

'The landlord and his missus see that someone's come for the merchant, they're afeared and they take to their heels. We hurry into the yard, hitch up the horses and make ourselves scarce.'

'But who was it banged the window?' asked Dymov.

'Oh, that. Some saint or angel, I reckon, for there weren't no one else. When we drove out of the yard there weren't no one in the street. 'Twas God's doing.'

Panteley told a few more yarns, 'long knives' figuring in all of them, and all having the same ring of fiction. Had he heard these tales from someone else, or had he made them up himself in the distant past, and then, beginning to lose his memory, confused fact and fiction till he could no longer tell one from the other? All things are possible. It is odd, though, that whenever he happened to tell a story, now and throughout the journey, he clearly favoured fantasy and never recounted his actual experiences. Yegorushka took it all at face value at the time, believing every word, but he wondered afterwards that one who had travelled the length and breadth of Russia in his time—who had seen and known so much, whose wife and children had been burnt to death—should so disparage his eventful life that when he sat by the camp-fire he either said nothing or spoke of what had never been.

Over the stew all were silent, thinking of what they had just heard. Life is frightening and marvellous, and so whatever fearful stories you may tell in Russia, and however you embellish them with highwaymen's lairs, long knives and such wonders, they will always ring true to the listener, and only a profoundly literate person will look askance, and even he will not say anything. The cross by the road, the dark bales, the vast expanse around them, the fate of those round the camp-fire—all this was so marvellous and frightening in itself that the fantastic element in fiction and folk-tale paled and became indistinguishable from reality.

Everyone ate out of the pot, but Panteley sat apart eating his stew from a wooden bowl. His spoon was different from the others', being of cypress wood with a little cross on it. Looking at him, Yegorushka remembered the lamp glass and quietly asked Styopka why the old fellow sat by himself.

'He's a Dissenter,' whispered Styopka and Vasya, looking as if they had mentioned a weakness or a secret vice.

All were silent, thinking. After the frightening tales they did not feel like talking about everyday things.

Suddenly in the silence Vasya drew himself upright, fixed his lustre-less eyes on one point and pricked up his ears.

'What is it?' Dymov asked.

'Someone's coming this way,' answered Vasya.

'Where do you see him?'

'There he is. A faint white shape.'

In the direction in which Vasya was looking nothing could be seen but darkness. All listened, but no steps were heard.

'Is he on the road?' asked Dymov.

'No, he's coming across country. He's coming this way.'

A minute passed in silence.

'Well, perhaps it's the merchant haunting the steppe, the one that's buried here,' said Dymov.

All cast a sidelong glance at the cross, but then they looked at each other and broke into a laugh, ashamed of their panic.

'Why should he haunt the place?' asked Panteley. 'The only ghosts are them that the earth don't accept. And the merchants were all right. They received a martyr's crown, them merchants did.'

But then hurrying footsteps were heard.

'He's carrying something,' said Vasya.

They could hear the grass rustle and the coarse weeds crackle under the walker's feet, but could see no one because of the fire's glare. At last the steps sounded close by and someone coughed. The flickering light seemed to yield, the veil fell from their eyes, and the carters suddenly saw before them a man.

Whether it was due to the flickering light, or because all were keen to make out the man's face, it turned out—oddly enough—that it was neither his face nor his clothes that struck everyone first, but his smile. It was an uncommonly good-natured, broad, gentle smile, as of a waking baby—infectious and tending to evoke an answering smile. When they had looked him over the stranger turned out to be a man of thirty, ugly and in no way remarkable. He was a southerner—tall, with a long nose, long arms and long legs. Everything about him seemed long except his neck—so short that it gave him a stooped look. He wore a clean white shirt with an embroidered collar, baggy white trousers and new riding boots, seeming quite a dandy by comparison with the carters. He was carrying a large white object, mysterious at first sight, and from behind his shoulder peeped out a gun barrel, also long.

Emerging from darkness into the circle of light, he stood stock-still and looked at the carters for half a minute as if calling on them to admire his smile. Then he went to the fire, grinned even more broadly and asked if a stranger might claim their hospitality, 'country fashion'.

'You're welcome indeed,' Panteley answered for everyone.

The stranger laid the object he was carrying near the fire—a dead bustard—and greeted them again.

All went up and examined the bustard.

'A fine big bird—how did you get it?' asked Dymov.

'Buckshot. Small shot's no use, you can't get near enough. Like to buy it, lads? It's yours for twenty copecks.'

'It ain't no use to us. 'Tis good enough roasted, but stewed—powerful tough it be, I reckon!'

'Oh, bother it. I could take it to the squire's lot on the estate. They'd give me half a rouble, but that's a way off—ten mile, it be.'

The stranger sat down, unslung his gun and put it by him. He seemed torpid and sleepy as he smiled and squinted in the light, evidently thinking agreeable thoughts. They gave him a spoon and he started eating.

'And who might you be?' asked Dymov.

Not hearing the question, the smiler neither answered nor even looked at Dymov. He probably could not taste the stew either, for he chewed lazily and rather automatically, his spoon sometimes chock full and sometimes quite empty as he raised it to his mouth. He was not drunk, but he did seem a trifle unhinged.

'I asked you who you were,' Dymov repeated.

'Me?' The stranger gave a start. 'I'm Constantine Zvonyk from Rovnoye, about three miles from here.'

To make it clear from the beginning that he was a cut above your average peasant, he hastened to add that he kept bees and pigs.

'Do you live with your father or in a place of your own?'

'Oh, I'm by myself now, set up on me own I have. I was married this month after St. Peter's Day. So now I'm a husband. 'Tis the eighteenth day since we was wed.'

'That's a fine thing,' said Panteley. 'No harm in having a wife. God has blessed you.'

'His young wife sleeps at home while he's a-wandering the steppes,' laughed Kiryukha. 'Strange doings!'

Constantine winced as though pinched in a sensitive place, laughed and flared up. 'Lord love us, she ain't at home,' he said, quickly taking the spoon from his mouth and surveying everyone with glad surprise. 'That she ain't. She's gone to her mother's for two days. Aye, off she's gone, and I'm a bachelor, like.'

Constantine dismissed the subject with a gesture and flexed his neck, wanting to go on thinking but hindered by the joy irradiating his face. He shifted his position, as if sitting was uncomfortable, laughed and then made another dismissive gesture. He was ashamed to betray his pleasant thoughts to strangers, yet felt an irresistible urge to share his happiness. 'She's gone to her mother's at Demidovo.' He blushed and moved his gun to another place. 'She'll be back tomorrow, she said she'd be back for dinner.'

'Do you miss her?' Dymov asked.

'Lord, yes—what do you think? I ain't been wed but a few days and she's already gone. See what I mean? And she's a little bundle of mischief, Lord love us. Aye, she's marvellous she is, marvellous, always a-laughing and a-singing, a proper handful she be. When I'm with her I don't know whether I'm on me head or me heels, and without her I feel as how I've lost something and I wander over the steppe like a fool. I've been at it since dinner—past praying for, I am.'

Constantine rubbed his eyes, looked at the fire and laughed.

'You must love her then,' said Panteley, but Constantine did not hear.

'She's marvellous, marvellous,' he repeated. 'She's such a good housewife, so clever, so intelligent—you couldn't find another woman like her in the whole county, not among us common folk you couldn't. She's gone away. But she misses me, I know. Aye, that she does, the naughty little thing. She said she'd be back by dinner tomorrow. But what a business it was.' Constantine almost shouted, suddenly pitching his voice higher and shifting his position. 'She loves me and misses me now, but she never did want to wed me, you know.'

'Have something to eat,' said Kiryukha.

'She wouldn't marry me,' Constantine went on, not hearing. 'Three years I spent arguing with her. I saw her at Kalachik fair, and I fell madly in love, I were downright desperate. I live at Rovnoye and she was at Demidovo nigh on twenty mile away and there weren't nothing I could do. I send matchmakers to her, but she says no, the naughty little creature. Well I try one thing and another. I send her ear-rings, cakes and twenty pound of honey, but it's still no. Can you believe it? But then again, when you come to think of it, I'm no match for her. She's young, beautiful and a proper little spitfire, but I'm old —I'll soon be thirty. And then I'm so handsome, ain't I—what with me fine beard the size of a matchstick and me face so smooth that it's one mass of pimples? What chance had I got with her? The only thing was, we are quite well off, but them Vakhramenkos live well too. They keep six oxen and two labourers.

'Well, I were in love with her, lads—proper crazy I was. Couldn't sleep, couldn't eat. God help us, I were that befuddled. I longed to see her, but she was at Demidovo. And do you know—I ain't lying, as God's my witness—I used to walk there about three times a week just to look at her. I stopped working, and I were in such a pother I even wanted to hire myself out as a labourer at Demidovo to be closer to her like. Sheer torture it was. My mother called in a village woman that could cast spells, and my father was ready to beat me a dozen times. Well, I put up with it for three years, and then I decided I'd go and be a cabbie in town, botheration take it! It weren't to be, I reckoned. At Easter I went to Demidovo for a last look at her.'

Constantine threw his head back and gave a peal of merry chuckles, as if he had just brought off a particularly cunning piece of deception. 'I see her with some lads near the stream,' he went on. 'And I feel proper angry. I call her to one side and I say all manner of things to her —for a full hour, maybe. And she falls in love with me! For three years she didn't love me, but she loved me for them words.'

'But what were them words?' Dymov asked.

'The words? I don't recall—how could I? At the time it all comes straight out like water from a gutter—blah, blah, blah, without me stopping to breathe. But I couldn't say one word of it now. So she weds me. And now she's gone to see her mother, the naughty lass, and here I am a-wandering the steppes without her. I can't stay at home, I can't abide to.'

Constantine awkwardly unwound his legs from under him, stretched out on the ground, propped his head on his fists, and then stood up and sat down again. By now everyone could clearly see that here was a man happy in love, poignantly happy. His smile, his eyes, his every movement reflected overwhelming bliss. He fidgeted, not knowing what posture to adopt or avoid, being drained of vitality through excess of delectable thoughts. Having poured his heart out to strangers, he settled down quietly at last, deep in thought as he gazed at the fire.

Seeing a happy man, the others felt depressed, wanting to be happy themselves, and fell to pondering. Dymov stood up and slowly strolled about near the fire, his walk and the movement of his shoulder-blades showing how weary and depressed he was. He stood still for a while, looked at Constantine and sat down.

The camp-fire was dying down by now, no longer flickering, and the patch of red had shrunk and dimmed. And the quicker the fire burnt out the clearer the moonlight became. Now the road could be seen in its full width—the bales of wool, the wagon shafts, the munching horses. On the other side was the hazy outline of the second cross.

Dymov propped his cheek on his hand and softly sang a mournful ditty. Constantine smiled drowsily, and joined in with his reedy little voice. They sang for less than a minute and fell silent. Yemelyan gave a start, flexed his elbows and flicked his fingers. 'I say, lads, let's sing a holy song,' he entreated them.

Tears came into his eyes and he pressed his hand to his heart, repeating his appeal to sing 'a holy song'. Constantine said he 'didn't know any', and everyone else refused. Then Yemelyan started on his own. He conducted with both hands, he tossed his head back and he opened his mouth, but from his throat burst only a hoarse, voiceless breath. He sang with his arms, head and eyes, and even with the swelling on his cheek. He sang fervidly and with anguish, and the more he strained his chest to extract a note, be it but a single one, the less sound did his breath carry.

Overcome by depression like everyone else, Yegorushka went to his wagon, climbed on the bales and lay down. He looked at the sky, thinking of lucky Constantine and his wife. Why do people marry? Why are there women in the world, the boy vaguely wondered, thinking how nice it must be for a man to have a loving, cheerful, beautiful woman constantly at his side. For some reason thoughts of Countess Dranitsky came into his head. How agreeable it must be to live with a woman like that! Perhaps he would have liked to marry her himself, had the notion not been so embarrassing. He recalled her eyebrows, the pupils of her eyes, her coach and the clock with the horseman. The quiet, warm night settled down over him, whispering something in his ear, and he felt as if that same beautiful woman was bending over him, looking at him, smiling, wanting to kiss him.

Nothing was left of the camp-fire but two little red eyes that dwindled and dwindled. The carters and Constantine sat round it—dark, still figures—and there seemed to be far more of them than before. The twin crosses were equally visible, and somewhere far away on the road a red light glowed—someone else cooking a meal, probably.

> 'Here's to good old Mother Russia,
> Finest nation in the world,'

Kiryukha suddenly sang out in a harsh voice, then choked and grew silent. The prairie echo caught his voice and carried it on so that the very spirit of stupidity seemed to be trundling over the steppe on heavy wheels.

'Time to go,' said Panteley. 'Up you get, mates.'

While they were hitching up Constantine was walking about by the wagons singing his wife's praises. 'Thanks for the hospitality, lads, and good-bye,' he shouted as the convoy moved off. 'I'll make for the other fire. It's all too much for me, it is.'

He quickly disappeared in the gloom, and could long be heard walking towards the glimmering light so that he could tell those other strangers of his happiness.

When the boy woke up next day it was early morning and the sun had not risen. The wagons had halted. Talking to Dymov and Kiryukha by the leading vehicle was a man on a Cossack pony—he wore a white peaked cap and a suit of cheap grey cloth. About a mile and a half ahead of the wagons were long, low white barns and cottages with tiled roofs. Neither yards nor trees were to be seen near them.

'What village is that?' Yegorushka asked the old man.

'Them farms are Armenian, young feller,' answered Panteley. ' 'Tis where the Armenians live—not a bad lot, they ain't.'

The man in grey finished talking to Dymov and Kiryukha, reined in his pony and looked at the farms.

' 'Tis a proper botheration,' sighed Panteley, also looking at the farms and shivering in the cool of the morning. 'He sent a man to the farm for some bit of paper, but he hasn't come back. He should have sent Styopka.'

'But who is he?' asked the boy.

'Varlamov.'

Varlamov! Yegorushka quickly jumped to his knees and looked at the white cap. It was hard to recognize the mysterious, elusive Varlamov, who was so much in demand, who was always 'knocking around', and who had far more money than Countess Dranitsky, in this short, grey, large-booted little man on the ugly nag who was talking to peasants at an hour when all decent people are abed.

'He's all right, a good sort he is,' said Panteley, looking at the farms. 'God grant him health, he's a fine gentleman, is Simon Varlamov. It's the likes of him as keeps the world a-humming, lad. Aye, that they do. It ain't cock-crow yet, and he's already up and about. Another man would be asleep, or he'd be at home gallivanting with his guests, but Varlamov's out on the steppe all day, knocking around like. Never misses a deal, he don't—and good for him, say I.'

Varlamov was staring fixedly at one of the farms, discussing something while his pony shifted impatiently from foot to foot.

'Hey, Mr. Varlamov!' shouted Panteley, taking off his hat. 'Let me send Styopka. Yemelyan, give a shout—send Styopka, tell 'em.'

But now at last a man on horseback was seen to leave the farm. Leaning heavily to one side and swinging his whip over his head, as if giving a rodeo performance and wanting to dazzle everyone with his horsemanship, he flew like a bird to the wagons.

'That must be one of his rangers,' said Panteley. 'A hundred of them he has, or more.'

Reaching the first wagon, the rider pulled up his horse, doffed his cap and gave a little book to Varlamov, who removed several papers from it and read them.

'But where's Ivanchuk's letter?' he shouted.

The horseman took the book back, looked at the papers and shrugged. He began saying something, probably in self-defence, and asked permission to go back to the farms. The pony suddenly gave a start as if Varlamov had become heavier, and Varlamov also gave a start.

'Clear out!' he shouted angrily, brandishing his whip at the rider. Then he turned his pony round and rode along the wagons at a walk, examining the papers in the book. When he reached the last wagon Yegorushka strained his eyes to get a good look. Varlamov was quite old. He had a small grey beard, and his simple, sunburnt, typically Russian face was red, wet with dew and covered with little blue veins.

He had exactly the same businesslike expression as Ivan Kuzmichov, and the same fanatical devotion to affairs. But what a difference you could feel between him and Kuzmichov! Besides wearing an air of businesslike reserve, Uncle Ivan always looked worried and afraid— of not finding Varlamov, of being late, of missing a bargain. But in Varlamov's face and figure there was nothing of your typical little man's dependent look. This man fixed the price himself. He didn't go round looking for people, and he depended on no one. Nondescript though his appearance might be, everything about him—even the way he held his whip—conveyed a sense of power and the habit of authority over the steppe.

He did not glance at the boy as he rode past. Only his pony deigned to notice Yegorushka, gazing at him with large, foolish eyes—and even the pony was not very interested. Panteley bowed to Varlamov, who noticed this but did not take his eyes off his papers and just said: 'Greetings, grandpa,' gargling the 'r's in his throat.

Varlamov's interchange with the horseman and the swish of his whip had evidently demoralized the whole party, for all looked grave. Quailing before the strong man's wrath, the horseman remained by the front wagon with his head bare, let his reins hang loose and said nothing, as if unable to believe that the day had begun so badly for him.

'He's a rough old boy,' muttered Panteley. 'Real hard. But he's all right—a good sort he is. He don't harm no one without reason. He's all right he is!'

After examining the papers, Varlamov thrust the book in his pocket. Seeming to understand his thoughts, the pony quivered and careered down the road without waiting for orders.

VII

On the following night the wagoners again halted to cook their meal, but on this occasion everything seemed tinged with melancholy from the start. It was sultry and they had all drunk a great deal, but without in the least quenching their thirst. The moon rose—intensely crimson and sullen, as if it were ailing. The stars were gloomy too, the mist was thicker, the distant prospect was hazier, and all nature seemed to wilt at some intimation of doom.

There was no more of the previous day's excitement and conversation round the camp-fire. All were depressed, all spoke listlessly and reluctantly. Panteley did nothing but sigh and complain of his feet, while occasionally invoking the topic of dying 'contumaciously'.

Dymov lay on his stomach, silently chewing a straw. He wore a fastidious expression as if the straw had a bad smell, and he looked ill-tempered and tired. Vasya complained that his jaw ached, and forecast bad weather. Yemelyan had stopped waving his arms, and sat still, looking grimly at the fire. Yegorushka was wilting too. The slow pace had tired him, and he had a headache from the day's heat.

When the stew was cooked Dymov began picking on his mates out of boredom. He glared spitefully at Yemelyan. 'Look at old Lumpy Jaws sprawling there! Always first to shove his spoon in, he is. Talk about greed! Can't wait to grab first place by the pot, can he? Thinks he's the lord of creation because he used to be a singer. We know your sort of choirboy, mister—there's tramps like you a-plenty singing for their suppers up and down the high road.'

Yemelyan returned the other's angry glare. 'Why pick on me?'

'To teach you not to dip in the pot before others. Who do you think you are?'

'You're a fool, that's all I can say,' wheezed Yemelyan.

Knowing from experience how such conversations usually ended, Panteley and Vasya intervened, urging Dymov to stop picking a quarrel.

'You—sing in a choir!' The irrepressible bully laughed derisively. 'Anyone can sing like that, rot you—sitting in the church porch a-chanting of your "Alms for Christ's sake!" '

Yemelyan said nothing. His silence exasperated Dymov, who looked at the ex-chorister with even greater hatred. 'I don't want to soil me hands, or I'd teach you not to be so stuck up.'

Yemelyan flared up. 'Why pick on me, you scum? What have I done to you?'

'What did you call me?' Dymov straightened up, his eyes blood-shot. 'What was that? Scum, eh? Very well—now you can go and look for that!'

He snatched the spoon from Yemelyan's hands and hurled it far to one side. Kiryukha, Vasya and Styopka jumped up and went to look for it, while Yemelyan fixed an imploring and questioning look on Panteley. His face suddenly shrinking, the former chorister frowned, blinked and wept like a baby.

Yegorushka, who had long hated Dymov, felt as if he had started to choke, and the flames of the fire scorched his face. He wanted to run quickly into the darkness by the wagons, but the bully's spiteful, bored eyes had a magnetic effect. Longing to say something exceedingly offensive, the boy took a step towards Dymov. 'You're the worst of the lot,' he panted. 'I can't stand you!'

That was when he should have run to the wagons, but he seemed rooted to the spot. 'You will burn in hell in the next world,' he continued. 'I'm going to tell Uncle Ivan about you. How dare you insult Yemelyan?'

'Now, ain't that a nice surprise, I must say!' Dymov laughed. 'A little swine, what ain't dry behind the ears, a-laying down the law! Want a clip on the ear-'ole?'

The boy felt as if there was no air to breathe. He suddenly shivered all over and stamped his feet, something that had never happened to him before.

'Hit him, hit him!' he yelled in a piercing voice. Tears spurted from his eyes, he felt ashamed and he ran staggering to the wagons. What impression his outburst produced he did not see. 'Mother, Mother!' he whispered, lying on the bale, weeping, jerking his arms and legs.

The men, the shadows round the camp-fire, the dark bales and the distant lightning flashing far away every minute—it all seemed so inhuman and terrifying now. He was horrified, wondering in his despair how and why he had landed in this unknown land in the company of these awful peasants. Where were his uncle, Father Christopher and Deniska? Why were they so long in coming? Could they have forgotten him? To be forgotten and abandoned to the whim of fate— the thought so chilled and scared him that he several times felt like jumping off the bale and running headlong back along the road without looking behind him. What stopped him was the memory of those grim, dark crosses that he was bound to meet on his way, and also the distant lightning flashes. Only when he whispered 'Mother, Mother!' did he feel a little better.

The carters must have been scared too. After the boy had run from the fire they said nothing for a while, and then spoke of something in hollow undertones, saying that 'it' was on its way, and that they must hurry up and get ready to escape it. They quickly finished supper, put out the fire and began hitching up the horses in silence. Their agitation and staccato speech showed that they foresaw some disaster.

Before they started off Dymov went up to Panteley. 'What's his name?' he asked quietly.

'Yegorushka,' answered Panteley.

Dymov put one foot on a wheel, seized the cord round a bale and hoisted himself. The boy saw his face and curly head—the face looked pale, weary and grave, but no longer spiteful. 'Hey, boy!' he said quietly. 'Go on, hit me!'

Yegorushka looked at him in amazement, and at that moment there was a flash of lightning.

'It's all right, hit me!' continued Dymov. Without waiting to see whether the boy would hit him or talk to him, he jumped down. 'I'm bored,' he said. Then, rolling from side to side and working his shoulder-blades, he slowly strolled down the wagon line.

'God, I'm bored,' he repeated in a tone half plaintive, half irritated. 'No offence, old son,' he said as he passed Yemelyan. 'It's cruel hard, our life.'

Lightning flashed on the right, and immediately flashed again far away, as if reflected in a mirror.

'Take this, boy,' shouted Panteley, handing up something large and dark from below.

'What is it?' asked Yegorushka.

'Some matting. Put it over you when it rains.'

The boy sat up and looked around. It had grown noticeably blacker in the distance, with the pale light now winking more than once a minute. The blackness was veering to the right as if pulled by its own weight.

'Will there be a storm, Grandad?' asked the boy.

'Oh, my poor feet, they're so cold,' intoned Panteley, not hearing him and stamping his feet.

On the left, as if a match had been struck on the sky, a pale phosphorescent stripe gleamed and faded. Very far away someone was heard walking up and down on an iron roof—barefoot, presumably, because the iron gave out a hollow rumble.

'Looks like a real old downpour,' shouted Kiryukha.

Far away, beyond the horizon on the right, flashed lightning so vivid that it lit up part of the steppe and the place where the clear sky met the black. An appalling cloud was moving up unhurriedly—a great hulk with large black shreds hanging on its rim. Similar shreds pressed against each other, looming on the horizon to right and left. The jagged, tattered-looking cloud had a rather drunken and disorderly air. There was a clearly enunciated clap of thunder. Yegorushka crossed himself, and quickly put on his overcoat.

'Real bored, I am.' Dymov's shout carried from the leading wagons, his tone showing that his bad temper was returning. 'Bored.'

There was a sudden squall of wind so violent that it nearly snatched the boy's bundle and matting off him. Whipping, tearing in all directions, the mat slapped the bale and Yegorushka's face. The wind careered whistling over the steppe, swerving chaotically and raising such a din in the grass that it drowned the thunder and creak of wagon wheels. It was blowing from the black thunderhead, bearing dust clouds, and the smell of rain and damp earth. The moon misted over, seeming dirtier, the stars grew dimmer still, dust clouds and their shadows were seen scurrying off somewhere back along the edge of the road. Eddying and drawing dust, dry grass and feathers from the ground, whirlwinds soared right into the upper heavens, it seemed. Uprooted plants must be flying around close by the blackest thunderhead, and how terrified they must feel! But dust clogged the eyes, blanking out everything except the lightning flashes.

Thinking the rain was just about to pour down, the boy knelt up and covered himself with his mat. From in front came a shout of 'Panteley', followed by some incomprehensible booming syllables.

'I can't hear!' loudly intoned Panteley in response, and the voice boomed out again.

An enraged clap of thunder rolled across the sky from right to left and then back again, dying away near the leading wagons.

'Holy, holy, holy, Lord God of Sabaoth,' whispered Yegorushka, crossing himself. 'Heaven and earth are full of thy glory.'

The sky's blackness gaped, breathing white fire, and at once there was another thunderclap. Barely had it died away when there was a flash of lightning so broad that the boy could see the whole road into the far distance, all the carters and even Kiryukha's waistcoat through the cracks in the matting. The black tatters on the left were already soaring aloft, and one of them—crude, clumsy, a paw with fingers—reached out towards the moon. Yegorushka decided to shut his eyes tightly, pay no attention and wait for it all to end.

The rain was long delayed for some reason, and the boy—hoping that the thunder cloud might pass over—peeped out from his mat. It was fearfully dark, and he could see neither Panteley nor the bale nor himself. He squinted towards where the moon had been, but it was pitch black there, as on the wagon. In the darkness the lightning flashes seemed whiter and more blinding, hurting the eyes.

He called Panteley's name, but there was no answer. Then, in the end, the wind gave a last rip at the mat and flew off. A low, steady throb was heard, and a large, cold drop fell on the boy's knee, while another crawled down his hand. Realizing that his knees were uncovered, he tried to rearrange the matting, but then came a pattering and a tapping of something on the road, and on the shafts and the bale. Rain. It seemed to have an understanding with the mat, for the two started some discussion—rapid, cheerful and exceedingly objectionable, like a couple of magpies.

Yegorushka knelt up—squatted, rather, on his boots. When the rain rapped the mat he leant forward to shield his suddenly soaked knees. He managed to cover them, but in less than a minute he felt an unpleasant penetrating wetness behind, on back and calves. He resumed his former position and stuck his knees out into the rain, wondering what to do and how to rearrange the mat that he could not see in the dark. But his arms were already wet, water was running down his sleeves and behind his collar, his shoulder-blades were cold. And so he decided to do nothing, but to sit still and wait for it all to end. 'Holy, holy, holy,' he whispered.

Suddenly, directly over his head, came an almighty deafening crash and the sky broke in two. He bent forwards—holding his breath, expecting the pieces to fall on his neck and back. He chanced to open his eyes, blinking half a dozen times as a penetrating, blinding light flared up, and he saw his fingers, his wet sleeves and the streams flowing off the mat, over the bale and down below on the earth. Then a new blow, no less mighty and awesome, resounded. No longer did the sky groan or rumble, but gave out crackles like the splitting of a dry tree.

The thunder's crash-bang beats were precisely enunciated as it rolled down the sky, staggered, and—somewhere by the leading wagons or far behind—tumbled over with a rancorous, staccato drumming.

The earlier lightning flashes had been awesome, but with thunder such as this they seemed downright menacing. The weird light penetrated your closed eyelids, percolating chillingly through your whole body. Was there a way to avoid seeing it? The boy decided to turn his face backwards. Carefully, as if afraid of being observed, he got on all fours, slid his palms over the wet bale and turned round.

The great drumming swooped over his head, collapsed under the wagon and exploded.

Again his eyes chanced to open and he saw a new danger. Behind the wagon stalked three giants with long pikes. The lightning flashed on the points of their pikes, distinctly lighting up their figures. These were people of vast dimensions with hidden faces, bowed heads and heavy footsteps. They seemed sad, despondent and lost in thought. Their aim in stalking the convoy may not have been to cause damage, but there was something horrible in their proximity.

The boy quickly turned forwards. 'Panteley! Grandad!' he shouted, shaking all over.

The sky answered him with a crash, bang, crash.

As he opened his eyes, to see whether the carters were there, the lightning flashed in two places, illuminating the road to the far horizon, the entire convoy and all the men. Rivulets streamed down the road, and bubbles danced. Panteley strode by his wagon, his high hat and shoulders covered with a small mat. His figure expressed neither fear nor alarm, as though he had been deafened by the thunder and blinded by the lightning.

'Grandad, see the giants!' the boy shouted at him, weeping.

But the old man heard nothing. Further ahead Yemelyan walked along, covered with a large mat from head to foot and triangular in shape. Vasya, who had nothing over him, stepped out in his usual clockwork style—lifting his feet high, not bending his knees. In the lightning the convoy seemed motionless, with the carters rooted to the spot and Vasya's raised leg frozen rigid in position.

Yegorushka called the old man again. Receiving no answer, he sat still, but he was no longer expecting it all to end. He was certain that the thunder would kill him that very instant, that he would open his eyes by accident and see those frightful giants. No longer did he cross himself, call the old man or think of his mother—he was simply numb with cold and the certainty that the storm would never end.

Suddenly voices were heard.

'Yegorushka, you asleep, or what?' shouted Panteley from below. 'Get down. Has he gone deaf, the silly lad?'

'Quite a storm!' It was a deep, unfamiliar voice, and the speaker cleared his throat as if he had tossed down a glassful of vodka.

The boy opened his eyes. Down near the wagon stood Panteley, triangle-shaped Yemelyan and the giants. The latter were now much shorter and turned out, when Yegorushka got a proper sight of them, to be ordinary peasants shouldering iron pitch-forks, not pikes. In the space between Panteley and the triangular Yemelyan shone the window of a low hut—the wagons must have halted in a village. Yegorushka threw off his mat, took his bundle and hurried down from the wagon. Now, what with people speaking near by and the lighted

window, he no longer felt afraid, though the thunder crashed as loudly
as ever and lightning scourged the whole sky.

'A decent storm—not bad at all, praise the Lord,' muttered Panteley.
'My feet have gone a bit soft in the rain, but no matter. Are you down,
boy? Well, go in the hut. It's all right.'

'It must have struck somewhere, Lord save us,' wheezed Yemelyan.
'You from these parts?' he asked the giants.

'Nay, from Glinovo. From Glinovo we be. We work at the squire's
place—name of Plater.'

'Threshers, are you?'

'We do different things. Just now we be getting in the wheat. But
what lightning, eh? There ain't been a storm like this for many a
moon.'

Yegorushka went into the hut, where he was greeted by a lean,
hunchbacked old woman with a sharp chin. She held a tallow candle,
screwing up her eyes and giving prolonged sighs.

'What a storm God has sent us!' she said. 'And our lads are spending
the night on the steppe—what a time they'll have of it, poor souls.
Now, take your clothes off, young sir—come on.'

Trembling with cold, shrinking fastidiously, the boy pulled off his
wet overcoat, spread his hands and feet far apart and did not move for
a long time. The slightest motion evoked a disagreeably damp, cold
sensation. The sleeves and the back of his shirt were sopping, his
trousers stuck to his legs, his head was dripping.

'Don't stand there splayed out like,' said the old woman. 'Come and
sit down, lad.'

Straddling his legs, Yegorushka went to the table and sat on a
bench near someone's head. The head moved, emitting a stream of air
through the nose, made a chewing sound and subsided. From the head
a mound covered with a sheepskin stretched along the bench—a sleeping peasant woman.

Sighing, the old woman went out and suddenly came back with a
big water-melon and a small sweet melon. 'Help yourself, young man,
I've nothing else for you.'

Yawning, she dug into a table drawer and took out a long, sharp
knife much like those used by highwaymen to cut merchants' throats
in inns. 'Help yourself, young sir.'

Trembling as if in fever, the boy ate a slice of sweet melon with
black bread, and then a slice of water-melon, which made him even
colder.

'Out on the steppe our lads are tonight,' sighed the old woman while he ate. ' 'Tis a proper botheration. I did ought to light a candle before the icon, but I don't know where Stepanida's put it. Help yourself, young man, do.' The old woman yawned, reached back with her right hand, and scratched her left shoulder. 'Two o'clock it must be,' she said. 'Time to get up soon. Our lads are outside for the night. Soaked to the skin they'll be, for sure.'

'I'm sleepy, Grannie,' said the boy.

'Then lie down, young man, do,' sighed the old woman, yawning. 'I was asleep meself, when—Lord God Almighty!—I hear someone a-knocking. I wake up and I see God's sent us a storm. I'd light a candle, dear, but I couldn't find one.'

Talking to herself, she pulled some rags off the bench, probably her bedding, took two sheepskins from a nail near the stove, and began making up a bed for the boy. ' 'Tis as stormy as ever,' she muttered. 'I'm afeared it might start a fire, you never can tell. The lads are out on the steppe all night. Lie down, young man, go to sleep. God bless you, my child. I won't clear away the melon—happen you'll get up and have a bite.'

The old soul's sighs and yawns, the measured breathing of the sleeping woman, the hut's dim light, the sound of rain through the window—it all made him sleepy. Shy of taking his clothes off in the old woman's presence, he removed only his boots, lay down and covered himself with the sheepskin.

A minute later Panteley's whisper was heard. 'Is the lad lying down?'

'Yes,' whispered the old woman. ' 'Tis a proper botheration. Bang, crash, bang—no end to it.'

'It'll soon be over,' wheezed Panteley, sitting down. 'It's quieter now. The lads have gone to different huts, and a couple have stayed with the horses. Aye, the lads. Have to do it, or else the horses will be stolen. Well, I'll stay a while, and then take my turn. Have to do it, or they'll be stolen.'

Panteley and the old woman sat side by side at Yegorushka's feet, talking in sibilant whispers punctuated by sighs and yawns. But the boy just could not get warm. He had a warm, heavy sheepskin over him, but his whole body shivered, his hands and legs were convulsed with cramps, his insides trembled. He undressed under the sheepskin, but it made no difference. The shivering became more and more pronounced.

Panteley left to take his turn with the horses and then came back again, but Yegorushka still could not sleep, and was still shivering all over. His head and chest felt crushed and oppressed by—by what he did not know. Was it the old people whispering or the strong smell of the sheepskin? The melons had left a nasty metallic taste in his mouth, besides which he was being bitten by fleas. 'I'm cold, Grandad,' he said, not recognizing his own voice.

'Sleep, son, sleep,' sighed the old woman.

Titus approached the bed on his thin legs, waved his arms, and then grew as tall as the ceiling and turned into a windmill. Father Christopher—not as he had been in the britzka, but in full vestments and carrying his aspergillum, walked around the mill, sprinkling it with holy water and it stopped turning. Knowing he was delirious, the boy opened his eyes. He called to the old man. 'Water!'

No answer. Finding it unbearably close and uncomfortable lying there, Yegorushka stood up, dressed and went out of the hut. It was morning now and the sky was overcast, but the rain had stopped. Trembling, wrapping his wet overcoat round him, he walked up and down the muddy yard, trying to catch a sound amid the silence. Then his eyes lighted on a small shed with a half-open door made of thatch. He looked in, entered and sat in a dark corner on a heap of dry dung.

His head felt heavy, his mind was in a whirl and there was a dry, unpleasant sensation in his mouth owing to the metallic taste. He looked at his hat, straightened its peacock feather, and remembered going to buy it with his mother. Putting his hand in his pocket, he took out a lump of brown, sticky paste. How did that stuff get in there? He thought, he sniffed it. A smell of honey. Ah, yes—the Jewish cake. How sodden the poor thing was!

The boy looked at his overcoat—grey with big bone buttons, cut like a frock-coat. A new and expensive garment, it had not hung in the hall at home, but with his mother's dresses in the bedroom. He was only allowed to wear it on holidays. The sight of it moved him to pity—he recalled that he and the overcoat had both been abandoned to their fate, and would never go home again. And he sobbed so loudly that he nearly fell off the dung pile.

A big white dog, sopping wet and with woolly tufts like curling papers on its muzzle, came into the shed and stared quizzically at the boy. It was obviously wondering whether to bark or not, but decided that there was no need, cautiously approached the boy, ate the lump of paste and went out.

'Them's Varlamov's men,' someone shouted in the street.

Having cried his eyes out, the boy left the shed, skirted a puddle and made his way to the street, where some wagons stood immediately in front of the gates. Wet carters with muddy feet, listless and drowsy as autumn flies, drifted near by or sat on the shafts. Looking at them, Yegorushka thought what a boring, uncomfortable business it was, being a peasant. He went up to Panteley and sat down on the shaft beside him. 'I'm cold, Grandad.' He shivered and thrust his hands into his sleeves.

'Never mind, we'll be there soon,' yawned Panteley. 'You'll get warm, never fear.'

It was quite cool, and the convoy made an early start. Yegorushka lay on his bale, trembling with cold, though the sun soon came out and dried his clothes, the bale and the ground. Barely had he closed his eyes when he saw Titus and the windmill again. Nauseated, feeling heavy all over, he fought to dispel these images, but as soon as they disappeared the bullying Dymov would pounce on him—roaring, red-eyed, his fists raised, or would be heard lamenting how 'bored' he was. Varlamov rode past on his Cossack pony, and happy Constantine walked by with his smile and his bustard. How depressing, intolerable and tiresome they all were!

In the late afternoon the boy once raised his head to ask for a drink. The wagons had halted on a large bridge over a wide river. Down below the river was shrouded in smoke through which a steamer could be seen towing a barge. Ahead, beyond the river, was a huge vari-coloured mountain dotted with houses and churches. At its foot a railway engine was being shunted round some goods wagons.

Never had the boy seen steamers, railway trains or wide rivers before, but as he glanced at them now he was neither frightened nor surprised. Nor did his face even express any semblance of curiosity. Nauseated, he quickly lay down with his chest on the bale's edge, feeling ready to vomit. Panteley saw him, grunted and shook his head.

'Our little lad's poorly,' said he. ' 'Tis a chill on the stomach, I'll be bound. Aye, and that far from home like. 'Tis a bad business.'

VIII

The wagons had stopped at a large commercial inn not far from the harbour. Climbing down from the wagon, Yegorushka heard a familiar voice and someone gave him a hand. 'We arrived yesterday evening. We've been expecting you all day. We meant to catch you up yesterday, but it didn't work out and we took a different route. Hey, what a mess you've made of your coat! Your uncle *will* give you what for!'

Gazing at the speaker's mottled face, Yegorushka remembered it as Deniska's.

'Your uncle and Father Christopher are in their room at the inn having tea. Come on.'

He took the boy to a big two-storey building—dark, gloomy, resembling the almshouse at N. By way of a lobby, a dark staircase and a long, narrow corridor Yegorushka and Deniska came to a small room where Ivan Kuzmichov and Father Christopher indeed were seated at a tea table. Both old men showed surprise and joy at seeing the boy.

'Aha, young sir! Master Lomonosov in person!' intoned Father Christopher.

'So it's the gentleman of the family,' said Kuzmichov. 'Pleased to see you.'

Taking his overcoat off, the boy kissed his uncle's hand and Father Christopher's, and sat down at the table.

'Well, how was the journey, *puer bone*?' Father Christopher showered him with questions, pouring him tea and smiling his habitual radiant smile. 'Sick of it, I'll be bound? Never travel with a wagon train or by ox-cart, God forbid. You go on, on, on, Lord help us, you glance ahead and the steppe's just as long-windedly elongated as ever, no end or limit to it. It's not travel, it's a downright travesty of it. But why don't you drink your tea? Go on! Well, while you were trailing along with the wagons we fixed things up to a tee here, thank God. We've sold our wool to Cherepakhin at tip-top prices—done pretty well, we have.'

On first seeing his own people, the boy felt an irresistible urge to complain. Not listening to Father Christopher, he wondered where to start and what exactly to complain of. But Father Christopher's voice, seeming harsh and disagreeable, prevented him from concentrating and confused his thoughts. After sitting for less than five minutes, he got up from table, went to the sofa and lay down.

Father Christopher was amazed. 'Well, I never! What about your tea?'

Still wondering what to complain of, Yegorushka pressed his forehead against the back of his sofa and burst into sobs.

'Well, I never!' repeated Father Christopher, getting up and going over to him. 'What's the matter with you, boy? Why the tears?'

'I—I'm ill.'

'Ill, eh?' Father Christopher was rather put out. 'Now, that's quite wrong, old son. You mustn't fall ill on a journey. Oh dear me, what a thing to do, old son, eh?'

He placed his hand on the boy's head and touched his cheek.

'Yes, your head's hot. You must have caught a chill, or else you've eaten something. You must pray to God.'

'We might try quinine.' Kuzmichov was somewhat abashed.

'No, he should eat something nice and hot. How about a nice bowl of soup, boy?'

'No—I don't want any,' answered Yegorushka.

'Feeling shivery, eh?'

'I was, but now I feel hot. I ache all over.'

Kuzmichov went over, touched the boy's head, cleared his throat in perplexity, and went back to the table.

'Well, you'd better get undressed and go to sleep,' said Father Christopher. 'What you need is a good rest.'

He helped the boy undress, gave him a pillow, covered him with a quilt with Kuzmichov's topcoat over it, and then tiptoed off and sat at the table. Closing his eyes, Yegorushka immediately imagined that he was not in an inn room but on the high road by the camp-fire. Yemelyan swung his invisible baton while red-eyed Dymov lay on his stomach looking sarcastically at Yegorushka.

'Hit him, hit him!' the boy shouted.

'He's delirious,' said Father Christopher in an undertone.

Kuzmichov sighed. 'Oh, what a nuisance!'

'We ought to rub him with oil and vinegar. Let's hope to God he'll be better tomorrow.'

Trying to shake off his irksome fancies, Yegorushka opened his eyes and looked at the light. Father Christopher and Kuzmichov had finished their tea and were having a whispered discussion. The former smiled happily, obviously unable to forget that he had netted a good profit on his wool. It was less the actual profit that cheered him than the prospect of assembling all his large family on his return, and of giving a knowing wink and a mighty chuckle. First he would mislead them, claiming to have sold the wool below its value, but then he'd give his son-in-law Michael a fat wallet. 'There you are,' he'd say. 'That's how to do a deal.' But Kuzmichov did not seem pleased, retaining his old air of businesslike reserve and anxiety. 'If only I'd known Cherepakhin would pay that much!' He spoke in an undertone. 'I wouldn't have sold Makarov that five tons at home, drat it. But who could have known that the price had gone up here?'

A white-shirted waiter cleared the samovar away, and lit the lamp before the icon in the corner. Father Christopher whispered something in his ear. He gave an enigmatic, conspiratorial look as if to say he understood, went out, came back a little later and placed a bowl under the sofa. Kuzmichov made up a bed on the floor, yawned several times, lazily said his prayers and lay down.

'I'm thinking of going to the cathedral tomorrow,' said Father Christopher. 'I know a sacristan there. I ought to go and see the Bishop after the service, but he's said to be ill.' He yawned and put out the lamp. Now only the icon lamp was burning. 'They say he doesn't see anyone.' Father Christopher was removing his robes. 'So I shall just leave without meeting him.'

When he took off his caftan he seemed just like Robinson Crusoe to Yegorushka. Crusoe mixed something in a dish, and went up to the boy. 'Asleep, are we, Master Lomonosov? Just sit up and I'll rub you with oil and vinegar. It'll do you good, but you must say a prayer.'

Yegorushka quickly raised himself and sat up. Father Christopher took the boy's shirt off and began rubbing his chest, cowering and breathing jerkily, as if it was he that was being tickled.

'In the name of the Father, the Son and the Holy Ghost,' he whispered. 'Now turn on to your face. That's the idea. You'll be well tomorrow, but don't let it happen again. Why, he's almost on fire! I suppose you were on the road in the storm.'

'Yes.'

'No wonder you're poorly. In the name of the Father, the Son and the Holy Ghost. No wonder at all.'

When the rubbing was finished Father Christopher put Yegorushka's shirt back on, covered him, made the sign of the cross over him, and went away. Then the boy saw him praying. The old man must know a lot of prayers because he stood whispering before the icon for quite a time. His devotions completed, he made the sign of the cross over the windows, the door, Yegorushka and Kuzmichov. Then he lay on a divan without a pillow, covering himself with his caftan. The corridor clock struck ten. Remembering how much time was left before morning, the boy miserably pressed his forehead against the sofa back, no longer trying to shake off his hazy, irksome fancies. But morning came much sooner than he expected.

He seemed to have been lying there with his forehead against the sofa back for only a short time, but when he opened his eyes sunbeams were slanting to the floor from the room's two windows. Father Christopher and Kuzmichov had gone out, and the place had been tidied. It was bright, comfortable and redolent of Father Christopher, who always smelt of cypress and dried cornflowers—at home he made his holy-water sprinklers out of cornflowers, also decorating icon cases with them, and that was why he had become saturated with their scent. Looking at the pillow, the slanting sunbeams and his boots—now cleaned and standing side by side near the sofa—the boy laughed. He found it odd that he was not on the bale of wool, that all around him was dry, and that there was no thunder or lightning on the ceiling.

Jumping up, he began to dress. He felt wonderful. Nothing remained of yesterday's illness but a slight weakness of the legs and neck. The oil and vinegar must have done the trick. Remembering the steamer, the railway engine and the wide river that he had dimly glimpsed yesterday, he was in a hurry to dress so that he could run to the quayside and look at them. He washed, and the door catch suddenly clicked as he was putting on his red shirt. On the threshold appeared the top-hatted Father Christopher wearing a brown silk cassock over his canvas caftan and carrying his staff. Smiling and beaming—old men are always radiant when just returning from church—he placed a piece of communion bread and a parcel on the table and prayed to the icon.

'God has been merciful,' he added. 'Better, are we?'

'All right now.' The boy kissed his hand.

'Thank God. I'm just back from service. I went to see my friend the sacristan. He asked me in for breakfast, but I didn't go. I don't like calling on people too early in the morning, dash it.'

He took his cassock off, stroked his chest and unhurriedly undid the bundle. The boy saw a tin of unpressed caviare, a piece of smoked sturgeon and a French loaf.

'I bought these as I was passing the fishmonger's,' said Father Christopher. 'It's an ordinary weekday and no occasion for a treat, but there's a sick person back there, thinks I to meself, so it may be forgiven. And the caviare is good—real sturgeon's roe.'

The waiter in the white shirt brought a samovar and a tray of crockery.

'Have some.' Father Christopher spread caviare on a piece of bread and gave it to the boy. 'Eat now and enjoy yourself, and in fullness of time you will study. But mind you do so with attention and zeal, that good may come of it. What you need to learn by heart, you learn by heart. And when you have to describe a basic concept in your own words without touching on its outer form, then you do it in your own words. And try to master all subjects. Some know mathematics well, but they've never heard of Peter Mogila, and there's those as know about Peter Mogila but can't tell you about the moon. No, you study so you understand everything. Learn Latin, French, German— geography, of course, and history, theology, philosophy and mathematics. And when you've mastered everything—slowly, prayerfully and zealously—then you go and take up a profession. When you know everything things will be easier for you in every walk of life. Do but study and acquire grace, and God will show you your path in life—a doctor it might be, or a judge or an engineer.'

Father Christopher spread a little caviare on a small piece of bread and put it in his mouth. 'The Apostle Paul says: "Be not carried about with divers and strange doctrines." Of course if so be you study the black arts, blasphemy, conjuring up spirits from the other world like Saul, or such-like lore—which is no good to you nor to anyone else, either—then better not study at all. You must apprehend only that which God has blessed. Take good thought. The holy apostles spoke in all tongues, so you learn languages. Basil the Great studied mathematics and philosophy, so you study them too. St. Nestor wrote history, so you study and write history. Take example from the saints.'

Father Christopher sipped tea from his saucer, wiped his whiskers, flexed his neck. 'Good,' said he. 'I'm one of the old school. I've forgotten a lot, but even so my way of life is different from others'— there's no comparison. For instance, in company—at dinner, say, or at a meeting—one may pass a remark in Latin, or bring in history or philosophy. It gives other people pleasure and me too. Or, again, when the assizes come round and you have to administer the oath, the other priests are all a bit bashful like, but me—I'm completely at home with the judges, prosecutors and lawyers. You say something in the learned line, you have tea with them, you have a laugh, and you ask them things you don't know. And they like it. That's the way of it, old son. Learning is light and ignorance is darkness. So you study. It won't be easy, mind, for it doesn't come cheap nowadays, learning doesn't. Your mother's a widow on a pension. And, well, obviously——'

Father Christopher looked fearfully at the door. 'Your Uncle Ivan will help,' he went on in a whisper. 'He won't abandon you. He has no children of his own and he'll take care of you, never fear.' He looked grave and began whispering even more quietly. 'Now, boy, as God may preserve you, see you never forget your mother and your Uncle Ivan. The commandment bids us honour our mother, and Mr. Kuzmichov's your benefactor and guardian. If you go in for book-learning and then—God forbid!—get irked with folks and look down on them because they're stupider than you, then woe, woe unto you!'

Father Christopher raised his hand aloft. 'Woe, woe unto you!' he repeated in a reedy voice. Having warmed to his theme, he was really getting into his stride, as they say, and would have gone on till dinner-time. But the door opened, and in came Uncle Ivan, who hastily greeted them, sat down at table and began rapidly gulping tea.

'Well, I've settled all my business,' said he. 'We might have gone home today, but there's more bother with Yegorushka here. I must fix him up. My sister says her friend Nastasya Toskunov lives some-where round about, and she might put him up.'

He felt inside his wallet, removed a crumpled letter and read it. ' "Mrs. Nastasya Toskunov, at her own house in Little Nizhny Street." I must go and look her up at once. What a nuisance!'

Soon after breakfast Uncle Ivan and Yegorushka left the inn. 'A nuisance,' muttered Uncle. 'Here I am stuck with you, confound you. It's studying to be a gentleman for you and your mother, and nothing but trouble for me.'

When they crossed the yard the wagons and carters were not there, having all gone off to the quay early in the morning. In a far corner of the yard was the dark shape of the familiar britzka. Near it stood the bays, eating oats.

'Good-bye, carriage,' thought the boy.

First came a long climb up a broad avenue, and then they crossed a big market square, where Uncle Ivan asked a policeman the way to Little Nizhny Street. The policeman grinned. 'Ar! That be far away. Out towards the common, that be.'

They met several cabs on the way, but Uncle Ivan permitted himself such weaknesses as cab drives only on exceptional occasions and major holidays. He and the boy walked along paved streets for a long time, and then along unpaved streets with paved sidewalks until they finally reached streets lacking both amenities. When their legs and tongues had got them to Little Nizhny Street both were red in the face, and they took their hats off to wipe away the sweat.

'Tell me, please!' Uncle Ivan was addressing a little old man sitting on a bench by a gate. 'Where is Nastasya Toskunov's house hereabouts?'

'No Toskunovs round here,' the old man answered, after some thought. 'Perhaps it's the Timoshenkos you want?'

'No, Mrs. Toskunov.'

'Sorry, there ain't no such missus.'

Uncle Ivan shrugged his shoulders and trudged on.

'No need to go a-looking,' the old man shouted from behind. 'When I say ain't I mean ain't.'

Uncle Ivan spoke to an old woman who was standing on a corner selling sunflower seeds and pears from a tray. 'Tell me, my dear, where's Nastasya Toskunov's house hereabouts?'

The old woman looked at him in surprise. 'Why, does Nastasya live in a house of her own then?' she laughed. 'Lord, it be seven years since she married off her daughter and gave the house to the son-in-law. It's him lives there now.' And her eyes asked how they could be such imbeciles as not to know a simple thing like that.

'And where does she live now?' Kuzmichov asked.

'Lord love us!' The old woman threw up her arms in surprise. 'She moved into lodgings ever so long ago. Nigh on eight years it be. Ever since she made her house over to the son-in-law. What a thing to ask!'

She probably expected that Kuzmichov would be equally surprised, and would exclaim that it was 'out of the question'. But he asked very calmly where her lodgings were.

The fruit-seller rolled up her sleeves, and pointed with her bare arm. 'You walk on, on, on,' she shouted in a shrill, piercing voice. 'You'll pass a little red cottage, and then you'll see a little alley on your left. Go down the alley and it will be the third gate on the right.'

Kuzmichov and Yegorushka reached the little red cottage, turned left down the alley and headed for the third gate on the right. On both sides of this ancient grey gate stretched a grey fence with wide cracks. It had a heavy outward list on the right, threatening to collapse, while the left side was twisted back towards the yard. But the gate itself stood erect, apparently still debating whether it was more convenient to fall forwards or backwards. After Uncle Ivan had opened a small wicket-gate he and the boy saw a big yard overgrown with burdock and other coarse weeds. There was a small red-roofed cottage with green shutters a hundred paces from the gate, and in the middle of the yard stood a stout woman with her sleeves rolled up and her apron held out. She was scattering something on the ground, shouting 'Chick, chick, chick!' in a voice as shrill and piercing as the fruit-seller's.

Behind her sat a red dog with pointed ears. Seeing the visitors, it ran to the wicket-gate and struck up a high-pitched bark—red dogs are all tenors.

'Who do you want?' shouted the woman, shielding her eyes from the sun with a hand.

'Good morning,' Uncle Ivan shouted back, waving his stick to keep off the red dog. 'Tell me, please, does Mrs. Toskunov live here?'

'She does! What do you want with her?'

Kuzmichov and Yegorushka went up to her, and she gave them a suspicious look. 'What do you want with her?' she repeated.

'Perhaps *you* are Mrs. Toskunov?'

'All right then, I am.'

'Very pleased to meet you. Your old friend Olga Knyazev sends her respects, see? This is her little son. And perhaps you remember me—her brother Ivan. We all come from N., you see. You were born in our town and you were married there.'

Silence ensued, and the stout woman stared blankly at Kuzmichov, as if not believing or understanding. But then she flushed all over and flung up her hands. Oats fell from her apron, tears sprang from her eyes. 'Olga!' she shrieked, panting with excitement. 'My darling, my darling! Heavens, why am I standing here like an idiot? My pretty little angel!' She embraced the boy, wet his face with her tears and broke down completely.

'Heavens!' She wrung her hands. 'Olga's little boy! Now that *is* good news! And isn't he like his mother—her very image, he is. But why are you standing out in the yard? Do come inside.' Weeping, gasping, talking as she went, she hurried to the house, with the guests plodding after her. 'It's so untidy here.' She ushered the visitors into a stuffy parlour crammed with icons and pots of flowers. 'Oh, good-ness me! Vasilisa, at least go and open the shutters. The little angel—now, isn't he just lovely! I had no idea dear Olga had such a dear little boy.'

When she had calmed down and got used to the visitors Kuzmichov asked to speak to her in private. The boy went into another room, containing a sewing-machine, a cage with a starling in the window, and just as many icons and flowers as the parlour. A little girl—sun-burnt, chubby-cheeked like Titus, wearing a clean little cotton frock —was standing stock-still near the sewing-machine. She looked at Yegorushka unblinkingly, obviously feeling very awkward. After gazing at her in silence for a moment he asked what her name was.

The little girl moved her lips, looking as if she was going to cry. 'Atka,' she answered softly.

This meant 'Katka'.

'He'll live here, if you will be so kind,' Kuzmichov whispered in the parlour. 'And we'll pay you ten roubles a month. The boy isn't spoilt, he's a quiet lad.'

'I really don't know what to say, Mr. Kuzmichov,' sighed Nastasya plaintively. 'Ten roubles is good money, but I'm afraid of taking on someone else's child, see? He might fall ill or something.'

When they called the boy back into the parlour his Uncle Ivan had stood up and was saying good-bye, hat in hand. 'Very well then, let him stay with you now.' He turned to his nephew. 'Good-bye, Yego-rushka, you're to stay here. Mind you behave yourself and do as Mrs. Toskunov says. Good-bye then. I'll come again tomorrow.'

And off he went.

Nastasya embraced the boy again, calling him a little angel and began tearfully laying the table. Three minutes later Yegorushka was sitting next to her, answering her endless questions and eating rich, hot cabbage stew.

In the evening he was back at the same table, resting his head on his hand as he listened to Nastasya. Now laughing, now crying, she talked of his mother's young days, her own marriage, her children. A cricket chirped in the stove and the lamp burner faintly buzzed. The mistress of the house spoke in a low voice, occasionally dropping her thimble in her excitement, whereupon her granddaughter Katka would crawl under the table after it, always staying down there a long time and probably scrutinizing Yegorushka's feet. He listened, he dozed, and he examined the old woman's face, her wart with hairs on it, the tear stains. And he felt sad, very sad. They made him a bed on a trunk, saying that if he was hungry in the night he should go into the corridor and take some of the chicken under a bowl on the win-dow-sill.

Next morning Ivan Kuzmichov and Father Christopher came to say good-bye. Mrs. Toskunov was pleased to see them and was going to bring out the samovar, but Kuzmichov was in a great hurry and dismissed the idea with a gesture.

'We've no time for tea, sugar and the rest of it, we're just leaving.'

Before parting, all sat in silence for a minute. Nastasya gave a deep sigh, gazing with tearful eyes at the icons.

'Well, well,' began Ivan, getting up. 'So you'll be staying here.'

The businesslike reserve suddenly vanished from his face. 'Now, mind you study.' He was a little flushed and smiled sadly. 'Don't forget your mother and obey Mrs. Toskunov. You study well, boy, and I'll stand by you.'

He took a purse from his pocket, turned his back to the boy, burrowed in the small change for a while, found a ten-copeck piece and gave it to him.

Father Christopher sighed and unhurriedly blessed Yegorushka. 'In the name of the Father, the Son and the Holy Ghost. Study, lad, work hard. Remember me in your prayers if I die. And here's ten copecks from me too.'

Yegorushka kissed his hand and burst into tears. Something inside him whispered that he would never see the old man again.

'I've already applied to the local high school,' Kuzmichov told Nastasya in a voice suggesting that there was a dead body laid out in the room. 'You must take him to the examination on the seventh of August. Well, good-bye and God bless you. Farewell, nephew.'

'You might have had a little tea,' groaned Nastasya.

Through the tears blinding his eyes the boy could not see Uncle Ivan and Father Christopher leave. He rushed to the window, but they were gone from the yard. The red hound had just barked, and was running back from the gate with an air of duty fulfilled. Not knowing why, the boy jumped up and rushed from the house, and as he ran out of the gate Kuzmichov and Father Christopher—the first swinging his stick with the curved handle and the second his staff—were just rounding the corner. Yegorushka felt that his entire stock of experience had vanished with them like smoke. He sank exhaustedly on a bench, greeting the advent of his new and unknown life with bitter tears.

What kind of life would it be?

AN AWKWARD BUSINESS

GREGORY OVCHINNIKOV was a country doctor of about thirty-five, haggard and nervous. He was known to his colleagues for his modest contributions to medical statistics and keen interest in 'social problems'. One morning he was doing his ward rounds in his hospital, followed as usual by his assistant Michael Smirnovsky—an elderly medical orderly with a fleshy face, plastered-down greasy hair and a single ear-ring.

Barely had the doctor begun his rounds when a trifling matter aroused his acute suspicions—his assistant's waistcoat was creased, and persistently rode up even though the man kept jerking and straightening it. His shirt too was crumpled and creased, and there was white fluff on his long black frock-coat, on his trousers, and even on his tie. The man had obviously slept in his clothes, and—to judge from his expression as he tugged his waistcoat and adjusted his tie—those clothes were too tight for him.

The doctor stared at him and grasped the situation. His assistant was not staggering, and he answered questions coherently, but his grim, blank face, his dim eyes, the shivering of his neck and hands, the disorder of his dress, and above all his intense efforts to control himself, together with his desire to conceal his condition—it all testified that he had just got up, had not slept properly and was still drunk, seriously drunk, on what he had taken the night before. He had an excruciating hangover, he was in great distress, and he was obviously very annoyed with himself.

The doctor, who had his own reasons for disliking the orderly, was strongly inclined to say: 'Drunk, I see.' He was suddenly disgusted by the waistcoat, the long frock-coat and the ear-ring in that meaty ear. But he repressed his rancour, and spoke gently and politely as always.

'Did Gerasim have his milk?'

'Yes, Doctor,' replied Smirnovsky, also softly.

While talking to his patient, Gerasim, the doctor glanced at the temperature chart, and felt another surge of hatred. He held his breath to stop himself speaking, but could not help asking in a rude, choking voice why the temperature had not been recorded.

'Oh, it was, Doctor,' said Smirnovsky softly. But on looking at the chart and satisfying himself that it indeed was not, he shrugged his shoulders in bewilderment.

'I don't understand, Doctor—it must be Sister's doing,' he muttered.

'It wasn't recorded last night either,' the doctor went on. 'All you ever do is get drunk, blast you! You're positively pie-eyed at this moment. Where *is* Sister?'

Sister Nadezhda Osipovna, the midwife, was not in the wards, though she was supposed to be on duty every morning when the dressings were changed. The doctor looked around him, and received the impression that the ward had not been tidied and was in an unholy mess, that none of the necessary routine had been carried out, and that everything was as bulging, crumpled and fluff-bedecked as the orderly's odious waistcoat. He felt prompted to tear off his white apron, rant, throw everything over, let it all go to hell, and leave. But he mastered himself and continued his rounds.

After Gerasim came a patient with a tissue inflammation of the entire right arm. He needed his dressing changed. The doctor sat by him on a stool and tackled the arm.

'They were celebrating last night—someone's name-day,' he thought, slowly removing the bandage. 'You just wait, I'll give you parties! What can I do about it, though? I can do nothing.'

He felt an abscess on the purple, swollen arm and called: 'Scalpel!'

Trying to show that he was steady on his feet and fit for work, Smirnovsky rushed off and quickly came back with a scalpel.

'Not this—a new one,' said the doctor.

The assistant walked mincingly to the box—which was on a chair—containing material for the dressings, and quickly rummaged about. He kept on whispering to the nurses, moving the box on the chair, rustling it, and he twice dropped something. The doctor sat waiting, and felt a violent irritation in his back from the whispering and rustling.

'How much longer?' he asked. 'You must have left them downstairs.'

The orderly ran up and handed over two scalpels, while committing the indiscretion of breathing in the doctor's direction.

'Not these!' snapped the doctor. 'I told you quite clearly to get me a new one. Oh, never mind, go and sleep it off—you reek like an alehouse. You're not fit to be trusted.'

'What other knives do you want?' asked the orderly irritably, slowly shrugging his shoulders. Annoyed with himself, and ashamed to have the patients and nurses staring at him, he forced a smile to conceal his embarrassment. 'What other knives do you want?' he repeated.

The doctor felt tears in his eyes and a trembling in his fingers. He made another effort to control himself. 'Go and sleep it off,' he brought out in a quavering voice. 'I don't want to talk to a drunk.'

'You can't tell me off for what I do off duty,' went on the orderly. 'Suppose I did have a drop—well, it don't mean anyone can order me about. I'm doing me job, ain't I? What more do you want? I'm doing me job.'

The doctor jumped to his feet, swung his arm without realizing what he was doing, and struck his assistant in the face with his full force. Why he did it he did not know, but he derived great pleasure from the punch landing smack on the man's face and from the fact that a dignified, God-fearing family man, a solid citizen with a high opinion of himself, had reeled, bounced like a ball and collapsed on a stool. He felt a wild urge to land a second punch, but the feeling of satisfaction vanished at the sight of the nurses' pale and troubled faces near that other hated face. With a gesture of despair he rushed out of the ward.

In the grounds he encountered the Sister on her way to the hospital —an unmarried woman of about twenty-seven with a sallow face and her hair loose. Her pink cotton dress was very tight in the skirt, which made her take tiny, rapid steps. She rustled her dress, jerking her shoulders in time with each step, and tossing her head as if humming a merry tune to herself.

'Aha, the Mermaid!' thought the doctor, recalling that the staff had given the Sister that nickname, and he savoured the prospect of taking the mincing, self-obsessed, fashion-conscious creature down a peg.

'Why are you never to be found?' he shouted as their paths crossed. 'Why aren't you at the hospital? The temperatures haven't been taken, the place is in a mess, my orderly is drunk, and you sleep till noon. You'd better find yourself another job—you're not working here any more.'

Reaching his lodgings, the doctor tore off his white apron and the piece of towelling with which it was belted, angrily hurled them both into a corner, and began pacing his study.

'Good grief, what awful people!' he said. 'They're no use, they're only a hindrance. I can't carry on, I really can't. I'm getting out.'

His heart was thumping, he was trembling all over, and on the brink of tears. To banish these sensations he consoled himself by considering how thoroughly justified he was, and what a good idea it had been to hit his assistant. The odious thing was, he reflected, that the fellow had not got his hospital job in the ordinary way, but through nepotism—his aunt worked for the Council Chairman as a children's nurse. And what a loathsome sight she was when she came in for treatment—this high-powered Auntie with her offhand airs and queue-jumping presumptions! The orderly was undisciplined and ignorant. What he did know he had no understanding of at all. He was drunken, insolent, unclean in his person. He took bribes from the patients and he sold the Council's medicines on the sly. Besides, it was common knowledge that he practised medicine himself on the quiet, treating young townsfolk for unmentionable complaints with special concoctions of his own. It would have been bad enough had he just been one more quack. But this was a quack militant, a quack with mutiny in his heart! He would cup and bleed out-patients without telling the doctor, and he would assist at operations with unwashed hands, digging about in the wounds with a perennially dirty probe—all of which served to demonstrate how profoundly and blatantly he scorned the doctor's medicine with all its lore and regulations.

When his fingers were steady the doctor sat at his desk and wrote a letter to the Chairman of the Council.

'Dear Leo Trofimovich,

'If, on receipt of this note, your Committee does not discharge the hospital orderly Smirnovsky, and if it denies me the right to choose my own assistants, I shall feel obliged—not without regret, I need hardly say—to request you to consider my employment as doctor at N. Hospital terminated, and to concern yourself with seeking my successor. My respects to Lyubov Fyodorovna and Yus.

'Faithfully,

G. OVCHINNIKOV'

Reading the letter through, the doctor found it too short and not formal enough. Besides, it was highly improper to send his regards to Lyubov Fyodorovna and Yus (nickname of the Chairman's younger son) in an official communication.

'Why the blazes bring in Yus?' wondered the doctor. He tore the letter up, and began planning another.

'Dear Sir,' he thought, sitting at his open window, and looking at the ducks and ducklings which hurried down the road, waddling and stumbling, and which must be on their way to the pond. One duckling picked a piece of offal from the ground, choked and gave a squeak of alarm. Another ran up to it, tore the thing out of its beak and started choking too. Far away, near the fence, in the lacy shadows cast on the grass by the young limes, Darya the cook was wandering about picking sorrel for a vegetable stew. Voices were heard. Zot the coachman, a bridle in his hand, and the dirty-aproned hospital odd-job-man Manuylo stood near the shed discussing something and laughing.

'They're on about me hitting the orderly,' thought the doctor. 'This scandal will be all over the county by tonight. Very well then. "Dear Sir, unless your Committee discharges——" '

The doctor was well aware that the Council would never prefer the orderly to him, and would rather dispense with every medical assistant in the county than deprive itself of so distinguished an individual as Doctor Ovchinnikov. Barely would the letter have arrived before Leo Trofimovich would undoubtedly be rolling up in his troika with his 'What crazy notion is this, old man?'

'My dear chap, what's it all about?' he would ask. 'May you be forgiven! Whatever's the idea? What's got into you? Where is the fellow? Bring the blackguard here! He must be fired! Chuck him out! I insist! That swine shan't be here tomorrow!'

Then he would dine with the doctor, and after dinner he would lie belly upwards on this same crimson sofa and snore with a newspaper over his face. After a good sleep he would have tea and drive the doctor over to spend the night at his house. The upshot would be that the orderly would keep his job and the doctor would not resign.

But this was not the result that the doctor secretly desired. He wanted the orderly's Auntie to triumph, he wanted the Council to accept his resignation without more ado—with satisfaction, even—and despite his eight years' conscientious service. He imagined leaving the hospital, where he had settled in nicely, and writing a letter to *The Physician*. He imagined his colleagues presenting him with an address of sympathy.

The Mermaid appeared on the road. With mincing gait and swishing dress she came up to the window.

'Will you see the patients yourself, Doctor?' she asked. 'Or do you want us to do it on our own?'

'You lost your temper,' said her eyes. 'And now that you've calmed down you're ashamed of yourself. But I'm too magnanimous to take any notice.'

'All right, I'll come,' said the doctor. He put on his apron again, belted it with the towelling and went to the hospital.

'I was wrong to run off after hitting him,' he thought on the way. 'It made me look embarrassed or frightened. I acted like a schoolboy. It was all wrong.'

He imagined the patients looking at him with discomfiture when he entered the ward, imagined himself feeling guilty. But when he went in they lay quietly in their beds, hardly paying him any attention. The tubercular Gerasim's face expressed total unconcern.

'He didn't do his job right, so you taught him what's what,' he seemed to be saying. 'That's the way to do things, old man.'

The doctor lanced two abscesses on the purple arm and bandaged it, then went to the women's wards and performed an operation on a peasant woman's eye, while the Mermaid followed him around, helping him as if nothing had happened and all was as it should be. His ward rounds done, he began receiving his out-patients. The window in the small surgery was wide open. You had only to sit on the sill and lean over a little to see young grass a foot or two below. There had been thunder and a heavy downpour on the previous evening, and so the grass was somewhat beaten down and glossy. The path running from just beyond the window to the gully looked washed clean, and the bits of broken dispensary jars and bottles strewn on both sides—they too had been washed clean, and sparkled in the sun, radiating dazzling beams. Farther on, beyond the path, young firs in sumptuous green robes crowded each other. Beyond them were birches with paper-white trunks, and through their foliage, as it gently quivered in the breeze, the infinite depths of the azure sky could be seen. As you looked out there were starlings hopping on the path, turning their foolish beaks towards your window and debating whether to take fright or not. Then, having decided on taking fright, they darted up to the tops of the birches, one after the other with happy chirps, as if making fun of the doctor for not knowing how to fly.

Through the heavy smell of iodoform the fresh fragrance of the spring day could be sensed. It was good to breathe.

'Anna Spiridonovna,' the doctor called.

A young peasant woman in a red dress entered the surgery and said a prayer before the icon.

'What's troubling you?' the doctor asked.

Glancing mistrustfully at the door through which she had come, and at the door to the dispensary, the woman approached the doctor.

'I don't have no children,' she whispered.

'Who else hasn't registered yet?' shouted the Mermaid from the dispensary. 'Report here!'

'What makes him such a swine is compelling me to hit someone for the first time in my life,' thought the doctor as he examined the woman. 'I was never involved in fisticuffs before.'

Anna Spiridonovna left. In came an old man with a venereal complaint, and then a peasant woman with three children who had scabies, and things began to hum. There was no sign of the orderly. Beyond the dispensary door the Mermaid merrily chirped, swishing her dress and clinking her jars. Now and then she came into the surgery to help with a minor operation, or to fetch a prescription—all with that same air of everything being as it should be.

'She's glad I hit the man,' thought the doctor, listening to her voice. 'Those two have always been at loggerheads, and she'll be overjoyed if we get rid of him. The nurses are glad too, I think. How revolting!'

When his surgery was at its busiest he began to feel that the Sister, the nurses, and the very patients, had deliberately assumed carefree, cheerful expressions. They seemed to realize that he was ashamed and hurt, but pretended not to out of delicacy. As for him, wishing to demonstrate that he was no whit disconcerted, he was shouting roughly.

'Hey, you there! Close that door, it's draughty.'

But ashamed and dejected he was, and after seeing forty-five patients he strolled slowly away from the hospital.

The Sister had already contrived to visit her lodgings. A gaudy crimson shawl round her shoulders, a cigarette between her teeth, and a flower in her flowing tresses, she was hurrying off, probably on a professional or private visit. Patients sat in the hospital porch, silently sunning themselves. Rowdy as ever, the starlings were hunting beetles.

Looking around him, the doctor reflected that among all these stable, serene lives only two stuck out like sore thumbs as obviously useless—the orderly's and his own. By now the orderly must have gone to bed to sleep it off, but was surely kept awake by knowing that he was in the wrong, had been maltreated, and had lost his job. His predicament was appalling. As for the doctor, having never struck anyone before, he felt as if he had lost his virginity. No longer did he blame his assistant, or seek to exculpate himself. He was merely perplexed. How had a decent man like himself, who had never even kicked a dog, come to strike that blow? Returning to his quarters, he lay on the study sofa with his face to the back.

'He's a bad man and a professional liability,' he thought. 'During his three years here I've reached the end of my tether. Still, what I did is inexcusable. I took advantage of my position. He's my subordinate, he was at fault and he was drunk to boot, whereas I'm his superior, I had right on my side and I was sober—which gave me the upper hand. Secondly, I struck him in front of people who look up to me, thus setting them a dreadful example.'

The doctor was called to dinner. After eating only a few spoonfuls of cabbage stew he left the table, lay on the sofa again and resumed his meditations.

'So what shall I do now? I must put things right with him as soon as possible. But how? As a practical man he probably thinks duelling stupid or doesn't recognize it. If I apologized to him in the same ward in front of the nurses and patients, that apology would only satisfy me, not him. Being a low type of person, he would put it down to cowardice, to fear of his complaining to the authorities. Besides, an apology would mean the end of hospital discipline. Should I offer him money? No, that would be immoral, and it would smack of bribery. Well, suppose we were to put the problem to our immediate superiors, the County Council, that is. They *could* reprimand or dismiss me, but they wouldn't. And, anyway, it wouldn't be quite the thing to involve the Council—which, incidentally, has no jurisdiction —in the hospital's domestic affairs.

Three hours after his meal the doctor was on his way to bathe in the pond, still thinking. 'Should I perhaps do what anyone else would do in the circumstances—let him sue me? Being unquestionably in the wrong, I shan't try to defend myself, and the judge will send me to gaol. Thus the injured party will receive satisfaction, and those who look up to me will see that I was in the wrong.'

The idea appealed to him. He was pleased, and felt that the problem had been solved in the fairest possible way.

'Well, that's fine!' he thought, wading into the water and watching shoals of golden crucians scurrying away from him. 'Let him sue. It will suit him all the better in that our professional relationship has been curtailed, and after this scandal one or other of us will have to leave the hospital anyway.'

In the evening the doctor ordered his trap, intending to drive over to the garrison commander's for bridge. When he had his hat and coat on, and stood in his study putting his gloves on ready to leave, the outer door opened creakingly, and someone quietly entered the hall.

'Who's there?' called the doctor.

A hollow voice answered. 'It's me, sir.'

The doctor's heart suddenly thumped. Embarrassment and a mysterious feeling of panic suddenly chilled him all over. Michael Smirnovsky, the orderly—it was he—coughed softly, and came timidly into the study.

'Please forgive me, Doctor,' he said in a hollow, guilty voice after a brief silence.

The doctor was taken aback, and did not know what to say. He realized that the man's reason for abasing himself and apologizing was neither Christian meekness, nor a wish to heap coals of fire on his ill-user, but simply self-interest. 'I'll make myself apologize, and with luck I won't get the sack and lose my livelihood.' What could be more insulting to human dignity?

'Forgive me,' repeated the man.

'Now then,' said the doctor, trying not to look at him, and still not knowing what to say. 'Very well, I assaulted you, and I, er, must be punished—must give you satisfaction, that is. You're not a duelling man. Nor am I, for that matter. I have given you offence and you, er, you can bring suit against me before the Justices of the Peace and I'll take my punishment. But we can't both stay on here. One of us—you or I—will have to go.'

('Oh God, I'm saying all the wrong things,' thought the doctor, aghast. 'How utterly stupid!')

'In other words, sue me. But we can't go on working together. It's you or me. You'd better start proceedings tomorrow.'

The orderly gazed sullenly at the doctor, and then his dark, dim eyes glinted with blatant contempt. He had always thought the doctor an unpractical, volatile, puerile creature, and he despised him now for being so nervous and talking so much fussy nonsense.

'Well, don't think I won't,' said he grimly and spitefully.

'Then go ahead.'

'You think I won't do it, don't you? Well, you're wrong! You have no right to raise your hand to me. You ought to be ashamed of yourself. Only drunken peasants hit people, and you're an educated man.'

Suddenly the doctor's hatred all boiled up inside him. 'You clear out of here!' he shouted in a voice unlike his own.

The orderly was reluctant to budge, as if having something else to say, but went into the hall and stood there, plunged in thought. Then, having apparently made up his mind to something, he marched resolutely out.

'How utterly stupid!' muttered the doctor after the other had gone. 'How stupid and trite it all is.'

His handling of the orderly had been infantile, he felt, and he was beginning to see that his notions about the lawsuit were all foolish, complicating the problem instead of solving it.

'How stupid!' he repeated as he sat in his carriage, and later while playing bridge at the garrison commander's. 'Am I really so uneducated, do I know so little of life, that I can't solve this simple problem? Oh, what shall I do?'

Next morning the doctor saw the orderly's wife getting into a carriage. 'She is off to Auntie's,' he thought. 'Well, let her go!'

The hospital was managing without an orderly, and though the Council should have been given notification, the doctor was still unable to frame a letter. It's tenor must now be: 'Kindly dismiss my orderly, though I am to blame, not he.' But to express the idea without it sounding foolish and ignominious—that was almost beyond any decent man.

Two or three days later the doctor was told that his assistant had gone and complained to Leo Trofimovich, the Chairman, who had not let him get a word out, but had stamped his feet and sent him packing.

'I know your sort!' he had shouted. 'Get out! I won't listen!'

From the Chairman the assistant had gone to the town hall, and had filed a complaint—neither mentioning the assault nor asking anything for himself—to the effect that the doctor had several times made disparaging comments about the Council and its Chairman in his presence, that the doctor's method of treating patients was incorrect, that he was neglectful in making his rounds of the district, and so on. Hearing of this, the doctor laughed and thought what a fool the man was. He felt ashamed and sorry for one who behaved so foolishly. The more stupid things a man does in his defence the more defenceless and feeble he must be.

Exactly one week later the doctor received a summons from the Justice of the Peace.

'Now this is idiocy run riot,' he thought as he signed the papers. 'This is the ultimate in sheer silliness.'

Driving over to the court-house on a calm, overcast morning, he no longer felt embarrassed, but was vexed and disgusted. He was furious with himself, with the orderly, with the whole business. 'I'll just tell the court that the whole lot of them can go to blazes,' he raged. ' "You're all jackasses, and you have no sense", I'll say.'

Driving up to the court-house, he saw three of his nurses and the Mermaid by the door. They had been called as witnesses. When he saw the nurses and that merry Sister—she was shifting from foot to foot in her excitement, and had even blushed with pleasure on seeing the protagonist of the impending trial—the incensed doctor wanted to pounce on them like a hawk and stun them with a 'Who said you could leave the hospital? Be so good as to return this instant.' But he took a hold on himself, tried to seem calm, and picked his way through the crowd of peasants to the court-house. The chamber was empty, and the judge's chain of office hung on the back of his armchair. Entering the clerk's cubicle, the doctor saw a thin-faced young man in a linen jacket with bulging pockets—the clerk—and the orderly, who sat at a table idly leafing through court records. The clerk stood up when the doctor came in. The orderly rose too, looking rather put out.

'Isn't Alexander Arkhipovich here yet?' the doctor asked uneasily.

'No, Doctor. He's at his house, sir,' the clerk answered.

The court-house was in one of the outbuildings of the judge's estate, and the judge himself lived in the manor house. Leaving the court-house, the doctor made his way slowly towards that residence, and found Alexander Arkhipovich in the dining-room, where a samovar was steaming. The judge wore neither coat nor waistcoat and had his shirt unbuttoned. He was standing by the table, holding a teapot in both hands and pouring tea as dark as coffee into a glass. Seeing his visitor, he quickly pulled up another glass and filled it.

'With or without sugar?' he asked by way of greeting.

A long time ago the judge had been a cavalryman. Now, through long service in elective office, he had attained high rank in the Civil Service, yet had never discarded his military uniform or his military habits. He had long whiskers like a police chief's, trousers with piping, and all his acts and words were military elegance personified. He spoke with his head thrown slightly back, larding his speech with your retired general's fruity bleats, flexing his shoulders and rolling his eyes.

When greeting someone or giving them a light he scraped his shoes, and when walking he clinked his spurs as carefully and delicately as if every jingle caused him exquisite pain. Having sat the doctor down to his tea, he stroked his broad chest and stomach and heaved a sigh.

'Hurrumph!' said he. 'Perhaps you'd like, m'yes, some vodka and a bite to eat, m'yes?'

'No thank you, I'm not hungry.'

Both felt that they were bound to discuss the hospital scandal, and both felt awkward. The doctor said nothing. With a graceful gesture the judge caught a gnat that had bitten his chest, scrutinized it keenly from all angles, and then let it go. Then he heaved a deep sigh and looked up at the doctor.

'Now then, why don't you get rid of him?' he asked succinctly.

The doctor sensed a note of sympathy in his voice, and suddenly pitied himself, jaded and crushed as he felt by the week's ructions. He rose from the table, frowned irritably and shrugged his shoulders, his expression suggesting that his patience had finally snapped.

'Get rid of him!' he said. 'Ye Gods, the mentality of you people! It really is remarkable! But how *can* I do that? You sit around here thinking I run my own hospital and can act as I please. The mentality of you people certainly is remarkable. Can I really sack an orderly whose aunt is nanny to our Chairman's children, and if our Chairman has a need for such toadies and blabbermouths as this Smirnovsky? What can I do if the Council doesn't care tuppence for us doctors, if it trips us up at every turn? I don't want their job, blast them, and that's flat—they can keep it!'

'There there, my dear chap. You're making too much of the thing, in a manner of speaking.'

'The Chairman tries his level best to prove we're all revolutionaries, he spies on us, he treats us as clerks. What right has he to visit the hospital when I'm away, and to question the nurses and patients? It's downright insulting. Then there's this pious freak of yours, this Simon Alekseyevich who does his own ploughing, rejects medicine because he's as strong as an ox—and eats as much!—vociferously calling us parasites to our faces and begrudging us our livelihood, blast him! I work day and night, I never take a holiday, I'm more necessary than all these prigs, bigots, reformers and buffoons put together! I've worked till I'm ill, and instead of any gratitude I'm told I'm a parasite. Thank you very, very much! Then again, everyone thinks himself entitled to poke his nose into other people's business, tell them how to do their job, order them about. Your pal Councillor Kamchatsky criticizes us doctors at the annual meeting for wasting potassium iodide, and advises us to be careful about using cocaine! What does he know about it, eh? What business is it of his? Why doesn't he teach you how to run your court?'

'But, but he's such a cad, old son—a bounder. You mustn't let him bother you.'

'He's a cad and a bounder, but it was you who elected this windbag to your Executive Committee, you who let him poke his nose into everything. All right, smile! These things are all trifles and pinpricks, think you. But so numerous are they that one's whole life now consists of them, as a mountain may consist of grains of sand—just you get that into your head! I can't carry on—I'm just about all in, Alexander Arkhipovich. Any more of this and I won't be punching faces, I'll be taking pot shots at people, believe you me! My nerves aren't made of steel, I tell you! I'm a human being like you——'

Tears came to the doctor's eyes, his voice shook. He turned away and looked through the window. Silence fell.

'Hurrumph, old fellow!' muttered the judge pensively. 'And then again, if one considers things coolly——'

He caught a gnat, squinted hard at it from all angles, squashed it and threw it in the slop-basin.

'——then, you see, there's no reason to dismiss him. Get rid of him and he'll be replaced by someone just like him, or even worse. You could run through a hundred of them and you wouldn't find one that was any good. They're all blackguards.' He stroked his armpits and slowly lit a cigarette. 'We must learn to put up with this evil. It's only among professional people and peasants—at the two poles of society, in other words—that one finds honest, sober, reliable workers nowadays, that's my opinion. A really decent doctor, a first-class teacher, a thoroughly honest ploughman or blacksmith—those you might, in a manner of speaking, find. But the in-betweeners, what you might call deserters from the peasantry who haven't acquired professional standing—they're the unreliable element. That's why it's so hard to find an honest, sober hospital orderly, clerk, farm bailiff and so on—exceedingly hard. I've been with the justice department since time immemorial, and I've never had one honest, sober clerk throughout my career, though I've booted them out by the sackful in my time. These people lack moral discipline, not to mention er, er, principles, in a manner of speaking——'

'What's all this in aid of?' wondered the doctor. 'What we're both saying is all beside the point.'

'Here's a trick my own clerk, Dyuzhinsky, played me only last Friday,' the judge continued. 'He got hold of some drunks—God knows who—and they spent all night boozing in my court-house. What do you say to that, now? I've nothing against drink. Let them guzzle themselves silly, confound them! But why bring strangers into my chambers? Just think—after all, would it take a second to steal a document, a promissory note or something, from the files? Well, believe it or not, after that orgy I had to spend two days checking all my files in case anything was missing. Now then, what will you do with this scallywag? Get rid of him? All right. And where's your guarantee that the next one won't be worse?'

'But how can he be got rid of?' the doctor asked. 'It's easy enough to talk, but how can I discharge him and take the bread out of his mouth when I know he's a family man with no resources. What would he and his family do?'

'I'm saying the wrong thing, damn it!' he thought, marvelling that he simply could not concentrate on any one definite idea or sentiment. 'That's because I'm shallow and illogical,' he reflected.

'The in-between man, as you call him, is unreliable,' he went on. 'We chase him out, we curse him, we slap his face, but shouldn't we try to see his point of view? He's neither peasant nor master, neither fish nor fowl. His past is grim and his present is a mere twenty-five roubles a month, a starving family and being ordered about, while his future is the same twenty-five roubles and the same inferior position even if he holds on for a hundred years. He has neither education nor property, he has no time to read and go to church, and he's deaf to us because we won't let him near us. And so he lives on from day to day till he dies without hoping for anything better, underfed, afraid of being turned out of his council flat, not knowing where to find a roof for his children. How can a man avoid getting drunk and stealing, how can he acquire principles in these conditions?

'Now we seem to be solving social problems,' he thought. 'And, my God, how clumsily! And what's the point of it all?'

Bells were heard as someone drove into the yard and bowled along to the court-house first, and then up to the porch of the big house.

'It's You-know-who,' said the judge, looking through the window. 'Well, you're for it!'

'Let's get it over quickly, please,' pleaded the doctor. 'Take my case out of turn if possible. I really can't spare the time.'

'Very well then. But I still don't know if the matter's within my jurisdiction, old man. After all, your relations with your assistant are, in a manner of speaking, official. Besides, you dotted him one when he was on official duty. I don't know for certain, actually, but now we can ask the Chairman.'

Hasty steps and heavy breathing were heard, and Leo Trofimovich, the Chairman, appeared in the doorway—a balding, white-haired old man with a long beard and red eyelids. 'Good day to you,' he panted. 'Phew, I say! Tell them to bring me some kvass, judge. This'll be the death of me.'

He sank into an armchair, but immediately sprang up, trotted over to the doctor, and glared at him furiously. 'Many, many thanks to you, Doctor.' He spoke in a shrill, high-pitched voice. 'You've done me no end of a good turn. Most grateful to you, I'm sure. I shan't forget you in a month of Sundays. But is this the way for friends to behave? Say what you like, but you haven't been all that considerate, have you? Why didn't you let me know? Do you take me for your enemy? For a stranger? Your enemy, am I? Did I ever refuse you anything, eh?'

Glaring and twiddling his fingers, the Chairman drank his kvass, quickly wiped his lips and continued.

'Thank you so very, very much! But why didn't you let me know? If you'd had any feelings for me at all you'd have driven over and spoken to me as a friend. "My dear Leo Trofimovich, the facts are this that and the other. What's happened is that et cetera et cetera." I'd have settled it all in two ticks, and there would have been no need for scandal. That imbecile seems to have gone clean off his rocker. He's touring the county muck-raking and gossiping with village women while you, shameful to relate, have stirred up one hell of a witch's brew, if you'll pardon my saying so, and have got this jackass to sue you. You should be downright ashamed of yourself. Everyone's asking me the rights and wrongs of it, and I—the Chairman!—don't know what you're up to. You have no use for me. Many, many thanks to you, Doctor.'

The Chairman bowed so low that he even turned purple. Then he went up to the window. 'Zhigalov, send Smirnovsky here,' he shouted. 'I want him this instant!' Then he came away from the window. 'It's a bad business, sir. Even my wife was upset, and you know how much she's on your side. You're all too clever by half, gentlemen. You're keen on logic, principles and such flapdoodle, but where does it get you? You just confuse the issue.'

'Well, you're keen on being illogical, and where does that get *you*?' the doctor asked.

'All right, I'll tell you. Where it gets me is this, that if I hadn't come here now you'd have disgraced both yourself and us. It's lucky for you I did come.'

The orderly entered and stood near the door. The Chairman stood sideways on to him, thrust his hands in his pockets and cleared his throat.

'Apologize to the doctor at once,' he said.

The doctor blushed and ran into another room.

'There, you see, the doctor doesn't want to accept your apology,' went on the Chairman. 'He wants you to show you're sorry in deeds, not words. Will you promise to do what he says and lead a sober life from this day onwards?'

'I will,' the orderly brought out in a deep, grim voice.

'Then watch your step, or heaven help you—you'll get the order of the boot double quick! If anything goes wrong you can expect no mercy. All right—off home with you.'

For the orderly, who had already accepted his misfortune, this turn of events was a delightful surprise. He even went pale with joy. He wanted to say something and put out his hand, but remained silent, smiled foolishly and went out.

'That's that,' said the Chairman. 'No need for a trial either.' He sighed with relief, surveyed the samovar and glasses with the air of one who has just brought off an extremely difficult and important *coup*, and wiped his hands.

'Blessed are the peacemakers,' said he. 'Pour me another glass, Alexander. Oh yes, and tell them to bring me a bite to eat first. And, well, some vodka——'

'I say, this just won't do!' Still flushed, the doctor came into the dining-room, wringing his hands. 'This, er—it's a farce, it's revolting. I can't stand it. Better have twenty trials than settle things in this cock-eyed fashion. I can't stand it, I tell you!'

'What do you want then?' the Chairman snapped back. 'To get rid of him? Very well, I'll fire him.'

'No don't do that. I don't know what I do want, but this attitude to life, gentlemen—— God, this is sheer agony!'

The doctor started bustling nervously, looked for his hat, could not find it, and sank exhausted in an armchair. 'Disgusting,' he repeated.

'My dear fellow,' whispered the judge. 'To some extent I fail to understand you, in a manner of speaking. The incident was your fault, after all. Socking folks in the jaw at the end of the nineteenth century! Say what you like, but, in a manner of speaking, it isn't, er, quite the thing. The man's a blackguard, but you must admit you acted incautiously yourself.'

'Of course,' the Chairman agreed.

Vodka and hors-d'œuvre were served. On his way out the doctor mechanically drank a glass of vodka and ate a radish. As he drove back to hospital his thoughts were veiled in mist like grass on autumn mornings.

How could it be, he wondered, that after all the anguish, all the heart-searching, all the talk of the past week, everything had fizzled out in a finale so banal? How utterly stupid!

He was ashamed of involving strangers in his personal problem, ashamed of what he had said to these people, ashamed of the vodka that he had drunk from the habit of idle drinking and idle living, ashamed of his insensitive, shallow mind.

On returning to hospital, he at once started on his ward rounds. The orderly accompanied him, treading softly as a cat, answering questions gently. The orderly, the Mermaid, the nurses—all pretended that nothing had happened, that all was as it should be. The doctor too made every effort to appear unaffected. He gave orders, he fumed, he joked with the patients, while one idea kept stirring in his brain.

'The sheer, the crass stupidity of it all.'

THE BEAUTIES

I

I REMEMBER driving with my grandfather from the village of Bolshaya Krepkaya, in the Don Region, to Rostov-on-Don when I was a high-school boy in the fifth or sixth form. It was a sultry August day, exhausting and depressing. Our eyes were practically gummed up, and our mouths were parched from the heat and the hot, dry wind that drove clouds of dust towards us. We did not feel like looking, speaking or thinking. When our dozing driver, a Ukrainian called Karpo, caught me on the cap with his whip while lashing at his horse, I neither protested nor uttered a sound, but just opened my eyes, half asleep as I was, and looked dispiritedly and mildly into the distance to see if a village was visible through the dust.

We stopped to feed the horse in the large Armenian settlement of Bakhchi-Salakh, at the house of a rich Armenian whom my grandfather knew. Never in my life have I seen anything more grotesque. Imagine a small, cropped head with thick, beetling eyebrows, a beaked nose, long white whiskers, and a wide mouth with a long cherry-wood chibouk sticking out of it. The small head has been clumsily tacked to a gaunt, hunched carcase arrayed in bizarre garb—a short red jacket and gaudy, sky-blue, baggy trousers. The creature walks about splaying its legs, shuffling its slippers, speaking with its pipe in its mouth, yet comporting itself with the dignity of your true Armenian—unsmiling, goggle-eyed, and trying to take as little notice of his visitors as possible.

The Armenian's dwelling was wind-free and dust-free inside, but it was just as disagreeable, stuffy and depressing as the prairie and the road. I remember sitting on a green chest in a corner, dusty and exhausted by the heat. The unpainted wooden walls, the furniture and the ochre-stained floorboards reeked of dry sun-baked wood. Wherever I looked there were flies, flies, flies. In low voices Grandfather and the Armenian discussed sheep, pasturage and grazing problems. I knew they would be a good hour getting the samovar going, and that Grandfather would spend at least another hour over his tea, after which he would sleep for two or three hours more. A quarter of my day would be spent waiting, and then there would be more heat, more dust, more jolting roads. Listening to the two mumbling voices, I felt as if I had long, long ago seen the Armenian, the cupboard full of crockery, the flies and the windows on which the hot sun beat, and that I should cease to see them only in the far distant future. I conceived a loathing for the steppe, the sun and the flies.

A Ukrainian woman wearing a shawl brought in a tray of tea things and then the samovar. The Armenian went slowly out into the lobby.

'Masha, Masha!' he shouted. 'Come and pour the tea! Where are you, Masha?'

Hurried footsteps were heard, and in came a girl of about sixteen wearing a simple cotton dress and a white shawl. Rinsing the crockery and pouring the tea, she stood with her back to me, and all I noticed was that she was slim-waisted and barefoot, and that her small heels were covered by long trousers.

The master of the house offered me tea. As I sat down at table I glanced at the face of the girl who was handing me my glass, and suddenly felt as if a fresh breeze had blown over my spirits and dispelled all the day's impressions, all the dreariness and dust. I saw the enchanting features of the loveliest face I have ever encountered either dreaming or waking. Here was a truly beautiful girl—and I took this in at first glance, like a lightning flash.

Though I am ready to swear that Masha—or 'Massya', as her father called her in his Armenian accent—was a real beauty, I cannot prove it. Clouds sometimes jostle each other at random on the horizon, and the hidden sun paints them and the sky every possible hue—crimson, orange, gold, lilac, muddy pink. One cloud resembles a monk, another a fish, a third a turbaned Turk. Embracing a third of the sky, the setting sun glitters on a church cross, and on the windows of the manor house. It is reflected in the river and the ponds, it quivers on the trees. Far, far away, against the sunset a flock of wild ducks flies off to its night's rest. The boy herding his cows, the surveyor driving along the mill dam in his chaise, the ladies and gentlemen who are out for a stroll—all gaze at the sunset, all find it awesomely beautiful. But wherein does that beauty lie? No one knows, no one can say.

I was not alone in finding the Armenian girl beautiful. My old grandfather, a man of eighty—tough, indifferent to women and the beauties of nature—gazed at her tenderly for a full minute.

'Is that your daughter, Avet Nazarovich?' he asked.

'Yes, she is,' the Armenian answered.

'A fine-looking young lady.'

An artist would have called the Armenian girl's beauty classic and severe. To contemplate such loveliness is to be imbued, heaven knows why, with the conviction that the regular features, that the hair, eyes, nose, mouth, neck and figure, together with all the motions of the young body, have been unerringly combined by nature in a harmonious whole without a single discordant note. You somehow fancy that the ideally beautiful woman must have a nose just like hers, straight but slightly aquiline, the same big, dark eyes, the same long lashes, the same languorous glance. The curly black hair and eyebrows seem ideally suited to the delicate white skin of the forehead and cheeks, just as green reeds and quiet streams go together. Her white neck and youthful bosom are not fully developed, but only a genius could sculpt them, you feel. As you gaze you gradually conceive a wish to say something exceedingly pleasant, sincere and beautiful to the girl—something as beautiful as herself.

At first I was offended and disconcerted by Masha taking no notice of me, but casting her eyes down all the time. It was as if some special aura, proud and happy, segregated her from me, and jealously screened her from my gaze.

'It must be because I'm covered with dust, because I'm sunburnt, because I'm only a boy,' I thought.

But then I gradually forgot myself and surrendered entirely to the sensation of beauty. I no longer remembered the dreary steppe and the dust, no longer heard the flies buzzing, no longer tasted my tea. All I was conscious of was the beautiful girl standing on the other side of the table.

My appreciation of her beauty was rather remarkable. It was not desire, not ecstasy, not pleasure that she aroused in me, but an oppressive, yet agreeable, melancholia—a sadness vague and hazy as a dream. I somehow felt sorry for myself, for my grandfather, for the Armenian —and even for the girl. I felt as if we had all four lost, irrecoverably, something vitally important. Grandfather too grew sad. He no longer spoke of sheep and grazing, but was silent, and glanced pensively at the girl.

After tea Grandfather took his nap, and I went out and sat on the porch. This house, like all the others at Bakhchi-Salakh, caught the full heat of the sun. There were no trees, no awnings, no shadows. Overgrown with goose-foot and wild mallow, the Armenian's big yard was lively and cheerful despite the intense heat. Threshing was in progress behind one of the low hurdles intersecting the large expanse at various points. Twelve horses, harnessed abreast and forming a single long radius, trotted round a pole fixed in the exact centre of the threshing area. Beside them walked a Ukrainian in a long waistcoat and broad, baggy trousers, cracking his whip and shouting as if to tease the animals and flaunt his power over them.

'Come on there, damn you. Aha! Come on, rot you! Afraid, are you?'

The horses—bay, grey and skewbald—had no idea why they were being forced to rotate in one spot and tread down wheat straw. They moved reluctantly, as though with difficulty, lashing their tails offendedly. The wind raised great clouds of golden chaff from under their hoofs and bore it far away across the hurdles. Women with rakes swarmed near the tall new ricks, and carts went to and fro. In a second yard beyond those ricks another dozen such horses trotted round their pole, while a similar Ukrainian cracked his whip and mocked them.

The steps on which I was sitting were hot. Owing to the heat glue was oozing here and there from the wood of the slender banisters and window-frames. In the streaks of shade beneath the steps and shutters tiny red beetles huddled together. The sun baked my head, chest and back, but I paid no attention to it, being conscious only of the rap of bare feet on the wooden floor of the lobby and the other rooms behind me. Having cleared away the tea, Masha ran down the steps, disturbing the air as she passed, and flew like a bird to a small, grimy outhouse—it must be the kitchen—whence proceeded the smell of roast mutton and the sound of angry Armenian voices. She disappeared through the dark doorway, where her place was taken by a bent, red-faced old Armenian woman wearing baggy green trousers, and angrily scolding someone. Then Masha suddenly reappeared in the doorway, flushed from the kitchen's heat, and carrying a big black loaf on her shoulder. Swaying gracefully under the bread's weight, she ran across the yard to the threshing floor, leapt a hurdle, plunged into a golden cloud of chaff, and vanished behind the carts. The Ukrainian in charge of the horses lowered his whip, stopped talking to them, and gazed silently towards the carts for a minute. Then, when the girl once more darted past the horses and jumped the hurdle, he followed her with his eyes, shouting at his horses in a highly aggrieved voice.

'Rot, you hell-hounds!'

After that I continually heard her bare feet, and saw her rushing round the place with a grave, preoccupied air. Now she ran down the steps, passing me in a gust of air, now to the kitchen, now to the threshing floor, now through the gate, and I could hardly turn my head fast enough to watch.

The more often I caught sight of this lovely creature the more melancholy I became. I felt sorry for myself, for her, and for the Ukrainian mournfully watching her as she ran through the chaff to the carts. Did I envy her beauty? Did I regret that the girl was not mine and never would be, that I was a stranger to her? Did I have an inkling that her rare beauty was accidental, superfluous, and—like everything else on earth—transitory? Was my grief that peculiar sensation which the contemplation of true beauty arouses in any human being? God only knows.

The three hours of waiting passed unnoticed. I felt that I had not had enough time to feast my eyes on Masha when Karpo rode off to the river, bathed the horse, and began to hitch it up. The wet animal snorted with pleasure and kicked his hoof against the shafts.

'Get back!' Karpo shouted.

Grandfather woke up, Masha opened the creaking gates, and we got into the carriage and drove out of the yard—in silence, as if angry with one another.

When Rostov and Nakhichevan appeared in the distance a couple of hours later, Karpo, who had said nothing all that time, looked round quickly.

'Splendid girl, the old Armenian's daughter,' said he, and whipped the horse.

II

On another occasion, after I had become a student, I was travelling south by rail. It was May. At a station—between Belgorod and Kharkov, I think—I got out of the carriage to stroll on the platform.

Evening shadows had already fallen on the station garden, on the platform and on the fields. The station building hid the sunset, but you could tell that the sun had not yet vanished completely by the topmost, delicately pink puffs of smoke from the engine.

While pacing the platform, I noticed that, of the other passengers who were taking an airing, the majority were strolling or standing near one of the second-class carriages, their attitude conveying the impression that someone of consequence must be sitting in it. Among these inquisitive persons I saw the artillery officer who was my travelling companion—an intelligent, cordial, likeable fellow, as is everybody with whom one strikes up a brief acquaintance on one's journeys.

I asked him what he was looking at.

He said nothing in reply, but just indicated a feminine figure with his eyes. It was a young girl of seventeen or eighteen in Russian national costume, bare-headed, with a lace shawl thrown carelessly over one shoulder. She was not a passenger, and I suppose she was the station-master's daughter or sister. She stood near a carriage window, talking to an elderly female passenger. Before I knew what was happening I was suddenly overwhelmed by the same sensation that I had once experienced in the Armenian village.

That the girl was strikingly beautiful neither I nor the others gazing at her could doubt.

Were one to describe her appearance item by item, as is common practice, then the only truly lovely feature was her thick, fair, undulating hair—loose on her shoulders and held back on her head by a dark ribbon. All her other features were either irregular or very ordinary. Her eyes were screwed up, either as a flirtatious mannerism or through short-sightedness, her nose was faintly *retroussé*, her mouth was small, her profile was feeble and insipid, her shoulders were narrow for her age. And yet the girl produced the impression of true loveliness. Gazing at her, I realized that a Russian face does not require strict regularity of feature to seem handsome. Indeed, had this young woman's up-tilted nose been replaced by another—regular and impeccably formed, like the Armenian girl's—I fancy her face would have lost all its charm.

Standing at the window, talking and shivering in the cool of the evening, the girl kept looking round at us. Now she placed her hands on her hips, now raised them to her head to pat her hair. She spoke, she laughed, she expressed surprise at one moment and horror at the next, and I don't recall a moment when her face and body were at rest. It was in these tiny, infinitely exquisite movements, in her smile, in the play of her expression, in her rapid glances at us that the whole mystery and magic of her beauty consisted—and also in the way this subtle grace of movement was combined with the fresh spontaneity and innocence that throbbed in her laughter and speech, together with the helplessness that so appeals to us in children, birds, fawns, young trees.

This was the beauty of a butterfly. It goes with waltzing, fluttering about the garden, laughing and merry-making. It does not go with serious thought, grief and repose. Had a gust of wind blown down the platform, had it started raining, then the fragile body would suddenly, it seemed, have faded, and the wayward loveliness would have been dispersed like pollen from a flower.

'Ah, well,' muttered the officer, sighing, as we went to our carriage after the second bell, but what his interjection meant I do not pretend to judge.

Perhaps he felt sad and did not want to leave the girl and the spring evening for the stuffy train. Or perhaps, like me, he was irrationally sorry for the lovely girl, for himself, for me, and for all the passengers as they drifted limply and reluctantly back to their compartments. We walked past a station window behind which a wan, whey-faced telegraphist, with upstanding red curls and high cheek-bones, sat at his apparatus.

'I'll bet the telegraph operator is in love with the pretty little miss,' sighed the officer. 'To live out in the wilds under the same roof as that ethereal creature and not fall in love—it's beyond the power of man. And what a misfortune, my dear chap, what a mockery to be round-shouldered, unkempt, dreary, respectable and intelligent, and to be in love with that pretty, silly little girl who never pays you a scrap of attention! Or, even worse: suppose the lovesick telegraphist is married, suppose his wife is as round-shouldered, unkempt and respectable as himself. What agony!'

A guard stood on the small open platform between our carriage and the next. Resting his elbows on the railing, he was gazing towards the girl, and his flabby, disagreeably beefy face, exhausted by sleepless nights and the train's jostling, expressed ecstasy combined with the most profound sorrow, as if he could see his own youth, his own happiness, his sobriety, his purity, his wife, his children reflected in the girl. He seemed to be repenting his sins, and to be conscious with every fibre of his being that the girl was not his, and that for him—prematurely aged, clumsy, fat-visaged—the happiness of an ordinary human being and train passenger was as far away as heaven.

The third bell rang, whistles sounded, the train trundled off. Past our window flashed another guard, the station-master, the garden, and then the lovely girl with her marvellous, childishly sly smile.

Putting my head out and looking back, I saw her watching the train as she walked along the platform past the window with the telegraph clerk, then patted her hair and ran into the garden. No longer did the station buildings hide the sunset. We were in open country, but the sun had already set and black puffs of smoke were settling over the green, velvety young corn. The spring air, the dark sky, the railway carriage—all seemed sad.

Our guard, that familiar figure, came in and began lighting the candles.

IT was Christmas Eve. Marya had long been snoring on the stove, and the paraffin in the little lamp had burnt out, but Theodore Nilov still sat over his work. He would have stopped long ago and gone out into the street, but a customer from Kolokolny Road, who had ordered some new vamps for his boots a fortnight ago, had come in on the previous day, sworn at him and told him to finish the work at once without fail, before morning service.

'It's a rotten life,' grumbled Theodore as he worked. 'Some folks have been asleep for ages, others are enjoying themselves, while I'm just a dogsbody cobbling away for every Tom, Dick or Harry.'

To stop himself falling asleep he kept taking a bottle from under the table and drinking, flexing his neck after each swallow. 'Pray tell me this,' he said in a loud voice. 'Why can my customers enjoy themselves while I'm forced to work for them. What sense is there in it? Is it because they have money and I'm a beggar?'

He hated all his customers, especially the one who lived in Kolokolny Road. This was a personage of lugubrious aspect—long-haired, sallow, with big blue-tinted spectacles and a hoarse voice. He had an unpronounceable German surname. What his calling might be, what he did, was a complete mystery. When Theodore had gone to take his measurements a fortnight ago, he had been sitting on the floor pounding away at a mortar. Before the cobbler could say good day the contents of the mortar suddenly flashed and blazed up with a bright red flame, there was a stench of sulphur and burnt feathers, and the room was filled with dense pink smoke that made Theodore sneeze five times.

'No God-fearing man would meddle with the likes of that,' he reflected on returning home.

When the bottle was empty he put the boots on the table and pondered. Leaning his heavy head on his fist, he began thinking of his poverty, and of his gloomy, cheerless life. Then he thought of the rich with their big houses, their carriages, their hundred-rouble notes. How nice it would be if the houses of the bloody rich fell apart, if their horses died, if their fur coats and sable caps wore threadbare. How splendid if the rich gradually became beggars with nothing to eat, while the poor cobbler turned into a rich man who went round bullying poor cobblers on Christmas Eve.

Thus brooding, he suddenly remembered his work and opened his eyes. 'What a business!' he thought, looking at the boots. 'The job was finished long ago, and here I sit. I must take them to the gentleman.'

He wrapped his work in a red handkerchief, put his coat on and went into the street. Fine, hard snow was falling and pricked his face like needles. It was cold, slippery and dark, the gas lamps were dim, and there was such a smell of paraffin in the street for some reason that he spluttered and coughed. Rich men drove up and down the road, each with a ham and a bottle of vodka in his hand. From the carriages and sledges rich young ladies peeped at Theodore, putting out their tongues and shouting.

'A beggar! A beggar! Ha ha ha!'

Students, officers, merchants and generals walked behind him, all jeering. 'Boozy bootmaker! Godless welt-stitcher! Pauper! But his soles go marching on, ha ha ha!'

It was all most offensive, but he said nothing and only spat in disgust. Then he met Kuzma Lebyodkin, a master bootmaker from Warsaw. 'I married a rich woman,' Kuzma told him. 'And I have apprentices working for me. But you're a pauper and have nothing to eat.'

Theodore could not resist running after him. He chased him until he found himself in Kolokolny Road, where his customer lived in a top-floor flat in the fourth house from the corner. To reach him you had to cross a long, dark courtyard, and then climb a very high slippery staircase that vibrated under your feet. When the cobbler entered, the customer was sitting on the floor pounding something in a mortar, just as he had been a fortnight earlier.

'I've brought your boots, sir,' said Theodore sullenly.

The other stood up without speaking and made to try the boots on. Wishing to help him, Theodore went down on one knee and pulled one of his old boots off, but immediately sprang up, aghast, and backed away to the door. In place of a foot the creature had a hoof like a horse's!

'Dear me!' thought the cobbler. 'What a business!'

The best thing would have been to cross himself, drop everything and run downstairs. But he immediately reflected that this was his first, and would probably be his last, encounter with the Devil, and that it would be foolish not to take advantage of his good offices.

Pulling himself together, he decided to chance his luck, and clasped his hands behind his back to stop himself making the sign of the cross.

'Folks say there's nothing more diabolical and evil on this earth than the Devil,' he remarked with a respectful cough. 'But to my way of thinking, your Reverence, the Prince of Darkness must be highly educated like. The Devil has hoofs and a tail, saving your presence, but he's a sight more brainy than many a scholar.'

'Thank you for those kind words,' said the customer, flattered. 'Thank you, cobbler. What do you desire?'

Losing no time, the cobbler began complaining of his lot, and started with having envied the rich since childhood. He had always resented folk not living alike in big houses, with fine horses. Why, he wondered, was he poor? How was he worse than Kuzma Lebyodkin from Warsaw who owned his own house, whose wife wore a hat? He had the same sort of nose, hands, feet, head and back as the rich, so why was he forced to work while others enjoyed themselves? Why was he married to Marya, not to a lady smelling of scent? He had often seen beautiful young ladies in the houses of rich customers, but they had taken no notice of him, except for laughing sometimes and whispering to each other.

'What a red nose that cobbler has!'

True, Marya was a good, kind, hard-working woman, but she was uneducated, wasn't she? She had a heavy hand, she hit hard, and you only had to speak of politics or something brainy in her presence for her to chip in with the most arrant nonsense.

'So what are your wishes?' broke in his customer.

'Well, seeing as how you're so kind, Mr. Devil, sir, I'd like your Reverence to make me rich.'

'Certainly. But you must give me your soul in return, you know. Before the cocks crow, go and sign this paper assigning your soul to me.'

'Now see here, your Reverence,' said Theodore politely. 'When you ordered the vamps done I didn't take money in advance. You must carry out the order first and ask for payment afterwards.'

'Oh, all right,' agreed the customer.

Bright flame suddenly flared in the mortar, followed by a gust of dense pink smoke and the smell of burnt feathers and sulphur. When the smoke had dispersed Theodore rubbed his eyes and saw that he was no longer Theodore the shoemaker but quite a different person—one who wore a waistcoat with a watch-chain, and new trousers—and that he was sitting in an armchair at a big table. Two footmen were serving him dishes with low bows and a 'Good appetite, sir'.

What wealth! The footmen served a large slice of roast mutton and a dish of cucumbers. Then they brought roast goose in a pan followed shortly afterwards by roast pork and horse-radish sauce. And how classy it was, all this—this was real politics for you! He ate, gulping a large tumbler of excellent vodka before every course like any general or count. After the pork, buckwheat gruel with goose fat was served, and then an omelette with bacon fat and fried liver, all of which he ate and thoroughly enjoyed. And what else? They also served onion pie and steamed turnips with kvass.

'I wonder the gentry don't burst with meals like this,' he thought.

Finally a large pot of honey was served, and after the meal the Devil appeared wearing his blue spectacles. 'Was dinner satisfactory, Mr. Cobbler?' he asked with a low bow.

But Theodore could not get a word out, for he was nearly bursting after his meal. He had the disagreeable, stuffed sensation that comes from overeating, and tried to distract himself by scrutinizing the boot on his left foot.

'I never charged less than seven-and-a-half roubles for boots like that,' he thought, and asked which cobbler had made it.

'Kuzma Lebyodkin,' answered a footman.

'Tell that imbecile to come here!'

Soon Kuzma Lebyodkin from Warsaw appeared.

'What are your orders, sir?' He stopped by the door in a respectful attitude.

'Hold your tongue!' cried Theodore, stamping his foot. 'Don't answer me back! Know your place, cobbler, and your station in life! Oaf! You don't know how to make boots! I'll smash your face in! Why did you come here?'

'For my money, sir.'

'What money? Be off with you! Come back on Saturday. Clout him one, my man!'

Then he immediately remembered what a life his own customers had led him, and he felt sick at heart. To amuse himself he took a fat wallet from his pocket and started counting his money. There was a lot of it, but he wanted even more. The Devil in the blue spectacles brought him another, fatter wallet, but he wanted more still, and the more he counted the more discontented he grew.

In the evening the Devil brought him a tall, full-bosomed lady in a red dress, explaining that she was his new wife. He spent the whole evening kissing her and eating gingerbreads, and at night he lay on a soft feather bed, tossing from side to side. But he just couldn't get to sleep, and he felt as if all was not well.

'We have lots of money,' he told his wife. 'But it might attract burglars. You'd better take a candle and have a look.'

He couldn't sleep all night, and kept getting up to see if his trunk was all right. In the morning he had to go to matins. Now, rich and poor receive equal honours in church. When Theodore had been poor he had prayed 'Lord forgive me, sinner that I am,' in church. He said the same prayer now that he was rich, so where was the difference? And when the rich Theodore died he wouldn't be buried in gold and diamonds, but in black earth like the poorest beggar. He would burn in the same fire as cobblers. All this he resented. And then again, he still felt weighed down by the meal, and his mind was not on worship, but was assailed by worries about his money chest, about burglars, and about his doomed and bartered soul.

He came out of church in a bad temper. To banish evil thoughts he followed his usual procedure of singing at the top of his voice, but barely had he begun when a policeman ran up and saluted.

'Gents mustn't sing in the street, squire. You ain't no cobbler!'

Theodore leant against a fence and began wondering how to amuse himself.

'Don't lean too hard on the fence, guv'nor, or you'll dirty your fur coat,' a doorkeeper shouted.

Theodore went into a shop, bought their best concertina, and walked down the street playing it. But everyone pointed at him and laughed.

'Cor, look at his lordship!' jeered the cabmen. 'He's carrying on like a cobbler.'

'We can't have the nobs disturbing the peace,' said a policeman. 'You'll be going to the ale-house next!'

'Alms for the love of Christ!' wailed beggars, surrounding Theodore on all sides. 'Give us something, mister.'

Beggars had never paid him any attention when he had been a cobbler, but now they wouldn't leave him alone.

At home he was greeted by his new wife, the lady. She wore a green blouse and a red skirt. He wanted a bit of a cuddle, and had raised his hand to give her a good clout on the back when she spoke angrily.

'Yokel! Bumpkin! You don't know how to treat a lady. Kiss my hand if you love me. Fisticuffs I do not permit.'

'What a bloody life!' thought Theodore. 'What an existence! It's all don't sing, don't play the concertina, don't have fun with your woman. Pshaw!'

No sooner had he sat down to tea with his lady than the Devil appeared in his blue spectacles. 'Now, Mr. Cobbler,' said he, 'I've kept my part of the bargain, so sign the paper and come with me. Now you know what being rich means, so that's enough of that!'

He dragged him off to hell, straight to the furnace, and demons flew up, shouting, from all sides.

'Idiot! Blockhead! Jackass!'

There was a fearful smell of paraffin in hell, it was fit to choke you.

But suddenly it all vanished. Theodore opened his eyes and saw his table, the boots and the tin lamp. The lamp glass was black, stinking smoke belched from the dimly glowing wick as from a chimney. The blue-spectacled customer stood near it.

'Idiot! Blockhead! Jackass!' he was yelling. 'I'll teach you a lesson, you rogue! You took my order a fortnight ago, and the boots still aren't ready! Expect me to traipse round here for them half a dozen times a day? Blackguard! Swine!'

Theodore tossed his head and tackled the boots while the customer cursed and threatened him for a time. When he at last calmed down Theodore sullenly enquired what his occupation was.

'Making Bengal lights and rockets—I'm a manufacturer of fireworks.'

Church bells rang for matins. Theodore handed over the boots, received his money and went to church.

Carriages and sledges with bearskin aprons careered up and down the street, while merchants, ladies and officers walked the pavement, together with humbler folk. But no longer did Theodore envy anyone, or rail against his fate. Rich and poor were equally badly off, he now felt. Some could drive in carriages, others could sing at the top of their voices and play concertinas, but one and the same grave awaited all alike. Nor was there anything in life to make it worth giving the Devil even a tiny scrap of your soul.

THE BET

I

ONE dark autumn night an elderly banker was pacing up and down his study and recalling the party that he had given on an autumn evening fifteen years earlier. It had been attended by a good few clever people, and fascinating discussions had taken place, one of the topics being capital punishment. The guests, including numerous academics and journalists, had been largely opposed to it, considering the death penalty out of date, immoral and unsuitable for Christian states. Several of them felt that it should be replaced everywhere by life imprisonment.

'I disagree,' said their host the banker. 'I've never sampled the death penalty or life imprisonment myself. Still, to judge *a priori*, I find capital punishment more moral and humane than imprisonment. Execution kills you at once, whereas life imprisonment does it slowly. Now, which executioner is more humane? He who kills you in a few minutes, or he who drags the life out of you over a period of several years?'

A guest remarked that both were equally immoral. 'Both have the same object—the taking of life. The state isn't God, and it has no right to take what it can't restore if it wishes.'

Among the guests was a young lawyer of about twenty-five. 'The death sentence and the life sentence are equally immoral,' said he when his opinion was canvassed. 'But, if I had to choose between them, I'd certainly choose the second. Any kind of life is better than no life at all.'

A lively argument had ensued. The banker, younger and more excitable in those days, had suddenly got carried away and struck the table with his fist. 'It's not true!' he shouted at the young man. 'I bet you two million you wouldn't last five years in solitary confinement.'

'I'll take you on if you mean it,' was the reply. 'And I won't just do a five-year stretch, I'll do fifteen.'

'Fifteen? Done!' cried the banker. 'Gentlemen, I put up two million.'

'Accepted! You stake your millions and I stake my freedom,' said the young man.

And so the outrageous, futile wager was made. The banker, then a spoilt and frivolous person, with more millions than he could count, was delighted, and he made fun of the lawyer over supper. 'Think better of it while there's still time,' said he. 'Two million is nothing to me, young man, but you risk losing three or four of the best years of your life, I say three or four because you won't hang on longer. And don't forget, my unfortunate friend, that confinement is far harder when it's voluntary than when it's compulsory. The thought that you can go free at any moment will poison your whole existence in prison. I'm sorry for you.'

Pacing to and fro, the banker now recalled all this. 'What was the good of that wager?' he wondered. 'What's the use of the man losing fifteen years of his life? Or of my throwing away two million? Does it prove that the death penalty is better or worse than life imprisonment? Certainly not! Stuff and nonsense! On my part it was a spoilt man's whim, and on his side it was simply greed for money.'

Then he recalled the sequel to that evening. It had been decided that the young man should serve his term under the strictest supervision in one of the lodges in the banker's garden. For fifteen years he was to be forbidden to cross the threshold, to see human beings, to hear the human voice, to receive letters and newspapers. He was allowed a musical instrument, and books to read. He could write letters, drink wine, smoke. It was stipulated that his communications with the outside world could not be in spoken form, but must take place through a little window built specially for the purpose. Anything he needed—books, music, wine and so on—he could receive by sending a note, and in any quantity he liked, but only through the window. The contract covered all the details and minutiae that would make his confinement strictly solitary, and compel him to serve precisely fifteen years from twelve o'clock on the fourteenth of November 1870 until twelve o'clock on the fourteenth of November 1885. The slightest attempt to break the conditions, even two minutes before the end, absolved the banker from all obligation to pay the two million.

So far as could be judged from the prisoner's brief notes, he suffered greatly from loneliness and depression in his first year of incarceration. The sound of his piano could be heard continually, day and night, from the lodge. He refused strong drink and tobacco. Wine stimulates desires, wrote he, and desires are a prisoner's worst enemy. Besides, is there anything drearier than drinking good wine and seeing nobody? And tobacco spoilt the air of his room. The books that he had sent during the first year were mostly light reading—novels with a complex love plot, thrillers, fantasies, comedies and so on.

In the second year there was no more music from the lodge, and the prisoner's notes demanded only literary classics. In the fifth year music was heard again, and the captive asked for wine. Those who watched him through the window said that he spent all that year just eating, drinking and lying on his bed, often yawning and talking angrily to himself. He read no books. Sometimes he would sit and write at night. He would spend hours writing, but would tear up everything he had written by dawn. More than once he was heard weeping.

In the second half of the sixth year the captive eagerly embraced the study of languages, philosophy and history. So zealously did he tackle these subjects that the banker could hardly keep up with his book orders—in four years some six hundred volumes were procured at his demand. During the period of this obsession the banker incidentally received the following letter from the prisoner.

'My dearest Gaoler,

'I write these lines in six languages. Show them to those who know about these things. Let them read them. If they can't find any mistakes I beg you to have a shot fired in the garden—it will show me that my efforts have not been wasted. The geniuses of all ages and countries speak different languages, but the same flame burns in them all. Oh, did you but know what a transcendental happiness my soul now experiences from my ability to understand them!'

The captive's wish was granted—the banker had two shots fired in the garden.

After the tenth year the lawyer sat stock-still at the table, reading only the Gospels. The banker marvelled that one who had mastered six hundred obscure tomes in four years should spend some twelve months reading a single slim, easily comprehensible volume. Theology and histories of religion followed the Gospels.

In the last two years of his imprisonment the captive read an enormous amount quite indiscriminately. Now it was the natural sciences, now he wanted Byron or Shakespeare. There were notes in which he would simultaneously demand a work on chemistry, a medical textbook, a novel and a philosophical or theological treatise. His reading suggested someone swimming in the sea surrounded by the wreckage of his ship, and trying to save his life by eagerly grasping first one spar and then another.

II

'He regains his freedom at twelve o'clock tomorrow,' thought the old banker as he remembered all this. 'And I should pay him two million by agreement. But if I do pay up I'm done for—I'll be utterly ruined.'

Fifteen years earlier he had had more millions than he could count, but now he feared to ask which were greater, his assets or his debts. Gambling on the stock exchange, wild speculation, the impetuosity that he had never managed to curb, even in old age—these things had gradually brought his fortunes low, and the proud, fearless, self-confident millionaire had become just another run-of-the-mill banker trembling at every rise and fall in his holdings.

'Damn this bet!' muttered the old man, clutching his head in despair. 'Why couldn't the fellow die? He's only forty now. He'll take my last penny, he'll marry, he'll enjoy life, he'll gamble on the Exchange, while I look on enviously, like a pauper, and hear him saying the same thing day in day out: "I owe you all my happiness in life, so let me help you." No, it's too much! My only refuge from bankruptcy and disgrace is that man's death.'

Three o'clock struck and the banker cocked an ear. Everyone in the house was asleep, and nothing was heard but the wind rustling the frozen trees outside. Trying not to make a noise, he took from his fireproof safe the key of the door that had not been opened for fifteen years, put his overcoat on, and went out.

It was dark and cold outside, and rain was falling. A keen, damp wind swooped howling round the whole garden, giving the trees no rest. Straining his eyes, the banker could not see the ground, the white statues, the lodge or the trees. He approached the area of the lodge, and twice called his watchman, but there was no answer. The man was obviously sheltering from the weather, and was asleep somewhere in the kitchen or the greenhouse.

'If I have the courage to carry out my intention the main suspicion will fall on the watchman,' the old man thought.

He found the steps to the lodge and the door by feeling in the dark, entered the hall, groped his way into a small passage, and lit a match. There was no one there—just a bedstead without bedding on it, and the dark hulk of a cast-iron stove in the corner. The seals on the door leading to the captive's room were intact. When the match went out the old man peered through the small window, trembling with excitement.

In the prisoner's room a candle dimly burned. He was sitting near the table, and all that could be seen of him were his back, the hair on his head and his hands. On the table, on two armchairs, and on the carpet near the table, lay open books.

Five minutes passed without the prisoner once stirring—fifteen years of confinement had taught him to sit still. The banker tapped the window with a finger, but the captive made no answering movement. Then the banker cautiously broke the seals on the door, and put the key in the keyhole. The rusty lock grated and the door creaked. The banker expected to hear an immediate shout of surprise and footsteps, but three minutes passed and it was as quiet as ever in there. He decided to enter.

At the table a man unlike ordinary men sat motionless. He was all skin and bones, he had long tresses like a woman's, and a shaggy beard. The complexion was sallow with an earthy tinge, the cheeks were hollow, the back was long and narrow, and the hand propping the shaggy head was so thin and emaciated that it was painful to look at. His hair was already streaked with silver, and no one looking at his worn, old-man's face would have believed that he was only forty. He was asleep, and on the table in front of his bowed head lay a sheet of paper with something written on it in small letters.

'How pathetic!' thought the banker. 'He's asleep, and is probably dreaming of his millions. All I have to do is to take this semi-corpse, throw it on the bed, smother it a bit with a pillow, and the keenest investigation will find no signs of death by violence. But let us first read what he has written.'

Taking the page from the table, the banker read as follows.

'At twelve o'clock tomorrow I regain my freedom and the right to associate with others. But I think fit, before I leave this room for the sunlight, to address a few words to you. With a clear conscience, and as God is my witness, I declare that I despise freedom, life, health and all that your books call the blessings of this world.

'I have spent fifteen years intently studying life on earth. True, I have not set eyes on the earth or its peoples, but in your books I have drunk fragrant wine, sung songs, hunted stags and wild boars in the forests, loved women. Created by the magic of your inspired poets, beautiful girls, ethereal as clouds, have visited me at night, and whispered in my ears magical tales that have made my head reel. In your books I have climbed the peaks of Elbrus and Mont Blanc, whence I have watched the sun rising in the morning, and flooding the sky, the ocean and the mountain peaks with crimson gold in the evening. From there I have watched lightnings flash and cleave the storm-clouds above me. I have seen green forests, fields, rivers, lakes, cities. I have heard the singing of the sirens and the strains of shepherds' pipes. I have touched the wings of beautiful devils who flew to me to converse of God. In your books I have plunged into the bottomless pit, performed miracles, murdered, burnt towns, preached new religions, conquered whole kingdoms.

'Your books have given me wisdom. All that man's tireless brain has created over the centuries has been compressed into a small nodule inside my head. I know I'm cleverer than you all.

'I despise your books, I despise all the blessings and the wisdom of this world. Everything is worthless, fleeting, ghostly, illusory as a mirage. Proud, wise and handsome though you be, death will wipe you from the face of the earth along with the mice burrowing under the floor. Your posterity, your history, your deathless geniuses—all will freeze or burn along with the terrestrial globe.

'You have lost your senses and are on the wrong path. You take lies for truth, and ugliness for beauty. You would be surprised if apple and orange trees somehow sprouted with frogs and lizards instead of fruit, or if roses smelt like a sweating horse. No less surprised am I at you who have exchanged heaven for earth. I do not want to understand you.

'To give you a practical demonstration of my contempt for what you live by, I hereby renounce the two million that I once yearned for as one might for paradise, but which I now scorn. To disqualify myself from receiving it I shall leave here five hours before the time fixed, thus breaking the contract.'

After reading this the banker laid the paper on the table, kissed the strange man on the head and left the lodge in tears. At no other time—not even after losing heavily on the stock exchange—had he felt such contempt for himself. Returning to his house, he went to bed, but excitement and tears kept him awake for hours.

Next morning the watchmen ran up, white-faced, and told the banker that they had seen the man from the lodge climb out of his window into the garden, go to the gate and vanish. The banker went over at once with his servants and made sure that the captive had indeed fled. To forestall unnecessary argument he took the document of renunciation from the table, went back to the house and locked it in his fireproof safe.

THIEVES

ONE evening in Christmas week the medical orderly Yergunov, a nonentity known in his district as a great braggart and drunkard, was returning from the township of Repino where he had been making purchases for his hospital. Since he might be late, the doctor had lent him his best horse to get him home in good time.

The evening was not bad at first—quite calm—but at about eight o'clock a violent snow-storm blew up, and the orderly completely lost his way only four miles or so from home.

Not knowing the road or how to guide his horse, he was riding at random, haphazardly, hoping that the horse would find its own way. Two hours passed, the horse was exhausted, Yergunov himself was cold—and now fancied that he was not on his way home any more, but returning to Repino. But then the muffled barking of dogs was heard through the storm's roar, and a vague red blur appeared ahead of him. A high gate gradually emerged in outline, then a long fence surmounted by nails, point uppermost, after which the slanted sweep of a well jutted out behind the fence. The wind chased away the snowy murk before his eyes, and a small, squat cottage with a high thatched roof loomed up where the red blur had been. There was a light in one of its three small windows, which had something red hanging inside.

What household was this? On the right of the road—four or five miles from the hospital—should be Andrew Chirikov's inn, Yergunov remembered. He remembered, too, that this Chirikov had been murdered by sledge-drivers recently, leaving an elderly widow and a daughter Lyubka, who had come to the hospital for treatment about two years previously. The inn had a bad name. Riding up late at night —and on someone else's horse at that—was a risky business, but that could not be helped. Yergunov fumbled for the revolver in his bag, coughed grimly, and rapped his whip butt on the window frame.

'Hey, anyone there?' he shouted. 'For God's sake let me in for a warm, old woman.'

Raucously barking, a black dog whizzed under the horse's hoofs, followed by a white one, then another black one—there must have been a dozen. Yergunov singled out the biggest, swung his whip, and lashed out with all his might, whereupon a small, long-legged tyke raised its sharp muzzle, setting up a shrill, piercing howl.

Yergunov stood by the window for some time, knocking. Then, beyond the fence, hoar-frost glowed pink on the trees by the house, the gate creaked and a muffled woman's figure appeared carrying a lantern.

'Let me in for a warm, old woman,' said Yergunov. 'I'm going back to hospital and I've lost my way. What weather, God help us! Never fear, old woman, we know each other.'

'Them we know's all at home, we've invited no strangers,' said the figure sternly. 'And why knock? The gate ain't bolted.'

Yergunov rode into the yard and stopped by the porch.

'Ask your man to stable my horse, old woman,' he said.

'I'm no old woman.'

Nor was she, indeed. As she put out the lantern the light fell on her face, and Yergunov knew Lyubka by the black eyebrows.

'None of the men are here now,' she said, going indoors. 'Some are drunk and asleep, the others went off to Repino this morning. Today's a holiday.'

Tethering his horse in an outhouse, Yergunov heard a neigh, and saw another horse in the dark. He felt the saddle—a Cossack's. So there must be someone else about besides the women of the house. To be on the safe side, the orderly unsaddled his horse, taking his saddle and purchases with him as he went indoors.

The first room he entered was large and well-heated, smelling of newly scrubbed floors. At the table under the icons sat a short, thin peasant, about forty years old, with a small, fair beard and navy-blue shirt. It was Kalashnikov, an arrant rogue and horse-thief whose father and uncle kept the tavern at Bogalyovka, dealing in stolen horses when they had the chance. He too had been to the hospital several times—not as a patient, but to talk horses with the doctor. Was there one for sale? Would 'Mister Doctor, sir' care to swap a bay mare for a dun gelding? Now his hair was greased, a silver ear-ring glittered in one ear, and altogether he had a festive look. He was poring over a large, dog-eared picture-book, frowning and dropping his lower lip. Stretched on the floor near the stove was another peasant, who had a short fur coat over his face, shoulders and chest, and who must be asleep. Near his new boots with shiny metal heel-plates melted snow had left two dark puddles.

Seeing the orderly, Kalashnikov bade him good day.

'Yes, what weather!' said Yergunov, rubbing his cold knees with the palms of his hands. 'I have snow inside my collar, I'm soaked—a proper drowned rat, I feel. My revolver too, I think, er——'

He took out his revolver, looked it all over and put it back in his bag, but the gun made no impression at all, and the peasant went on looking at his book.

'Yes, what weather! I lost my way, and I do believe it would have been the death of me but for the dogs here. It would have been quite a business. But where are the women of the house?'

'The old woman's gone to Repino, and the girl's cooking supper,' Kalashnikov answered.

Silence followed. Shivering, gulping, Yergunov blew on his palms and cringed, making a show of being very cold and exhausted. The dogs, still restless, were heard howling outside. This was becoming boring.

'You a Bogalyovka man?' Yergunov asked the peasant sternly.

'Yes, I am.'

To pass the time, Yergunov thought about Bogalyovka—a large village set in a gulley so deep that when you drove along the high road on a moonlit night and looked down into the dark ravine, and then up at the sky, the moon seemed to hang above a bottomless pit, and it was like the end of the world. The road down was steep, winding, and so narrow that when you went to Bogalyovka during an epidemic or to do vaccinations, you must whistle all the time, or bellow at the top of your voice—for if you met a cart coming up you would never get by. The Bogalyovka peasants are known as expert gardeners and horse-thieves. Their gardens are well-stocked, with the whole village buried under white cherry-blossom in spring, and cherries sold at three copecks the pail in summer—you pay your three copecks and pick your own. The peasants' wives are good-looking and sleek, and they like wearing their best clothes. Even on working days they do nothing but sit on the banks by their huts searching each others' heads for insects.

Then footsteps were heard, and Lyubka came in—a barefoot girl of about twenty in a red dress.

She gave Yergunov a sidelong glance, and walked from one corner of the room to another a couple of times—in no ordinary manner, but with tiny steps, thrusting her bosom forward. She obviously enjoyed padding about in bare feet on the newly scrubbed floor, having taken off her shoes on purpose.

Laughing at something, Kalashnikov beckoned her with his finger. She came up to the table, and he showed her the prophet Elijah in his book—driving a carriage drawn by three horses hurtling into the sky. Lyubka leant her elbows on the table. Her hair flew over her shoulder

—a long auburn plait tied with red ribbon at the end—and almost touched the floor. She laughed too.

'What a fine picture—marvellous!' said Kalashnikov.

'Marvellous!' he repeated, moving his hands as if he wanted to take the reins in Elijah's place.

The wind soughed in the stove. There was a growl and a squeak, as if a big dog had killed a rat.

'Whew! We must be haunted,' Lyubka said.

'It's the wind,' said Kalashnikov. He paused and raised his eyes to the orderly.

'What do you think, Mr. Yergunov, you being a scholar?' he asked. 'Are there such things as devils or aren't there?'

'Now, how can I put it, my dear fellow?' answered the orderly with a shrug of one shoulder. 'Scientifically speaking, there ain't no such thing as devils of course, because that's all superstition. But taking a plain man's view, as you and I are now—yes, devils do exist, to cut a long story short. I've been through a lot in my time. After my training I was posted to the dragoons as medical orderly, and I was in the war, of course—I have a medal and a decoration from the Red Cross. But after San Stefano I came back to Russia and took a job with the rural council. Having been around such a lot in my day, I've seen more things than some have even dreamt of. I've seen devils too sometimes. I don't mean with horns or a tail—that's all rubbish—but ordinary ones, as you might say, or something of the sort.'

'Where?' asked Kalashnikov.

'In various places—no need to go far afield. Last year, between you and me, I met one right here—by this very inn, like. I'm driving to Golyshino, as I recall, to do some vaccinations and all that. Well, you know how it is, I have my racing sulky as usual, my horse, the various trappings I need, besides which I have my watch on me and so forth, so I'm on my guard as I drive along, just in case something happens— there are enough tramps about. I come to that blasted Snake Gulch, and I start going down. Then, suddenly, I notice someone or other on foot and all that—black hair, black eyes, his whole face seeming smutted with soot. He comes up to my horse and takes the left rein.

'"Stop!" says he.

'He looks the horse over, then me, see? Then he throws down the rein, doesn't utter a bad word.

'"Where are you off to?" he asks, his teeth bared and his eyes vicious.

'"Ah," thinks I, "you devil, you!"'

'"I'm going to do smallpox vaccinations," say I. "And what business is it of yours?"'

'"Well, if that's how it is," he says, "then you can vaccinate me too,"—and he bares his arm and shoves it under my nose.'

'I don't stop to argue of course, I just vaccinate to get rid of him. Then I look at my lancet—and it's rusty all over.'

The peasant sleeping by the stove suddenly turned over and threw off his coat. To his amazement, Yergunov recognized the very stranger whom he had met that day in Snake Gulch. The peasant's hair, beard and eyes were black as soot, and his face was swarthy, besides which he had a black spot the size of a lentil on his right cheek. He looked at Yergunov contemptuously.

'I did take hold of your left rein,' said he. 'That's quite true. But about the vaccination you are lying, sir. We never even mentioned vaccination, you and I.'

The orderly was taken aback.

'I wasn't talking about you,' he said. 'So if you're lying down, lie down.'

The swarthy peasant had never been to the hospital, and Yergunov did not know who he was or where he came from. Looking at the man now, he decided that he must be a gypsy. The peasant stood up, stretched himself, gave a loud yawn, went up to Lyubka and Kalashnikov, sat down beside them and also started looking at the book. Rapture and envy appeared on his sleepy face.

'Look, Merik,' said Lyubka to him, 'you bring me horses like that, and I'll drive to heaven.'

'Sinners can't go to heaven,' said Kalashnikov. 'You have to be a saint.'

Then Lyubka laid the table, serving a large hunk of bacon fat, salted gherkins and a wooden platter of stewed meat cut in small pieces, followed by a frying-pan with sausage and cabbage hissing in it. A cut-glass spirits decanter also appeared on the table, wafting a smell of orange peel through the room after everyone had been poured a glass.

Yergunov was annoyed that Kalashnikov and the dark-skinned Merik should talk to each other and ignore him—he might just as well not have been there. And he wanted to talk to them, wanted to brag, have a drink and a good meal—and a spot of fun with Lyubka if possible. While they supped, she sat down near him half a dozen times, touching him with her lovely shoulders as if by accident, and stroking her broad hips with her hands. She was a hearty, laughing, flighty, restive girl who kept sitting down and standing up. While sitting, she would keep turning her breast or her back to her neighbour—she was a proper fidget—and was always brushing against him with elbow or knee.

Yergunov was also displeased by the peasants drinking only a glass apiece, and it was somehow awkward for him to drink on his own. But he could not stop himself taking a second glass, then a third, and he ate up all the sausage. Not wanting the peasants to cold-shoulder him, he decided on flattery so as to be accepted as one of the boys.

'You've some great lads in Bogalyovka!' he said with a wag of his head.

'Great in what way?' Kalashnikov asked.

'Oh, you know, take that horse business. Great rustlers, that lot are!'

'What's so great about them? They're drunkards and thieves, more like.'

'That's all over and done with,' said Merik after a short pause. 'Old Filya's about the only one of them left now, and he's blind.'

'Yes, there's only Filya,' sighed Kalashnikov. 'He must be about seventy now, I reckon. Some German settlers put out one of his eyes, and he doesn't see too well with the other. Wall-eyed, he is. There was a time when the police inspector would see him, and—"Hallo there, Shamil!" he'd shout. And the peasants all said the same. Shamil, they always called him, but now he's only known as One-eyed Filya. He was a proper lad! He and old Andrew—Lyubka's father that was— made their way into Rozhnovo one night when some cavalry regiments were stationed there. They stole nine military mounts, the pick of the bunch, and they weren't frightened of the sentries. And that very morning they sold all these horses to Gypsy Afonka for twenty roubles. Aye! But nowadays your thief is more concerned to steal a horse from someone who's drunk or asleep. He's lost to shame, he'll steal the very boots off a drunkard—and then he's so grasping he'll take the horse over a hundred miles away, and try to sell it in a market, haggling like a Jew till the police sergeant arrests him, the fool. That's no fun, it's a thorough disgrace. They're a miserable lot, I must say!'

'What about Merik?' asked Lyubka.

'Merik ain't one of us,' said Kalashnikov. 'He comes from the Kharkov country, from Mizhirich. But it's true he's quite a lad—a good man he is, we ain't got no complaints.'

Lyubka gave Merik a sly, gleeful look.

'Yes, no wonder he was ducked in that ice-hole,' she said.

'How was that?' asked Yergunov.

'Well, it was this way,' said Merik with a laugh. 'Filya stole three horses off some tenant farmers in Samoylovka, and they thought it was me. In Samoylovka there were about ten of these farmers all told, and with their labourers that made thirty men, all of the Molokan sect.

'"Come and have a look, Merik," says one of them at the market. "We've brought some new horses from the fair".

'Well, I'm interested, naturally, so along I go. Then the whole lot of them, all thirty, tie my hands behind me and take me to the river.

'"We'll give you horses!" say they.

'There's one hole in the ice already, and they cut another next to it, seven feet away. Then they take a rope, see? They put a noose under my armpits and tie a crooked stick to the other end, so it will go through both holes see? Well, they shove the stick through and haul, while I—just as I am in fur coat and high boots—crash into that ice-hole with them standing there kicking me in or ramming me with a chopper. Then they drag me under the ice and haul me out of the other hole.'

Lyubka shuddered and hunched herself together.

'First thing I felt was the cold shock,' Merik went on. 'But when they pull me out I'm helpless, I just lie on the snow with them Molokans standing by hitting my knees and elbows with their sticks. It doesn't half hurt! When they've beaten me they go away, but everything on me's frozen, my clothes is all ice. I stand up, but I ain't got no strength. Then a peasant woman drives past, thank God, and gives me a lift.'

Meanwhile Yergunov had drunk five or six glasses. Feeling light-hearted, he too had an urge to spin some weird and wonderful yarn, showing that he was a bit of a lad himself and afraid of nothing.

'Once at home in Penza Province—' he began.

Because he had drunk a lot and was rather tipsy—and perhaps because he had been caught out lying a couple of times—the peasants took not the slightest notice of him, and even stopped answering his questions. What's more, they permitted themselves such outspokenness in his presence—ignoring him, in other words—that a creepy, cold feeling came over him.

Kalashnikov had the dignified bearing of a solid, respectable citizen. He spoke at length, making the sign of the cross over his mouth whenever he yawned, and no one could have known that he was a thief, a cruel bandit who robbed the poor, had been to prison twice already, and had been sentenced to Siberian exile by his village community, except that his father and uncle—robbers and good-for-nothings like himself—had bought him off. But Merik had a dashing air. Seeing Lyubka and Kalashnikov admiring him, and thinking himself no end of a lad, he kept putting his arms akimbo, puffing out his chest, and stretching so violently that the bench creaked.

After supper Kalashnikov faced the icon and said grace without standing up, and shook Merik's hand. Merik said grace too, and shook Kalashnikov's hand. Lyubka cleared away supper, threw some peppermint cakes, roast nuts and pumpkin seeds on the table, and served two bottles of sweet wine.

'May old Andrew rest in peace,' said Kalashnikov, clinking glasses with Merik, 'and may the Kingdom of Heaven be his. When he was alive we used to meet here, or at his brother Martin's, and—what men those were, heaven help us, what talk we had! Wonderful talk! Martin would be there, with Filya and Theodore Stukotey. It was all right and proper—but what a time we had, we didn't half have fun!'

Lyubka went out and came back a little later wearing a green kerchief and beads.

'Look, Merik,' she said. 'See what Kalashnikov brought me today.'

She looked at herself in the mirror, tossing her head several times to make the beads jingle. Then she opened a chest and began taking out . . . first a cotton dress with red and blue polka-dots, then another—red, with flounces, rustling and swishing like paper—then a new kerchief, navy-blue shot with rainbow colours. She displayed all these things, laughing and flinging up her arms as if amazed that such treasures should be hers.

Kalashnikov tuned the balalaika and started playing, and Yergunov simply could not make out what kind of song he was singing, gay or sad—for it was so very sad at times that you felt like crying, but then it would brighten up again. Suddenly Merik shot up and began stamping his heels on one spot. Then he spread his arms and strutted on his heels from table to stove and from stove to chest, after which he flew up as if stung, clicking heel-plates in mid-air and launching himself into a squatting dance. Lyubka threw up both hands with a frantic squeak and followed suit. First she moved sideways—viciously, as if wanting to creep up on someone and hit them from behind. She rapidly clattered her bare heels as Merik had clattered his boot-heels, spun top-like and crouched, her red dress billowing like a bell. Glaring at her angrily and baring his teeth, Merik swooped towards her, doing squatting steps, and wanting to destroy her with his terrible legs, but she jumped up and tossed back her head. Waving her arms as a big bird flaps its wings, she floated across the room, scarce touching the floor.

'Phew, that girl has spirit!' Yergunov thought, sitting on the chest and observing the dance from there. 'What fire! Nothing's too good for her.'

He regretted being a medical orderly instead of an ordinary peasant. Why must he wear a coat and a watch-chain with a gilt key, and not a navy-blue shirt with a cord belt—in which case, he, like Merik, could have sung boldly, danced, drunk and thrown both arms round Lyubka?

The rat-tat-tat, the shouts, the whoops set crockery jingling in the cupboard and made the candle-light dance. The thread broke, and Lyubka's beads flew all over the floor, the green kerchief slipped off her head, and she was less like a girl than a red cloud whipping by with dark eyes flashing, while Merik's hands and feet looked ready to fly off at any moment.

Then Merik gave a last stamp and stood like one rooted to the spot.

Exhausted, scarcely breathing, Lyubka stooped over his chest, leaning on him as on a post, while he embraced her, looked into her eyes, and spoke tenderly and affectionately as if in jest.

'I'll find out where your old mother's money's hidden later on. I'll kill her, I'll cut your little throat with my little knife, and then I'll set fire to the inn. It'll be thought you both died in the fire, and I'll take your money to the Kuban and keep droves of horses, and raise sheep.'

Not answering, Lyubka only looked at him guiltily.

'Is it nice in the Kuban, Merik?' she asked.

He said nothing, but went to the chest and sat down, deep in thought—dreaming about the Kuban, most likely.

'It's time I was going, though,' said Kalashnikov, standing up. 'Filya must be expecting me by now. Good-bye, Lyubka.'

Yergunov went out into the yard to make sure that Kalashnikov did not take his horse. Still the blizzard raged. Their long tails clinging to weeds and bushes, white clouds floated about the yard, while in the fields beyond the fence, giants in broad-sleeved white shrouds whirled and fell, then stood up again to wave their arms and fight. And what a gale was blowing! Unable to endure its rude caresses, bare birches and cherry-trees bowed down to the ground.

'Oh Lord,' they wept, 'what sin have we committed that Thou hast bent us to the ground and wilt not set us free?'

'Whoa there!' said Kalashnikov sternly, mounting his horse.

One half of the gate was open, and by it lay a deep snowdrift.

'Come on then, gee up!' shouted Kalashnikov.

Starting off, his small, short-legged nag sank belly deep in the drift. White with snow, Kalashnikov and horse soon vanished through the gate.

When Yergunov came back into the room, Lyubka was crawling about the floor picking up her beads, and Merik was not there.

'A glorious girl,' Yergunov thought, lying on the bench and placing his coat under his head. 'Oh, if only Merik wasn't here!'

Lyubka aroused him as she crawled about the floor near the bench. He would most certainly get up and embrace her, he thought, if Merik wasn't there, and what happened after that would remain to be seen. She was still a girl, admittedly, but hardly a virgin—and even if she were, need one stand on ceremony in this robbers' lair?

Lyubka picked up her beads and went out. The candle was burning low, and the flame caught a piece of paper in the candle-stick. Yergunov placed his revolver and matches beside him, and put out the candle. The icon-lamp was flickering so much that it hurt his eyes. Patches of light danced on ceiling, floor and cupboard, and among them he had visions of Lyubka—a buxom, full-breasted girl. Now she spun like a top. Now she panted, exhausted by the dance.

'Oh, if only Merik would go to the devil!' he thought.

The lamp gave a last flicker, sputtered and went out. Someone who could only be Merik came in and sat on the bench. He drew at his pipe, and his dark cheek with its black spot was lit up for a moment. The foul tobacco smoke tickled Yergunov's throat.

'What filthy tobacco, damn it!' he said. 'It makes me feel quite sick.'

'I mix my tobacco with oat blooms,' Merik answered after a short pause. 'It's better for the chest.'

He smoked, spat and went out again. About half an hour passed, then a light suddenly flashed in the lobby, and Merik appeared in a short fur coat and cap, followed by Lyubka carrying a candle.

'Don't go away, Merik,' Lyubka implored.

'No, Lyubka. Don't keep me.'

'Listen, Merik,' said Lyubka, her voice growing soft and tender. 'I know you'll find Mother's money, you'll kill us both, you'll go to the

Kuban and you'll love other girls. But I don't care, I ask only one thing of you, darling—stay with me.'

'No, I want to go and celebrate,' said Merik, fastening his belt.

'But you have no mount. You walked here, didn't you? So what will you ride?'

Merik bent down and whispered in Lyubka's ear. She looked at the door, and laughed through her tears.

'And he's asleep, the pompous swine,' she said.

Merik embraced her, kissed her hard and went out. Yergunov stuck his revolver in his pocket, jumped up quickly and ran after him.

'Get out of my way!' he told Lyubka, who had hurriedly bolted the lobby door and stood across the threshold. 'Let me through, don't stand there!'

'Why go out?'

'To look at my horse.'

Mischievously and fondly, Lyubka gazed up at him.

'Why look at that, when you can look at me?' she asked, bending down and touching the gilt key on his watch-chain.

'Let me through or he'll take my horse,' Yergunov said. 'Let go, you bitch!' he shouted, hitting her angrily on the shoulder, and barging as hard as he could with his chest to shove her off the door. But she clung hard to the bolt, and seemed made of iron.

'Let me go!' he shouted, exhausted. 'He'll go off with it, I tell you!'

'Why should he? Not he.'

Panting and rubbing her shoulder, which hurt, she looked up at him again, blushed and laughed.

'Don't leave, darling,' she said. 'I'm bored on my own.'

Yergunov gazed into her eyes, hesitated and then put his arms round her. She did not resist.

'Now, no more silliness, let me go,' he said.

She did not speak.

'I heard you just now,' he said, 'telling Merik you loved him.'

'He's not the only one. Who I love—that's my secret.'

She touched his watch-key again.

'Give me that,' she asked softly.

Unfastening the key, Yergunov gave it her. She suddenly craned her neck, listening with a serious expression, and her look struck the orderly as cold and calculating. Remembering his horse, he now easily pushed her to one side and ran out into the yard. In the shed a sleepy pig grunted in lazy rhythm, and a cow banged her horn.

Yergunov lit a match. He saw the pig, the cow, the dogs streaking towards his light from all sides, but of his horse there was no trace. Shouting, shaking his fists at dogs, stumbling into drifts, floundering in snow, he ran through the gate and stared into darkness. He strained his eyes, but could see only the flying snow, its flakes distinctly forming various figures. Now the white, laughing face of a corpse peeped through the gloom. Now a white horse galloped past, ridden by an Amazon in a muslin dress. Or a string of white swans flew overhead.

Shaking with rage and cold, baffled, Yergunov fired his revolver at the dogs, hitting none of them, and rushed back indoors.

As he entered the lobby, he distinctly heard someone dart out of the room beyond, banging the door. It was dark in there. Yergunov pushed the door, but it was bolted. Then, lighting match after match, he rushed back to the lobby, and thence to the kitchen, and on from there to a little room where the walls were all draped with petticoats and dresses, where there was a smell of cornflower and dill, and where, in the corner near the stove, stood someone's bed with a great mound of pillows on it. This must be the old mother's room. He passed through to another room, also a small one, where he saw Lyubka—lying on a chest, covered with a gaudy patchwork cotton quilt and pretending to be asleep. Above the head of her bed an icon-lamp was burning.

'Where's my horse?' asked the orderly grimly.

Lyubka did not stir.

'Where's my horse, I ask you?' Yergunov repeated in an even grimmer voice, and tore the quilt off her. 'I asked you a question, you bitch!' he shouted.

She started up and rose to her knees. She held her shift with one hand, and tried to grasp the quilt with the other, crouching against the wall. She looked at Yergunov with loathing and fear as she warily followed his slightest move with eyes like a trapped animal's.

'Tell me where my horse is,' shouted Yergunov, 'or I'll beat the living daylights out of you!'

'Go away, damn you!' she wheezed hoarsely.

Seizing her shift near the neck, Yergunov wrenched, then lost control of himself and embraced the girl as hard as he could. Hissing with rage, she slithered in his clutches, freed one arm—the other was caught in the torn shift—and punched him on the top of his head.

Pain numbed his senses, there was a ringing and a banging in his ears. Lurching backwards, he received another blow—on the temple. He reeled, clutched the door-posts to stop himself falling, made his way to the room where his things were, and lay on the bench. He lay there for a while, then took the match-box from his pocket, and began lighting one match after another quite aimlessly. He would light one, blow it out and throw it under the table—until all the matches were gone.

Outside, meanwhile, the sky was turning blue and the cocks had started crowing. But Yergunov's head still ached, and his ears roared as if he was under a railway bridge with a train passing overhead. Somehow he got his coat and hat on. He could not find his saddle and bundle of shopping, and his bag was empty. No wonder someone had scurried out of that room when he had come in from the yard not so long ago.

He picked up a poker in the kitchen to keep off the dogs, and went out into the yard, leaving the door wide open. The blizzard had subsided, the weather was calm.

When he had passed through the gate, the white fields seemed dead, there was not one bird in the morning sky. On both sides of the road, and in the far distance, were dark blue copses of small trees.

Yergunov tried to consider his forthcoming reception in the hospital, and what the doctor would say. He must certainly give thought to that and have his answers ready in advance, but such thoughts dissolved and eluded him. Walking along, he could think only of Lyubka and the peasants that he had spent the night with. He remembered, too, how Lyubka's plait had swung loose to the floor as she bent down for the quilt after hitting him for the second time. His mind was in such a muddle. Why are there doctors and medical orderlies, he wondered, why are there merchants, clerks and peasants in this world? Why aren't there just free men? The birds and beasts are free, aren't they? So is Merik. They fear no one, they need no one. Now, whose idea was it—who says we have to get up in the morning, have a meal at midday and go to bed at night? That a doctor is senior to an orderly? That one must live in a room and love no one but one's wife? Why shouldn't things be the other way round—lunch at night and sleep by day? Oh, to leap on a horse, not asking whose it is, and race the wind down fields, woods and dales like some fiend out of hell! Oh, to make love to girls, to laugh at everyone!

Yergunov threw the poker in the snow and pressed his forehead on the cold, white trunk of a birch tree, lost in thought. And his grey, monotonous life, his wages, his subordinate position, his dispensary, the everlasting fussing over jars and poultices, seemed contemptible and sickening.

'Who says it's wrong to have a bit of fun?' he wondered ruefully. 'Those who talk that way have never lived a free life like Merik or Kalashnikov, they haven't loved Lyubka. They've spent all their lives on their knees, they haven't enjoyed themselves. And they've loved no one but their frog-like wives.'

If he still wasn't a burglar, a swindler—a highway robber, even— that was only through lack of ability or suitable opportunity. Such was his present view of himself.

Some eighteen months passed. In spring, after Easter, Yergunov— long since dismissed from his hospital and drifting around out of work —left the tavern at Repino late one night and wandered aimlessly down the street.

He walked into the country. There was a scent of spring and the breath of a warm, caressing breeze. From the sky the quiet, starlit night gazed down on earth. God, how deep that sky is, how infinitely broad its canopy over the world! The world is well enough made, thought Yergunov. But why do people divide each other into sober and drunk, employed and discharged, and so forth. What right have they? Why do the sober and well-fed sleep comfortably in their homes, while the drunken and the starving must roam the country without shelter? The man who doesn't work, and doesn't earn wages—why must he necessarily go hungry, unclothed, without boots? Whose idea was this? Why don't the birds and forest beasts have jobs or earn wages—but enjoy themselves instead?

Unfurled over the horizon, a magnificent crimson glow quivered in the far sky, and Yergunov stood watching it for a long time. Why, he kept wondering, should it be a sin if he had run off with someone's samovar yesterday and drunk the proceeds in the tavern? Why?

Two carts drove past on the road. In one a peasant woman slept, in the other sat a bare-headed old man.

'Where's the fire, old man?' asked Yergunov.

'At Andrew Chirikov's inn,' the old man replied.

Then Yergunov remembered his winter adventure of eighteen months ago in that same inn, remembered Merik's boastful threat. Picturing the old woman and Lyubka with their throats cut, burning, he envied Merik. On his way back to the tavern, he looked at the houses of rich inn-keepers, cattle-dealers and blacksmiths. It would be a good idea to burgle some rich man's house at night, he reflected.

GUSEV

I

It is getting dark, and will soon be night.

Gusev, a discharged private soldier, sits up in his bunk.

'I say, Paul Ivanovich,' he remarks in a low voice. 'A soldier in Suchan told me their ship ran into a great fish on the way out and broke her bottom.'

The nondescript person whom he addresses, known to everyone in the ship's sick-bay as Paul Ivanovich, acts as if he has not heard, and says nothing.

Once more quietness descends.

Wind plays in the rigging, the screw thuds, waves thrash, bunks creak, but their ears have long been attuned to all that, and they feel as if their surroundings are slumbering silently. It is boring. The three patients—two soldiers and one sailor—who have spent all day playing cards, are already dozing and talking in their sleep.

The sea is growing rough, it seems. Beneath Gusev the bunk slowly rises and falls, as if sighing—once, twice, a third time.

Something clangs on to the floor—a mug must have fallen.

'The wind's broken loose from its chain,' says Gusev, listening.

This time Paul Ivanovich coughs.

'First you have a ship hitting a fish,' he replies irritably. 'Then you have a wind breaking loose from its chain. Is the wind a beast, that it breaks loose, eh?'

'It's how folk talk.'

'Then folk are as ignorant as you, they'll say anything. A man needs a head on his shoulders—he needs to use his reason, you senseless creature.'

Paul Ivanovich is subject to sea-sickness, and when the sea is rough he is usually bad-tempered, exasperated by the merest trifle. But there is absolutely nothing to be angry about, in Gusev's opinion. What is there so strange or surprising in that fish, even—or in the wind bursting its bonds? Suppose the fish is mountain-sized, and has a hard back like a sturgeon's. Suppose, too, that there are thick stone walls at the world's end, and that fierce winds are chained to those walls. If the winds haven't broken loose, then why do they thrash about like mad over the whole sea, tearing away like dogs? What happens to them in calm weather if they aren't chained up?

For some time Gusev considers mountainous fish and stout, rusty chains. Then he grows bored and thinks of the home country to which he is now returning after five years' service in the Far East. He pictures a large, snow-covered pond. On one side of the pond is the red-brick pottery with its tall chimney and clouds of black smoke, and on the other side is the village. Out of the fifth yard from the end his brother Alexis drives his sledge with his little son Vanka sitting behind him in his felt over-boots together with his little girl Akulka, also felt-booted. Alexis has been drinking, Vanka is laughing, and Akulka's face cannot be seen because she is all muffled up.

'He'll get them kids frostbitten if he don't watch out,' thinks Gusev. 'O Lord,' he whispers, 'grant them reason and the sense to honour their parents, and not be cleverer than their mum and dad.'

'Those boots need new soles,' rambles the delirious sailor in his deep voice. 'Yes indeed.'

Gusev's thoughts break off. Instead of the pond, a large bull's head without eyes appears for no reason whatever, while horse and sledge no longer move ahead, but spin in a cloud of black smoke. Still, he's glad he's seen the folks at home. His happiness takes his breath away. It ripples, tingling, over his whole body, quivers in his fingers.

'We met again, thanks be to God,' he rambles, but at once opens his eyes and tries to find some water in the darkness.

He drinks and lies back, and again the sledge passes—followed once more by the eyeless bull's head, smoke, clouds.

And so it goes on till daybreak.

II

First a dark blue circle emerges from the blackness—the port-hole. Then, bit by bit, Gusev can make out the man in the next bunk—Paul Ivanovich. Paul sleeps sitting up because lying down makes him choke. His face is grey, his nose is long and sharp, and his eyes seem huge because he has grown so fearfully thin. His temples are sunken, his beard is wispy, his hair is long.

From his face you cannot possibly tell what class he belongs to—is he gentleman, merchant or peasant? His expression and long hair might be those of a hermit, or of a novice in a monastery, but when he speaks he doesn't sound like a monk, somehow. Coughing, bad air and disease have worn him down and made breathing hard for him as he mumbles with his parched lips.

He sees Gusev watching him, and turns to face him.

'I'm beginning to grasp the point,' says he. 'Yes, now I see it all.'

'See what, Paul Ivanovich?'

'I'll tell you. Why aren't you serious cases kept somewhere quiet, that's what's been puzzling me? Why should you find yourselves tossing about in a sweltering hot steamship—a place where everything endangers your lives, in other words? But now it's all clear, indeed it is. Your doctors put you on the ship to get rid of you. They're sick of messing around with such cattle. You pay them nothing, you only cause them trouble, and you spoil their statistics by dying. Which makes you cattle. And getting rid of you isn't hard. There are two requisites. First, one must lack all conscience and humanity. Second, one must deceive the steamship line. Of the first requisite the less said the better—we're pastmasters at that. And the second we can always pull off, given a little practice. Five sick men don't stand out in a crowd of four hundred fit soldiers and sailors. So they get you on board, mix you up with the able-bodied, hurriedly count you and find nothing amiss in the confusion. Then, when the ship's already under way, they see paralytics and consumptives in the last stages lying around on deck.'

Not understanding Paul Ivanovich, and thinking he was being told off, Gusev spoke in self-defence.

'I lay around on deck because I was so weak. I was mighty chilly when they unloaded us from the barge.'

'It's a scandal,' Paul Ivanovich goes on. 'The worst thing is, they know perfectly well you can't survive this long journey, don't they? And yet they put you here. Now, let's assume you last out till the Indian Ocean. What happens next doesn't bear thinking of. And such is their gratitude for loyal service and a clean record!'

Paul Ivanovich gives an angry look, frowning disdainfully.

'I'd like a go at these people in the newspapers,' he pants. 'I'd make the fur fly all right!'

The two soldier-patients and the sailor are already awake and at their cards. The sailor half lies in his bunk, while the soldiers sit on the floor near him in the most awkward postures. One soldier has his right arm in a sling, with the hand bandaged up in a regular bundle, so he holds his cards in his right armpit or in the crook of his elbow, playing them with his left hand. The sea is pitching and rolling heavily—impossible to stand up, drink tea or take medicine.

'Were you an officer's servant?' Paul Ivanovich asks Gusev.

'Yes sir, a batman.'

'God, God!' says Paul Ivanovich, with a sad shake of his head. 'Uproot a man from home, drag him ten thousand miles, give him tuberculosis and—and where does it all lead, I wonder? To making a batman of him for some Captain Kopeykin or Midshipman Dyrka. Very sensible, I must say!'

'It's not hard work, Paul Ivanovich. You get up of a morning, clean the boots, put the samovar on, tidy the room—then there's no more to do all day. The lieutenant spends all day drawing plans, like, and you can say your prayers, read books, go out in the street—whatever you want. God grant everyone such a life.'

'Oh, what could be better! The lieutenant draws his "plans, like", and you spend your day in the kitchen longing for your home. "Plans, like!" It's not plans that matter, it's human life. You only have one life, and that should be respected.'

'Well, of course, Paul Ivanovich, a bad man never gets off lightly, either at home or in the service. But you live proper and obey orders— and who needs harm you? Our masters are educated gentlemen, they understand. I was never in the regimental lock-up, not in five years I wasn't, and I wasn't struck—now let me see—not more than once.'

'What was that for?'

'Fighting. I'm a bit too ready with my fists, Paul Ivanovich. Four Chinamen come in our yard, carrying firewood or something—I don't recall. Well, I'm feeling bored, so I, er, knock 'em about a bit, and make one bastard's nose bleed. The lieutenant sees it through the window. Right furious he is, and he gives me one on the ear.'

'You wretched, stupid man,' whispers Paul Ivanovich. 'You don't understand anything.'

Utterly worn out by the pitching and tossing, he closes his eyes. His head keeps falling back, or forward on his chest, and he several times tries to lie flat, but it comes to nothing because the choking stops him.

'Why did you hit those four Chinamen?' he asks a little later.

'Oh, I dunno. They comes in the yard, so I just hits 'em.'

They fall silent.

The card players go on playing for a couple of hours with much enthusiasm and cursing, but the pitching and tossing wear even them out, they abandon their cards and lie down. Once more Gusev pictures the large pond, the pottery, the village.

Once more the sledge runs by, and again Vanka laughs, while that silly Akulka has thrown open her fur and stuck out her legs.

'Look, everyone,' she seems to say. 'I have better snow-boots than Vanka. Mine are new.'

'Five years old, and still she has no sense,' rambles Gusev. 'Instead of kicking your legs, why don't you fetch your soldier uncle a drink? I'll give you something nice.'

Then Andron, a flint-lock gun slung over his shoulder, brings a hare he has killed, followed by that decrepit old Jew Isaiah, who offers a piece of soap in exchange for the hare. There's a black calf just inside the front door of the hut, Domna is sewing a shirt and crying. Then comes the eyeless bull's head again, the black smoke.

Overhead someone gives a loud shout, and several sailors run past—dragging something bulky over the deck, it seems, or else something has fallen with a crash. Then they run past again.

Has there been an accident? Gusev lifts his head, listening, and sees the two soldiers and the sailor playing cards again. Paul Ivanovich is sitting up, moving his lips. He chokes, he feels too weak to breathe, and he is thirsty, but the water is warm and nasty.

The boat is still pitching.

Suddenly something strange happens to one of the card-playing soldiers.

He calls hearts diamonds, he muddles the score and drops his cards, then he gives a silly, scared smile and looks round at everyone.

'One moment, lads,' says he and lies on the floor.

Everyone is aghast. They call him, but he doesn't respond.

'Maybe you feel bad, eh, Stephen?' asks the soldier with his arm in a sling. 'Should we call a priest perhaps?'

'Have some water, Stephen,' says the sailor. 'Come on, mate, you drink this.'

'Now, why bang his teeth with the mug?' asks Gusev angrily. 'Can't you see, you fool?'

'What is it?'

'What is it?' Gusev mimics him. 'He has no breath in him, he's dead. That's what it is. What senseless people, Lord help us!'

III

The ship is no longer heaving, and Paul Ivanovich has cheered up. He is no longer angry, and his expression is boastful, challenging and mocking.

'Yes,' he seems about to say, 'I'm going to tell you something to make you all split your sides laughing.'

The port-hole is open and a soft breeze blows on Paul Ivanovich. Voices are heard, and the plashing of oars.

Just beneath the port-hole someone sets up an unpleasant, shrill droning—a Chinese singing, that must be.

'Yes, we're in the roadstead now,' Paul Ivanovich says with a sardonic smile. 'Another month or so and we'll be in Russia. Yes indeed, sirs, gentlemen and barrack-room scum. I'll go to Odessa, and then straight on to Kharkov. I have a friend in Kharkov, a literary man. I'll go and see him.

'"Now, old boy," I'll say, "you can drop your loathsome plots about female amours and the beauties of nature for the time being, and expose these verminous bipeds. Here are some subjects for you."'

He ponders for a minute.

'Know how I fooled them, Gusev?' he asks.

'Fooled who, Paul Ivanovich?'

'Why, those people we were talking about. There are only two classes on this boat, see, first and third. And no one's allowed to travel third class except peasants—the riff-raff, in other words. Wear a jacket and look in the least like a gentleman or bourgeois—then you must go first class, if you please! You must fork out your five hundred roubles if it kills you.

'"Now why," I ask, "did you make such a rule? Trying to raise the prestige of the Russian intelligentsia, I assume?"

'"Not at all. We don't allow it because no respectable person should travel third—it's very nasty and messy in there."

'"Oh yes? Grateful for your concern on behalf of respectable persons, I'm sure! But nice or nasty, I haven't got five hundred roubles either way. I've never embezzled public funds, I haven't exploited any natives. I've not done any smuggling—nor have I ever flogged anyone to death. So judge for yourself—have I any right to travel first class, let alone reckon myself a member of the Russian intelligentsia?"

'But logic gets you nowhere with these people, so I'm reduced to deception. I put on a workman's coat and high boots, I assume the facial expression of a drunken brute, and off I go to the agent. "Gimme one o' them tickets, kind sir!"'

'And what might your station be in life?' asks the sailor.

'The clerical. My father was an honest priest who always told the powers that be the truth to their faces—and no little did he suffer for it.'

Paul Ivanovich is tired of speaking. He gasps for breath, but still goes on.

'Yes, I never mince my words, I fear nothing and no one—there's a vast difference between me and you in this respect. You're a blind, benighted, down-trodden lot. You see nothing—and what you do see you don't understand. People tell you the wind's broken loose from its chain—that you're cattle, savages. And you believe them. They punch you on the neck—you kiss their hand. Some animal in a racoon coat robs you, then tips you fifteen copecks—and, "Oh, let me kiss your hand, sir," say you. You're pariahs, you're a pathetic lot, but me— that's another matter. I live a conscious life, and I see everything as an eagle or hawk sees it, soaring above the earth. I understand it all. I am protest incarnate. If I see tyranny, I protest. If I see a canting hypocrite, I protest. If I see swine triumphant, I protest. I can't be put down, no Spanish Inquisition can silence me. No sir. Cut out my tongue and I'll protest in mime. Wall me up in a cellar and I'll shout so loud, I'll be heard a mile off. Or I'll starve myself to death, and leave that extra weight on their black consciences. Kill me—my ghost will still haunt you. "You're quite insufferable, Paul Ivanovich"—so say all who know me, and I glory in that reputation. I've served three years in the Far East, and I'll be remembered there for a century. I've had rows with everyone. "Don't come back," my friends write from European Russia. So I damn well will come back and show them, indeed I will. That's life, the way I see it—that's what I call living.'

Not listening, Gusev looks through the port-hole. On limpid water of delicate turquoise hue a boat tosses, bathed in blinding hot sunlight. In it stand naked Chinese, holding up cages of canaries.

'Sing, sing,' they shout.

Another boat bangs into the first, and a steam cutter dashes past. Then comes yet another boat with a fat Chinese sitting in it, eating rice with chopsticks. The water heaves lazily, with lazy white gulls gliding above it.

'That greasy one needs a good clout on the neck,' thinks Gusev, gazing at the fat Chinese and yawning.

He is dozing, and feels as if all nature is dream-bound too. Time passes swiftly. The day goes by unnoticed, unnoticed too steals on the dark.

No longer at anchor, the ship forges on to some further destination.

IV

Two days pass. Paul Ivanovich no longer sits up. He is lying down with his eyes shut, and his nose seems to have grown sharper.

'Paul Ivanovich!' Gusev shouts. 'Hey, Paul Ivanovich!'

Paul Ivanovich opens his eyes and moves his lips.

'Feeling unwell?'

'It's nothing, nothing,' gasps Paul Ivanovich in answer. 'On the contrary, I feel better, actually. I can lie down now, see? I feel easier.'

'Well, thank God for that, Paul Ivanovich.'

'Comparing myself with you poor lads, I feel sorry for you. My lungs are all right, this is only a stomach cough. I can endure hell, let alone the Red Sea. I have a critical attitude to my illness and medicines, what's more. But you—you benighted people, you have a rotten time, you really do.'

There is no motion and the sea is calm, but it is sweltering hot, like a steam bath. It was hard enough to listen, let alone speak. Gusev hugs his knees, rests his head on them and thinks of his homeland. Heavens, what joy to think about snow and cold in this stifling heat! You're sledging along, when the horses suddenly shy and bolt.

Roads, ditches, gulleys—it's all one to them. Along they hurtle like mad, right down the village, over pond, past pottery, out through open country.

'Hold him!' shout pottery hands and peasants at the top of their voices. 'Hold hard!'

But why hold? Let the keen, cold gale lash your face and bite your hands. Those clods of snow kicked up by horses' hooves—let them fall on cap, down collar, on neck and chest. Runners may squeak, traces and swingletrees snap—to hell with them! And what joy when the sledge overturns and you fly full tilt into a snowdrift, face buried in snow— then stand up, white all over, with icicles hanging from your moustache, no cap, no mittens, your belt undone.

People laugh, dogs bark.

Paul Ivanovich half opens one eye and looks at Gusev.

'Did your commanding officer steal, Gusev?' he asks softly.

'Who can tell, Paul Ivanovich? We know nothing, it don't come to our ears.'

A long silence follows. Gusev broods, rambles deliriously, keeps drinking water. He finds it hard to speak, hard to listen, and he is afraid of being talked to. One hour passes, then a second, then a third.

Evening comes on, then night, but he notices nothing, and still sits dreaming of the frost.

It sounds as if someone has come into the sick-bay, and voices are heard—but five minutes later everything is silent.

'God be with him,' says the soldier with his arm in a sling. 'May he rest in peace, he was a restless man.'

'What?' Gusev asks. 'Who?'

'He's dead, they've just carried him up.'

'Ah well,' mumbles Gusev with a yawn. 'May the Kingdom of Heaven be his.'

'What do you think, Gusev?' asks the soldier with the sling after a short pause. 'Will he go to heaven or not?'

'Who?'

'Paul Ivanovich.'

'Yes, he will—he suffered so long. And then he's from the clergy, and priests always have a lot of relations—their prayers will save him.'

The soldier with the sling sits on Gusev's bunk.

'You're not long for this world either, Gusev,' he says in an undertone. 'You'll never get to Russia.'

'Did the doctor or his assistant say so?' Gusev asks.

'It's not that anyone said so, it's just obvious—you can always tell when someone's just going to die. You don't eat, you don't drink, and you're so thin—you're a frightful sight. It's consumption, in fact. I don't say this to upset you, but you may want to have the sacrament and the last rites. And if you have any money you'd better give it to the senior officer.'

'I never wrote home,' sighs Gusev. 'They won't even know I'm dead.'

'They will,' says the sick sailor in a deep voice. 'When you're dead an entry will be made in the ship's log, they'll give a note to the Army Commander in Odessa, and he'll send a message to your parish or whatever it is.'

This talk makes Gusev uneasy, and a vague urge disturbs him. He drinks water, but that isn't it. He stretches towards the port-hole and breathes in the hot, dank air, but that isn't it either. He tries to think of home and frost—and it still isn't right.

He feels in the end that one more minute in the sick-bay will surely choke him to death.

'I'm real bad, mates,' says he. 'I'm going on deck—help me up, for Christ's sake.'

'All right,' agrees the soldier with the sling. 'You'll never do it on your own, I'll carry you. Hold on to my neck.'

Gusev puts his arms round the soldier's neck, while the soldier puts his able arm round Gusev and carries him up. Sailors and discharged soldiers are sleeping all over the place on deck—so many of them that it is hard to pass.

'Get down,' the soldier with the sling says quietly. 'Follow me slowly, hold on to my shirt.'

It is dark. There are no lights on deck or masts, or in the sea around them. Still as a statue on the tip of the bow stands the man on watch, but he too looks as if he is sleeping. Left to its own devices, apparently, the ship seems to be sailing where it lists.

'They're going to throw Paul Ivanovich in the sea now,' says the soldier with the sling. 'They'll put him in a sack and throw him in.'

'Yes. That's the way of it.'

'But it's better to lie in the earth at home. At least your mother will come and cry over your grave.'

'Very true.'

There is a smell of dung and hay. Bullocks with lowered heads are standing by the ship's rail. One, two, three—there are eight of them. There is a small pony too. Gusev puts his hand out to stroke it, but it tosses its head, bares its teeth, and tries to bite his sleeve.

'Blasted thing!' says Gusev angrily.

The two of them, he and the sailor, quietly thread their way to the bows, then stand by the rail and look up and down without a word. Overhead are deep sky, bright stars, peace, quiet—and it is just like being at home in your village. But down below are darkness and disorder. The tall waves roar for no known reason. Whichever wave you watch, each is trying to lift itself above the others, crushing them and chasing its neighbour, while on it, with a growling flash of its white mane, pounces a third roller no less wild and hideous.

The sea has no sense, no pity. Were the ship smaller, were it not made of stout iron, the waves would snap it without the slightest compunction and devour all the people, saints and sinners alike. The ship shows the same mindless cruelty. That beaked monster drives on, cutting millions of waves in her path, not fearing darkness, wind, void, solitude. She cares for nothing, and if the ocean had its people this juggernaut would crush them too, saints and sinners alike.

'Where are we now?' Gusev asks.

'I don't know. In the ocean, we must be.'

'Can't see land.'

'Some hope! We shan't see that for a week, they say.'

Silently reflecting, both soldiers watch the white foam with its phosphorescent glint. The first to break silence is Gusev.

'It ain't frightening,' says he. 'It does give you the creeps a bit, though—like sitting in a dark forest. But if they was to lower a dinghy into the water now, say, and an officer told me to go sixty miles over the sea and fish—I'd go. Or say some good Christian was to fall overboard, I'd go in after him. A German or a Chinaman I wouldn't save, but I'd go in after a Christian.'

'Are you afeared of dying?'

'Aye. It's the old home that worries me. My brother's none too steady, see? He drinks, he beats his wife when he didn't ought to, and he don't look up to his parents. It'll all go to rack and ruin without me, and my father and my old mother will have to beg for their bread, very like. But I can't rightly stand up, mate, and it's so stuffy here. Let's go to bed.'

V

Gusev goes back to the sick-bay and gets in his bunk. Some vague urge still disturbs him, but what it is he wants he just can't reckon. His chest feels tight, his head's pounding, and his mouth's so parched, he can hardly move his tongue. He dozes and rambles. Tormented by nightmares, cough and sweltering atmosphere, he falls fast asleep by morning. He dreams that they have just taken the bread out of the oven in his barracks. He has climbed into the stove himself, and is having a steam bath, lashing himself with a birch switch. He sleeps for two days. At noon on the third, two soldiers come down and carry him out of the sick-bay.

They sew him up in sail-cloth and put in two iron bars to weigh him down. Sewn in canvas, he looks like a carrot or radish—broad at the head and narrow at the base.

They carry him on deck before sundown, and place him on a plank. One end of the plank rests on the ship's rail, the other on a box set on a stool. Heads bare, discharged soldiers and crew stand by.

'Blessed is the Lord's name,' begins the priest. 'As it was in the beginning, is now, and ever shall be.'

'Amen,' chant three sailors.

Soldiers and crew cross themselves, glancing sideways at the waves.

Strange that a man has been sewn into that sail-cloth and will shortly fly into those waves. Could that really happen to any of them?

The priest scatters earth over Gusev and makes an obeisance. *Eternal Memory* is sung.

The officer of the watch tilts one end of the plank. Gusev slides down it, flies off head first, does a somersault in the air and—in he splashes! Foam envelops him, and he seems swathed in lace for a second, but the second passes and he vanishes beneath the waves.

He moves swiftly towards the bottom. Will he reach it? It is said to be three miles down. He sinks eight or nine fathoms, then begins to move more and more slowly, swaying rhythmically as if trying to make up his mind. Caught by a current, he is swept sideways more swiftly than downwards.

Now he meets a shoal of little pilot-fish. Seeing the dark body, the fish stop dead. Suddenly all turn tail at once and vanish. Less than a minute later they again pounce on Gusev like arrows and stitch the water round him with zig-zags.

Then another dark hulk looms—a shark. Ponderous, reluctant and apparently ignoring Gusev, it glides under him and he sinks on to its back. Then it turns belly upwards, basking in the warm, translucent water, and languidly opening its jaw with the two rows of fangs. The pilot-fish are delighted, waiting to see what will happen next. After playing with the body, the shark nonchalantly puts its jaws underneath, cautiously probing with its fangs, and the sail-cloth tears along the body's whole length from head to foot. One iron bar falls out, scares the pilot-fish, hits the shark on the flank and goes swiftly to the bottom.

Overhead, meanwhile, clouds are massing on the sunset side—one like a triumphal arch, another like a lion, a third like a pair of scissors.

From the clouds a broad, green shaft of light breaks through, spanning out to the sky's very centre. A little later a violet ray settles alongside, then a gold one by that, and then a pink one.

The sky turns a delicate mauve. Gazing at this sky so glorious and magical, the ocean scowls at first, but soon it too takes on tender, joyous, ardent hues for which human speech hardly has a name.

PEASANT WOMEN

Just opposite the church in the village of Raybuzh stands an iron-roofed, two-storey house with a stone foundation. The owner, Philip Kashin, also known as Dyudya, lives on the ground floor with his family, while on the upper storey—extremely hot in summer, extremely cold in winter—are lodgings for passing officials, merchants and country gentlemen. Dyudya rents plots of land, keeps a tavern on the highway, deals in tar, honey, cattle and bonnets, and has saved about eight thousand roubles which he keeps in the town bank.

His elder son Theodore is foreman mechanic in a factory—having gone up in the world, as the locals say, and left the rest of them standing. Theodore's wife Sophia, a plain woman in poor health, makes her home with her father-in-law, is always crying, and drives over to hospital for treatment every Sunday. Dyudya's second son, hunchbacked Alyoshka, lives at home with his father, and was recently married to a girl from a poor family called Barbara—a pretty young thing who enjoys the best of health and likes to dress smartly. When officials and merchants put up at the house, they always insist on Barbara serving the samovar and making their beds.

One June evening—the sun was setting and a scent of hay, warm dung and fresh milk filled the air—a plain cart with three occupants drove into Dyudya's yard. There was a man of about thirty in a sail-cloth suit sitting beside a boy of seven or eight in a long, black coat with big bone buttons, and there was a red-shirted youth as driver.

The youth unhitched the horses and walked them up and down the street, while the man washed, faced the church to say a prayer, spread out a rug by the cart, and sat down with the boy to have supper.

He ate with leisurely dignity. Having seen plenty of travellers in his day, Dyudya recognized his bearing as that of a businesslike, serious man who knows his own worth.

Dyudya sat in his porch in his waistcoat, without a cap, waiting for the traveller to speak—he was used to visitors telling various bed-time stories of an evening, and liked listening to them. His wife, old Afana-syevna, and his daughter-in-law, Sophia, were milking in the cow-shed, while Barbara—the other daughter-in-law—sat upstairs by an open window eating sunflower seeds.

'Would the little boy be your son, then?' Dyudya asked the traveller.

'No, he's adopted—an orphan. I took him in for my soul's salvation.'

They fell into conversation, and the visitor turned out a talkative man with quite a turn of phrase. From what he said Dyudya learnt that he was a local townsman of the lower sort and a householder, that he went by the name of Matthew Savvich, that he was now on his way to look at some allotments which he had rented from some German settlers, and that the boy was called Kuzka. It was a hot, stifling evening, and no one felt like sleep. When it was dark, and pale stars twinkled here and there in the sky, Matthew Savvich began telling the story of how Kuzka had come into his care. Afanasyevna and Sophia stood a little way off listening, and Kuzka went to the gate.

'It's a complicated story in the extreme, old man,' Matthew began. 'To tell you all of it would take all night and more. Ten years ago there lived in our street, in the cottage next to mine—where the chandlery and dairy now are—an old widow called Martha Kapluntsev, who had two sons. One was a railway guard. The other, Vasya, was about my age, and lived at home with his mother. Old Kapluntsev had kept horses, about five pair, and had a carting business in town. The widow carried on her husband's business, and was as good at managing her carriers as the old man, so that the carting cleared about five roubles' profit some days. The lad made a bit of money too, breeding pedigree pigeons and selling them to fanciers. He was forever standing on the roof, throwing up a broom and whistling, while his tumblers flew right up in the sky—but not high enough for him, he wanted them higher still. He caught goldfinches and starlings, and made them cages.

'It seemed a waste of time, but his time-wasting was soon bringing in ten roubles a month. Well now, in course of time the old lady loses the use of her legs and takes to her bed, for which reason the house has no woman to run it, and that's about as good as a man having no eyes! So the old lady bestirs herself and decides to get Vasya married. They call in the matchmaker at once, one thing leads to another, there's lots of women's talk, and Vasya goes to inspect the local girls. He picks on Mashenka, Widow Samokhvalikha's daughter. They're betrothed without much ado, and it's all fixed up in one week. She's a young girl of about seventeen, a small, short little thing, but fair-complexioned and attractive, with all the makings of a high-class young lady, and her dowry isn't bad—about five hundred roubles in cash, a cow and a bed. But the old lady knew what was coming, and two days after the wedding she departs for that heavenly Jerusalem where there's neither illness nor sighing. The young couple bury her and settle down. For six months everything's fine, but then disaster suddenly strikes again— it never rains but it pours. Vasya's summoned to an office for the conscription balloting, and they take him for a soldier, poor boy—won't even grant him any exemptions, but shave his head and pack him off to Poland. God's will it was, it couldn't be helped. He's all right as he says good-bye to the wife in his yard, but when he takes his last look at his pigeon-loft he weeps buckets—a sorry sight he is. At first Mashenka gets her mother to live with her to keep her company, and the mother stays on till the confinement, when this boy Kuzka is born. But then she goes to another married daughter in Oboyan, leaving Mashenka alone with her baby. There are the five carters—a drunken, rowdy crew. She has the horses and drays on her hands, besides which there's her fence falling down, or her chimney catching fire, see? It's not woman's work, so she turns to me for every little thing, since we're neighbours. I go and fix things up, give her a few tips.

'Well, of course, all this means going indoors, having tea and a chat. I'm a young chap—a bit brainy, like, fond of talking about this and that—and she's a cultured, polite girl too. She dresses nicely and carries a parasol in summer. I'll start talking religion or politics, which flatters her and she'll give me tea and jam.

'In fact, old man, to cut a long story short, within a twelve-month the devil, the adversary of mankind, has me in a proper muddle, I can tell you. I notice that if I don't go and see her, I never feel right that day—I'm bored. And I keep thinking of excuses to call.

'"It's time to put in your window-frames for winter," I say. And I hang around all day with her—putting in her frames, but taking care to leave a couple over for next day.

'"I'd better count Vasya's pigeons," I say, "and see that none of them gets lost"—and so on.

'I keep talking to her over the fence, and end by making a little gate in it as a short cut. There's a lot of evil and nastiness in this world from the female sex—even saints have been led astray, let alone us sinners. Mashenka doesn't keep me at arm's length, and instead of thinking of her husband and keeping herself for him, she falls in love with me. I begin noticing that she misses me too, and is always walking near the fence and looking into my yard through the cracks. My mind reels at the thought of her. Early one morning, at dawn on a Thursday in Easter Week, I'm going past her gate on my way to market when up pops the Evil One. I look through the trellis thing at the top of her gate, and there she is—already awake and feeding her ducks in the middle of the yard. I can't resist calling her. She comes and looks at me through the trellis, her little face all pale, her eyes soft and sleepy-looking.

'I find her very attractive and begin complimenting her, like as if we were at a party instead of standing by that gate, while she blushes, laughs and looks me straight in the eye without blinking. I lose all sense and begin declaring my amorous feelings.

'She opens the gate to let me in, and we live together as man and wife from that morning on.'

Hunchbacked Alyoshka came into the yard from the street, and ran gasping into the house without looking at anyone. A minute later he ran out of doors again with his accordion and vanished through the gate, jingling copper coins in his pocket and cracking sunflower seeds on his way.

'Who's that?' asked Matthew Savvich.

'It's my son Alyoshka,' answered Dyudya. 'The rascal's off on a spree. He's a hunchback, God having afflicted him that way, so we don't ask much of him.'

'He's always with the lads, always having his bit of fun,' sighed Afanasyevna. 'We married him off just before Shrovetide, and thought he'd improve—but he's even worse, I do declare.'

'It didn't work out,' Dyudya said. 'We only made a strange girl's fortune when we didn't need to.'

Beyond the church someone began singing a magnificent, sad song. The words were inaudible, and only the voices could be heard—two tenors and a bass. While everyone listened, the yard grew as quiet as can be.

Two of the singers suddenly broke off with a peal of laughter, but the third—a tenor—went on singing, taking so high a note that all felt impelled to gaze upwards as if the voice had reached the very height of heaven. Barbara came out of doors and looked at the church, shading her eyes with her hand as if blinded by sunlight.

'It's the priest's sons and the schoolmaster,' she said.

The three voices once more sang in unison. Matthew Savvich sighed.

'Well, that's the way of it, old man,' he went on. 'Two years later we get a letter from Vasya in Warsaw. He's being invalided out of the army, he writes—he isn't well. By this time I've banished all that nonsense from my head, and arrangements are under way to marry me to a decent young woman, but what I don't know is how to be rid of this wretched love affair. I make up my mind to speak to Mashenka every day, but I don't know how I can do it without a lot of female squawking. The letter frees my hands. Mashenka and I read it together, and she turns white as a sheet.

'"Thank God," says I. "This means you can be an honest woman again."

'"I won't live with him," she tells me.

'"He's your husband, ain't he?" says I.

'"It ain't so simple. I never loved him—I married him against my will because Mother made me."

'"Now don't try and wriggle out of it, you little fool," I say. "Just tell me this—were you married in church or weren't you?"

'"Yes I was," says she. "But it's you I love, and I'll live with you till my dying day. People may laugh at me, but I don't care."

'"You're a God-fearing woman," say I. "You've read what the Scripture says, haven't you?"'

'If she's married, she should cleave to her husband,' said Dyudya.

'Yes, husband and wife are one flesh.

'"You and I have sinned," I tell her, "and we must stop. We must repent and fear God. Let's beg Vasya's pardon," say I. "He's a quiet, mild fellow—he won't kill us. And it's better," I say, "to suffer agonies from a lawful husband in this world than gnash your teeth on the Day of Judgement."

'The woman won't listen, she's set on having her own way, and takes no notice.

'"I love you," says she, and that was that.

'Vasya arrives home on the Saturday before Trinity Sunday, early in the morning—I can see everything through the fence. He runs into the house, and comes out a minute later with Kuzka in his arms, laughing and crying. He kisses Kuzka and looks at his pigeon loft—he wants to go to his pigeons, but hasn't the heart to put Kuzka down. A soft, sentimental sort of fellow, he was. The day passes off all right, quietly and uneventfully. The bells are rung for evening service.

'"Tomorrow's Trinity Sunday," I think. "So why don't they decorate their gate and fence with green boughs? Something's wrong," thinks I.

'So I go over. I look, and there he is sitting on the floor in the middle of the room, rolling his eyes as if he was drunk, with tears streaming down his cheeks and his hands trembling. He takes some cracknels, necklaces, gingerbread and various sweets out of his bundle, and throws them all over the floor. Kuzka, about three years old at the time, crawls around munching gingerbread, while Mashenka stands by the stove, pale and shuddering.

'"I'm no wife to you, I don't want to live with you," she mutters, and all sorts of silly rubbish.

'I bow low to Vasya.

'"We have done you wrong, Vasya," I say. "Forgive us, for Christ's sake!"

'Then I get up and speak to Mashenka.

'"You, Mashenka, must now wash Vasya's feet and drink the dirty water. Be his obedient wife, and pray God for me that He may forgive my transgressions in His mercy."

'As if inspired by an angel in heaven, I read her a lecture and speak with such feeling that I actually break down and cry. Well, two days later Vasya comes to see me.

'"I'll forgive you, Matthew, and forgive my wife too," he says. "God help you both. She's a soldier's wife, it's a common way of behaving for a young female, it's hard to keep yourself to yourself. She ain't the first and she won't be the last. The only thing is," says he, "I ask you to act as if there had never been anything between you—don't let on. And I," says he, "will try to please her every way I can, so she'll love me again."

'He shakes hands with me, has some tea and goes away looking happy. Well, thinks I, thank God for that, and I'm glad it's all turned out so well. But no sooner is Vasya out of my yard than in comes Mashenka—something terrible, it was. She hangs on my neck, crying.

'"Don't leave me, for Christ's sake," she begs. "I can't live without you."'

'The shameless hussy!' sighed Dyudya.

'I shout at her, I stamp my feet, I drag her out in the lobby, and I put the door on the latch.

'"Go to your husband," I shout. "Don't shame me in public. Have some fear of God in your heart."

'So it goes on every day. One morning I'm standing in my yard by the stable, mending a bridle, and suddenly I see her run in through the gate, barefoot, just as she was in her petticoat, coming straight towards me. She picks up the bridle and gets tar all over her, trembling and crying.

'"I can't live with that hateful creature, I can't bear it. If you don't love me, kill me."

'I get angry and hit her twice with the bridle, and meanwhile Vasya runs in through the gate.

'"Don't hit her, don't hit her!" he shouts, quite frantic.

'But he runs up himself and lashes out like a maniac, punching her with all his might, then throws her on the ground and starts kicking her. I try to protect her, but he picks up the reins and goes for her with those. And all the time he's thrashing her, he's squealing and whinnying like a foal.'

'I'd give you reins if I had my way!' muttered Barbara, moving off. 'Torturing us women, you rotten swine!'

'Shut up, bitch!' shouted Dyudya.

'Squealing away he was,' Matthew Savvich went on. 'One of the carters runs out of his yard, I call my own workman, and the three of us take Mashenka away from him and lead her home by the arms. Disgraceful, it was! That evening I go along to see how she is, and she's lying in bed all wrapped up with fomentations on her. Only her eyes and nose can be seen, and she's looking at the ceiling.

'"Hello, Mashenka," I say. No answer.

'Vasya's sitting in the next room clutching his head.

'"I'm a wicked man, I've ruined my life!" he weeps. "Let me die, O Lord!"

'I sit with Mashenka for half an hour and read her a lecture—put the fear of God into her.

'"The righteous will go to heaven in the next world," say I. "But you'll go into the fiery Gehenna along with all the other whores. Don't disobey your husband—down on your knees to him!"

'But not a word does she answer, she doesn't even wink an eye—I might have been talking to a stone. Next day Vasya sickens with something like cholera, and by evening I hear he's dead. They bury him.

'Not wanting to show people her shameless face and bruises, Mashenka doesn't go to the cemetery. And soon the rumour spreads among the townsfolk that Vasya's death wasn't natural, and that Mashenka did him in. The story reaches the authorities, who dig up Vasya, slit his guts and find arsenic in his belly—an open and shut case, it was. The police come and take Mashenka away together with that little innocent Kuzka, and put them in prison. That's where her flighty ways got her, it was punishment from God.

'They tried her eight months later. I remember her sitting in the dock wearing a white kerchief and grey prison coat. She was thin, pale, sharp-eyed—a pathetic sight. Behind her was a soldier with a gun. She wouldn't plead not guilty. There were some in court who said she'd poisoned her husband, while others argued that her husband had taken the poison himself in his grief. I was one witness. When they cross-examined me, I told the whole truth.

'"She done it, the sinful creature," said I. "She didn't love her husband, you can't get away from it—and she was used to having her own way."

'They began the trial in the morning, and that night they sentenced her to thirteen years' hard labour in Siberia. After the sentence, Mashenka was in the local prison for three months, and I used to go and see her—take her tea and sugar out of common humanity. But when she sees me she trembles all over and throws her arms about.

'"Go away," she mutters. "Go away!"

'And she clasps Kuzka to her as if afraid I might take him off her.

'"Now," I say, "see what you've sunk to! Oh Mashenka, Mashenka, you lost soul! You wouldn't listen when I tried to talk sense into you, and now you must pay for it. It's your fault," say I, "you've only yourself to blame."

'I read her a lecture, and she keeps telling me to go away, go away, huddling against the wall with Kuzka and shivering. When they're taking her to our county town, I go to see her off at the railway station and slip a rouble in her bundle to save my soul. But she never got to Siberia—she fell sick of a fever in the county town and died in gaol.'

'Serve the bitch right!' said Dyudya.

'They brought Kuzka back home. I thought it over, and decided to adopt him. And why not? Gaol-bird's spawn he may be—still he's a living soul, a Christian. I felt sorry for him. I'll make him a clerk, and if I don't have children of my own I'll make him a merchant. Nowadays I take him with me wherever I go, so he can learn something.'

All the time while Matthew Savvich was telling his story, Kuzka sat on a stone near the gate, his head cupped in his hands, and looking at the sky. In the darkness he looked like a tree-stump from a distance.

'Go to bed, Kuzka,' Matthew Savvich yelled.

'Yes, it's time,' said Dyudya, getting up and yawning noisily. 'They all try to be too clever,' he added. 'They won't listen, and then they end up getting what they asked for.'

The moon was already sailing in the sky above the yard. It was moving swiftly to one side, while the clouds below it sped the other way. The clouds drifted off, but the moon was still clearly seen above the yard. Matthew Savvich turned towards the church and prayed, then wished them good night and lay down on the ground near the cart. Kuzka also said his prayers, then lay in the cart, covering himself with his coat. To make himself comfortable, he burrowed in the hay, curling up with his elbows touching his knees. From the yard Dyudya could be seen lighting a candle in a downstairs room, putting on his spectacles, and standing in the corner with a book. For a long time he read, bowing before the icon.

The visitors fell asleep. Afanasyevna and Sophia went up to the cart and looked at Kuzka.

'He's asleep, poor little orphan,' the old woman said. 'He's thin and pale, nothing but skin and bones. He has no mother, and no one to feed him properly.'

'My Grishutka's two years older, I reckon,' Sophia said. 'He's no better than a slave, living in that factory without his mother. The master beats him, I'll warrant. When I looked at this little boy just now, I remembered Grishutka, and it made my blood turn cold.'

A minute passed in silence.

'He won't remember his mother, I reckon,' said the old woman. 'How could he?'

Huge tears flowed from Sophia's eyes.

'He's curled up like a kitten,' she said, sobbing and laughing with tender pity. 'Poor little orphan.'

Kuzka started, and opened his eyes. He saw an ugly, wrinkled, tear-stained face before him, and next to it another, an old woman's—toothless, sharp-chinned, hook-nosed. Above was the fathomless sky with its racing clouds and moon. He screamed in terror, and Sophia screamed too. Echo answered both of them, and their alarm flashed through the stifling air. A neighbouring watchman started banging, and a dog barked. Matthew Savvich muttered in his sleep, and turned over.

Late at night, when Dyudya, the old woman and the watchman next door were all asleep, Sophia went out through the gate and sat on a bench. The heat was stifling, and her head ached from crying. Broad and long—with two verst-posts visible on the right, and another two on the left—the street seemed to go on for ever. The moon had abandoned the yard to stand behind the church, and one side of the street was bathed in moonlight, while the other was black with shadows. The long shadows of poplars and starling-cotes spanned the entire street, and the church's shadow, black and menacing, lay in a broad band, clasping Dyudya's gate and half his house. There was no one about and it was quiet. From time to time faint strains of music were wafted from the end of the street—Alyoshka playing his accordion, no doubt.

In the shadow near the church fence someone was walking. Was it man or cow—or no more than a large bird rustling in the trees? One could not tell. Then a figure emerged from the shadows, paused, said something in a man's voice and vanished down the church lane. A little later another figure appeared about five yards from the gate. This person was moving straight to the gate from the church, and stopped still on seeing Sophia on the bench.

'Is that you, Barbara?' Sophia asked.

'What if it is?'

Barbara it was. She stood still for a minute, then came and sat on the bench.

'Where have you been?' asked Sophia.

Barbara made no answer.

'You mind you don't get into trouble,' Sophia said. 'Playing around like this, and you only just married. Did you hear how they kicked Mashenka and whipped her with the reins? You mind that don't happen to you.'

'I don't care.'

Barbara laughed into her handkerchief.

'I've been having a bit of fun with the priest's son,' she whispered.

'You don't mean it!'

'It's God's truth.'

'That's a sin,' Sophia whispered.

'Who cares? Why bother? Sin or no sin, I'd rather be struck by lightning than live this way. I'm young and healthy, and I have a hunchbacked husband that I can't abide—he's that pig-headed, he's worse than that blasted Dyudya. I never had enough to eat as a girl, and I went barefoot. To escape such misery I took the bait of Alyoshka's money, and became a slave. I was caught like a rat in a trap, and now I'd rather sleep with a viper than with that rotten Alyoshka. And your life too—it don't bear thinking of! Your Theodore threw you out of the factory—sent you to his father's—and took up with another woman. They took your boy off you and made a slave out of him. You work like a horse, and never hear a kind word. Better pine away as an old maid all your life, better take your half-roubles from the priest's sons, better go begging, better throw yourself head first down a well——'

'That's a sin,' Sophia whispered again.

'Who cares?'

Somewhere beyond the church the same three voices—the two tenors and the bass—started another sad song. Once again the words were inaudible.

'They're making quite a night of it,' Barbara laughed.

She began whispering about the fun she was having with the priest's son of a night—what he said, what his friends were like, and about how she also carried on with officials and merchants who stayed at the house. The sad song bore a whiff of freedom, and Sophia began laughing. It was all very sinful and frightening and sweet to the ear. She envied Barbara, sorry that she hadn't sinned herself when she was young and beautiful.

Midnight struck in the old church by the cemetery.

'We'd better go to bed, or else Dyudya may miss us,' said Sophia, getting up.

Both went quietly into the yard.

'I went away and missed the end of his story about Mashenka,' said Barbara, making her bed under the window.

'She died in gaol, he said. She'd poisoned her husband.'

Barbara lay down by Sophia and thought for a moment.

'I could kill Alyoshka,' she said. 'I'd think nothing of it.'

'You don't mean that, God help you.'

As Sophia was dropping off, Barbara huddled up to her.

'Let's do away with Dyudya and Alyoshka,' she whispered in her ear.

Sophia shuddered and said nothing, then opened her eyes and stared at the sky for a long time without winking.

'They'd find out,' she said.

'No, they wouldn't. Dyudya's an old man, he's not long for this world. And they'll say Alyoshka died of drink.'

'I'm afraid—. God would strike us dead.'

'Who cares?'

Both lay awake, silently thinking.

'It's cold,' said Sophia, shivering all over. 'It'll soon be morning, I reckon. Are you asleep?'

'No. Don't take any notice of me, dear,' whispered Barbara. 'I'm so angry with them swine, I don't know what I'm saying. Go to sleep, it's nearly daylight. Sleep.'

Both were silent. They calmed down and soon fell asleep.

The old woman was the first to wake up. She woke Sophia, and they both went to the shed to milk the cows. Hunchbacked Alyoshka walked in, dead drunk, without his accordion, his chest and knees covered with dust and straw—so he must have fallen down on the way. He staggered into the shed, flopped on to a sledge without undressing, and started snoring at once. When the crosses on the church, and then the windows, were blazing in the bright flame of the rising sun, and the shadows from trees and well-sweep spanned the dewy grass of the yard, Matthew Savvich jumped up and bestirred himself.

'Get up, Kuzka!' he shouted. 'Time to harness up! Look slippy there!'

The morning's bustle began. A young Jewish woman in a flounced brown dress led a horse into the yard to water it. The pulley of the well creaked piteously, the pail rattled.

Sleepy, listless, covered with dew, Kuzka sat in the cart, lazily putting on his coat, listening to water splashing out of the pail in the well, and shivering with cold.

'Give my lad a nudge, missus, so he'll go and harness up,' shouted Matthew Savvich to Sophia.

Then Dyudya yelled from a window. 'Sophia, charge that woman a copeck for watering her horse. They're always doing that, the Jewish scum.'

In the street sheep were running to and fro, bleating. Women shouted at the shepherd, who played his pipe, cracked his whip, or answered them in a heavy, rough, deep voice. Three sheep ran into the yard, couldn't find the gate, butted the fence—and the noise woke Barbara, who seized her bedding in both arms and made for the house.

'You might have driven the sheep out,' the old woman shouted at her. 'You're too high and mighty, I suppose!'

'There she goes again—why should I work for such monsters?' muttered Barbara as she went indoors.

The cart was greased, the horses harnessed. Dyudya came out of the house carrying an abacus, and sat in the porch working out what to charge the visitor for his night's lodging, oats and water.

'That's a lot for oats, old man,' said Matthew Savvich.

'Then don't take them. No one's forcing you, Mister Merchant.'

Just as the travellers were going to get in the cart and leave, something held them up for a moment—Kuzka had lost his cap.

'Where did you put it, you little swine?' Matthew Savvich roared angrily. 'Where is it?'

Kuzka's face was contorted with terror as he rushed this way and

that near the cart. Not finding it there, he ran to the gate, then to the
cowshed. The old woman and Sophia helped him look.

'I'll tear your ears off!' shouted Matthew Savvich. 'Little bleeder!'

The cap was found at the bottom of the cart. Brushing off the hay
with his sleeves, Kuzka put it on and mounted the cart—nervously,
still looking terrified, as if fearing to be struck from behind. Matthew
Savvich crossed himself, the lad tugged the reins. The cart moved off
and rolled out of the yard.

OLD Simon—or 'Foxy', as he was called—and a young Tatar whose name no one knew, were sitting by a bonfire on the river bank, and the other three ferrymen were inside the hut. Simon was an old fellow of about sixty, lean and toothless, but broad-shouldered and still husky, from the look of him. He was drunk and would have gone off to sleep long ago but for the pint bottle of vodka in his pocket—he was afraid of his hut-mates asking for a swig. The Tatar was ill and depressed. He wrapped his rags around him, saying how good life had been in Simbirsk Province and what a beautiful, clever wife he had left behind. He was about twenty-five at most. Pale, ill-looking, sad-faced, he seemed no more than a boy in the firelight.

'Now, this ain't no heaven on earth, I grant you,' said Foxy. 'There's just water, see? There's bare banks, there's clay everywhere, and that's all. It's long past Easter, but the ice is still coming down river and it snowed this morning.'

'This bad, bad place,' said the Tatar, casting a fearful glance around him.

Some ten paces away the dark, cold river flowed, grumbling, lapping the rutted clay bank, sweeping swiftly on to the distant sea. Just by the bank loomed the dark hulk of the big boat which the ferry-men called their barge. Far away on the opposite bank lights snaked, now dimming, now flickering as last year's grass was burnt. Beyond the snakes was yet more blackness. Small chunks of ice rapped the barge. It was damp and cold.

The Tatar looked at the sky. There were as many stars as at home, there was the same blackness everywhere, but something was missing. The stars were quite different at home in Simbirsk Province, and so was the sky.

'This bad, bad place,' he repeated.

'You'll settle down,' said Foxy with a laugh. 'You're young and stupid yet, you ain't dry behind the ears, like, and you're daft enough to think you're the unluckiest man on earth. In time, though, you'll say it's a great life, this. Take me, for instance. We'll have clear water in a week and we'll get the other ferry-boat started. The rest of you'll be tramping Siberia, but I'll stay here and ply from one bank to the other. Twenty-two years I've been at it, day and night. There's pike down in the water and our local salmon, but I'm above water, praise the Lord. I don't need nothing. It's a great life, this is.'

The Tatar put some wood on the fire and lay down closer to the heat.

'My father sick man,' he said. 'When he die my mother and wife come here. They promise.'

'What do you need with mother and wife?' asked Foxy. 'That's all daft, mate, it's the devil befuddling you, damn his black soul. Don't you heed the bastard, don't you give in to him. If it's your woman he's on about, you do him down—you don't want her, say. If it's freedom, don't you give way—you don't want any, say. You don't need anything: no father, no mother, no wife, no freedom, no homestead, no nothing. You don't need a thing, blast their rotten souls!'

Foxy took a swig from his bottle.

'I ain't just another yokel, mate,' he went on. 'I ain't a bumpkin, like. I'm a verger's son, I am. When I lived in Kursk before losing my freedom I wore a frock-coat, but now I've trained myself to sleep uncovered on the ground and eat grass. Oh, it's a great life, this is. I need nothing, I fear nobody. The way I see it, I'm the richest man on earth, and the freest. When they sent me here from European Russia I dug my heels in on the first day. I don't want nothing, says I. The devil's on at me about a wife, a family, my freedom, but I don't want nothing, I tell him. I stood firm and now I'm all right, see, I ain't got no complaints. But the man that gives way to the devil and heeds him but once—he's a goner, there's no saving him. Up to his neck in the bog he'll stick and he'll never get out. And it ain't just us stupid peasants that comes a cropper, it's gentry too and educated folk.

'Fifteen years ago a certain squire was sent out here to Siberia. There was some property quarrel with his brothers back there, he forged a will or something. They did say he was a titled gentleman, like, but maybe he was just an official. Who cares? Well, the squire turns up here and the first thing he does, he buys a house and land in Mukhortinskoye.

'"I want to earn my own living," says he, "in the sweat of my face, seeing as how I'm a gentleman no more, but an exile."

'"All right," says I, "and good luck to you. It's a good idea, that is."

'He was young then. Very spry he was and always on the go. He did his own reaping, he fished and he'd ride his horse forty mile. The trouble was, though, that from his first year he begins going over to Gyrino, to the post office. He'll stand on my ferryboat.

'"Oh, Simon," he'll sigh, "it's quite a time since they sent me money from home."

'"You don't need money, Mr. Vasily," says I. "What good is it? You drop that old stuff, forget it. You put it from your mind as if it was all a dream, like, and start a new life."

'Don't you heed the devil, I tell him. He'll do you no good, he'll put a noose round you. Now it's money you're after, says I, but a bit later it'll be something else, see? And then something else again. If you want to be happy, says I, then the main thing is—don't have no wants. Yes, indeed. If fate's played us a rotten trick, you and me, there's no call to beg for mercy, says I, and crawl on our bellies, we should despise it, laugh at it, or else fate will have the last laugh, and I tell him so.

'About two years later I ferry him over here, and he's rubbing his hands and laughing.

'"I'm off to Gyrino to meet my wife," says he. "She's taken pity on me and come out," he says. "She's a good woman, very kind."

'Fair panting with joy, he was. Then, a day later, back he comes with this wife. She's a beautiful young lady with a little hat on and she has a little baby girl in her arms. And there's all sorts of baggage. My Mr. Vasily is dancing around her, he can't take his eyes off her, he can't— he fair dotes on her.

'"Yes, Simon old man, life's not so bad even in Siberia."

'All right, thinks I, but you'll have no joy of it.

'After that he was off to Gyrino every week, I reckon, to see if any money had come from home. Oh, he needed a mint of money.

'"She has sacrificed her youth and beauty for me out here in Siberia," says he. "She's sharing my wretched lot and so I'm bound to do what I can to please her."

'To keep his lady amused he meets up with officials and various riff-raff. But of course he has to feed that lot and give them their drink, then there has to be a piano, like, and some fluffy little dog on the sofa, rot its guts!

'It was all extravagance, in other words, sheer self-indulgence. His lady didn't stay long either. What else could you expect, what with the clay, the water, the cold, not a vegetable nor a fruit to be had, drunken boors all around, no proper manners—and her a spoilt lady from the metropolis, like? No wonder she took it bad. And, say what you like, her husband was a squire no longer, but an exile, and a bit of a come-down that made!

'Three years later, I recall, about the middle of August, there was shouting from the other side. I take the ferry over, and there's the lady all wrapped up, and with her a young gent, an official. They've come in a troika.

'I ferry them over, they get in their carriage and make themselves scarce. Gone without trace, they had. Towards morning up gallops Mr. Vasily with his carriage and pair.

'"Simon," he asks, "has my wife driven past with a gentleman in spectacles?"

'"She has that," says I, "and they've vanished into thin air."

'Off he gallops after them, and he chases them five days and nights. When I take him back to the other side later he flops down in the ferry and starts banging his head on the boards and yelling.

'"I told you so," says I with a laugh. "Life ain't so bad, even in Siberia," I reminds him. But he only bangs his head the harder.

'Then he wanted his freedom. His wife had made for European Russia, so he felt he must go there to see her and get her away from her lover. And believe me, mate, he took to galloping off to the post office or town authorities practically every day. He kept putting in for a pardon and applying to be sent home—he reckoned he'd spent a couple of hundred roubles on telegrams alone. He sold his land, he mortgaged his house to the Jews. He grew grey and bent, and yellow-complexioned, like as if he had consumption. He talks to you and all the time he's coughing and choking, and there's tears in his eyes. Eight years he spent traipsing to and fro with his applications, but now he's bucked up again and become cheerful. He's off on a new lark now. His daughter's grown up, see, and she's the very apple of his eye, like. And she ain't bad, I give her that, a pretty little thing with black eyebrows, and high-spirited with it. Every Sunday he drives her to church in Gyrino. They stand on the ferry side by side, her laughing and him feasting his eyes on her.

'"Yes, Simon," says he, "life ain't so bad, even in Siberia. Even in Siberia you can be happy. See what a fine daughter I have," says he. "You won't find her like within a thousand mile, I reckon."

'"Your daughter's all right," says I, and that's true enough.

'But just you wait, thinks I to myself. She's a young girl, she's hot-blooded, she wants a bit of fun—and what kind of life is there here? And then she began pining away, mate. She withered and withered and wasted right away, she fell sick and now she's bed-ridden. It's the consumption. There's your Siberian happiness, rot it, there's your life ain't so bad even in Siberia for you! He keeps visiting all the doctors and bringing them to his house. When he hears of a doctor or quack within a couple of hundred mile, he'll go and see him. He's spent a fortune on doctors, but he might as well have spent it on drink if you ask me. She'll die anyway. She'll die as sure as sure can be, and then he really *is* done for. He'll either hang himself in his misery or he'll try to escape, and we know what that means: he'll run for it, he'll be caught, he'll be tried, he'll get hard labour and a taste of the lash.'

'Good, good,' muttered the Tatar, hugging himself in fever.

'What's good?' asked Foxy.

'Wife and daughter. Never mind prison, never mind misery—he has seen wife and daughter. You say you don't need nothing. But not need nothing is bad. His wife live with him three years, God gave him that. Nothingness is bad, but three years is good. Why you not understand?'

Shivering, straining as he chose the Russian words of which he knew so few, stuttering, the Tatar said he hoped that God would save him from falling ill in foreign parts, from dying and being buried in the cold, rusty earth. If his wife visited him for but a single day, for a single hour, even . . . to gain such happiness he said he would accept any tortures whatever and would thank God for them. Better one day's happiness than nothing.

He spoke once more of the beautiful, clever wife he had left at home. Then he clutched his head in both hands, burst into tears, and began telling Simon that he was innocent and was suffering unjustly. His two brothers and his uncle had stolen a peasant's horses and had nearly beaten the old man to death, but the community court had judged dishonestly, sentencing all three brothers to Siberia while their rich uncle stayed at home.

'You'll settle down,' said Simon.

The Tatar was silent, staring at the fire with tears in his eyes. He looked baffled and scared as if he still couldn't see why he should be among strangers in this dark, damp place instead of in Simbirsk Province. Foxy lay down near the fire, gave a laugh and started humming a song.

'How can she be happy with her father?' he said a little later. 'He loves her, she's a comfort to him—granted. But he's an ugly customer too, mate, he's strict and hard, that old man is. But strictness ain't for young girls. Cuddles, giggles, titters, scent and pomade—that's more their line. Yes, indeed.

'Oh, what a business,' sighed Simon and stood up heavily. 'The vodka's finished, so it's time for bed, eh? I'm off, mate.'

Now alone, the Tatar put on more wood, lay down, looked at the fire and began thinking of his native village, of his wife. If only she would come out for a month, or just for one day. Then let her go home again if she liked. Better a month, or just a day, than nothing. But supposing his wife did keep her word and come out, how would he feed her? Where would she live here?

'If there's no food, how she live?' the Tatar asked aloud.

For plying an oar here right round the clock he was paid only ten copecks a day. Travellers did give tips, true, but the other lads shared this tea and vodka money among themselves. They gave the Tatar nothing, they only laughed at him. Being destitute, he was also famished, frozen and frightened. Now that his whole body ached and shook he should go in the hut and sleep there, but he had nothing to put over him and it was colder in there than out on the bank. Here too there was nothing to cover up with, but he could at least make up the fire.

In a week's time the water would fall and they would launch the smaller ferry-boat. Then none of the ferrymen would be needed except Simon, and the Tatar would start tramping from village to village, begging alms and work. His wife was only seventeen, a beautiful, spoilt, shy girl. Could she really trudge round the villages begging, with her face unveiled? No, the very thought was terrifying.

Dawn was breaking. Barge, willow-clumps in the water, ripples . . . all showed clearly, and if you looked the other way there was a clay cliff with a little brown-thatched hovel at the bottom and the village huts clinging higher up. The village cocks crowed.

Reddish clay cliff, barge, river, unkind strangers, hunger, cold, illness . . . perhaps none of it was real. It was probably all a dream, the Tatar thought. He sensed that he was asleep and heard himself snore. Ah, of course—he was back home in Simbirsk Province, he had but to call his wife's name for her to answer and his mother was in the next room. But how frightening some dreams can be! What are they for? The Tatar smiled and opened his eyes. What river was this? The Volga?

It was snowing.

'Hey, let's be having you!' someone bellowed on the other side. 'Ba-a-arge!'

The Tatar came to and went to rouse his comrades so that they could cross the river. Donning their tattered sheepskins as they went, half-asleep, swearing hoarsely, hunched in the cold, the ferrymen appeared on the bank. Woken from sleep, they found the river's piercing, frozen breath repulsive and unnerving. They took their time about jumping into the barge. The Tatar and three other rowers seized the long, broad-bladed oars which seemed like crayfish claws in the dark. Simon thrust his belly against the long rudder, while shouting continued on the far side and they twice fired a revolver—thinking the ferrymen asleep, most likely, or gone to the local pub.

'All right, there's no hurry.' Foxy spoke as one convinced that there is time for everything in this world. Not that there's any point in any of it, either, he seemed to say.

Detaching itself from the shore, the heavy, clumsy barge glided between willow-clumps, and only the slowly retreating willow showed that it was in motion at all. The ferrymen plied their oars in measured unison while Foxy laid his belly on the rudder, flitting from one side to the other and describing an arc in the air. In the darkness they seemed to be mounted on some long-pawed prehistoric beast as they floated off to that cold, dismal clime which sometimes figures in one's worst dreams.

Leaving the willow behind, they came out into open river. Those on the far shore could now hear the slap and measured plashing of oars, and shouted to them to get a move on. Ten minutes later the barge bumped heavily into a jetty.

'Will it ever, ever stop snowing?' muttered Simon, wiping snow off his face. 'Lord alone knows where it all comes from.'

On the bank a short, thin old man was waiting. He wore a short fox-fur coat and a white astrakhan cap, and stood quite still some way from his horses with a grim, tense look, as if trying to recall something and annoyed with his faulty memory. Simon went up to him and smilingly doffed his cap.

'I must get to Anastasyevka quickly,' the old man said. 'My daughter's worse again and I'm told they have a new doctor there.'

They lugged his four-wheeler on to the barge and set off back. During the crossing the man whom Simon called Mr. Vasily stood quite still, firmly pursing his thick lips and staring at one spot. When his driver asked permission to smoke he gave no answer and seemed not to have heard. Lying belly-forward on the rudder, Simon looked at him derisively.

'Things ain't so bad, even in Siberia,' said he. 'It's a life of sorts.'

Foxy looked triumphant, as if he had just scored a point, and he seemed glad that things had turned out just as he had expected. The wretched, helpless look of the man in the fox coat gave him great pleasure, that was obvious.

'It's dirty travelling now, Mr. Vasily,' he said after they had harnessed the horses on the bank. 'You should have waited a couple of weeks for drier weather. Or, better still, you should have stayed at home altogether. It's not as if there was any point your going. As you well know, sir, people have been travelling day in day out for donkeys' years, but no good ever came of it, believe you me.'

Vasily tipped him silently, climbed into his carriage and drove off.

'He's off to fetch a doctor, see?' said Simon, doubled up with cold. 'But looking for a proper doctor round here . . . it's like looking for a needle in a haystack. Oh, it's a real wild-goose chase, that is, may you rot in hell! People are funny, Lord forgive me, sinner that I am.'

The Tatar went up to Foxy and looked at him with loathing and disgust.

'Him good, good. You bad,' he said, shivering and mixing Tatar words with his broken Russian. 'You bad. Squire him good soul, him fine man, but you wild beast, you bad. Squire alive, you dead. God made man to be alive, to have joy and grief and sorrow, but you not want anything. So you not alive—you stone, you clay! Stone need nothing, you need nothing.

'You stone. God not love you, God love squire.'

Everyone laughed. The Tatar frowned squeamishly, made an impatient gesture, gathered his rags around him and went to the fire. Simon and the ferrymen trudged off to the hut.

'It's cold,' wheezed one man, stretching himself on the straw laid on the damp clay floor.

'Well, it ain't warm,' another agreed. 'Oh, it's a dog's life, this is.'

All lay down. The door blew open and snow drifted in, but no one felt like getting up and closing the door. It was cold and they couldn't bother.

'I feel fine,' said Simon as he fell asleep. 'It's a great life, this.'

'You're a real old lag, we all know that. The devils wouldn't have you in hell, they wouldn't.'

From outside came noises like a hound's baying.

'What's that? Who's there?'

'The Tatar's crying.'

'Is he now? He's an odd one.'

'He'll settle down,' said Simon and fell straight asleep.

Soon the others too fell asleep and the door just stayed open.

It was a small town, more wretched than a village, and almost all the inhabitants were old folk with a depressingly low death rate. Nor were many coffins required at the hospital and gaol. In a word, business was bad. Had Jacob Ivanov been making coffins in a county town he would probably have owned a house and been called 'mister'. But in this dump he was plain Jacob, his street nickname was 'Bronze' for whatever reason, and he lived as miserably as any farm labourer in his little old one-roomed shack which housed himself, his Martha, a stove, a double bed, coffins, his work-bench and all his household goods.

Jacob made good solid coffins. For men—village and working-class folk—he made them to his own height, and never got them wrong because he was taller and stronger than anyone, even in the gaol, though now seventy years old. For the gentry, though, and for women he made them to measure, using an iron ruler. He was not at all keen on orders for children's coffins, which he would knock up contempt-uously without measuring. And when paid for them he would say that he 'quite frankly set no store by such trifles'.

His fiddle brought him a small income on top of his trade. A Jewish band usually played at weddings in the town, conducted by the tinker Moses Shakhkes who took more than half the proceeds. And since Jacob was a fine fiddler, especially with Russian folk tunes, Shakhkes sometimes asked him to join the band for fifty copecks a day plus tips. Straight away it made his face sweat and turn crimson, did sitting in the band. It was hot, there was a stifling smell of garlic, his fiddle squeaked. By his right ear wheezed the double-bass, by his left sobbed the flute played by a red-haired, emaciated Jew with a network of red and blue veins on his face. He was known as Rothschild after the noted millionaire. Now, this bloody little Jew even contrived to play the merriest tunes in lachrymose style. For no obvious reason Jacob became more and more obsessed by hatred and contempt for Jews, and for Rothschild in particular. He started picking on him and swearing at him. Once he made to beat him, whereat Rothschild took umbrage.

'I respect your talent, otherwise I am long ago throwing you out of window,' he said with an enraged glare.

Then he burst into tears. This was why Bronze wasn't often asked to play in the band, but only in some dire crisis, when one of the Jews was unavailable.

Jacob was always in a bad mood because of the appalling waste of money he had to endure. For instance, it was a sin to work on a Sunday or a Saint's Day, while Mondays were unlucky, so that made two hundred odd days a year when you had to sit around idle. And that was all so much money wasted. If someone in town held a wedding without music, or Shakhkes didn't ask Jacob to play, that meant still more losses. The police superintendent had been ill for two years now. He was wasting away, and Jacob had waited impatiently for him to die, but the man had left for treatment in the county town, and damned if he didn't peg out there. Now, that was at least ten roubles down the drain, as his would have been an expensive coffin complete with brocade lining. Thoughts of these losses hounded Jacob mostly at night. He would put his fiddle on the bed beside him, and when some such tomfoolery preyed on his mind he would touch the strings and the fiddle would twang in the darkness. That made him feel better.

On the sixth of May in the previous year Martha had suddenly fallen ill. The old woman breathed heavily, drank a lot of water, was unsteady on her feet, but she would still do the stove herself of a morning, and even fetch the water. By evening, though, she would already be in bed. Jacob fiddled away all day. But when it was quite dark he took the book in which he listed his losses daily and began, out of sheer boredom, to add up the annual total. It came to more than a thousand roubles. This so shocked him that he flung his abacus on the floor and stamped his feet. Then he picked up the abacus and clicked away again for a while, sighing deep, heartfelt sighs. His face was purple and wet with sweat. He was thinking that if he had put that lost thousand in the bank he would have received at least forty roubles' interest a year. So that was forty more roubles down the drain. However hard you tried to wriggle out of it, everything was just a dead loss in fact.

Then he suddenly heard Martha call out. 'Jacob, I'm dying.'

He looked round at his wife. Her face was flushed in the heat, her expression was exceptionally bright and joyous. Accustomed to her pale face and timid, unhappy expression, Bronze was put out. She really did look as if she was dying, glad to be saying a permanent good-bye to hut, coffins and Jacob at long last.

Gazing at the ceiling and moving her lips, she looked happy, as if she could actually see her saviour Death and was whispering to him.

It was dawn and the first rays were seen through the window. As he looked at the old woman, it vaguely occurred to Jacob that for some reason he had never shown her any affection all his life. Never had he been kind to her, never had he thought of buying her a kerchief or bringing her sweetmeats from a wedding. All he had done was yell at her, blame her for his 'losses', threaten to punch her. True, he never had hit her. Still he had frightened her, she had always been petrified with fear. Yes, he had said she couldn't have tea because they had enough other expenses without that, so she only drank hot water. And now he knew why she looked so strangely joyous, and a chill went through him.

When it was fully light he borrowed a neighbour's horse and drove Martha to hospital. There were not many patients, so he did not have long to wait. Only about three hours. To his great joy the patients were not received on this occasion by the doctor, who was ill himself, but by his assistant Maxim, an old fellow said by everyone in town to be better than the doctor, drunken brawler though he was.

'I humbly greet you,' said Jacob, taking his old woman into the consulting-room. 'You must excuse us troubling you with our trifling affairs, sir. Now, as you see, guv'nor, my old woman has fallen sick. She's my better half in a manner of speaking, if you'll pardon the expression——'

Frowning, stroking his side-whiskers, the white-eyebrowed assistant examined the old woman, who sat hunched on a stool, wizened, sharp-nosed, open-mouthed, her profile like a thirsty bird's.

'Hurrumph. Well, yes,' the assistant slowly pronounced, and sighed. 'It's influenza, fever perhaps. There's typhus in town. Ah well, the old woman's lived her life, praise the Lord. How old is she?'

'Seventy come next year, guv'nor.'

'Ah well, her life's over. Time she was on her way.'

'It's true enough, what you just said, sir.' Jacob smiled out of politeness. 'And we thanks you most kindly for being so nice about it, like. But, if you'll pardon the expression, every insect wants to live.'

'Not half it does.' The assistant's tone suggested that it depended on him whether the old woman lived or died. 'Now then, my good man, you put a cold compress on her head and give her one of these powders twice a day. And now cheerio to you. A very bong jour.'

From his face Jacob could tell that it was all up, and that no powders would help now. Obviously Martha was going to die soon, either today or tomorrow. He gave the assistant's elbow a push and winked.

'We ought to cup her, Mr. Maxim sir,' he said in a low voice.

'Haven't the time, my good man. Take your old woman and be off with you. So long and all that.'

'Begging your kindness, sir,' implored Jacob. 'As you know, mister, if it was her guts or her innards, like, what was sick, then it's powders and drops she should have. But this here is a chill, and the great thing with chills is to bleed 'em, sir.'

But the assistant had already called for his next patient, and a village woman with a little boy had come into the consulting-room.

'Buzz off you, beat it!' The assistant frowned at Jacob. 'Don't hang around.'

'Then at least put some leeches to her. I'll be grateful to you all my life, I will.'

The assistant lost his temper.

'Don't you bandy words with me,' he yelled. 'D-damned oaf!'

Jacob lost his temper too, and turned completely crimson. But he grabbed Martha's arm without a single word and took her out of the room. Only when they were getting into their cart did he cast a stern, mocking look at that hospital.

'They're a high and mighty lot round here,' he said. 'He'd have cupped a rich man, I'll be bound, but for a poor one he grudges even a single leech. Bastards!'

They arrived home, and Martha, after entering the house, stood for about ten minutes gripping the stove. If she was to lie down Jacob would talk about all the money he'd lost and blame her for lolling about and not wanting to work—or so she thought. And Jacob looked at her miserably, remembering that tomorrow was St. John's Day, and the day after that was St. Nicholas's Day, after which came Sunday and Unlucky Monday. That made four days when he couldn't work. But Martha was sure to die on one of those days, so he must make the coffin today. He took his iron ruler, went up to the old woman and measured her. Then she lay down and he crossed himself and started on the coffin.

When the work was finished, Jacob put on his spectacles and wrote in his book.

'Martha Ivanov: to one coffin, 2 roubles 40 copecks.'

He sighed. The old woman lay there all the time silently, her eyes shut, but when it grew dark that evening she suddenly called the old man.

'Remember fifty years ago, Jacob?' She looked at him happily. 'God gave us a little fair-haired baby, remember? We were always

sitting by the river, you and I, singing songs under the willow tree.'
She laughed bitterly. 'The little girl died.'

Jacob cudgelled his brains, but could recall neither baby nor willow.
'You're imagining things.'

The priest came and gave the last rites, whereupon Martha mumbled
something or other. By morning she was gone.

Old women neighbours washed her, dressed her, laid her in her
coffin. So as not to waste money on the sexton, Jacob read the lesson
himself, and he got the grave for nothing because the cemetery caretaker was a crony of his. Four peasants bore the coffin to the cemetery
out of respect, not for money. It was followed by old women, beggars
and two village idiots while people in the street crossed themselves
piously. Jacob was delighted that it was all so right and seemly, that it
didn't cost much or hurt anyone's feelings. As he said good-bye to
Martha for the last time he touched the coffin.

'Good workmanship, that,' he thought.

But on his way back from the cemetery he was overcome by a great
sorrow. He felt vaguely unwell. His breath came hot and heavy, his
legs were weak, he felt thirsty. Then various thoughts began to prey
on his mind. He again remembered that never in his life had he been
kind to Martha or shown her affection. The fifty-two years of their life
together in one hut—it seemed such a long, long time. But somehow
he had never given her a thought in all that time, he had no more
noticed her than a cat or dog. But she had made up the stove every day,
hadn't she? She had cooked, baked, fetched water, cut wood, shared
his bed. And when he came back from weddings drunk she would
reverently hang his fiddle on the wall and put him to bed—all this in
silence, looking scared and troubled.

Rothschild approached Jacob, smiling and bowing.

'I been looking for you, mister,' he said. 'Mister Moses sends his
respects, says he vonts you at once.'

Jacob wasn't interested. He wanted to cry.

'Leave me alone.' He walked on.

'Vot are you doing?' Rothschild ran ahead, much alarmed. 'Mister
Moses'll be offended. You're to come at once, said he.'

Out of breath, blinking, with all those red freckles, the Jew disgusted Jacob. The green frock-coat with the black patches, his whole
frail, puny figure—what a loathsome sight.

'Keep out of my way, Garlick-breath,' shouted Jacob. 'You leave
me alone.'

The Jew, angered, also shouted. 'You are being quiet please or I am throwing you over fence.'

'Out of my sight, you!' bellowed Jacob, pouncing on him with clenched fists. 'Proper poison, them greasy bastards are.'

Scared to death, Rothschild crouched down, waving his hands above his head as if warding off blows, then jumped up and scampered off as fast as he could, hopping about and flapping his arms as he ran. You could see the quaking of his long, thin back. At this the street urchins gleefully rushed after him shouting 'Dirty Yid!' Barking dogs chased him too. Someone roared with laughter and then whistled, the dogs barked louder and in closer harmony.

Then a dog must have bitten Rothschild, for a shout of pain and despair was heard.

Jacob walked on the common, then started off along the edge of the town without knowing where he was going. 'There's old Jake, there he goes,' shouted the boys. Then he came to the river. Here sandpipers swooped and twittered, ducks quacked. The sun's heat beat down and the water sparkled till it hurt the eyes. Walking along the tow-path, Jacob saw a buxom, red-cheeked woman emerge from a bathing hut.

'Damn performing seal,' he thought.

Not far from the bathing hut boys were fishing for crayfish, using meat as bait. They saw him.

'Hey, there's old Jake,' they shouted nastily.

Then came the broad old willow tree with its huge hollow and crows' nests.

Suddenly Jacob's memory threw up a vivid image of that fair-haired baby and the willow that Martha had spoken of. Yes, it was the same willow—so green, so quiet, so sad.

How old it had grown, poor thing.

He sat beneath it and began remembering. On the other bank, now a water meadow, had been a silver-birch forest, and over there on that bare hill on the horizon the dark blue bulk of an ancient pine wood. Barges had plied up and down the river. But now it was all flat and bare with the one little silver birch on the near side, slim and youthful as a young girl. There were only ducks and geese on the river, and it was hard to think that barges had ever passed here. Even the geese seemed fewer. Jacob shut his eyes and pictured vast flocks of white geese swooping towards each other.

How was it, he wondered, that he had never been by the river in the last forty or fifty years of his life. Or, if he had, it had made no impression on him. Why, this was a proper river, not just any old stream. You could fish it, you could sell the fish to shopkeepers, clerks and the man who kept the station bar, you could put the money in the bank. You could sail a boat from one riverside estate to another playing your fiddle, and all manner of folk would pay you for it. You could try starting up the barges again—better than making coffins, that was. Then you could breed geese, slaughter them and send them to Moscow in winter. 'The down alone would fetch ten roubles a year, I'll be bound.' But he had let all this go by, he had done nothing about it. Oh, what a waste, what a waste of money! If you put it all together —fishing, fiddling, barging, goose-slaughtering—what a lot of money you'd have made. But none of it had happened, not even in your dreams. Life had flowed past without profit, without enjoyment— gone aimlessly, leaving nothing to show for it. The future was empty. And if you looked back there was only all the awful waste of money that sent shivers down your spine. Why couldn't a man live without all that loss and waste? And why, he wondered, had they cut down the birch forest? And the pine wood? Why wasn't that common put to use? Why do people always do the wrong things? Why had Jacob spent all his life cursing, bellowing, threatening people with his fists, ill-treating his wife? And what, oh what, was the point of scaring and insulting that Jew just now? Why are people generally such a nuisance to each other? After all, it's all such a waste of money, a terrible waste it is. Without the hate and malice folks could get a lot of profit out of each other.

That evening and night he had visions of baby, willow, fish, dead geese, of Martha with her thirsty bird's profile, and of Rothschild's wretched, pale face, while various other gargoyle-like faces advanced on him from all sides muttering about all the waste of money. He tossed and turned, he got out of bed half a dozen times to play his fiddle.

Next morning he forced himself to get up and went to the hospital. That same Maxim told him to put a cold compress on his head and gave him powders, but his look and tone made Jacob realize that it was all up and that no powders would help now. Later, on his way home, he reckoned that death would be pure gain to him. He wouldn't have to eat, drink, pay taxes or offend folk. And since a man lies in his grave not just one but hundreds and thousands of years, the profit would be colossal. Man's life is debit, his death credit. The argument was correct, of course, but painfully disagreeable too. Why are things so oddly arranged? You only live once, so why don't you get anything out of it?

He didn't mind dying, but when he got home and saw his fiddle his heart missed a beat and he felt sorry. He couldn't take his fiddle with him to the grave, so it would be orphaned and go the way of the birches and the pines. Nothing in this world has ever come to any-thing, nothing ever will. Jacob went out of the hut and sat in the door-way clasping the fiddle to his breast. Thinking of his wasted, profitless life, he started playing he knew not what, but it came out poignantly moving and tears coursed down his cheeks. The harder he thought the sadder grew the fiddle's song.

The latch squeaked twice and Rothschild appeared at the garden gate. He crossed half the yard boldly, but when he saw Jacob he suddenly stopped, cringed and—through fear, no doubt—gesticulated as if trying to indicate the time with his fingers.

'Come along then,' said Jacob kindly, beckoning him. 'It's all right.'

Looking at him mistrustfully and fearfully, Rothschild began to approach but stopped a few feet away.

'Don't hit me, I beg you.' He squatted down. 'It's Mister Moses has sent me again. Never fear, says he, you go to Jacob again—tell him we can't do without him, he says. There's a vedding on Vednesday. Aye, that there is. Mister Shapovalov is marrying his daughter to a fine young man. A rich folks' vedding this, and no mistake!' The Jew screwed up one eye.

'Can't be done.' Jacob breathed heavily. 'I'm ill, son.'

He again struck up, his tears spurting on to the fiddle. Rothschild listened carefully, standing sideways on, arms crossed on his breast. His scared, baffled look gradually gave way to a sorrowful, suffering expression. He rolled his eyes as if in anguished delight.

'A-a-ah!' he said as the tears crawled down his cheeks and splashed on his green frock-coat.

After that Jacob lay down all day, sick at heart. When the priest heard his confession that evening and asked whether he remembered committing any particular sin he exerted his failing memory and once more recalled Martha's unhappy face and the desperate yell of the Jew bitten by a dog.

'Give my fiddle to Rothschild,' he said in a voice barely audible.

'Very well,' the priest answered.

Now everyone in town wants to know where Rothschild got such a fine fiddle. Did he buy it, did he steal it? Or did someone leave it with him as a pledge? He only plays the fiddle now, having given up the flute long ago. From his bow there flow those same poignant strains which used to come from his flute. But when he tries to repeat the tune Jacob had played in his doorway the outcome is so sad and mournful that his listeners weep and he ends by rolling his eyes up with an 'A-a-ah!'

So popular is this new tune in town that merchants and officials are always asking Rothschild over and making him play it a dozen times.

THE weather was fine and calm at first. Thrushes were singing, and in the near-by swamps some creature droned piteously as if blowing into an empty bottle. A woodcock flew over and a shot reverberated merrily in the spring air. But when darkness fell on the wood an unwelcome, piercing cold wind blew up from the east and everything grew silent. Ice needles formed on the puddles and the wood seemed inhospitable, abandoned, empty. It smelt of winter.

Ivan Velikopolsky, a student at a theological college and a sexton's son, was returning home along the path through the water meadow after a day's shooting. His fingers were numb, his face burned in the wind. This sudden onset of cold seemed to have destroyed the order and harmony of things, striking dread into Nature herself and causing the shades of night to thicken faster than was needful. Everything was so abandoned, so very gloomy, somehow. Only in the widows' allotments near the river did a light gleam. But far around, where the village stood about three miles away, everything drowned in the dense evening mist. The student remembered that, when he had left the house, his mother had been sitting barefoot on the lobby floor cleaning the samovar, while his father lay coughing on the stove. There was no cooking at home because today was Good Friday, and he felt famished. Cringing in the cold, he reflected that just such a wind had blown in the days of Ryurik, Ivan the Terrible and Peter the Great. Their times had known just such ferocious poverty and hunger. There had been the same thatched roofs with the holes in them, the same ignorance and misery, the same desolation on all sides, the same gloom and sense of oppression. All these horrors had been, still were, and would continue to be, and the passing of another thousand years would make things no better. He did not feel like going home.

The allotments were called widows' because they were kept by two widows, a mother and daughter. A bonfire was burning briskly—crackling, lighting up the plough-land far around. Widow Vasilisa, a tall, plump old woman in a man's fur jacket, stood gazing pensively at the fire. Her short, pock-marked, stupid-looking daughter Lukerya sat on the ground washing a cooking pot and some spoons. They had just had supper, obviously. Men's voices were heard, some local labourers watering their horses by the river.

'So winter's come back,' said the student, approaching the fire. 'Good evening.'

Vasilisa shuddered, but then saw who it was and smiled a welcome.

'Goodness me, I didn't recognize you,' she said. 'That means you'll be rich one day.'

They talked. Vasilisa, a woman of some experience—having been wet-nurse to gentlefolk and then a nanny—spoke delicately, always smiling a gentle, dignified smile. But her daughter Lukerya, a peasant whose husband had beaten her, only screwed up her eyes at the student, saying nothing and wearing an odd look as if she was deaf and dumb.

'On a cold night like this the Apostle Peter warmed himself by a fire.' The student held out his hands towards the flames. 'So it must have been cold then. What a frightening night that was, Granny, what a very sorrowful, what a very long night.'

He looked at the darkness around and abruptly jerked his head. 'Were you in church yesterday for the Twelve Gospel Readings?'

'Yes,' Vasilisa answered.

'At the Last Supper, you'll remember, Peter said to Jesus, "Lord, I am ready to go with Thee, both into prison, and to death." And the Lord said, "I say unto thee, Peter, before the cock crow twice, thou shalt deny me thrice." After supper Jesus prayed in mortal agony in the garden, while poor Peter was weary in spirit, and enfeebled. His eyes were heavy, he couldn't fight off sleep and he slept. Then, as you have heard, Judas that night kissed Jesus and betrayed Him to the torturers. They bound Him, they took Him to the high priest, they smote Him, while Peter—worn, tormented, anguished, perturbed, you understand, not having slept properly, foreseeing some fearful happening on this earth—went after them. He loved Jesus passionately, to distraction, and now, afar, he saw Him being buffeted.'

Lukerya put down the spoons and stared at the student.

'They went to the high priest,' he continued. 'They put Jesus to the question, and meanwhile the workmen had kindled a fire in the midst of the hall, as it was cold, and were warming themselves. Peter stood with them near the fire—also warming himself, as I am now. A certain maid beheld him, and said, "This man was also with Jesus." In other words she was saying that he too should be taken for questioning. All the workmen round the fire must have looked at him suspiciously and sternly because he was confused and said, "I know him not." A little later someone recognized him as one of Jesus' disciples and said,

"Thou also wast with him." But he denied it again. And for the third time someone addressed him. "Did I not see thee in the garden with Him this day?" He denied Him for the third time. And after that the cock straightway crowed, and Peter, looking at Jesus from afar, remembered the words which He had said to him at supper. He remembered, his eyes were opened, and he went out of the hall and shed bitter tears. The Gospel says, "And he went out, and wept bitterly." I can imagine it was a very quiet, very dark garden and his hollow sobs could hardly be heard in the silence.'

The student sighed, plunged deep in thought. Still smiling, Vasilisa suddenly sobbed and tears, large and profuse, flowed down her cheeks. She shielded her face from the fire with her sleeve as if ashamed of the tears, while Lukerya, staring at the student, blushed and her expression became distressed and tense as if she was holding back a terrible pain.

The workmen returned from the river. One of them, on horseback, was already near and the light from the fire quivered on him. The student said good night to the widows and moved on. Again darkness came upon him, and his hands began to freeze. A cruel wind blew, it was real winter weather again, and it did not seem as if Easter Sunday could be only the day after tomorrow.

The student thought of Vasilisa. Her weeping meant that all that had happened to Peter on that terrible night had a particular meaning for her.

He looked back. The lonely fire quietly flickered in the darkness, no one could be seen near it. Again the student reflected that, if Vasilisa had wept and her daughter had been moved, then obviously what he had just told them about happenings nineteen centuries ago— it had a meaning for the present, for both women, and also probably for this God-forsaken village, for himself, for all people. It had not been his gift for poignant narrative that had made the old woman weep. It was because Peter was near to her, because she was bound up heart and soul with his innermost feelings.

Joy suddenly stirred within him. He even stopped for a moment to catch his breath.

'The past', thought he, 'is linked to the present by an unbroken chain of happenings, each flowing from the other.'

He felt as if he had just seen both ends of that chain. When he touched one end the other vibrated.

Crossing the river by ferry, and then climbing the hill, he looked at his home village and at the narrow strip of cold crimson sunset shining in the west. And he brooded on truth and beauty—how they had guided human life there in the garden and the high priest's palace, how they had continued without a break till the present day, always as the most important element in man's life and in earthly life in general. A sensation of youth, health, strength—he was only twenty-two years old—together with an anticipation, ineffably sweet, of happiness, strange, mysterious happiness, gradually came over him. And life seemed enchanting, miraculous, imbued with exalted significance.

THERE was a flower sale at Count and Countess N's greenhouse. But there were not many buyers, just myself, my landowning neighbour and a young timber merchant. While labourers carried our magnificent purchases out and packed them on carts, we sat by the greenhouse door discoursing of this and that. To sit in a garden on a warm April morning, to listen to the birds, and to see the flowers sunning themselves now that they had been brought outside—how very delightful.

The stowage of the plants was handled by the head gardener Michael Karlovich—a venerable, full-faced, clean-shaven old fellow in a fur waistcoat—he had taken off his frock-coat. He said nothing all this time, but listened to our conversation in case we might say anything new. He was an intelligent, easy-going, universally respected man. Somehow everyone thought he was German, though he was Swedish on his father's side and Russian on his mother's. He was an Orthodox church-goer, he knew Russian, Swedish and German, he read a lot in these languages, and you could give him no greater delight than lending him a new book or talking to him about Ibsen, for instance.

He had his foibles, but innocent ones. For instance, he called himself a 'head' gardener, though there were no under-gardeners. His expression was highly dignified and haughty. He did not permit contradictions, he liked to be listened to seriously and attentively.

'Now, that young spark over there—he's a frightful rogue, I can tell you.' My neighbour pointed to a workman with a florid gipsy's face riding past on a water-cart. 'He was had up in town for robbery last week and got off on grounds of insanity. But just look at the blackguard's face, he's as sane as can be. Russian courts are always acquitting scoundrels nowadays, explaining everything by ill health and temporary insanity, but these acquittals, this blatant leniency, this aiding and abetting—it bodes no good. It demoralizes the masses, blunting everyone's sense of justice because they're used to seeing vice going unpunished, so that one can boldly apply to our own day Shakespeare's lines.

> "For in the fatness of these pursy times
> Virtue itself of vice must pardon beg." '

'True, true,' agreed the merchant. 'These acquittals have caused a boom in murder and arson. Just ask the peasants.'

The gardener Michael Karlovich turned to us.

'For myself I'm always delighted with an acquittal, gentleman,' said he. 'A not guilty verdict doesn't make me fear for morality and justice. Far from it, it pleases me. Even when my conscience tells me that a jury has been wrong to acquit a criminal, even then I feel exultant. Judge for yourselves, gentlemen—if judges and juries believe more in *man* than in clues, circumstantial evidence and speeches, then is not this *faith in man* itself superior to all mundane considerations? Such faith is accessible only to those few who understand Christ and feel His presence.'

'A fine thought,' said I.

'But not a new one. I even remember once hearing a story on this theme long long ago, a most delightful story.' The gardener smiled. 'My old grandmother, now passed away—my father's mother, a wonderful old woman—used to tell me it. She told it in Swedish, but it doesn't sound as well in Russian, it's less classic.'

Still, we asked him to tell the story undeterred by the crudeness of the Russian language. Well pleased, he slowly lit his pipe, looked angrily at the labourers, and began.

In a certain small town there lived an elderly, ugly bachelor called Thomson or Wilson. The name doesn't matter, it's beside the point. He practised the noble calling of doctor, was always grim and unsociable, spoke only when his profession required it. He never made social visits, never carried acquaintanceship beyond a silent bow, lived as humbly as any hermit. He was a scholar, in fact, and in those days scholars were unlike ordinary people. They would spend their days and nights contemplating, reading books, healing sickness, rating all else mere frivolity and being too busy to speak without need. The townsfolk appreciated this, trying not to pester him with their visits and idle chat. They were overjoyed that God had sent them a healer at last, they were proud to have so remarkable a man living in their town.

They used to say that he 'knew everything'.

Nor was this all. We should also add his love for everyone. In the scholar's breast beat a wondrous, angelic heart. And in any case the townsfolk were strangers to him, they weren't his kith and kin after all, yet he loved them like his children, was ready to give his very life for them. He suffered from tuberculosis, he was always coughing, but when called to a patient he would forget his illness, not sparing himself, and would puff his way up mountains however high. He spurned heat and cold, despised hunger and thirst, never accepted money, and—odd, isn't it?—when one of his patients died he would follow the coffin with the relatives and weep.

He soon became so vital to the town that folk wondered how they had ever managed without him. Their gratitude knew no bounds. Adults and children, the good-natured and ill-natured, the honest men and rogues—everyone, in a word—respected him, valued him. No one in the little town and its environs would have done him an ill turn, or even thought of it. He never locked his doors and windows when leaving his quarters, being absolutely assured that no thief would venture to harm him. As a doctor he often had to walk highways, forests and mountains, the haunts of hungry vagabonds, but felt completely safe. One night on his way home from a patient he was waylaid in a wood by highwaymen who, when they saw who it was, respectfully doffed their hats and asked if he was hungry. When he said he was not, they gave him a warm cloak and escorted him all the way to town, happy that fortune had granted them this chance of conveying their thanks to one so noble-spirited. Then again, if you take my drift, my grandmother used to say that even horses, cows and dogs knew him and showed how glad they were to see him.

Yet this man whose saintliness seemed a bulwark against all evil, this man whom the very robbers and madmen wished well—he was found murdered one morning. Covered with blood, his skull smashed in, he lay in a gulley with a surprised look on his pale face. No, it was not horror but surprise which had frozen on his face when he saw his murderer before him. Now, imagine how heart-broken the townsfolk and locals were. All were in despair, not believing their eyes, wondering who could kill such a man. The court officers who conducted the investigation and examined the corpse pronounced as follows.

'Here is every evidence of murder. Since, however, no one on earth could bring himself to kill our doctor, it obviously cannot be murder and the accumulated clues must derive from pure coincidence. We must assume that the doctor stumbled into the gulley in the dark and died from the fall.'

With this opinion the whole town concurred. The doctor was buried, and there was no more talk of death by violence. The very existence of someone base and foul enough to murder him seemed improbable. After all, even vileness does have its limits, doesn't it?

But then suddenly, believe it or not, chance revealed the murderer. A certain scallywag, who had often stood trial and was known for his dissolute life, was seen in an inn with a snuff-box and watch, once the doctor's, which he was using to obtain drink. When questioned he showed embarrassment and told some blatant lie. His home was searched, and in his bed were found a shirt with blood-stained sleeves and the doctor's lancet in a golden case. What more clues were needed? They put the villain in prison, and the townsfolk were perturbed while claiming it as 'most unlikely' and 'impossible'.

'Look, there may have been a mistake. Clues can be misleading, after all.'

The murderer stubbornly denied his complicity in court. Everything was against him. His guilt was as plain as that this soil is black, but the magistrates had apparently taken leave of their senses. Ten times they weighed every clue, viewing the witnesses with suspicion, blushing, drinking water.

They began trying the case early in the morning, and did not finish until evening.

The presiding magistrate addressed the murderer. 'Prisoner in the dock, the court finds you guilty of the murder of Doctor Such-and-Such and sentences you——'

The chief magistrate was about to say 'to death', but dropped the paper on which the sentence had been written and wiped off cold sweat.

'No,' he shouted. 'May God punish me if this judgement is wrong, but I swear he is not guilty. That anyone would dare kill our friend the doctor I do not concede. Man cannot sink so low.'

'No indeed,' the other magistrates concurred.

'No,' echoed the crowd. 'Let him go.'

They let the murderer go scot free, and not a soul reproached the court with a miscarriage of justice. According to my grandmother God forgave all the townsfolk their sins because of their great faith in man. He rejoices when folk believe that man is His own image and likeness, and He is grieved if men forget their human dignity and judge their fellows to be worse than dogs. Even if the acquittal should harm the townsfolk, yet just consider how beneficent an influence their faith in man has had on them. That faith is no dead formula, now is it? It educates us in noble sentiments, always prompting us to love and respect everyone. Everyone—that's what's so important.

Michael Karlovich ended. My neighbour wanted to offer some objection, but the head gardener made a gesture signifying a dislike of all objections, and went over to the carts to continue supervising the loading with an expression of great dignity on his face.

PATCH

A HUNGRY she-wolf got up to go hunting. Her three cubs were all fast asleep, huddled together in each other's warmth. She gave them a lick and went off.

It was already March—spring in fact—but at night trees cracked in the cold as though it was still December. Stick out your tongue and it felt as if it had been bitten. The wolf was in bad health and very wary—the least sound made her start. She feared that someone might hurt her cubs while she was away from home. She was scared by the scent of men and horses, by tree stumps, wood piles, and by the dark road with animal droppings on it. She seemed to sense men standing in the darkness behind the trees and dogs howling beyond the wood somewhere.

She was quite old and was losing her scent, so she sometimes took a fox's track for a dog's and even lost her way, betrayed by her scent —which had never happened when she was young. Being unwell, she had stopped hunting calves and big rams, as of old, and kept well out of the way of mares with foals, feeding only on carrion. Only very seldom did she have fresh meat—in spring when she met a doe hare and made off with her babies or got among the lambs in a peasant's barn.

By the post road, about three miles from her lair, was a forest lodge. This was the home of Ignat, an old watchman of about seventy who was always coughing and talking to himself. He usually slept at night and wandered through the forest in daytime with a shot-gun, whistling at the hares. He must have had something to do with engines once because he never came to a halt without shouting 'Brakes on!' and he would not go on without a 'Full steam ahead!' He had a big black mongrel bitch called Arapka, and when she ran too far ahead he shouted, 'Reverse!' Sometimes he sang, staggering violently, and he often fell—blown over by the wind, thought the wolf—and shouted, 'We've run off the rails!'

The wolf remembered a ram and two ewes grazing near the lodge in summer and autumn and she fancied she had heard bleating in the shed not long ago as she ran past. As she went up to the hut, she considered that it was now March—the season when there must be lambs in the shed. Tortured by hunger, she thought how ravenously she would devour a lamb, and such thoughts made her teeth snap and her eyes glint in the dark like two lamps.

Ignat's hut, barn, cattle-shed and well had deep snow piled all round them. It was quiet and Arapka must be sleeping under the barn.

The wolf climbed over a snowdrift onto the shed roof and began scratching the thatch away with her paws and muzzle. The straw was rotten and crumbling, and she nearly fell through. Suddenly the smell of warm steam, dung and sheep's milk hit her straight in the muzzle. Feeling the cold, a lamb gently bleated down below. The wolf jumped through the hole and her four paws and chest hit something soft and warm. That must be the ram. Meanwhile something in the shed suddenly whined and barked and there was a lot of shrill yapping. The sheep all crashed back against the wall and the terrified wolf seized something in her teeth at random and rushed out. . . .

She ran as fast as she could. Scenting wolf, Arapka howled furiously, frightened hens clucked inside the lodge, and Ignat went out into the porch.

'Full steam ahead!' he shouted. 'Sound the whistle!'

He whistled like an engine and then shouted several times. The forest echoed back all these noises.

When things had grown quieter the wolf calmed down a little. Holding the prey in her teeth and dragging it along the snow, she noticed that it was heavier and somehow harder than lambs usually are at that season. It seemed to have a different smell and there were strange noises.

The wolf stopped and laid her burden on the snow, so that she could rest and start eating—then suddenly leapt back in disgust. This was no lamb, but a puppy—black, with a big head and long legs, of some large type, with a white patch over his whole forehead like Arapka. Judging by his manners, he was an ordinary ignorant farm dog. He licked his injured back, wagged his tail, quite unimpressed, and barked at the wolf. She growled like a dog and ran off. He ran after her. She looked back and clicked her teeth. He stopped, baffled, and must have decided that she was having a game with him because he stretched his muzzle back towards the lodge and gave a joyous, ringing peal of barks as if asking his mother Arapka to come and play with him and the wolf.

It was already growing light and as the wolf made her way home through a thick aspen copse, each aspen-tree could be clearly seen. Woodcocks were waking already and the puppy kept putting up magnificent cock birds which were startled by its barks and careless gambols.

'Why does he run after me?' wondered the wolf, annoyed. 'He must want me to eat him.'

She and her cubs lived in a shallow lair. Three years ago a tall old pine had been torn up by the roots in a great storm, and that was how the hole had been made. Now there were dead leaves and moss at the bottom and it was strewn with bones and bullocks' horns, the cubs' playthings. The cubs were awake and all three of them, very much alike, stood in a row on the edge of the hole, wagging their tails and watching their mother come back. Seeing them, the puppy stopped some way off and stared for a while. When he noticed them staring back at him, he barked angrily at them because they were strangers.

It was light now and the sun was up. Snow sparkled all around and still he stood apart, barking. The mother suckled her cubs, who prodded her emaciated belly with their paws while she gnawed a white, dry horse's bone. She was frantic with hunger, the puppy had given her a headache with his barking, and she felt like pouncing on the intruder and rending him in pieces.

In the end the puppy grew tired and hoarse. Seeing that no one was afraid of him or even noticing him, he timidly approached the cubs, now squatting down, now bouncing forward. Now that it was light it was easy to see what he was like.

He had a large white forehead with a bump on it—usually the sign of an extremely stupid dog. He had tiny, dull, light blue eyes and his whole expression was idiotic. Going up to the cubs, he stretched out his broad paws, put his muzzle on them and set up a sort of champing, mumbling noise.

This made no sense to the cubs, but they wagged their tails. Then the puppy cuffed one of the cubs on its large head and the cub cuffed him back. The puppy stood sideways on, looking at the cub out of the corner of his eye, wagging his tail—then suddenly dashed off and circled a few times on the frozen snow. The cubs chased after him. He fell on his back, kicking up his legs and all three pounced, squealing with joy, and began playfully biting him, not trying to hurt. Crows perched on a tall pine looked down at this engagement in great agitation. It was all very noisy and it was all great fun. There was warm spring sunshine. Game birds flew over the fallen pine from time to time, emerald-coloured in the brilliant sunshine.

Wolves usually teach their cubs to hunt by giving them some of their prey to play with, and as the wolf watched her cubs chasing the puppy on the snow and wrestling with him, she thought that they might as well pick up a few hints.

Having played long enough, the cubs went to their lair and lay down to sleep. The puppy howled a little because he was hungry, then he too stretched out in the sun. When they woke up they started playing again.

All day and evening the wolf could not forget the night before—the lamb bleating in the shed and the smell of sheep's milk. She kept snapping her teeth from hunger and went on gnawing greedily at the old bone, pretending that it was a lamb. The cubs sucked and the puppy, hungry, ran round sniffing the snow.

'I think I'll eat him . . .' decided the wolf.

She went up to him. He gave her muzzle a lick and yapped, thinking that she wanted to play. She had eaten dog in the old days, but the pup had a strong doggy smell, and now that she was unwell she could not stand that smell any more. It sickened her, so she went away. . . .

Towards night it grew cold. The pup felt bored and set off home.

When the cubs were fast asleep the wolf went hunting again. As on the night before, the faintest sound startled her and she was scared of tree-stumps, timber and dark, lonely juniper bushes which looked at a distance like men. She ran over the frozen snow, keeping off the road. Suddenly, on the road far ahead, something black moved.

She looked hard and pricked up her ears. Yes, something was moving ahead of her. She could even hear a rhythmical padding. A badger? Cautiously, scarcely breathing, keeping well to one side, she overtook the dark blob, looked back and saw what it was. It was the puppy with the white forehead making his leisurely way home to the lodge.

'I hope he won't be in my way again,' thought the wolf, running quickly ahead.

But she had almost reached the lodge already. She climbed once more over the snow-drift onto the shed. Yesterday's gap had been mended with straw and there were two new beams across the roof. The wolf began working rapidly with feet and muzzle, looking round in case the puppy was coming. But hardly had she scented the warm steam and reek of dung before a joyous peal of barks rang out behind her. The puppy was back. He jumped onto the roof after the wolf, then through the hole. Feeling at home in the warm and recognizing his own sheep, he barked even louder.

Under the barn Arapka awoke and set up a howl as she scented wolf. There was a clucking of hens, and when Ignat appeared in the porch with his shot-gun, the terrified wolf was already far from the lodge.

'Got away!' whistled Ignat. 'Got away, eh? Full steam ahead!'

He pressed the trigger, but the gun misfired. He pressed it again. It misfired again. He pressed a third time and a great shaft of fire flew from the barrel, there was a deafening boom, and the hard kick of the recoil against his shoulder. He took his gun in one hand and his axe in the other and went to see what the noise was all about. . . .

A little later he came back to the hut.

'What is it?' someone asked hoarsely—a pilgrim who was there for the night and had been woken by the noise.

'It doesn't matter . . .' answered Ignat. 'It's nothing at all. Our Patch has taken to sleeping in the warm with the sheep. But he hasn't the sense to use the door—has to try and get through the roof. The other night he made a hole in the roof and went larking about, the young varmint. Now he's back he's made another hole in the roof.'

'Must be stupid.'

'Yes, he has a screw loose. I can't abide stupidity!' sighed Ignat, climbing onto the stove. 'Well, mister pilgrim, it's too early to get up, so let's sleep. Full steam ahead. . . .'

Next morning he called Patch, pulled his ears till it hurt and then beat him with a switch.

'Use the door, can't you,' he kept saying. 'Use the door!'

THE SAVAGE

IVAN Zhmukhin was a retired officer of Cossacks who now lived on his farm after seeing service in the Caucasus. Once he had been a strong, hefty young man, but he was a dry old stick nowadays—with drooping shoulders, shaggy eyebrows and a white moustache tinged with green.

One hot summer day he was on his way back to his farm from town, where he had been to church and seen a lawyer about his will, having had a slight stroke about a fortnight earlier. Now that he was on the train, he was haunted by solemn, melancholy thoughts. He would soon die, he thought, all is vanity and nothing on this earth lasts for ever.

At Provalye, a station on the Donets Line, a man came into his carriage and sat down opposite. He was fair-haired, middle-aged, stout, and carried a shabby brief-case. They fell into conversation.

'Aye, it's not a thing to rush into, marriage isn't,' said Zhmukhin, looking thoughtfully through the window. 'I was married when I was forty-eight and was told it was too late in life. It was neither late nor early as it turned out—I just shouldn't have married at all. A man soon gets bored with a wife, but there's them that won't let on, being ashamed to have an unhappy family life, see what I mean? They try to keep quiet about it. A man may be all over his wife with lots of "Mary this" and "Mary that", when what he'd really like would be to pop Mary in a sack and drop her in a lake. A wife's a bore. Where's the sense of it all? And children are no better, you take my word for it, I've two of the wretched things. There's no schooling for them out here in the steppe and I can't afford to send them to school at Novocherkassk. So they live round here like a couple of young wolves. They'll soon be cutting people's throats on the highway, the way they're going.'

The fair-haired man listened attentively and replied briefly in a low voice. He seemed a quiet, unassuming sort and described himself as a solicitor on a business trip to the village of Dyuyevka.

'Why, that's only six miles from me, by heaven!' said Zhmukhin. From the way he spoke you would have thought that someone was denying the fact. 'Now look here, you'll find no horses at the station now. If you ask me, your best plan is to come straight over to my place, see what I mean? Stay the night, see? Then you can drive over to-morrow morning with my horses, and jolly good luck to you.'

The solicitor accepted after a moment's thought.

When they reached the station the sun was low over the steppe. On the way to the farm they said nothing at all, jolted beyond speech as the trap bobbed up and down, squealing and apparently sobbing, as though all this bumping really hurt it. The solicitor found it a most uncomfortable ride and kept staring ahead, longing for the farm to come into sight. After about five miles there came a distant view of a low house and yard with a wall of dark stone slabs round it. The house had a green roof, peeling stucco and tiny slits of windows like screwed-up eyes. This farm stood in the full blaze of the sun and no water or trees were to be seen anywhere near. Local squires and peasants had called it 'Savage Farm', ever since a surveyor had stayed there on his way through many years ago and spent the whole night talking to Zhmukhin.

The surveyor had not been impressed.

'Sir!' he had told Zhmukhin severely as he drove off in the morning. 'You are a savage!'

Hence the name 'Savage Farm', which caught on all the more when Zhmukhin's boys grew up and took to raiding near-by orchards and melon-plots. Zhmukhin himself was called 'See-what-I-mean?' because he talked so much and was always using that expression.

Zhmukhin's sons were standing in the yard near the barn, both barefoot and bare-headed, one about nineteen and the other a little younger. Just as the trap was coming into the yard, the younger boy threw a hen high in the air. It clucked and took wing, describing an arc. The elder fired a gun and it crashed to the ground, dead.

'That's my lads learning to shoot,' said Zhmukhin.

The travellers were greeted in the hall by a thin little woman with a pale face, still young and good-looking, who might have been a servant, to judge by her clothes.

'Now, may I do the honours?' asked Zhmukhin. 'This is the mother of my two sons of bitches.' He turned to his wife. 'Come on, Missus,' he said. 'Do get a move on, and look after your guest. Let's have supper! Look sharp, Mother!'

The house consisted of two parts. One contained the parlour with old Zhmukhin's bedroom next door—stuffy rooms with low ceilings and hordes of flies and wasps. The kitchen, where they cooked, did the laundry and fed the men, was in the other part. There were geese and hen turkeys hatching eggs under the benches. Mrs. Zhmukhin's bed was in there and so were her two sons' beds. The furniture in the parlour was unpainted and had obviously been roughly put together by a carpenter. On the walls hung guns, game-bags and whips, all old rubbish grey with dust, covered with the rust of ages. There were no pictures. In the corner was a dingy board that had started life as an icon.

A young Ukrainian peasant-woman laid the table and served ham followed by beetroot soup. The guest refused vodka and would eat only bread and cucumbers.

'Have some ham,' said Zhmukhin.

'No thank you. I never touch it,' the guest answered. 'I don't eat meat.'

'Why is that?'

'I'm a vegetarian and killing animals is against my principles.'

Zhmukhin thought for a moment.

'Aye. . . . I see what you mean . . . ' he brought out with a sigh. 'I met someone else in town once who didn't eat meat. It's a kind of new belief that's caught on. And why not? It's a good idea. After all, there's other things in life beside slaughtering and shooting, see what I mean? It's time we took things easy and gave the beasts a bit of peace and quiet. It's a sinful thing, is killing, it stands to reason. Sometimes if you shoot a hare in the leg, it screams like a baby. So it must hurt.'

'Of course it does. Animals feel pain like we do.'

'You're quite right,' said Zhmukhin. 'I get your point,' he went on thoughtfully. 'But I must say, there's one thing I don't see. Suppose everyone stops eating meat? What'll happen to farm animals and things like hens and geese, see what I mean?'

'Hens and geese will live free like wild birds.'

'Oh, I see. Well, it's quite true crows and jackdaws get on very well without us. . . . Aye. . . . Hens, geese, hares, sheep—they'll all be free to enjoy themselves, see, and praise God and not fear us. We'll all have a bit of peace and quiet. Only, you know, there's one thing I don't see,' Zhmukhin went on with a glance at the ham. 'What'll become of pigs? What shall we do with them?'

'The same thing. They'll be free like other animals.'

'Aye, I see. But look here, if we don't slaughter them, they'll breed, see? Then you can say goodbye to your pastures and kitchen-gardens. Let a pig loose, you know, and take your eye off it and it'll wreck your whole place in a day. A pig's a pig. It's not called a pig for nothing, you know. . . .'

They finished supper. Zhmukhin got up from table and stalked up and down the room for a long time. He kept on and on talking.

He liked a serious, earnest talk and he liked to meditate. And he felt the need of something to hold on to in his old age, something to reassure him so that he need not be so afraid of dying. He wanted to be gentle, relaxed and self-confident like his guest, who had just made a meal of bread and cucumbers and thought himself a better man for it. He sat on a trunk, healthy and stout, saying nothing, patient in his boredom. When you looked at him from the hall in the dusk he seemed like a rock that could not be budged. A man's all right if he has something to hang on to in life.

Zhmukhin went through the hall to the porch and was heard sighing, deep in thought.

'Aye. . . . To be sure,' he said to himself.

It was growing dark and a few stars had come out. Indoors no lights had yet been lit. Someone slipped quietly into the parlour and stopped by the door. It was Lyubov—Zhmukhin's wife.

'Are you from town?' she asked timidly, not looking at the visitor.

'Yes, I live in town.'

'Maybe you're something of a scholar, sir, and can tell us what to do. Please help us. We ought to send in an application.'

'What do you mean?' asked the guest.

'We've two sons, kind sir. They should have gone to school long ago, but no one ever comes here and there's no one to advise us. And I don't know about these things. You see, if they don't learn anything, they'll be called up in the Cossacks as privates. It's not right, sir! They can't read and write. They're worse than peasants and Mr. Zhmukhin himself turns up his nose at them. He won't have them in the house. But it's not their fault, is it? If we could only send the younger one to school, oh it is such a shame.'

As she dragged out the words her voice quavered. How could a woman so small and young possibly have grown-up children?

'Oh, it is such a shame!'

'You know nothing about it, Mother, and it's no business of yours,' said Zhmukhin, appearing in the doorway. 'Stop annoying our guest with your wild talk. Out you go, Mother.'

Mrs. Zhmukhin went out.

'Oh, it is such a shame!' she said again in the hall in her thin little voice.

They made up a bed for the guest on a sofa in the parlour and lit a lamp in front of the icon so that he should not be in the dark. Zhmukhin went to bed in his own room.

He lay and thought of his soul, of old age, of the recent stroke that had so frightened him and made him so conscious of death. He was given to abstract speculation when alone in the quiet. At such times he fancied himself a very deep, serious thinker whose sole concern on this earth was with things that really matter. And now as he meditated he wanted to fix on some single idea, different from all others—something significant to serve him as a sign-post in life. He wanted to work out principles that would make his life as deep and serious as he was himself. It would not be a bad thing for an old man like him to give up meat and other luxuries. Sooner or later men would stop killing other men and animals, it was bound to come. He imagined it happening, pictured himself living in peace with the animal kingdom—but then suddenly thought of pigs again and that thoroughly bewildered him.

'What a business, great heavens above,' he muttered with a deep sigh, and asked, 'Are you awake?'

'Yes.'

Zhmukhin got out of bed and stood in the doorway with only his shirt on. His guest could see his stringy legs, as thin as sticks.

'Nowadays,' he began, 'we have things like the telegraph, see what I mean? And there's telephones and other miracles of one sort and another as you might say, but people are no better. In my day, thirty or forty years ago, men were rough and cruel, it's said. But isn't it just the same nowadays? In my time we never stood on ceremony, it's true. I remember being stationed for four solid months in the Caucasus by a small river. We had absolutely nothing to do—I was only a sergeant at the time—and something happened then that was as good as a story book. Right on the river bank, see, just where our company was stationed, some minor chief was buried—we'd killed him ourselves not long before. At night the chief's widow used to visit the grave and cry, if you see what I mean. Her moaning and groaning fair gave us the willies and we just couldn't sleep. Two nights that went on, and we were fed up with it. Why should we lose our sleep for damn all reason, pardon my language? What sense does that make? So we took that widow and flogged her. She stopped coming then, you take my word.

'Oh, you get a different type nowadays of course. They don't flog people, they're more clean-living and there's a lot more studying. But human nature hasn't changed, see? Not a bit of it.

'Take a case in point. There's a landowner round these parts, owns some mines, see? He has all sorts of riff-raff working for him—men

with no papers and nowhere to go. Saturday's pay day, but he doesn't
want to pay them, see? Grudges the money. So he gets hold of a
foreman—another tramp, even if he does wear a hat. "Don't pay them
a thing," he says. "Not one copeck. They'll beat you up," says he.
"Well, let them. Just put up with it, and I'll pay you ten roubles of
a Saturday."

'Well, Saturday evening rolls on and the workers duly come along,
as the custom is, for their wages. "Nothing doing!" says the foreman.
Well, one thing leads to another, and they start swearing and knocking
him about a bit. . . . They punch him, they kick him—men can be
like beasts, see, when they're starving. They beat him senseless and
clear off. The boss tells someone to pour water over the foreman. He
chucks him his ten roubles, and he's glad to take it—in fact he'd be
quite prepared to jump off a cliff for three. Aye. . . . On Monday
along comes a new gang of workers. Why? Because they've nowhere
else to go. . . . And on Saturdays it's the same story over again. . . .'

The guest turned over to face the back of the sofa and muttered
something.

'Take another case,' Zhmukhin went on. 'We once had anthrax
here, see? Cattle were dying off like flies, believe you me. We had
the vets going round and there were strict orders to bury the dead
cattle deep in the earth a long way off, pour lime over them and all
that—on a proper scientific basis, see what I mean? A horse of mine
died of it as well. I buried it with proper precautions, poured three or
four hundredweight of lime over it—and what do you think? Those
young sparks, those dear lads of mine, dug up the horse at night, see,
skinned it and sold the hide for three roubles, and that's a fact. So
people haven't got any better. A leopard doesn't change his spots,
and that's a fact. Makes you think, though, eh? What do you say?'

Through the cracks in the window-shutters on one side of the room
lightning flashed. The air was heavy with the threat of thunder, mos-
quitoes were biting, and Zhmukhin lay deep in thought in his room,
sighing, groaning and talking to himself. 'Aye. . . . To be sure,' he
said. And he could not sleep. Thunder growled somewhere in the
far distance.

'Are you awake?'

'Yes,' answered the visitor.

Zhmukhin got up, his heels clattering through the parlour and hall
as he went to the kitchen for a drink of water.

'There's nothing worse than stupidity, see?' he said a bit later, coming back with a dipper. 'The missus kneels down and prays. She prays every night, see—bangs her head on the floor. The main thing is, she wants the boys to go to school. She's afraid of them being ordinary Cossacks and getting a sabre or two laid across their backs. But schooling means money and that doesn't grow on trees. You can bang your head on the floor till it goes right through, but if you haven't got it you haven't got it.

'The other reason she prays is that every woman thinks she's the unhappiest person in the world, see? I'm a blunt man and I'll not keep anything from you. She comes of a poor family. Her father's a priest, so she's a daughter of the cloth as you might say. I married her when she was seventeen. They let her marry me chiefly because they had nothing to eat. They were hard up and times were bad and I at least had land and a farm, see what I mean? And then I was an officer when all's said and done and she was flattered to marry me, see? She cried on our wedding day and since then she's hardly stopped the whole twenty years—oh, she's a proper cry-baby, is our Lyubov. She sits and thinks all the time. And what does she think about, I ask you? What *can* a woman think about? Nothing. But then women aren't really human to my way of thinking.'

The solicitor sat up abruptly.

'I'm sorry, it's a bit close in here,' he said. 'I must go outside.'

Still talking about women, Zhmukhin drew the bolt in the hall and they both went out. As it happened a full moon was sailing through the sky over the farm, and the house and barns seemed whiter by moonlight than by day. There were also bright streaks of silver moonlight, crossing the grass between black shadows. Away to the right the steppe could be seen for miles, with stars softly glowing above it. All was mysterious and infinitely remote, as though you were looking down into a deep abyss. But to the left heavy, pitch-black storm-clouds were stacked on top of one another above the steppe, their edges lit by the moon, and they looked like snow-capped mountains, dark forests, the sea. Lightning flashed, thunder faintly rumbled, and it seemed like a battle in the mountains. . . .

Just outside the grounds was a small night owl. 'To sleep! To sleep!' it cried monotonously.

'What time is it?' asked the visitor.

'Just after one.'

'Heavens, it won't be light for ages.'

They went back to the house and lay down again. They should

have slept—you usually sleep so well just before rain—but the old man was hankering after solemn, portentous ideas. Just thinking was not enough, he wanted to meditate. And he meditated that he would soon die, and ought for the good of his soul to shake off the laziness that caused day after day and year after year to be engulfed unnoticed, leaving no trace. He should plan some heroic exploit, like going on foot to some far-distant place or giving up meat like this young fellow. Once again he pictured the time when people would not kill animals any more. He saw it clearly and distinctly as if he was actually there, but his confusion suddenly returned, and all was blurred.

The storm passed over, but they were caught by some outlying clouds, and rain pattered lightly on the roof. Zhmukhin got up and looked into the parlour, groaning from sheer old age and stretching himself. His guest was still awake, he saw.

'We had a colonel in the Caucasus,' he said, 'a vegetarian like you, see what I mean? He didn't eat meat, never went hunting and wouldn't let his men fish. I see the point of course. Every animal should be free to enjoy life. But how can you let a pig go where it likes without keeping a eye on it, that's what I don't see . . . ?'

The guest sat up, his pale, haggard face showing annoyance and fatigue. He was obviously suffering, and only his natural good manners prevented him from putting his annoyance into words.

'It's getting light,' he said mildly. 'Would you please let me have a horse now?'

'But why? Wait till it stops raining.'

'No, really, please,' begged the guest fearfully. 'I must go right now.'

He started quickly dressing.

By the time they brought the horse the sun was rising. It had just stopped raining, clouds raced past, there were more and more blue patches in the sky and down in the puddles the first rays of sunlight timidly glinted.

The solicitor took his brief-case and went through the hall to get in the trap, while Mrs. Zhmukhin, tearful and pale—paler, seemingly, than the day before—gave him a careful, unblinking stare, looking as innocent as a little girl. Her dejected face showed how she envied his freedom—what joy it would be for her if she could escape from the place! And she obviously wanted to speak to him and must want his advice about the boys. She was so pathetic. She wasn't a wife, she wasn't the mistress of the house or even a servant, she was more of a dependant—an unwanted poor relation, a nobody.

Her husband made a great fuss of seeing his guest off, talking non-stop and constantly darting ahead of him, while she huddled, timid and apologetic, against a wall, waiting her chance to speak.

'Do come again,' the old man kept saying. 'You're always welcome, see what I mean?'

The guest got quickly into the trap, clearly relieved, but looking scared as if he feared some last-minute hitch, but the trap lurched and squealed as on the day before and a pail tied to the back-board banged furiously.

The solicitor looked back at Zhmukhin with an odd expression. It seemed as if he, like the surveyor before him, felt the urge to call Zhmukhin a savage or some such name, but being too kind he held himself back and said nothing. However, in the gateway he could suddenly stand it no longer and raised himself slightly.

'You're a bore!' he yelled angrily.

He vanished through the gate.

Zhmukhin's sons were standing near the barn. The elder had a gun and the younger held a grey cockerel with a beautiful bright comb. The younger threw the cockerel up as hard as he could and the bird flew higher than the house and turned over in the air like a pigeon. The elder boy fired and the cockerel fell like a stone.

Greatly put out, baffled by his guest's odd, unexpected outcry, the old man slowly made his way indoors. He sat at a table, reflecting for a while on current intellectual trends, universal immorality, the telegraph, the telephone and the bicycle—what use was all that stuff? He gradually calmed down, had a leisurely breakfast, drank five glasses of tea and went to bed.

IN THE CART

THEY left town at half-past eight in the morning.

The road had dried out and there was a glorious, hot April sun, but snow still lay in the ditches and among the trees. The long, dark, foul winter had only just ended and here, suddenly, was spring. It was so warm. The sleepy trees with their bare boughs basked in the breath of springtime and black flocks of birds flew over open country where vast pools lay like lakes. What joy, you felt, to disappear into the un-fathomable depths of that marvellous sky! But to Marya as she sat in the cart these things had nothing fresh or exciting to offer. For thirteen years she had been a schoolmistress, and during those years she had gone into town for her salary time without number. It might be spring, as now. It might be a rainy autumn evening or winter. What difference did it make? All she ever wanted was to get it over with.

She seemed to have lived in these parts for so long—a hundred years or more—and felt as if she knew every stone and tree on the way from town to her school. Her whole life, past and present, was bound up with the place, and what did the future hold? The school, the road to town, the school, the road to town again, and that was all. . . .

By now she had given up thinking of her life before she was a teacher and had forgotten about most of it. Once she had had a father and mother who lived in a big flat near the Red Gates in Moscow, but that period had only left a vague, blurred, dreamlike memory. Her father had died when she was ten, her mother soon after.

There was a brother, an army officer, and they had corresponded for a time, but then her brother lost the habit of answering. All she had left from those days was a snapshot of her mother and that had faded, as the schoolhouse was so damp—all you could see of Mother now was hair and eyebrows.

After a mile or two her driver, old Simon, turned round.

'They've run in some official in town,' he said. 'Sent him away, they have. They say he helped some Germans in Moscow to kill Mayor Alekseyev.'

'Who told you?'

'Someone read it out from the newspaper at Ivan Ionov's inn.'

Another long silence followed. Marya thought of her school and of the forthcoming examinations, for which she was entering four boys and one girl. She was just thinking about these examinations when Squire Khanov passed her in his carriage and four—the Khanov who had examined at her school last year. He recognized her as he drew level and bowed.

'Good morning,' he said. 'On your way home?'

This Khanov, a man of about forty, with a worn face and a bored look, had begun to show his age, but was still handsome and attractive to women. He lived alone on his large estate. He had no job and it was said that he did nothing at home but stride about whistling or play chess with an old manservant. He also drank a lot, it was said. And true enough, even the papers that he had brought to last year's examinations had smelt of scent and spirits. He had been wearing new clothes and Marya had thought him very attractive and felt rather shy sitting beside him. She was used to callous, businesslike examiners, but this one had forgotten all his prayers and did not know what questions to ask. He was most polite and tactful and everyone got full marks.

'Well, I'm going to see Bakvist,' he went on, addressing Marya. 'But I'm told he may be away.'

They turned off the highway into a country lane, Khanov leading and Simon bringing up the rear. The four horses plodded down the lane, straining to haul the heavy carriage out of the mud, while Simon zig-zagged and made detours up hill and down dale, often jumping off to help the horse.

Marya thought of the school and wondered how difficult the examination questions would be. She was annoyed with the rural council because she had not found anyone in the office the day before. What inefficiency! She had been on to them for the last two years to sack her caretaker, who was rude and idle and beat the children. But no one would listen. It was hard to catch the council chairman in his office, and even if you succeeded he only told you with tears in his eyes that he had not a moment to spare. The inspector visited the school only once in three years and was right out of his depth—he had been an excise officer before that and was only made inspector because he had friends in the right places. The education committee met very seldom, and then you could never find out where. The school manager was a peasant who could hardly write his name, and owned a tannery—a dull, uncouth fellow and a crony of the caretaker. So where on earth could you complain? Or find anything out . . . ?

'He really is a good-looking man,' she thought, with a glance at Khanov.

The track went from bad to worse.

They entered woods where no more detours were possible. There were deep ruts with swishing, gurgling water and prickly branches that lashed you in the face.

'Call this a road!' Khanov said with a laugh.

The schoolmistress stared at him.

Why was he fool enough to live round here? That's what she couldn't see. What use were his money, good looks and sophistication to him in this dismal, filthy dump? He got nothing out of life! He was slowly jogging along the same ghastly track as Simon here and putting up with just the same discomforts. Why live here when you could live in St. Petersburg or abroad? He was rich, and it might have been thought worth his while to improve this foul track and spare himself all the bother, and that look of despair on his coachman's face and Simon's. But he only laughed. He obviously didn't care—wasn't interested in any better life. He was kind, gentle, innocent. He didn't understand this rough life. He knew no more about it than he had about his prayers at the examinations. All he ever gave the school was terrestrial globes, yet he genuinely thought that this made him a useful citizen and a leading light in popular education. A lot of use his globes were here!

'Hold tight, miss,' said Simon.

The cart gave a great lurch and nearly overturned. Something heavy crashed onto Marya's feet—her bundles of shopping. Then came a steep climb on clay with water rushing and roaring down winding ruts as if it had gnawed into the track. What a place to drive through! The horses snorted. Khanov got down from his carriage and walked by the side of the track in his long overcoat. He was hot.

'Call this a road!' he said with another laugh. 'At this rate we'll soon have no carriage left.'

'Well, why go out in such weather?' asked Simon sternly. 'Stay at home, can't you?'

'Home's a bore, old fellow. I hate being cooped up there.'

He looked fit and keen enough beside old Simon, but there was a hint of something in the way he walked which showed that he was really a feeble, poisoned creature well on the road to ruin. And from the forest, sure enough, came a sudden whiff of spirits. Marya was horrified. She was sorry for the man, and could see no good reason why he should be so hopeless. It struck her that if she was his wife or sister she would very likely give her whole life to saving him.

'His wife?' He lived alone on his large estate, the way things had worked out, while she also lived alone—in her godforsaken village. But could they be friends and equals? The very idea—impossible, absurd! Such is life, that's what it comes down to. People's relationships have grown so complex, they make so little sense. They are too frightful to contemplate—too depressing altogether.

'Why, oh why,' she thought, 'does God give these weak, unhappy, useless people such good looks, delightful manners and beautiful, melancholy eyes? Why are they so charming?'

'This is where we turn right,' said Khanov, getting back in his carriage. 'Goodbye and good luck.'

Once more she thought of pupils, of the examinations, the caretaker and the education committee. Then she heard the departing carriage rumbling somewhere on her right, its noise borne on the wind—and these thoughts fused with others. She wanted to dream of beautiful eyes, love and happiness that was not to be. . . .

To be a wife? It was cold in the mornings with the caretaker out and no one to light the stoves. The children began arriving at crack of dawn, bringing in snow and mud and making a noise. It was all so hideously uncomfortable. She had only a bed-sitting-room in which she also did her cooking. She had headaches every day after school and after dinner she always had heartburn. She had to collect money from the children for firewood and for the caretaker and hand it to the manager—then practically go down on her knees to that smug, insolent lout before he let her have the wood. Examinations, peasants, snowdrifts—they filled her dreams at night. The life had aged and coarsened her—made her ugly, awkward, clumsy, as if her veins were filled with lead. She was so scared of things. If the school manager or a local councillor came in, she would rise to her feet and did not dare sit down. And she called them 'sir'. No one found her attractive and life rolled wretchedly on without affection, sympathy or interesting friends. For her to fall in love, placed as she was, would be a disaster.

'Hold tight, miss!'

Another steep rise. . . .

She had become a teacher because she was hard up, not because she had any vocation for it. She never thought of education as a calling, or as something of value. She always felt that examinations were the main thing in her job, not pupils or education, and anyway, what time had she to think of her calling or of the value of education? Teachers, badly paid doctors and their assistants do a tough enough

job, yet are so worried about where their next meal is coming from—
or about fuel, bad roads and illness—that they even miss the satisfaction
of thinking that they are serving an ideal or working for the people.
It is a hard, dull life and no one puts up with it for long except silent
drudges like Marya. Vivacious, highly strung, sensitive souls may talk
of their vocation and service to ideals, but they soon enough wilt and
throw in their hand.

Simon tried to pick the driest and shortest route through fields or
back yards, but at one place the villagers would not let him pass,
another place was priest's land and no thoroughfare, while somewhere
else again Ivan Ionov had bought a plot from the squire and dug a ditch
round it. They kept turning back.

They came to Lower Gorodishche. Near the inn, in a place where
the snow was spread with dung, stood carts loaded with oil of vitriol
in carboys. The inn was full of people, all waggoners, and smelt of
vodka, tobacco and sheepskins. People were talking at the top of
their voices and the door, which had a weight-and-pulley to keep it
shut, kept slamming. In the off-licence next door there was an accordion playing, and it never let up for a second. Marya sat down and
drank tea, while peasants at the next table—half stewed already, what
with the tea they had had and the stuffy ale-house atmosphere—were
swilling vodka and beer.

Discordant voices rang out. 'Hey, Kuzma!' 'Eh?' 'Lord, save us!'
'That I can, Ivan, my boy!' 'Watch it, mate!'

A short, pock-marked peasant with a little black beard, who had
been drunk for a long time, suddenly showed surprise at something
and swore vilely.

Simon was sitting at the far end of the room. 'Hey, you! What
do you mean by swearing!' he shouted angrily. 'Can't you see the
young lady?'

'Young lady, eh?' sneered someone in the other corner.

'Clumsy swine!'

'Sorry, I didn't mean no harm . . . ' said the little peasant sheepishly.
'I was minding my own business, just as the young lady was minding
hers. . . . Good morning to you, miss.'

'Good morning,' answered the teacher.

'And uncommonly obliged to you I am.'

Enjoying her tea, Marya went red in the face like the peasants while
she brooded yet again on the firewood and the caretaker. . . .

'Just a moment, mate,' came a voice from the next table. 'It's her

that teaches at Vyazovye . . . we know her—and a nice young lady
she is too.'

'Oh, yes, she's not bad at all.'

The door kept banging as people came and went. Marya sat, still
thinking the same old thoughts, while the accordion next door went
on and on and on. On the floor had been patches of sunlight. They had
moved to the counter, crawled up the wall and disappeared altogether.
So it must be past noon. The men at the next table made ready to go.
Swaying slightly, the little peasant went up and shook hands with
Marya. The others took their cue from him and also shook hands and
then went out one after another. Nine times the door squeaked and
slammed.

'Get ready, miss!' shouted Simon.

They drove off, but could still only move at walking pace.

'They built a school not long back here in Lower Gorodishche,' said
Simon, turning round. 'What a swindle!'

'Why, what happened?'

'They say the chairman of the council pocketed a thousand, the
manager another thousand, and the teacher got five hundred.'

'But the whole school only cost a thousand. You shouldn't tell such
tales, old fellow. You're talking rubbish.'

'I wouldn't know. . . . I only got it from the others.'

But Simon clearly didn't believe the teacher. The peasants never did
trust her, they always thought that she was paid too much—a cool
twenty-one roubles a month where five would have done—and they
thought that she hung on to most of what she collected from the
children for firewood and the caretaker. The manager thought like
the peasants. He himself made a bit on the firewood and was also
paid by the peasants for managing the school, of which the authorities
knew nothing.

The forest ended, thank God, and now it was all level going to
Vyazovye. They were nearly there—just the river to cross and the
railway line—and that would be it.

'Hey! Where are you off to?' Marya asked Simon. 'Why didn't you
go to the right across the bridge?'

'Eh? We can get across here. It ain't very deep.'

'Mind we don't drown the horse then.'

'Eh?'

'Look—there's Khanov crossing the bridge,' said Marya, spotting
a carriage and four far to the right. 'It is him, isn't it?'

'That it is. Bakvist must have been out. Pig-headed fool, Lord help us, going all that way when this be two mile nearer.'

They drove down to the river. In summer it was a shallow brook, easily forded, and by August it had usually dried up, but now the spring floods had made it a cold, muddy torrent about forty feet across. On the bank, right up to the water's edge, were fresh wheel tracks, so someone must have crossed here.

'Come on!' shouted Simon, angry and worried, tugging hard at the reins and flapping his elbows like wings. 'Gee up!'

The horse waded in up to its belly and stopped, but then plunged on again, straining every sinew, and Marya felt a cold shock on her feet.

She stood up. 'Come on,' she shouted. 'Gee up!'

They came out on the other bank.

'Gawd help us, what with one thing and another,' muttered Simon, putting the harness to rights. 'A proper botheration—'tis all the council's doing. . . .'

Marya's galoshes and boots were full of water, the bottom of her dress and coat and one sleeve were sopping wet—and worst of all, her sugar and flour were soaked. She could only throw up her hands in horror.

'Oh, Simon . . . ' she said. 'Simon, how could you . . . ?'

The barrier was down at the level-crossing and an express was ready to leave the station. Marya stood by the crossing and waited for it to pass, trembling with cold in every limb. Vyazovye was in view—the school with its green roof and the church, its crosses ablaze in the evening sun. The station windows blazed too and the smoke from the engine was pink.

Everything seemed to be shivering with cold.

The train came past, its windows ablaze like the church crosses—it hurt to look at them. On the small platform at the end of a first-class carriage stood a woman and Marya glanced at her. It was her mother! What a fantastic likeness! Her mother had the same glorious hair, exactly the same forehead and set of the head. Vividly, with striking clarity, for the first time in thirteen years, she pictured her mother and father, her brother, their Moscow flat, the fish-tank and goldfish—all down to the last detail. Suddenly she heard a piano playing, heard her father's voice and felt as she had felt then—young, pretty, well-dressed in a warm, light room, with her family round her. In a sudden surge of joy and happiness she clasped her head rapturously in her hands.

'Mother,' she cried tenderly, appealingly.

For some reason she burst into tears, at which moment Khanov drove up with his coach and four. Seeing him, she imagined such happiness as has never been on earth. She smiled and nodded to him as to her friend and equal, feeling that the sky, the trees and all the windows were aglow with her triumphant happiness. No, her father and mother had not died, she had never been a schoolmistress. It had all been a strange dream, a long nightmare, and now she had woken up. . . .

'Get in, miss.'

Suddenly it all vanished. The barrier slowly rose. Shivering, numb with cold, Marya got into the cart. The coach and four crossed the line, followed by Simon. The crossing-keeper raised his cap.

'Well, here we are. Vyazovye.'

NEW VILLA

I

A HUGE bridge was under construction two miles from Obruchanovo village. From the village, which stood high on a steep bank, the trellised skeleton could be seen: a picturesque—indeed, a fantastic—sight in misty weather and on quiet winter days, when the thin iron struts and all the surrounding scaffolding were frost-covered. Engineer Kucherov, who was building the bridge—a stout, broad-shouldered, bearded man with a crumpled soft cap—sometimes drove through the village in a fast droshky or carriage. Sometimes the navvies employed on the bridge came along on their days off—begged for money, jeered at the local women, occasionally absconded with something. That was exceptional, though. Usually the days passed as quietly and uneventfully as if no construction was in progress at all. Only in the evenings, when bonfires blazed near the bridge, was the navvies' singing borne faintly on the breeze. In daytime there was an occasional sad, metallic clanking.

Mrs. Kucherov, the engineer's wife, chanced to come over on a visit. Much taken with the river banks and the gorgeous view of the green valley with its hamlets, churches and cattle, she asked her husband to buy a small plot of land and build a villa. He did. They bought fifty acres, and on the high bank, in a meadow where once the village cows had strayed, they put up a handsome two-storey house with terrace, balconies, tower . . . and a spire which flew a flag on Sundays. After building it in about three months they planted large trees through the winter. Then, when spring came with all the fresh greenery, the new garden already had its paths. A gardener and his two white-aproned assistants dug near the house, a fountain played and a globe made of looking-glass gleamed so fiercely that it hurt the eyes. The estate already had its name: New Villa.

One fine warm morning at the end of May two horses were brought to Obruchanovo for shoeing by the local blacksmith, Rodion Petrov. They came from New Villa, they were snow-white, graceful, well-fed, and they bore a striking resemblance to each other.

'Like swans, they are,' said Rodion, awe-struck.

His wife Stepanida, his children, his grand-children . . all came out of doors to see, and a crowd gradually collected. The Lychkovs, father and son—both naturally beardless, both puffy-faced and hatless—came along. So did Kozov: a tall, scraggy old boy with a long, narrow beard, carrying a walking-stick. He kept winking sly winks and smiling sardonic, knowing smiles.

'They're white, but they're no good,' said he. 'Put mine on oats, and they'd be just as sleek. I'd make 'em plough—whip 'em too.'

The coachman just gave him a look of scorn and said nothing. Then, as the smithy furnace was heated up, the coachman talked and smoked cigarettes. The villagers learnt many details. His master and mistress were rich. Before her marriage the mistress, Helen Kucherov, had been a poor governess in Moscow. She was kind, she was soft-hearted, she liked helping the poor. There was to be no ploughing or sowing on the new estate, said he. They were just going to enjoy themselves—breathing fresh air, that was their sole aim in life.

When he had finished and started leading the horses back home, a crowd of urchins followed him. Dogs barked. Kozov watched him go, winking sarcastically.

'Think they own everything!' he jeered. 'They build a house, they keep horses—but they're the lowest of the low, believe you me. Think they're the lords of creation, do they?'

Kozov had somehow conceived an immediate loathing for the new estate, for those white horses, for that sleek, handsome coachman. He was a lonely man, was Kozov, a widower. He led a dull life—couldn't work because of some illness: 'me rheumatics' he would call it, or 'the worms'. The money for his keep came from a son who worked at a Kharkov confectioner's. He would stroll idly along the river bank or village from dawn to dusk. If he saw someone carting a log, say —or fishing—he would tell him that his wood was 'dry, rotten stuff', or that he would 'never catch anything on a day like this'. During droughts he would say that there would be no rain before the frosts came, and when it did rain he would say that the crops would all rot, they were all ruined. And he would wink knowingly the while.

On the estate Bengal lights and rockets were set off in the evenings, and a boat with red lamps would sail past Obruchanovo. One morning the engineer's wife, Helen Kucherov, brought her little daughter to the village in a yellow-wheeled trap drawn by a pair of dark bay ponies. Mother and daughter both wore broad-brimmed straw hats turned down over their ears.

This happened at mucking-out time, and Blacksmith Rodion—a

tall, scraggy, bare-headed, barefoot old man with a pitchfork over his shoulder—stood near his nasty, dirty cart, staring flabbergasted at those ponies. He had never seen such small horses in his life . . . that was written on his face.

'Look at 'er in the trap!' the whisper was heard on all sides. 'It's that there Kucherov woman.'

Scanning the huts quizzically, Helen Kucherov halted her horses near the poorest of all, where there were masses of children's heads—fair, dark, red—in the windows. Out of the hut ran Rodion's wife, Stepanida, a stout old girl, her kerchief slipping off her grey hair. She peered at the trap against the sun, smiling and frowning like a blind person.

'This is for your children, my good woman,' said Helen Kucherov. And gave her three roubles.

Suddenly bursting into tears, Stepanida bowed to the ground, while Rodion too flopped down, showing his broad, brown pate and almost catching his wife in the side with his pitchfork. Helen Kucherov felt awkward and went home.

II

The Lychkovs, father and son, caught two cart-horses straying in their meadow, together with one pony and a broad-muzzled Aalhaus bull-calf. These they drove off to the village, helped by 'Ginger' Volodka—Blacksmith Rodion's son. They called the village elder, they collected witnesses, they went to assess the damage.

'Very well, let 'em try it on!' Kozov winked. 'Just let 'em try, that's all. Let's see them engineers wriggle out of this! Think themselves above the law, do they? Very well, we'll send for the sergeant, make out a charge.'

'Make out a charge,' echoed Volodka.

'I ain't a-going to overlook it,' shouted the younger Lychkov. His voice sounded louder and louder, seeming to make his beardless face bulge increasingly. 'A fine to-do, this is! Ruin all the pasture, they will, if we let 'em! They ain't got no right to harm the common man. We ain't living in the dark ages.'

'No, that we ain't,' echoed Volodka.

'We've got on without a bridge so far,' said Lychkov Senior gloomily. 'We never asked for one, we don't need one and we won't 'ave one!'

'They ain't getting away with this, mates!'

'Just let 'em try it on!' winked Kozov. 'Let 'em squirm! Who do they think they are?'

They turned back towards the village, and as they went Lychkov Junior pounded his chest with his fist, shouting, while Volodka also shouted, echoing his words. Meanwhile, in the village, a crowd had formed round the pedigree bull-calf and horses. The calf glowered in embarrassment, but suddenly dropped his head to the ground and ran, kicking up his back legs. Taking fright, Kozov swung his stick and everyone laughed. Then they locked the animals up and waited.

That evening the engineer sent five roubles in compensation, where-upon both horses, pony and bull-calf returned home: unfed, unwatered, hanging their heads in guilt as if on their way to execution.

Having received the five roubles, the Lychkovs Senior and Junior, the village elder and Volodka crossed the river by boat, set off for Kryakovo village on the other side, where there was a pub, and spent a long time whooping it up. Their singing and young Lychkov's shouting were heard. Back at the village the women couldn't sleep all night for worrying. Nor could Rodion.

'A bad business,' he sighed, tossing from side to side. 'He'll have the law on 'em, will Squire, if he be vexed. They done him wrong, oh, that they have. A bad business.'

One day the men, Rodion included, went into their wood to decide who should reap what plot of land. On their way home they met the engineer. He wore a red calico shirt and high boots, he was followed by a setter with its long tongue stuck out.

'Good day, my lads,' said he.

The peasants stopped, doffed their caps.

'I've been wanting to talk to you for some time, lads,' he went on. 'The thing is, your cattle have been in my garden and woods every day since early spring. It's all been trampled up. Your pigs have dug up the meadow, they're ruining the vegetable plot, and I've lost all the saplings in my wood. I can't get on with your shepherds, they bite your head off if you ask them anything. You trespass on my land every day, but I do nothing, I don't get you fined, I don't complain. Now you've taken my horses and bull—*and* my five roubles.

'Is it fair, is it neighbourly?' he went on, his voice soft and pleading, his glance anything but stern. 'Is this how decent men behave? One of you cut down two young oaks in my wood a week ago. You've dug up the Yeresnevo road, and now I have to go two miles out of my way. Why are you always injuring me? What harm have I done you?

For God's sake tell me. My wife and I have tried our level best to live in peace and harmony with you—we help the village as much as we can. My wife is a kind, warm-hearted woman, she doesn't refuse to help—she longs to be useful to you and your children. But you repay good with evil. You are unfair, my friends. Now, you just think it over, I beg you—think it over. We're treating you decently, so why can't you pay us back in the same coin?'

He turned and walked off. The peasants stood a little longer, put their hats on, and left. Rodion—who misinterpreted everything, always putting his own twist on things—gave a sigh.

'We'll have to pay, says he. Pay in coin, mates.'

They walked to the village in silence. At home Rodion said his prayers, took his boots off, and sat on the bench beside his wife. Stepanida and he always did sit side by side at home, and they always walked down the street side by side. They always ate, drank and slept together, and the more they aged the more they loved each other. It was hot and crowded in their hut, and there were children everywhere: on floor, window-ledges and stove.

Stepanida was still having babies despite her advanced years, and it was hard to tell which, in that huddle of children, were Rodion's and which Volodka's. Volodka's wife Lukerya—an ill-favoured young woman with bulging eyes and a beaky nose—was mixing dough in a tub. Her husband sat on the stove, feet dangling.

'On the road near Nikita's buckwheat, er . . . the engineer and his dog,' began Rodion after resting and scratching his sides and elbows. 'We must pay, says he. In coin, he says. I dunno about no coins, but ten copecks a hut—that we should collect. We're treating Squire right badly, we are. 'Tis a shame——'

'We've done without a bridge so far,' said Volodka, looking at no one. 'We don't want no bridge.'

'Oh, get away with you! 'Tis a government bridge.'

'We don't want none of it.'

'Who asked you? What's it got to do with you?'

' "Who asked you?" ' mimicked Volodka. 'We have nowhere to go, so what do we want with a bridge? We can cross by boat if we want.'

Someone outside banged the window so loudly that the whole hut seemed to shake.

'Volodka in?' said the voice of Lychkov Junior. 'Come out, Volodka. On our way!'

Volodka jumped down from the stove, looked for his cap.

'Don't go, Volodka,' Rodion said nervously. 'Don't go with them, son. You're such a silly boy, you're a proper baby, and they won't teach you no good. Don't go.'

'Don't go, son,' begged Stepanida, blinking on the brink of tears. 'They want to take you to the pub, I'll be bound.'

' "To the pub",' Volodka mimicked.

'You'll come back drunk again, you filthy hell-hound.' Lukerya gave him an angry look. 'You go! And may the vodka rot your guts, you blasted tailless wonder!'

'You hold your tongue!' Volodka shouted.

'I'm married to a half-wit, my life's been ruined—oh, I'm so alone and unhappy! You ginger-haired sot!' lamented Lukerya, wiping her face with a dough-covered hand. 'I wish I'd never set eyes on you.'

Volodka hit her on the ear and left.

III

Helen Kucherov and her little daughter went for a stroll and arrived in the village on foot. It happened to be a Sunday, and the women and girls were out and about in their bright dresses. Sitting side by side on their porch, Rodion and Stepanida gave Helen and her little girl a friendly bow and smile, while over a dozen children watched them from the windows, their faces expressing bafflement and curiosity. Whispering was heard.

'It's that there Kucherov woman.'

'Good morning,' said Helen and stopped.

'Well, how are you?' she asked after a pause.

'Can't complain, praise be,' answered Rodion rapidly. 'We manage, that's true enough.'

'Oh, it's no end of a life, lady, ours is,' Stepanida laughed. 'You can see how poor we are, love. We've fourteen in the family, and only two at work. It ain't much of a trade, a smith's ain't. People bring their horses for shoeing, but there's no coal—we can't afford it. It's a terrible life, lady,' she went on with a laugh. ' 'Tis a proper botheration!'

Helen sat on the porch and put her arms broodily round her little girl. The child too looked as if she was subject to gloomy musings, and pensively played with the smart lace parasol which she had taken from her mother.

'We're so poor,' said Rodion. 'We have lots of trouble and no end of work. And now God won't send us rain. It's a rotten life, that's plain enough.'

'You suffer in this life,' said Helen. 'But you'll be happy in the next.'

Not understanding, Rodion only coughed into his fist.

'The rich are well off, lady,' said Stepanida. 'Even in the next world they are, love. Your rich man pays for his church candles, he has his special services held. And he gives to the poor, does the rich man. But your peasant hasn't time to make the sign of the cross over his forehead, even. He's poor as a church mouse—so how *can* he save his soul? It makes for a mort of sinning, does poverty. Oh, it's a dog's life, ours—sheer howling misery, I call it! We've a good word for no one, missus. And the goings-on round here, love—well, all I say is, God 'elp us! There's no happiness for us in this world *or* the next. The rich have took it all.'

She spoke good-humouredly, obviously long accustomed to retailing her miseries. Rodion smiled too. He liked feeling that his old woman was so clever, that she had the gift of the gab.

'The rich aren't really so well off, appearances are deceptive,' said Helen. 'Everyone has some trouble or other. Now, we—my husband and I—don't live poorly, we do have means. But are we happy? I'm still young, but I have four children already. They're always ill. I'm ill too—I'm always seeing the doctor.'

'What's the matter with you then?' Rodion asked.

'It's a woman's complaint. I can't sleep, I'm plagued by headaches. Here I sit talking to you, but my head feels rotten, my body's weak all over, and I'd rather do the hardest labour than be in such a state. I'm worried too. You fear for your children and your husband all the time. Every family has some trouble or other, and we have ours. I'm not really a lady. My grandfather was an ordinary peasant, and my father a Moscow tradesman—so he was lower class too. But my husband has rich, well-connected parents. They didn't want him to marry me, but he disobeyed them, quarrelled with them. And they still haven't forgiven us. This bothers my husband—upsets him, makes him edgy all the time. He loves his mother, loves her very much. So I'm upset too, my feelings are hurt.'

Near Rodion's hut men and women now stood around listening. Up came Kozov. He halted, shook his long narrow beard. Up came the Lychkovs, father and son.

'And another thing—you can't be happy and contented if you feel out of place,' went on Helen. 'Each of you has his plot of land—you all

work, and you do know what you're working for. My husband
builds bridges. Everyone has his own job, in other words. But I just
drift, I have no bit of land, I don't work, I feel out of it. I'm telling you
all this so you shan't judge from appearances. If a person has expensive
clothes, and is well off, it doesn't follow that he's contented with his
lot.'

She got up to go away, taking her daughter's hand.

'I do like being with you here,' she smiled: a feeble, timid smile
which showed how unwell she really was—and how young and pretty.
She had a pale, thin face, dark brows and fair hair. The little girl was
just like her mother: thin, fair-haired, slender. They smelt of scent.

'I like the river, the woods, the village,' Helen went on. 'I could
spend all my life here. I feel as if I could get well here, and find a place
in life. I want, I do so much want, to help you: to be useful and close
to you. I know how poor you are, and what I don't know I can feel
and sense by instinct. I'm ill and weak myself—perhaps it's too late
for me, now, to change my life as I should like. But I do have children,
and I shall try to educate them to know you and like you. I shall always
impress on them that their lives belong to you, not to themselves. But
I beg most earnestly, I implore you—do trust us, do live in friendship
with us. My husband is a good, kind man. Don't upset and irritate him.
He's so sensitive to every trifle. Take yesterday—your cattle got into
our vegetable garden, and one of you broke the fence by our bee-
hives. It's your attitude to us . . . it drives my husband frantic.

'I beg you,' she pleaded, crossing her hands on her breast, 'do please
be good neighbours, do let us live in peace. A bad truce is better than a
good war, they say, and it's always neighbours you buy rather than a
house. My husband is, I repeat, a good, kind man. If all goes well we'll
do our utmost, I promise you: we'll mend roads, we'll build a school
for your children. You have my promise.'

'We thanks you kindly, lady—stands to reason,' said Lychkov
Senior, looking at the ground. 'You're educated, like, and you know
what's best. It's just that a rich villager—name of "Raven" Voronov—
once said he'd build a school in Yeresnevo, like. He too kept saying
he'd give this and he'd give that. But all he did was put up the framework and walk out. Them peasants had to build the roof and finish it
off—a thousand roubles, it cost 'em. Raven didn't care, just stroked his
beard—but it was kind of hard on the lads.'

'That was Master Raven's doing,' winked Kozov. 'Now it's Mrs.
Rook's turn!'

Laughter was heard.

'We don't need no school,' said Volodka gloomily. 'Our kids go to Petrovskoye. Let 'em! We don't want one.'

Helen suddenly felt nervous. She blenched, her face looked pinched, she flinched as at the touch of something coarse, and she went off without another word. She walked faster and faster without looking round.

'Lady,' called Rodion, going after her. 'Wait a moment, missus, I want to talk to you.'

He followed her, hatless. 'I've something to say, missus,' he told her quietly, as if begging for alms.

They left the village, and Helen stopped in the shadow of an old mountain-ash near somebody's cart.

'Don't you take offence, missus,' said Rodion. 'Don't you take no notice. Just have patience, put up with things for a couple of years. Stay on here and put up with it, it'll be all right. We're decent, quiet folk. The peasants are all right, I'll take my oath. Never mind Kozov and the Lychkovs, never mind my Volodka—that boy's an idiot, listens to the first that speaks. The rest are peaceable, quiet folk. One or two of them wouldn't mind putting in a good word and standing up for you, like, but they can't. They have feelings and consciences, but they ain't got no tongues. Don't you take offence, you just put up with it. What does it matter?'

Helen looked pensively at the broad, calm river, tears streaming down her cheeks. Embarrassed by her weeping, Rodion almost wept himself.

'Don't you take no notice,' he muttered. 'Put up with it for a couple of years. We can have the school and the roads—but not just yet. Suppose you wanted to sow crops on this hillock, say. You'd first have to grub up the roots and pick out all the stones. Then you'd plough it—for ever a-coming and a-going you'd be. Folk are the same, like, there's a lot of coming and going before you get things to rights.'

A crowd detached itself from Rodion's hut, and moved off up the road towards the mountain-ash. They began singing, an accordion struck up. They kept coming nearer and nearer.

'Do let's leave here, Mother,' said the little girl—pale, huddling up to her mother and trembling all over. 'Let's go away!'

'Where to?'

'Moscow. Let's go away, Mother.'

The child burst into tears. Rodion, his face sweating profusely, was utterly taken aback. He removed a cucumber from his pocket—a little, twisted, crescent-shaped cucumber covered with rye crumbs—and thrust it into the girl's hands.

'There there,' he muttered, frowning sternly. 'Take the cucumber and eat it, dear. Don't cry, now, or Mummy will smack you—she'll tell your father of you. There, there.'

They walked off. He followed, wanting to say something kind and persuasive. Then, seeing that both were too engrossed in their thoughts and grief to notice him, he stopped. Shielding his eyes from the sun, he watched them for a while until they vanished into their wood.

IV

The engineer had evidently grown irritable and niggling, now seeing in every trifle some act of robbery or other outrage. He kept his gates bolted even in daytime, and at night two watchmen patrolled his garden beating boards. He hired no more labour from Obruchanovo. And then, as ill luck would have it, someone—peasant or navvy, no one knew which—took the new wheels off his cart and replaced them with old ones. A little later two bridles and a pair of tongs were taken, and murmurs were heard even in the village. The Lychkovs' place and Volodka's ought to be searched, it was said. But then both tongs and bridles turned up under the engineer's garden hedge, where someone had thrown them.

Going from the wood one day, a crowd of peasants met the engineer on the road again. He stopped without saying good day.

'I have asked you not to pick mushrooms in my park and near my place, but to leave them for my wife and children,' said he, looking angrily from one to the other. 'But your girls come before dawn, and we're left without any. Whatever we ask or don't ask, it makes no difference. Pleading, kindness, persuasion . . . they're all useless, I see.'

He fixed his indignant gaze on Rodion.

'My wife and I have treated you as human beings, as equals,' he went on. 'But what about you? Oh—what's the use of talking? We shall end up looking *down* on you, very likely—what else can we do?'

Making an effort to keep his temper, in case he said too much, he turned on his heel and marched off.

Rodion went home, prayed, took his boots off, sat on his bench beside his wife.

'Aye,' said he when he was rested. 'We're walking along just now, and there's Squire Kucherov coming our way. Aye! He saw them girls at dawn. Why, says he, don't they pick some mushrooms for my wife and children? Then he looks at me. "Me and the wife, we're a-going to look *after* you," says he. I want to fall down at his feet, but I don't make so bold. God save him, Lord bless him——'

Stepanida crossed herself and sighed.

'Squire and his lady are so nice and kind, like,' Rodion went on. ' "We shall look after you"—he promises me that before them all. In our old age, er—. Not a bad thing, either—. I'd always remember them in my prayers. Holy Mother, bless him——'

The Fourteenth of September—the Feast of the Exaltation of the Cross—was the local church festival. After going over the river in the morning, Lychkov Senior and Lychkov Junior came back towards afternoon drunk. They lurched about the village for a while, singing and swapping obscenities, they had a fight, and they went up to the manor to complain. First Lychkov Senior entered the grounds carrying a long aspen stick. He halted indecisively, doffed his cap.

'What do you want?' shouted the engineer, who happened to be having tea on the terrace with his family.

'Begging your pardon, Squire,' began Lychkov, bursting into tears. 'Have mercy on me, sir—don't let me down. My son'll be the death of me. Ruined me, he has. He's always picking on me, sir——'

In came Lychkov Junior, hatless, also carrying a stick. He paused, he fixed a drunken, mindless stare on the terrace.

'It's not my job to deal with you,' said the engineer. 'Go and see the police, go to the magistrate.'

'I've been everywhere, I've made me applications,' said Lychkov Senior, sobbing. 'Where can I turn now? He can murder me now, I suppose. Do anything he likes, can he? And to his father? His own father?'

He raised his stick and hit his son on the head. Then Junior raised *his* stick and struck the old man straight on his bald pate so hard that the stick actually rebounded. Without so much as a wince, Lychkov *père* again hit Junior, again on the head. They just stood there clouting each other on the head—it looked more like some game than a fight. Massing beyond the gates, village men and women stared silently into the yard, all looking very serious. They had come to offer their holiday greetings, but when they saw the Lychkovs they were too ashamed to go in.

Next morning Helen left for Moscow with her children, and rumour had it that the engineer had put his house up for sale.

V

The bridge has long been a familiar sight—it is hard, now, to imagine this bit of river without its bridge. The heaps of building rubble have long been covered with grass, the navvies are a thing of the past, and instead of their shanties the noise of a passing train is heard almost hourly.

New Villa was sold long ago. It belongs, now, to a civil servant who brings his family over on his days off, has tea on his terrace and drives back to town. He wears a cockade on his cap, he talks and coughs like a bureaucrat of consequence, whereas in fact he's very much of a junior. When the villagers bow to him he makes no reply.

Everyone in Obruchanovo has aged. Kozov has died, Rodion has even more children in his hut, Volodka has grown a long ginger beard. They are just as poor as ever.

Early one spring the Obruchanovites are sawing wood near the station. See them going home after work: walking slowly, in single file. The wide saws sway on their shoulders, reflecting sunlight. Nightingales sing in the bushes on the river's bank, larks trill in the sky. At New Villa all is quiet, not a soul is to be seen—nothing but golden pigeons . . . golden because they are flying in the sunshine high above the house. Everyone—Rodion, both Lychkovs, Volodka— remembers white horses, little ponies, fireworks, lamp-lit boat. They remember the engineer's wife, so handsome and elegant, coming to the village, speaking to them so kindly. Yet none of it might ever have happened, it is all like a dream or legend.

They trudge along wearily, pensively.

We're decent, quiet, reasonable, god-fearing folk in the village, they reflect. Helen Kucherov had been a quiet, kind, gentle person too— you couldn't help liking her, poor thing. So why had they been on such bad terms, why had they parted as enemies? What was this mist which veiled everything of real importance, while disclosing only such trifles as trespass, bridles, tongs? Such nonsense it all seems when you remember it now! How is it that they can get on with the new owner when they were on such bad terms with the engineer?

Knowing no answer to these questions, they remain silent. Only Volodka mutters something.

'What's that?' asks Rodion.

'We've managed without a bridge,' says Volodka gloomily. 'We never asked for no bridge and we don't need none.'

No one answers. They trudge on silently, heads bowed.

An acting coroner and a country doctor were on their way to hold an inquest in the village of Syrnya when they were overtaken by a snowstorm. For a while they went round in circles, and instead of turning up (as intended) at noon they did not arrive until evening, when it was dark. They were to stay the night in a hut, the rural district council 'offices'. Now, it chanced that these same 'offices' housed the corpse: that of the council's insurance representative Lesnitsky, who had reached Syrnya three days earlier, settled down in the hut, ordered a samovar and shot himself much to everyone's surprise. The strange manner of his end—over that samovar, after he had spread his food out on the table—had given rise to widespread suspicions of murder. An inquest there must be.

Doctor and coroner shook the snow off in the passage, stamping their feet, while the elderly village constable, Eli Loshadin, stood near them holding a light: a tin lamp. There was a stink of paraffin.

'Who are you, my man?' asked the doctor.

'Conshtible,' answered the constable. That was how he signed his name in the post-office: conshtible.

'And where are the witnesses?'

'Gone for their tea, sir, I reckon.'

On the right was the parlour, or 'reception'—for persons of genteel rank—and on the left was the room for the vulgar, with its big stove and its shelf for sleeping on. Doctor and coroner, followed by the constable with the lamp above his head, went into 'reception'. Here, on the floor close to the table legs, a long, white-shrouded body lay stock still. Besides that white covering the dim lamp-light clearly showed some new rubber galoshes. It was all very eerie and nasty: the dark walls, the silence, those galoshes, the stillness of the corpse. On the table was the samovar, long cold, and around it were certain packets—the food, presumably.

'Shooting himself on council property—very tactless, that,' said the doctor. 'If he wanted to put a bullet through his brains he might have done it at home in some shed or other.'

Just as he was—in fur cap, fur coat, felt boots—he lowered himself on to the bench. His companion the coroner sat opposite.

'They're so selfish, these hysterical neurotics,' the doctor went on sadly. 'When a neurotic sleeps in the same room as you, he'll rustle a newspaper. When you dine together he'll start a row with his wife without minding you. And when he fancies shooting himself he does it like this: in a village, on official premises, just to create as much trouble as possible. No matter where they are they think only of Number One, these birds do—oh, they're a selfish lot. That's why old folk so dislike what they call this "nervous" age.'

'Old folk dislike so many things,' yawned the coroner. 'Why don't you tell the older generation about the difference between suicides as they used to be and as they are today? In the old days your gentleman, so-called, would shoot himself because he'd embezzled public money, but your present-day suicide does it because he's fed up with life and depressed. Which is better?'

'The fed-up-and-depressed brigade. Still, he didn't have to shoot himself on council property, now, did he?'

'Oh it's real vexing—more than flesh and blood can stand,' said the constable. 'The peasants are very upset, sir, they haven't slept these three nights. Their kids are crying. Their cows need milking, but the women are scared to go to the shed—afraid they'll see the gent's ghost in the dark. They're just silly women, I know, but there's some of the men scared too. They won't pass this hut on their own of an evening, they all troop by in a bunch. Them witnesses are the same.'

Middle-aged, dark-bearded, bespectacled Dr. Starchenko and Coroner Lyzhin—fair-haired, quite young, having taken his degree only two years previously and looking more like a student than an official—sat deep in silent thought. They were annoyed at arriving late. Now they had to wait till morning and spend the night here, but it wasn't even six o'clock yet, and they were faced with a long evening followed by a long, dark night, boredom, uncomfortable sleeping arrangements, cockroaches and the cold of early morning. Harking to the blizzard howling in chimney and loft, both thought how far this was from the life which they would have chosen, and of which they had once dreamed. How little they resembled their contemporaries who were now strolling down brightly-lit town streets not noticing the bad weather, who were getting ready for the theatre or sitting over books in their studies. What they would have given, now, just to stroll along the Nevsky Prospekt in St. Petersburg or down Moscow's Petrovka Street, to listen to decent singing, to spend an hour or so in a restaurant!

The blizzard whined and droned in the loft, there was a furious slamming outside: the office signboard, no doubt.

'I don't know about you, but I don't want to spend the night here.' Starchenko stood up. 'It's not six yet, it's too early for bed, so I'm off. There's a von Taunitz lives near by, only a couple of miles from Syrnya. I'll drive over for the evening. Constable, go and tell our driver not to take the horses out.

'Now, what about you?' he asked Lyzhin.

'I don't know. I'll go to sleep, I suppose.'

The doctor wrapped his fur coat round him and went out. He was heard talking to the driver. Sleigh-bells jingled on cold horses. He drove off.

'It ain't right for you to sleep here, mister,' said the constable. 'You go in the other room. It ain't clean, but that won't matter for one night. I'll just get a samovar from the caretaker and put it on. Then I'll make a pile of this here hay for you, sir, and you can have a nice sleep.'

A little later the coroner was sitting in the other room drinking tea while Constable Loshadin stood by the door talking. He was an old man: turned sixty, short, very thin, hunched, pale, with a naïve smile and watery eyes. And he was for ever smacking his lips as if sucking sweets. He wore a short sheepskin coat and felt boots, he always held a stick. He was evidently touched by the coroner's youth, which must be why he spoke to him in this familiar way.

'Old Theodore, the gaffer on the parish council . . . he told me to report when the police inspector or the coroner arrived,' he said. 'Oh well, I suppose I must be on my way. It's nearly three miles to his place, there's a blizzard and there's drifts. Proper awful it is—I won't get there before midnight, belike. Hark at that howling!'

'I don't need your gaffer,' said Lyzhin. 'There's nothing for him to do here.'

He looked at the old man inquisitively. 'I say, old fellow, how long have you been constable round here?'

'How long? Why, thirty year, it must be. Five years after the serfs were freed I started the job, so you can reckon it yourself. Since then I've been at it every day. Others have their holidays, but I never have no day off. It may be Easter over there, with church bells ringing and Christ getting Himself resurrected, but I'm doing me rounds with me little bag. I go to the accounts department, the post-office, the police inspector's place. I visit the magistrate, the tax man, the town hall, the ladies and gentlemen, the peasants and all other god-fearing Russian folks. I carry parcels, notices, tax papers, letters, all sorts of forms, registers. These days, my dear good sir, there's all these form things—red, white, yellow—what you write figures on. Every squire, parson and rich villager must write down a dozen times a year what he's sown and reaped, how many bushels or hundredweight of rye he has, how much oats and hay—and also about the weather, different insects and that. They put down what they please, of course—it's only a form—but it's me as has to go round handing out them bits of paper and then go round again collecting them. Now, take this dead gentleman here. There ain't no call to cut his guts out—there's no point, as you know yourself, it's only dirtying your hands for nothing. But you've been put to this trouble—you've come out here—because of them forms, sir. It can't be helped. Thirty year I've been traipsing round with forms. Summer's all right, it's warm and dry—but in winter or autumn it's a nuisance. I've known times when I near drowned and froze, there's nothing as hasn't happened to me. There was that time when some villains stole me bag in a wood and beat me up. And I've been had up in court——'

'What ever for?'

'Fraud.'

'What do you mean, fraud?'

'Well, what happened is, our clerk—Khrisanf Grigoryev—sells a contractor some boards as weren't his . . . cheats him, like. I'm there when it's going on, and they send me out to the pub for some vodka. Well, the clerk doesn't cut me in—never even offers me a glass—but seeing as I'm poor and don't look reliable, seeing I'm kind of no good, like, they takes us both to court. He goes to prison, but I'm let off on all counts, thank God. They read out one of them bits of paper at the trial, and they're all wearing uniform—in court, that is. Now, you take it from me, sir, my kind of work . . . for someone as ain't used to it, it's hell on earth, God help me, but it ain't nothing to the likes of us. It's when you're *not* doing your rounds that your feet ache! And it's worse for us indoors. Back at the parish offices it's make up the clerk's stove, fetch the clerk's water, clean the clerk's boots.'

'What wages do you get?' Lyzhin asked.

'Eighty-four rouble a year.'

'But you must make a bit on the side, surely?'

'Bit on the side? No fear! Gentlefolk don't tip much these days. They're hard-hearted nowadays, are gentlefolk—proper touchy they are. Bring 'em a form and they take it amiss. Doff your hat to 'em, and they take that amiss. "You didn't use the proper entrance," they say. "You're a drunkard," they say. "You stink of onion, you oaf, you son of a bitch." There's some kind ones of course, but what good are they? They only laugh at you, call you names. Take that Mr. Altukhin, now. He's kind and he looks sober, like, he has his head screwed on. But when he sees you he starts shouting things he don't even understand himself. He gives me a nickname, er ——'

The constable pronounced a word, but so quietly that it made no sense.

'What?' asked Lyzhin. 'Say it again.'

'Mr. Administrator,' the constable repeated aloud. 'He's been calling me that for a long time, about six years. "Hallo there, Mr. Administrator." But it's all right, I don't mind—let 'im! And a lady will sometimes send you out a glass of vodka and a bit of pie—so you drink her health, like. The peasants give most. He's more warm-hearted, your peasant is, he fears God. He'll give you a bit of bread, a sup of cabbage stew, or a glass of something. Or the gaffers give you tea in the pub. Like now, say—them witnesses have gone for their tea. "You stay and keep watch, Loshadin," they tell me. And they give me a copeck each. They're scared because they ain't used to these things. And yesterday they gave me fifteen copecks and a glass of tea.'

'And you—aren't *you* afraid?'

'I am that, mister, but it's all part of the job, ain't it? That's service life for you. Last year I was taking a prisoner to town, when he suddenly starts beating me up—he doesn't half lam into me! There's open country and forests all around, no refuge anywhere. Now, take this business here. I remember Mr. Lesnitsky when he was only so high, I knew his father and his mum. I come from Nedoshchotovo village, and they—the Lesnitsky family—live half a mile away . . . less, in fact, their land joins ours. Now, old Mr. Lesnitsky had an unmarried sister, a god-fearing, kind-hearted soul—Lord, remember Thy servant Julia, may her name live for ever! She never married, and when she was dying she split her property, leaving the monastery two hundred and fifty acres, and giving us—Nedoshchotovo village— five hundred to remember her by. But they do say as how the old squire her brother hid that paper—burnt it in his stove, he did, and took all the land himself. He's doing himself a good turn, thinks he. But that ain't so, mate. You can't live by injustice, brother, not on this earth you can't. And the old squire didn't go to confession for twenty year, he turned against the church, like, and he died unrepentant. Burst himself he did—he wasn't half fat. Right along his whole length he burst. Then they take everything away from the young master here—name of Seryozha—to pay them debts. They take the lot. Well, seeing he hasn't much book-learning—or sense, either—his uncle, who's Council Chairman, thinks he'll take him on as insurance man. "Let Seryozha try it," says he. "It's easy enough, is the insurance." But the young master's proud, he is. He wants something with a bit more scope too, a bit more stylish, a bit more free and easy. Traipsing round the county in some broken-down cart talking to peasants . . . it's rather a come-down. When he's on his rounds he always has his eyes fixed on the ground. He don't say nothing. "Mr. Seryozha!" you can shout right into his ear, and he'll just look round with an "Eh?" And he'll fix his eyes on the ground again. And now he's done himself in, see? It's awkward, sir—it ain't right. The things that happen . . . you can't make head nor tail of them, God help us. Say your father was rich, but you're poor—well, it's real hard on you, true enough, but you must put up with it. I once lived well myself, sir, I've kept my two horses, my three cows, my twenty head of sheep. But a time came when I was left with only me little bag—even that wasn't mine but the government's. And now I've got what you might call the rottenest house in our village. Fell off me perch, I did—came down with a bump: it was king of the castle one day and dirty rascal the next!'

'What made you so poor?' the coroner asked.

'My sons don't half knock back the vodka. The amount they shift . . . if I told you, you'd never believe it.'

Lyzhin realized as he listened that he himself would be back in Moscow sooner or later, whereas this old boy would be stuck here doing his rounds for ever. How many more of them would he meet in life . . . these bedraggled, unkempt, 'no good' old men in whose consciousness the concept of the fifteen-copeck piece was somehow indissolubly fused with that of their glass of tea and a profound faith that honesty is the only possible policy in life? Then he grew tired of listening and told the old man to bring hay for his bedding. Though there was an iron bedstead, with pillow and blanket, in 'reception', and though it could have been brought in, the corpse—the man who had perhaps sat on that bed before he died—had lain alongside for nearly three days. To sleep in it now would be unpleasant.

'Only half-past seven, how awful!' thought Lyzhin, looking at his watch.'

He was not sleepy, but having nothing else to do he lay down and pulled a rug over himself—just to pass the time. Loshadin cleared away the tea things, popping in and out several times, smacking his lips, sighing, fidgeting near the table. He took his lamp and went out in the end. Looking at that long grey hair and bent body from behind, Lyzhin thought that the old man was just like a wizard in an opera.

It was dark. There must have been a moon behind the clouds because the windows and the snow on their frames could be so clearly seen. The blizzard howled and howled.

'Oh lord, lord, lord—' moaned a woman in the loft. Or so it seemed.

Then something struck the outside wall with a great thudding crash.

The coroner pricked up his ears. That was no woman but the howling wind. Feeling chilly, he put his fur coat over the rug, reflecting as he warmed up on all this stuff: blizzard, hut, old man, corpse next door. What a far cry, all this, from the life of his dreams—how alien, how petty, how dull! If the man had killed himself in Moscow or those parts, if the coroner had had to hold *that* inquest, how interesting and important it would all have been. He might even have been scared to sleep in the next room to a corpse. Here, though, more than six hundred miles from Moscow, all these things appeared in different guise. This wasn't life, these weren't people—they were just 'things on forms' (as Loshadin would put it). None of this would leave the faintest trace in the memory, it would be forgotten as soon as Lyzhin left Syrnya. His country—real Russia—was Moscow and St. Peters-burg. This place was just a provincial outpost. When you dream of making a stir, becoming popular—being an ace investigator, say, prosecuting at the assizes, making a splash socially—you're bound to think of Moscow. Moscow . . . that's where the action is! Whereas here you want nothing, you easily come to terms with your own insignificance, and you expect only one thing of life: just let it hurry up and go away. Borne in imagination along Moscow streets, Lyzhin called at friends' houses, met relatives and colleagues. His heart leapt for joy to think that he was only twenty-six—and if he escaped from here and reached Moscow in five or ten years it still wouldn't be too late, there would still be a whole life ahead of him. Sinking into unconsciousness, his thoughts now more and more confused, he imagined the long corridors of the Moscow court-house, himself giving a speech, his sisters, and an orchestra which was droning away for some reason.

And again he heard the same howling, again the same thudding crashes.

Then he suddenly remembered talking to a cashier once at the council offices, when a certain thin, pale, dark-eyed, black-haired individual had approached the counter. He had that unpleasant look about the eyes which you see in people who have slept too long after lunch—it spoilt his subtle, intelligent profile. He wore jack-boots which didn't suit him: they looked too rough. The cashier had introduced him as 'our insurance man'.

So that was who Lesnitsky had been—the very same, Lyzhin now reckoned. He remembered Lesnitsky's quiet voice, pictured his walk . . . and seemed to hear someone walking near him now: someone who walked just like Lesnitsky.

Suddenly he panicked, his head went cold.

'Who's there?' he asked in alarm.

'The conshtible.'

'What do you want?'

'It's just a question, sir. You said just now you didn't need the gaffer here, but I'm afraid he might get vexed, like. He told me to fetch him, so hadn't I better?'

'Oh, bother you,' said Lyzhin, testily, covering himself up again. 'I'm fed up with you.'

'He might get vexed, like. I'll be on my way, sir, and you make yourself at home here.'

Loshadin left. There was coughing and murmuring in the passage— the witnesses must be back.

'We'll let those poor fellows off early tomorrow,' thought the coroner. 'We'll start the inquest at daybreak.'

Then, just as he was losing consciousness, more footsteps—not timid, these, but swift and noisy—were heard. A door slammed, there were voices, a match was struck.

'Asleep, eh?' rapped Dr. Starchenko crossly, lighting match after match. He was completely covered with snow and brought a chill air in with him. 'Asleep, eh? Get up, we're going to von Taunitz's, he's sent his own horses for you. Come on, you'll at least get your supper and a decent sleep. I've come for you myself, you see. The horses are splendid, and we'll make it in twenty minutes.'

'What time is it?'

'A quarter past ten.'

Sleepy and disgruntled, Lyzhin donned boots, coat, cap and hood, and went out with the doctor. Though the cold was not intense, a piercing gale blew, driving clouds of snow down the road before it— seemingly in panic-stricken rout. There were already deep snowdrifts by fences and doorways. Doctor and coroner got into the sledge, and a white driver bent over them to button up the cover. They were both hot.

'We're off!'

Off they drove through the village. The coroner idly watched the trace-horse's legs working, and thought of Pushkin's 'He clove the snow in powdered furrows'. There were lights in all the huts, as on the eve of a major festival: the villagers were too scared of the corpse to go to bed. Bored, no doubt, by his wait outside the hut—brooding, too, on the dead body—their driver preserved a sullen silence.

'When Taunitz's people realized you were staying overnight in that hut,' said Starchenko, 'they all went on at me for not bringing you along.'

On a bend at the end of the village the driver suddenly yelled at the top of his voice that someone should 'get out of the way!' They glimpsed a figure knee-deep in snow: someone who had stepped off the road and was watching the sledge with its three horses. The coroner saw a crook, a beard, a slung satchel. It was Loshadin, it struck him, a Loshadin who was actually smiling! It was just a glimpse and then he vanished.

The road first skirted a wood, then ran down a broad forest ride. They glimpsed old pines, young birches and tall, gnarled young oaks standing alone in clearings where timber had recently been felled, but soon the air was all a-blur with snow flurries. The driver claimed to see trees, but the coroner saw only the trace-horse. The wind blew against their backs.

Suddenly the horses halted.

'What is it this time?' asked Starchenko crossly.

The driver silently climbed off his box and ran round the sledge, digging in his heels. He described ever wider circles further and further from the sledge, and seemed to be dancing. At last he came back and turned right.

'Missed the road, did you, my man?' asked Starchenko.

'We're all right——'

Here was some village without a single light. Then came more woods, more fields, they lost the road again, the driver climbed off the box and danced again. The sledge careered down a dark avenue, flying rapidly on while the heated trace-horse kicked into the front of the bodywork. Here the trees gave a hollow roar. It was terrifying, pitch black—as if they were hurtling into an abyss. Then, suddenly, the bright light of a drive and windows struck their eyes, a welcoming bark rang out, there were voices.

They had arrived.

As they took off their coats and boots in the hall, someone was playing the waltz 'Un petit verre de Cliquot' on a piano upstairs, and the stamp of children's feet was heard. Warm air suddenly breathed on the travellers the scent of rooms in an old manor where life is always so snug, clean and comfortable, never mind the weather outside.

'Capital, capital!' said von Taunitz, a fat man with side-whiskers and an unbelievably broad neck, as he shook the coroner's hand. 'Now do come in—delighted to meet you. After all, we're colleagues in a way, you and I. I was deputy prosecutor once, but not for long—only two years. I came here to run this place, and I've grown old here. I'm an old fogy, in fact.

'Do come in,' he went on, obviously trying not to speak too loud, and took the guests upstairs. 'I have no wife. She died, but here are my daughters. May I introduce you?'

He turned round. 'Tell Ignatius to bring the sledge round for eight o'clock tomorrow,' he shouted downstairs in a voice of thunder.

His four daughters were in the drawing-room: pretty young girls, all in grey dresses, all with the same hair style. There was an attractive young cousin too, with her children. Having met them already, Starchenko at once asked them to sing something, and two of the young ladies assured him at length that they couldn't sing and had no music. Then the cousin sat down at the piano and they rendered a quavering duet from The Queen of Spades. 'Un petit verre de Cliquot' was played again, while the children skipped and beat time with their feet. Starchenko pranced a bit too, and everyone laughed.

Then the children said good night and went to bed. The coroner laughed, danced a quadrille, flirted, and wondered if he was dreaming. The peasants' quarters in the council hut, the hay pile in the corner, the rustle of cockroaches, the revoltingly mean appointments, the witnesses' voices, the wind, the snowstorm, the danger of losing one's way—then, suddenly, these superb, brightly-lit rooms, piano-playing, lovely girls, curly-haired children and gay, happy laughter! The transformation seemed magical. And for it to be accomplished within a couple of miles or so, a single hour . . . that seemed incredible. Dismal thoughts marred his enjoyment. This wasn't life around him, he mused, it was only scraps of life—mere fragments. You could draw no conclusions, things were all so arbitrary. He even felt sorry for these girls who lived, who would end their lives, out here in this provincial dump, far from the sort of cultured setting where nothing is arbitrary, where everything makes sense and conforms with its own laws—and where, for instance, every suicide is intelligible, where one can explain why it happened, and what part it plays in the general scheme of things. If he couldn't make sense of the life around him in this backwater, if he couldn't even see it—then there couldn't *be* any life round here, he supposed.

Conversation at supper turned to Lesnitsky.

'He left a wife and child,' said Starchenko. 'These neurotics and other mentally unstable persons . . . I wouldn't let them marry, I'd deny them the right and opportunity to reproduce their kind. It's a crime to bring mentally disturbed children into the world.'

'Poor young fellow,' von Taunitz sighed quietly, shaking his head. 'What brooding, what agony one must suffer before finally venturing to take one's life—a young life. It can happen in any family, such a disaster. It's terrible, it's hard to endure, it's unbearable——'

The girls all listened silently, with grave faces, looking at their father. Lyzhin felt that he was expected to comment too, but all he could think of was that, yes, suicides were an 'undesirable phenomenon'.

He slept in a warm room on a soft bed with a quilt above him and a finely woven fresh sheet beneath, but somehow failed to appreciate these amenities—perhaps because the doctor and von Taunitz kept up a long conversation next door while the storm was making just as big a racket above the ceiling and in the stove as it had back in the hut. It was that same old droning, piteous whine.

Taunitz's wife had died two years before. He still hadn't resigned himself to the fact, and kept mentioning her no matter what he was talking about. There was nothing of the lawyer about him any longer.

'Could *I* ever be reduced to such a state?' wondered Lyzhin as he fell asleep, hearing the other's subdued and bereaved-sounding voice through the wall.

The coroner slept badly. He was hot and uncomfortable. In his sleep he seemed not to be in Taunitz's house, or in a soft clean bed—but still back in the hut on the hay, listening to the witnesses' muffled voices. He felt as if Lesnitsky was near: about fifteen paces away. In his dreams he once more remembered the insurance man—black-haired, pale, in dusty boots—approaching the cashier's counter. ('This is our insurance man.') Then he imagined Lesnitsky and Constable Loshadin walking side by side through the snow-fields, supporting each other. The blizzard whirled above them, the wind blew at their backs, while they went on their way quietly singing that they were 'marching along, marching along'.

The old man looked like an operatic wizard, and both were singing as though on stage.

'We're marching, marching along. You're warm, you have light and comfort, but we are marching into the freezing cold and blizzard through the deep snow. We know no peace, no joy. We bear all the burdens of this life, our own and yours.

'We are marching, marching along,' they droned.

Lyzhin woke and sat up in bed. What a confused, evil dream! Why had he dreamt of the insurance man and the constable together? What nonsense! But while Lyzhin's heart throbbed, while he sat up in bed clutching his head in his hands, it occurred to him that the insurance man and the constable really did have something in common. Had they not indeed been marching along through life side by side, clinging to each other? There was some link—invisible, but significant and essential—between the two, between them and Taunitz, even . . . between all men. Nothing in this life, even in the remotest backwater, is arbitrary, everything is imbued by a single common idea, everything has but one spirit, one purpose. Thinking and reasoning are not enough to furnish insights into these things. Very likely one also needs the gift of penetrating life's essence—a gift which has obviously not been granted to everyone. The miserable, broken-down, suicidal 'neurotic' (the doctor's word for him), the old peasant who had spent every day of his life wandering from one person to another . . . only to someone who also finds his own existence arbitrary are these arbitrary fragments of life. To him who sees and understands his own life as part of the common whole these things are all part of a single miraculous and rational organism. Thus did Lyzhin brood, such was his own long-cherished secret idea. But only now had it unfurled itself so broadly and clearly in his mind.

He lay down, began dozing off. Then, suddenly, they were walking along together again.

'We're marching, marching along,' they sang. 'We take upon ourselves all the hardest and bitterest elements in life. We leave you the easy, enjoyable things, and so you can sit at your supper table coldly and sensibly discussing why we suffer and perish, why we are less healthy and happy than you.'

The burden of their song had occurred to him before, but as an idea somehow masked by other ideas. It had flickered timidly like a distant light in foggy weather. This suicide, this village tragedy . . . they lay heavy on his conscience, he felt. To resign oneself to the fact that these people, so submissive to their fate, have taken on the burden of everything most grim and black in life . . . how horrible! To resign oneself to that while yet desiring a bright, lively life for oneself amid happy, contented people, and while yearning constantly for such a life . . . this was to desire yet more suicides among those crushed by toils and tribulations, among the weak and the outcast: among those very people who may be the subject of the occasional annoyed or sardonic mention over the supper-table . . . yet without anyone ever going to their help.

Once again he heard their 'marching, marching along', and he felt as if someone was banging his temples with a hammer.

Next morning he woke early with a headache, roused by a noise.

'You can't leave now,' von Taunitz was shouting at the doctor in the next room. 'Just look out of doors! Don't argue, you ask the driver—he won't take you in this weather for a million roubles.'

'But it is only two miles, isn't it?' the doctor pleaded.

'I don't care if it's two hundred yards. What can't be done can't be done. The moment you're through those gates all hell will break loose, you'll be off that road inside a minute. Say what you like, but nothing would induce me to let you go.'

'It'll quieten down by evening, I reckon,' said the peasant who was tending the stove.

The doctor next door was talking about Russia's rugged climate influencing her national character, about the long winters impeding freedom of movement and thus retarding the people's intellectual growth. Meanwhile Lyzhin listened with vexation to these disquisitions, gazing through the windows at the snowdrifts against the fence, at the white dust filling all visible space, at the trees bending desperately to right and left. He listened to the howling and banging.

'Well, what moral can we draw?' he wondered gloomily. 'That this is a blizzard, that's all.'

They lunched at noon, then wandered aimlessly about the house and went to the windows.

'Lesnitsky lies there,' thought Lyzhin, looking at the snow flurries whirling furiously above the drifts. 'There he lies, while the witnesses wait.'

They talked about the weather, saying that a snowstorm usually lasts forty-eight hours, rarely longer. They dined at six, then played cards, sang, danced and finally had supper. The day was over, they went to bed.

The storm dropped just before dawn. When they got up and looked out of the windows, bare willows with their feebly drooping branches stood completely still. It was overcast and quiet, as if nature was now ashamed of her orgy, of her mad nights, of giving vent to her passions. Harnessed in tandem, the horses had been waiting at the front door since five o'clock that morning. When it was fully daylight, doctor and coroner put on their coats and boots, said good-bye to their host, and went out.

By the porch, near the driver, stood the familiar figure of the 'conshtible'. Hatless, with his old leather bag across his shoulder, Eli Loshadin was covered with snow. His face was red and wet with sweat.

A footman—he had come out to help the guests into the sledge and wrap up their feet—looked at the old man sternly. 'Why are you hanging around, you old devil? Clear out!'

'The village people are upset, sir,' said Loshadin, smiling innocently all over his face—and obviously glad to see, at last, those whom he had so long awaited. 'Very restive, them peasants are, and the kids are crying. They thought you'd gone back to town, sir. Have pity on them, good, kind sirs——'

Doctor and coroner said nothing, got in the sledge and drove to Syrnya.

AT CHRISTMAS

I

'TELL me what to write,' said Yegor as he dipped his pen in the ink.

Not for four years had Vasilisa seen her daughter. The daughter, Yefimya, had gone to St. Petersburg with her husband after their wedding, and she had written home twice. But not a word had been heard of her after that, she might have vanished into thin air. Milking the cow at dawn, making up the stove, dreaming at night, the old woman had only one thing on her mind: how was Yefimya getting on, was she alive? Vasilisa ought to send a letter, but her old man couldn't write—and there was no one else to ask.

Well, when Christmas came round Vasilisa could bear it no longer, and went to see Yegor at the inn. This Yegor was the landlady's brother who had been hanging round that pub doing nothing ever since he had come home from the army. He was said to turn out a good letter if he was properly paid. Vasilisa first had a word with the pub cook, and then with the landlady, and finally with Yegor himself. A fifteen-copeck fee was agreed.

And now, in the pub kitchen on Boxing Day, Yegor sat at the table holding a pen. Vasilisa stood before him brooding. She had a care-worn, grief-stricken air. Her old husband, Peter—very thin, tall, brown-pated—had come in with her and stood staring straight before him like a blind man. On the stove a pan of pork was frying. It hissed, it spurted, it even seemed to be saying 'flue', 'flu', 'flew' or some such word. The room was hot and stuffy.

'What shall I write?' Yegor repeated.

'None of that, now!' said Vasilisa with an angry and suspicious look. 'Don't you rush me. You ain't doing us no favour. You're being paid, ain't you? So you write "to our dear son-in-law Andrew and our only beloved daughter Yefimya our love, a low bow and our parental blessing which shall abide for ever and ever."'

'O.K. Carry on shooting!'

'We also wish you a Happy Christmas. We are alive and well, and we wish the same to you from Our Lord, er, and Heavenly King.'

Vasilisa pondered, exchanged glances with the old man.

'We wish the same to you from Our Lord, er, and Heavenly King,' she repeated—and burst into tears.

That was all she could say. And yet, when she had lain awake at night thinking, a dozen letters hadn't seemed enough to say it all. Since the daughter and her husband had left, a great deal of water had flowed under the bridge, and the old people had lived a life of utter loneliness, sighing deeply of a night as if they had buried their daughter. So many things had happened in the village since then, what with all the weddings and funerals. How long the winters had seemed, how long the nights!

'It's hot in here,' said Yegor, unbuttoning his waistcoat. 'About seventy degrees, I reckon.

'All right then—what else?' he asked.

The old people said nothing.

'What's your son-in-law's job?' asked Yegor.

'He was a soldier, sir, as you know,' answered the old man in a frail voice. 'He left the service same time as you. He was a soldier, but now he works in St. Petersburg, like—in the hydropathetics. There's a doctor cures the sick with the waters, and he's a doorman at that doctor's institution.'

'It's all written here,' said the old woman, taking a letter out of her kerchief. 'This came from Yefimya, God knows when. Perhaps they ain't alive no more.'

Yegor reflected and wrote rapidly.

'At the present juncture,' he wrote, 'seeing as how destinny has been determined in the Soldiering Feild we advises you to look in the Regulations of Disciplinnary Penalties and the Criminal Law of the War Department and you will see in them said Laws the civilization of the Higher Ranks of the War Deppartment.'

After writing this, he read it out aloud while Vasilisa was thinking that he ought to write how miserable they had been last year, when their grain hadn't even lasted till Christmas and they'd had to sell the cow. She ought to ask for money, she ought to write that the old man was often poorly—and was bound, soon, to be called to his Maker.

But how could she put it in words? What did you say first and what next?

'Pay attenshon,' Yegor went on writing. 'In Volume Five of Milittary Regulations. Soldier is a genneral Term as is well known your most important Genneral and the least importtant Private is both called Soldiers.'

The old man moved his lips.

'It would be nice to see our grandchildren,' he said softly.

'What grandchildren?' the old woman asked, looking at him angrily. 'Perhaps there ain't none.'

'Ain't none? But perhaps there is. Who can tell?'

'By which you can judge,' Yegor hurried on, 'which enemy is Foreign and which Internnal the most important Internnal Enemy is Bacchus.'

The pen squeaked, making flourishes like fish-hooks on the paper. Yegor was in a hurry and read out each line several times. He sat on a stool, legs sprawling under the table: a smug, hulking, fat-faced, red-necked creature. He was the very soul of vulgarity—of vulgarity brash, overbearing, exultant, and proud of having been born and bred in a pub. That this indeed was vulgarity Vasilisa fully realized, though she could not put it into words, but only looked at Yegor angrily and suspiciously. His voice, his meaningless words, the heat, the stuffiness . . . they made her head ache and muddled her thoughts, so she said nothing, thought nothing, and only waited for that pen to stop squeaking. But the old man was looking at Yegor with absolute faith. He trusted them both: his old woman who had brought him here, and Yegor. And when he had mentioned the 'hydropathetics' institution just now, his faith—alike in that institution and in the curative power of 'the waters'—had been written all over his face.

Yegor finished, stood up and read out the whole letter from the beginning. Not understanding, the old man nodded trustingly.

'Pretty good, a smooth job,' said he. 'God bless you. Pretty good.'

They put three five-copeck pieces on the table and left the pub. The old man stared straight before him as if he was blind, absolute faith written on his face, but as they came out of the pub Vasilisa swung her fist at the dog.

'Ugly brute!' she said angrily.

The old woman got no sleep that night for worrying. At dawn she rose, said her prayers and set off for the station to post the letter—a distance of between eight and nine miles.

II

Dr. B. O. Moselweiser's Hydro was open on New Year's Day, as on any ordinary day, the only difference being that Andrew the doorman wore a uniform with new galloons. His boots had an extra special shine and he wished everyone who came in a Happy New Year.

It was morning. Andrew stood by the door reading a newspaper. At exactly ten o'clock in came a general whom he knew—one of the regulars—followed by the postman.

'Happy New Year, sir,' said Andrew, helping the general off with his cloak.

'Thank you, my good fellow. Same to you.'

On his way upstairs the general nodded towards a door and asked a question which he asked every day, always forgetting the answer.

'What goes on in there?'

'Massage room, sir!'

When the general's steps had died away, Andrew examined the postal delivery and found one letter addressed to himself. He opened it, read several lines. Glancing at the newspaper, he sauntered to his room which was down here on the ground floor at the end of the passage. His wife Yefimya sat on the bed feeding a baby. Another child, the eldest, stood near her with his curly head on her lap while a third slept on the bed.

Entering his room, Andrew gave his wife the letter.

'This must be from the village.'

Then he went out, not taking his eyes off the newspaper, and paused in the corridor near his door. He could hear Yefimya read out the first lines in a quavering voice. After reading them she couldn't carry on—those few lines were quite enough for her, she was bathed in tears. Hugging and kissing her eldest child, she began to speak—crying or laughing, it was hard to say which.

'This is from Granny and Grandpa,' she said. 'From the village. May the Holy Mother and the Blessed Saints be with them. They have snow drifts right up to the roofs now, and the trees are white as white. The children are sliding on their tiny toboggans. And there's dear old bald Grandpa on the stove. And there's a little yellow dog. My lovely darlings.'

As he listened, Andrew remembered that his wife had given him letters three or four times, asking him to post them to the village, but some important business had always prevented him. He had not posted those letters, and they had been left lying around somewhere.

'There's little hares running about them fields,' Yefimya chanted, bathed in tears and kissing her boy. 'Grandpa is quiet and gentle, and Granny is also kind and loving. In the village they live a godly life and fear the Lord. There's a little church, with such nice peasants singing in the choir. Holy Mother, our protector, take us away from this place!'

Andrew came back to his room for a smoke before anyone else arrived, and Yefimya suddenly stopped talking, quietened down and wiped her eyes. Only her lips quivered. She was so afraid of him, oh dear she was! His footsteps, his glance . . . they made her tremble with fright. She dared not utter a word in his presence.

No sooner had Andrew lit a cigarette than there was a ring from upstairs. He put out his cigarette, adopted an expression of great solemnity, and ran to his front door.

The general was descending from aloft, pink and fresh from his bath.

'What goes on in there?' he asked, pointing at a door.

Andrew drew himself up to attention, and announced in a loud voice that it was the 'Charcot showers, sir!'

FRAGMENT

KOZEROGOV, a senior civil servant, retired, bought a small estate and
settled down on it. Here, in partial emulation of Cincinnatus but also of
Professor Kaygorodov, he worked in the sweat of his brow and noted
down his observations of nature. After his death these notes were
inherited by his housekeeper Martha, as also were his other effects. As
everyone knows, that respectable old woman pulled down the manor
farm and built an excellent inn, licensed for spirits, on the site. There
was a special saloon bar for travelling landowners and officials, and the
deceased owner's diary was kept on a table in this bar for convenience,
should customers perchance require paper. One sheet of these notes has
come into my possession. It evidently refers to the very beginning of
the deceased's agricultural activities and it contains the following
entries.

3 March. Spring. The birds have begun to fly back. Yesterday I saw
some sparrows. Greetings, feathered children of the south! In your
sweet twittering I seem to hear the words: 'Wishing you every
happiness, sir.'

14 March. Today I asked Martha why a cock crows so often. 'Because
it has a throat,' she told me. I have a throat too, I told her, but I don't
crow. Nature holds so many mysteries. When working in St. Petersburg, I frequently ate turkey, but yesterday was the first time I ever
saw a live turkey. Most remarkable bird.

22 March. The local police officer called. We had a long conversation
about virtue: I seated, he standing. 'Would you like to have your youth
restored, sir?' he asked, among other things. 'No, I wouldn't,' I
answered, 'because if I was young again I shouldn't hold my present
high rank.' He agreed and went away visibly moved.

16 April. I personally dug two beds in my kitchen garden and sowed
buckwheat in them. I didn't say a word about it as I wanted to surprise
Martha, to whom I owe so many happy moments of my life. Yesterday
at tea she complained bitterly of her build, claiming that increasing
corpulence now prevented her going through the larder door.

'On the contrary, dearest,' I noted in reply, 'the fullness of your figure
serves to adorn you and only disposes me more favourably towards you.'

She blushed, and I stood up and embraced her with both arms, for
one arm alone wouldn't go round her.

28 May. An old fellow saw me near the women's bathing place and asked what I was doing there. 'I'm making sure no young men loiter and hang around,' I answered.

'Let's make sure of it together.' With these words the old man sat down by my side and we started to talk about virtue.

ANDREW SIDEROV inherited four thousand roubles from his mother and decided to open a bookshop with the money. Such a shop was greatly needed, for the town was stagnating in ignorance and prejudice. Old men did nothing but visit the public baths, civil servants played their cards and knocked back their vodka, ladies gossiped, young people lacked ideals, unmarried girls thought about getting married and ate porridge all day long, husbands beat their wives, pigs wandered the streets.

'Ideas, and then more ideas!' thought Siderov. 'That's what we need.'

Having rented premises for his shop he went to Moscow and brought back numerous authors, old and new, and plenty of textbooks, and arranged all these wares on shelves.

In the first three weeks he had no customers at all. Siderov sat behind the counter, read his Mikhaylovsky and tried to think high-minded thoughts. Whenever he suddenly felt like buying some bream and gruel, say, he would immediately find himself thinking how very cheap such thoughts were.

Every day a frozen wench, in kerchief and leather galoshes on bare feet, rushed headlong into his shop and asked for two copecks' worth of vinegar.

'You have come to the wrong address, madam,' Siderov would answer scornfully.

Whenever a friend visited him he adopted a portentous, enigmatic expression, took down Volume Three of Pisarev from the remotest shelf, blew off the dust and spoke, his expression hinting that he had a few other items in the shop, but was afraid to show them.

'Yes, old man. That's quite something, I assure you, er . . . . Yes, er . . . . At this point, old man, in a word, I must say, er, you understand, er, you'll be really shaken if you read this, indeed you will.'

'You mind you don't get into trouble, old boy.'

Three weeks later the first customer arrived. This was a fat, white-haired individual with side-whiskers, wearing a peaked cap with a red band and looking like a country squire. He demanded Part Two of *Our Native Word* and asked for slate pencils.

'I don't keep them.'

'Well, you should. It's a pity you don't. One doesn't want to go to market for a little thing like that.'

'Now, I really should keep slate pencils,' thought Siderov after his customer had left. 'One shouldn't specialize too narrowly here in the provinces, one should sell anything connected with education: anything which fosters it in some way or other.'

He wrote to Moscow and within a month his window display included pens, pencils, fountain-pens, exercise-books, slates and other school requisites. Boys and girls took to dropping in occasionally, and there was even a day when he made one rouble forty copecks. Once the girl in leather galoshes hurtled in. He had already opened his mouth to tell her scornfully that she had come to the wrong address, but——

'Give me one copeck's worth of paper and a seven-copeck stamp!' she shouted.

Thereafter Siderov started keeping postage and revenue stamps, and also forms for promissory notes. About eight months after the opening of the shop a lady came in to buy pens and asked if he kept school-children's satchels.

'No, alas, madam.'

'Oh, what a pity! Then show me your dolls: just the cheap ones.'

'I don't keep dolls either, madam,' said Siderov dolefully.

He wrote to Moscow without more ado and soon satchels, dolls, drums, sabres, mouth-organs, balls and various other toys appeared in his shop.

'This is all rubbish,' he told his friends. 'But just wait till I get some teaching aids and educational toys. My educational section shall be grounded, so to speak, in the most refined deductions of science, see, in other words——'

He ordered dumb-bells, croquet and backgammon sets, a child's billiard-table, gardening tools for children and a couple of dozen highly ingenious educational games. Then, to their immense delight, passing townsfolk noticed two bicycles, one large, the other smaller. Business picked up splendidly. Trade was particularly brisk at Yuletide when Siderov put up a notice in his window stating that he sold Christmas tree decorations.

'I'll slip in a spot of hygiene too, see?' he told his friends, and rubbed his hands. 'Just wait till my next trip to Moscow. I'll have filters and sundry scientific gadgets—you'll be crazy about them, in a word. One mustn't ignore science, old man, that one mustn't.'

Having made a tidy profit, he went to Moscow and bought various wares there for about five thousand roubles, cash and credit.

There were filters, there were first-rate desk-lamps, there were guitars. There were hygienic underpants for children, babies' dummies, purses, sets of toy animals. And he incidentally bought some excellent crockery for five hundred roubles, and was glad of that because hand-some things develop refined tastes and make for mellow manners. Returning home from Moscow, he got down to arranging his new wares on shelves and stands. Once when he climbed up to clear his top shelf there was a bit of a commotion and ten volumes of Mikhaylovsky fell down one after the other. One volume hit him on the head, the others fell straight on to the lamps and broke two globes.

'But what, er, great thick books people do write,' muttered Siderov, scratching himself.

He picked up all the books, tied them tightly with string and put them under the counter. A couple of days later he learnt that the grocer next door had been sentenced to penal servitude for causing his nephew bodily harm and that his shop was up to let in consequence. Delighted, Siderov took an option on it. A door was soon made in the wall, the two shops were joined together and were crammed with goods. Since the customers in the second shop demanded tea, sugar and paraffin through force of habit, Siderov did not hesitate to stock up with groceries.

He is now one of the town's leading shopkeepers. He deals in crockery, tobacco, tar, soap, rolls, dress-making material, haberdashery, chandlery, guns, leatherware and ham. He has rented a wine-cellar in the market and he is said to be about to open family baths with individual cubicles. The books which once lay on his shelves, including Volume Three of Pisarev, have long since been sold off at three roubles per hundredweight.

At name-day parties and weddings Siderov's former friends, whom he now sneeringly dubs 'Americans', occasionally talk to him about progress, literature and other lofty topics.

'Read the latest *European Herald*, Siderov?' they ask.

'No, I have not,' he answers, screwing up his eyes and toying with his thick watch-chain. 'That does not interest us, we have more substantial concerns.'

FROM A RETIRED TEACHER'S NOTEBOOK

IT is argued that family and school should work hand in glove. Very true, but only if the family is a respectable one unconnected with trade or shop-keeping, inasmuch as proximity to the lower orders may hinder a school's progress. On grounds of humanity, however, one should not deprive shopkeepers and the wealthier tradesfolk of their occasional pleasures—such as asking teachers to a party, shall we say?

The words 'proposition' and 'conjunction' make schoolgirls modestly lower their eyes and blush, but the terms 'organic' and 'copulative' enable schoolboys to face the future hopefully.

As the vocative case and certain rare letters of the Russian alphabet are practically obsolete, teachers of Russian should in all fairness have their salaries reduced, inasmuch as this decline in cases and letters has reduced their work load.

Our teachers try to persuade their pupils not to waste time reading novels and newspapers since this hampers concentration and distracts them. Besides, novels and newspapers are useless. But why should pupils believe their mentors if the latter spend so much time on newspapers and magazines? Physician, heal thyself! As for me, I am completely in the clear, not having read a single book or paper for thirty years.

When teaching science one should above all ensure that one's pupils have their books bound, inasmuch as one cannot bang them on the head with the spine of an unbound book.

Children! What bliss it is to receive one's pension!

A FISHY AFFAIR

STRANGE as it may sound, the only carp in the pond near General Pantalykin's cottage fell head over heels in love with a holiday visitor, Sonya Mamochkin. But is that really so very remarkable? Lermontov's Demon fell in love with Tamara, after all, and the swan loved Leda. And don't clerks occasionally fall for the boss's daughter? Sonya Mamochkin came for a bathe with her aunt each morning and the lovesick carp swam near the pond edge watching her. Close proximity to the foundry of Krandel and Sons had turned the water brown ages ago, yet the carp could see everything. He saw white clouds and birds soaring through the azure sky, he saw bathing beauties undressing, he saw peeping toms watching them from bushes on the bank and he saw a fat old woman sitting on a rock complacently stroking herself for five minutes before going in the water.

'Why am I such a great fat cow?' she said. 'Oh, I do look awful!'

Doffing her ethereal garments, Sonya dived into the water with a shriek, swam about, braced herself against the cold—and there, sure enough, was the carp. He swam up to her and began avidly kissing her feet, shoulders, neck.

Their dip over, the girls went home for tea and buns while the solitary carp swam round the enormous pond.

'There can be no question of reciprocity, of course,' he thought. 'As if a beautiful girl like that would fall in love with a carp like me! No, no, a thousand times no! So don't indulge in such fancies, O wretched fish! You have only one course left: death. But what death? This pond lacks revolvers and phosphorous matches. There is only one possible death for us carp: a pike's jaws. But where can I find a pike? There was a pike in this pond once, but even it died of boredom. Oh, I am so miserable!'

Brooding on death, the young pessimist buried himself in mud and wrote a diary.

Late one afternoon Sonya and her aunt were sitting at the edge of the pond fishing. The carp swam near the floats, feasting his eyes on his beloved. Suddenly an idea flashed through his head.

'I shall die by her hand,' thought he with a gay flip of the fins. 'How marvellous, how sweet a death!'

Resolute yet blenching slightly, he swam up to Sonya's hook and took it in his mouth.

'Sonya, you have a bite!' shrieked Aunty. 'You've caught something, my dear!'

'Oh, oh!'

Sonya jumped up and tugged with all her might. Something golden flashed in the air and flopped on the water, making ripples.

'It got away!' both women shouted, turning pale. 'It got away! Oh, my dear!'

They looked at the hook and saw a fish's lower lip on it.

'Oh, you shouldn't have pulled so hard, dear,' said Aunty. 'Now that poor fish has no lip.'

After snatching himself off the hook our hero was flabbergasted and it was some time before he realized what was happening to him. Then he came to.

'To live again!' groaned he. 'Oh, mockery of fate!'

But noticing that he was minus a lower jaw, the carp blenched and uttered a wild laugh. He had gone mad.

It may seem odd, I fear, that I should wish to detain the serious reader's attention with the fate of so insignificant and dull a creature as a carp. What is so odd about that, though? After all, ladies in literary magazines describe utterly futile tiddlers and snails. And I am imitating those ladies. Perhaps I may even *be* a lady and am just hiding behind a man's pseudonym.

So our carp went mad. That unhappy fish is still alive. Most carps like to be served fried with sour cream, but my hero would settle for any death now. Sonya Mamochkin has married a man who keeps a chemist's shop and Aunty has gone to her married sister's in Lipetsk, though there is nothing odd in that because the married sister has six children and they all adore their aunt.

But let us continue. Engineer Krysin is director of the foundry of Krandel and Sons. He has a nephew Ivan, well known as a writer of verse which he eagerly publishes in all the magazines and papers. Passing the pond one hot noontide, our young poet conceived the notion of taking a dip, removed his clothes and entered the pond. The mad carp took him for Sonya Mamochkin, swam up and tenderly kissed his back. That kiss had most fatal consequences: the carp infected our poet with pessimism. Suspecting nothing, the poet climbed out of the water and went home uttering wild guffaws. Several days later he went to St. Petersburg. Having visited some editorial offices there, he infected all the poets with pessimism, from which time onwards our poets have been writing gloomy, melancholy verse.

NOTES

1 *a school of the type intended for gentlemen's sons*: in the context this phrase effectively translates the original *gimnaziya*. These 'high schools', as the word is elsewhere rendered, were maintained by the State, set exacting standards, and though originally intended for sons of the gentry (*dvoryanstvo*), were not exclusive to them. Chekhov, himself a shopkeeper's son, had graduated from the *gimnaziya* at Taganrog in south Russia in 1879.

a minor official: literally, 'a Collegiate Secretary': Class Ten in the Table of Ranks instituted for the civil service by Peter the Great in 1722. It provided grades for all officials of the government and the court, with equivalents in the armed forces.

2 *the day of Our Lady of Kazan*: according to tradition the Kazan Icon of the Virgin had been miraculously discovered in the ground at Kazan in 1579 by a 10-year-old girl. This event was celebrated annually, on 8 July, from 1595 onwards.

3 *Lomonosov*: M. V. Lomonosov (1711–65) was the son of a fisherman in the north Russian port of Archangel. He ran away to Moscow at the age of 17, and became famous as a scientist, educationist, poet, and grammarian.

8 *on the saint's day of our most pious Sovereign Alexander the First of Blessed Memory*: reference is to the Emperor Alexander I (1777–1825), who succeeded to the Russian throne in 1801, his saint's day being 30 August.

10 *And the Cherubims*: Ezekiel 10: 19.

17 *the Two-Headed Eagle*: the emblem of Imperial Russia.

the Molokan's farm: the Molokans were members of a religious sect that arose in about 1765, and are sometimes said to derive their name from a habit of drinking milk (*moloko*) during Lent.

19 *an official application form*: in order to possess legal validity official applications of certain types had to be transcribed on *gerbovaya bumaga*: special paper bearing the Imperial Russian crest and sold

at a price that constituted a form of taxation on the given transaction.

20 *Chernigov*: large town in the Ukraine, about 80 miles north of Kiev.

31 *giants with seven-league boots*: literally, 'broad-striding people like Ilya Muromets and Solovey the Brigand': two heroes from Russian folk myth.

33 *Slavyanoserbsk*: small town in the Donbass, about 100 miles north of Taganrog.

St. Georgie-Porgie: St George, the patron saint of England, martyred in Palestine, probably in the third or fourth century AD. The name 'Yegor' (of which 'Yegorushka' is a derivative) is an alternative form to Russian 'Georgy' (George); the speaker here employs other variants: 'Yegory' and the comically eccentric form 'Yegorgy'.

Tim in Kursk County: Tim is a small town, about 400 miles south of Moscow, near the administrative centre of Kursk in central European Russia.

34 *St. Barbara*: martyred under Maximinus Thrax (235–8) according to legend; the patron saint of pyrotechnicians.

36 *Lugansk*: large town in the Ukraine, about 100 miles north of Taganrog.

Donets: river in the Ukraine and the south of European Russia, a tributary of the Don.

43 *Vyazma*: large town about 160 miles west of Moscow.

45 *Nizhny Novgorod*: large town, about 250 miles east of Moscow, now called Gorky.

47 *Oryol*: large town, about 200 miles south of Moscow.

50 *Morshansk*: small town, about 240 miles south-east of Moscow.

54 *a Dissenter*: an adherent of the 'Old Belief'—the ritual of the Russian Orthodox Church as practised before the reforms of the Patriarch Nikon in the mid-seventeenth century.

56 *St Peter's Day*: 29 June.

76 *Peter Mogila*: a leading seventeenth-century cleric and educationist (1596–1647), who became Metropolitan of Kiev in 1632.

Be not carried about . . .: Hebrews 13: 9.

Basil the Great: leading fourth-century churchman (329–79).

St. Nestor: ancient Russian historian and chronicler whose exact dates are unknown but who was probably a monk at the Monastery of the Caves, Kiev, in the late eleventh century.

AN AWKWARD BUSINESS

86 *The Physician*: *Vrach*: a monthly medical newspaper, published in St Petersburg from 1880 onwards.

92 *had attained high rank*: literally, 'held the rank of Actual State Councillor': Class Four in the Table of Ranks.

97 *Blessed are the peacemakers*: Matthew 5: 9.

THE BEAUTIES

99 *Don Region . . . Rostov-on-Don*: Rostov-on-Don, a large town on the River Don, about 13 miles from its mouth in the Sea of Azov.

103 *Nakhichevan*: Nakhichevan-on-Don was a small town, an Armenian colony founded in 1780 near Rostov-on-Don, with which it is now merged.

Belgorod: town about 40 miles north-east of Kharkov.

Kharkov: large city in the Ukraine.

105 *The second bell*: passengers on Russian railways were warned of a train's departure by a succession of three rings. The first (single) ring took place a quarter of an hour before departure, the second (double) ring gave five minutes' warning, and on the third (triple) peal the train pulled out.

THE BET

118 *Elbrus*: the highest mountain (18,470 ft.) in the main Caucasian range.

THIEVES

123 *the war . . . San Stefano*: the Russo-Turkish War which broke out in 1877, and ended with the Treaty of San Stefano in 1878.

125 *Shamil*: Shamil (1797–1871) was political and religious leader of

the Moslem peoples of the Caucasus in their resistance to conquest by the Russians, who captured him in 1859.

126 *Samoylovka*: village in the Province of Kharkov.

   Penza: town, about 500 miles south-east of Moscow.

127 *Village community*: the village community, or *mir*, took decisions about village affairs, and was charged with certain administrative responsibilities.

128 *Kuban*: the area of the River Kuban, north of the Caucasus.

GUSEV

134 *Suchan*: town in the far east of Siberia, about 60 miles east of Vladivostok.

137 *Captain Kopeykin*: a comic Captain Kopeykin figures in Gogol's novel *Dead Souls*, Part I (1842).

   Midshipman Dyrka: a comic Midshipman Dyrka is described by Zhevakin, hero of Gogol's play *Marriage* (1842).

139 *Odessa*: large Russian port on the Black Sea.

PEASANT WOMEN

148 *Oboyan*: small town, about 340 miles south of Moscow.

154 *watchman started banging . . .*: in order to warn thieves that they were about, and show their masters that they were awake, Russian watchmen used to bang a stick against a wall, or use some kind of improvised rattle.

IN EXILE

159 *Simbirsk Province*: this was situated on the middle Volga, the provincial capital (Simbirsk; modern Ulyanovsk) being over 400 miles east of Moscow. The province had a sizeable Tatar element in its population.

160 *Kursk*: city in central Russia, about 300 miles south of Moscow.

163 *community court*: the legal provision whereby a village commune (*mir, obshchestvo*, or *obshchina*) was empowered to sentence offending members to exile in Siberia, flogging, etc.

ROTHSCHILD'S FIDDLE

170 *St. John's Day* . . .: 8 May—the day of St John the Evangelist.

St. Nicholas's Day . . .: 9 May—the day of the Transference of the Remains of St Nicholas the Miracle-Worker.

THE STUDENT

176 *Ryurik*: Rurik, or Ryurik, a late ninth-century Viking prince of Novgorod, was traditionally the founder of the Rurikid line—the Russian ruling house from 862 to 1598.

Ivan the Terrible: Ivan IV, Tsar of Muscovy; born 1530, acceded 1533, died 1584.

Peter the Great: Peter I, the first Russian emperor; born 1672, acceded 1682, died 1725.

177 '*At the Last Supper* . . .': in the account which follows Chekhov's student quotes or paraphrases material from the Gospels (Mark 14; Luke 22; John 18), and the translation draws on the Authorized Version at the appropriate points.

THE HEAD GARDENER'S STORY

180 *Ibsen*: the Norwegian playwright Henrik Ibsen (1828–1906).

'*For in the fatness* . . .': Shakespeare, *Hamlet*, III. iv.

PATCH

185 *watchman*: owing to the great demand for wood as fuel and building material, it was customary to appoint watchmen to guard the forests against thieves.

THE SAVAGE

190 *officer of Cossacks*: originally frontiersmen and grouped in various specific localities, of which the area of the River Don and its tributaries was one, the Cossacks enjoyed special status and privileges in return for which they were obliged to serve in special Cossack military units.

Provalye: name of a small station about 75 miles north of Rostov-on-Don on the Donets Railway line west of Zverevo.

190 *the Donets Line*: the network of railway lines serving the Donets Basin in the south of European Russia

Novocherkassk: town in southern Russia, founded in 1805 as capital of the Don Cossack Region.

IN THE CART

203 *Lower Gorodishche*: possibly suggested by Old [Staroye] Gorodishche, name of village about 30 miles south-east of Melikhovo, east of the River Kashirka, a tributary of the Oka.

ON OFFICIAL BUSINESS

221 *The Nevsky Prospekt*: the main thoroughfare of St Petersburg.

Petrovka Street: a street running north from central Moscow.

222 *the gaffer on the parish council*: literally, the cantonal elder: a peasant elected to perform certain administrative duties within a *volost* (group of villages or canton).

five years after the serfs were freed: Loshadin is saying that his appointment dates from 1866: i.e. five years after the Emancipation of the Serfs.

225 *Fell off me perch, I did—came down with a bump: it was king of the castle one day and dirty rascal the next*: a literal translation would be: 'Mokey had four lackeys, but now Mokey is himself a lackey. Petrak had four men working for him, but now Petrak himself is working for someone else.'

228 *Pushkin's 'He clove the snow in powdered furrows'*: the quotation is of line 5, verse II, Canto Five of Pushkin's verse novel *Eugene Onegin* (1823–31).

229 *The Queen of Spades*: the opera (1890) by P. I. Tchaikovsky (1840–93), based on Pushkin's short story with the same title.

AT CHRISTMAS

238 *Charcot*: Jean Martin Charcot (1825–93), the French physician and pioneer of psychotherapy.

FRAGMENT

239 *a senior civil servant*: literally 'an actual state councillor', grade four in the Table of Ranks.

Cincinnatus: Lucius Quinctius Cincinnatus, the early Roman politician famous for his addiction to farm labour in intervals between serving the Republic as consul (460 BC) and dictator (458 BC).

Kaygorodov: D. N. Kaygorodov (b. 1846) was a professor at the St Petersburg Forestry Institute and author of numerous learned works.

THE STORY OF A COMMERCIAL VENTURE

241 *Mikhaylovsky*: the Russian political thinker and literary critic N. K. Mikhaylovsky (1842–1904).

Our Native Word: *Rodnoye slovo* (untraced) was possibly a school reader.

243 *European Herald*: *Vestnik Yevropy*: a historico-political and literary monthly of liberal complexion published in St Petersburg/ Petrograd, 1866–1918.

A FISHY AFFAIR

245 *Lermontov's Demon fell in love with Tamara*: in the long poem *The Demon* (1839) by M. Yu. Lermontov (1814–41), the devil's kiss destroys Tamara, the girl whom he loves.

246 *Lipetsk*: town about 230 miles south of Moscow.